BLACK SILK HANDKERCHIEF

VOLUME ONE

HOM-ASTUBBY MYSTERY SERIES

BLACK SILK HANDKERCHIEF

A Hom-Astubby Mystery

by

D. L. BIRCHFIELD

UNIVERSITY OF OKLAHOMA PRESS : NORMAN

Also by D. L. Birchfield

The Oklahoma Basic Intelligence Test: New and Collected Elementary,
Epistolary, Autobiographical, and Oratorical Choctologies (Green-
field Center, N.Y., 1997)
Field of Honor: A Novel (Norman, 2004)

This is a work of fiction. Names, characters, places, and incidents
are either the product of the author's imagination or are used ficti-
tiously, and any resemblance to actual events, locales, or persons,
living or dead, is entirely coincidental.

Library of Congress Cataloging-in-Publication Data

Birchfield, D. L., 1948–
　Black silk handkerchief : a Hom-Astubby mystery / by D. L.
Birchfield.
　　p. cm.
　ISBN 0-8061-3751-7 (alk. paper)
　1. Choctaw Indians—Fiction.　2. Colorado—Fiction.　I. Title.
　PS3602.I725B57 2006
　813'.6—dc22　　　　　　　　　　　　　　　　　　2005054888

The paper in this book meets the guidelines for permanence and
durability of the Committee on Production Guidelines for Book
Longevity of the Council on Library Resources, Inc. ∞

1　2　3　4　5　6　7　8　9　10

TREATY WITH THE CHOCTAW, 1802

. . . and the said Choctaw nation, for, and in consideration of one dollar, to them in hand paid by the said United States, the receipt whereof is hereby acknowledged, do hereby release to the said United States, and quit claim for ever, to all that track of land . . .

At Fort Confederation, October 17, 1802
Ratified by the U.S. Senate, 7 stat., 73
Proclaimed by the President of the
United States, January 20, 1803

TREATY WITH THE CHOCTAW, 1803

We the commissioners of the Choctaw nation . . . do acknowledge to have received from the United States of America . . . as a consideration in full for the confirmation of the above concession, the following articles, viz., : fifteen pounds of strouds, three rifles, one hundred and fifty blankets, two hundred and fifty pounds of powder, two hundred and fifty pounds of lead, one bridle, one man's saddle, and one black silk handkerchief.

At Ho-Buckin-too-pa, August 31, 1803
Ratified by the U.S. Senate, 7 stat., 80
Proclaimed by the President of the
United States, December 26, 1803

CONTENTS

BLACK SILK HANDKERCHIEF

PART 1

The Purple Pentagon

(Monday afternoon, Tuesday, Wednesday morning)

The world is filled with mystery, filled with fleeting secrets. They dance before our eyes at the speed of light, too swift for full appreciation. But a little bit of trapped light can stop a secret in its flight and illuminate for our contemplative study even the darkest mystery.

—WILLIAM H. MALLORY
Basic 35 MM Photography

CHAPTER ONE

Monday, 2 P.M.—Early August
Crystal Fork of the Dolores River
Devon County
Southwestern Colorado

om-Astubby fidgeted beside the pay phone beneath the tall trees in the sprawling parking lot of the big log-walled Purple Pentagon restaurant and bar. He was feeling the pressure of the ticking of white man's time, wishing the sheriff would hurry up.

Hom-Astubby was so anxious for the sheriff to get there that he barely noticed the stark mountain ruggedness of the granite spires and scrub-timbered ridges of the remote and mysterious Ghazis Range that nearly surrounded Devon County.

It was ordinarily a place of sun-splashed beauty, but a large bank of low-scudding clouds had blocked out the sun, giving the whole countryside an eerie and foreboding cast, which matched Hom-Astubby's mood.

He also paid no attention to the most visible penetration of that once-isolated place—the heavy tourist traffic crossing the river on the highway bridge near the Purple Pentagon. Most of that traffic was streaming toward Telluride, which was just beyond Lizard Head Pass in the distance to the north. Those tourists would be seeking a modest taste of the expensive and internationally sophisticated diversions that were a magnet for the wealthy of the world, who arrived at Telluride in sleek private jets.

The sheriff's dispatcher had told Hom-Astubby that no deputies were available and that the sheriff himself would handle the call. But the sheriff was at a car wreck at the south end of the county. He would get there as soon as he could.

Hom-Astubby would have preferred waiting with a cup of coffee inside the Purple Pentagon. A brisk wind had sprung up suddenly, with the arrival of the clouds, about an hour ago. The wind had gotten stronger and was now blowing dust across the big gravel parking lot.

But he held his ground, keeping his remarkably expressive brown eyes focused downriver on a dense clump of brush in the distance, where he had found the woman's body, being guarded by her dog. He also kept watch on the dirt road that led from the highway down to that clump of brush.

Hom-Astubby knew the importance of preserving a crime scene. After taking a degree in photojournalism, he had worked as a newspaper photographer while moonlighting as a civilian auxiliary crime scene photographer.

He hadn't done that now for a few years, but he hadn't forgotten anything he'd learned about crime scenes. In fact, he had learned how to look at homicide investigation with a lot more sophistication when he had gone back to college, to law school.

Hom-Astubby viewed himself as a victim of luck. He had returned to college as a last resort after a prolonged period of bad luck had driven him to try doing something to change his luck. He had gone to law school mostly out of frustration at being blacklisted by an aggressively expanding newspaper chain that, as part of a media empire, had made his life miserable.

For several years he had the extraordinary bad luck of staying just a step or two ahead of their next newspaper acquisition, getting fired again nearly every time he turned around. He had tried to view that as a chance to get acquainted with a number of different places, mostly small cities all over the West, work for a lot of different newspapers, and moonlight for a variety of law enforcement agencies.

But having to pull up, move, and find a new job every few months, sometimes every few weeks, had been frustrating beyond anything he could tolerate. The more it happened, the more he was convinced that the people running that newspaper chain were actually hounding him from place to place, just so they could buy that paper and fire him again. He had finally gotten so fed up with it that he'd gone to law school to find out if there was any way he could fight back.

During that bad-luck period he had also endured a horrifying run-in with the bloodless bureaucrats who called themselves Internal Revenue Service income tax auditors—who had demonstrated all the compassion and humanity of an asteroid on a collision course with earth. They had rubbed their hands with glee at discovering that Hom-Astubby treated nit-picking paperwork requirements as merely rough guidelines.

The ordeal of that income tax audit had dragged on for so long and had turned into such a nightmare that he had been willing to spend three years of his life in law school to find out whatever he needed to know to ensure that he would never again see the inside of an IRS office.

After law school, he hadn't quite gotten around to practicing law, for reasons he didn't like thinking about too much. That blacklisting, aggressively expanding newspaper chain had become a distant, receding memory, and law school had turned out to be a lot different than he had expected.

To his horror, he had learned that there could be no assurance that any taxpayer, with anything other than the most routine tax return, was abiding by the tax laws, because there couldn't be anybody in the entire Internal Revenue Service who could possibly make any sense out of the mountainous volumes of convoluted and contradictory tax codes, let alone anybody, anywhere else.

Long before his last year of law school he was asking himself why he kept trying to do things he didn't really want to do.

All he had ever wanted to do was outdoor photography, something he had done off and on, part-time, with quite a bit of success since before he had first entered college. Why he had wasted his time trying to do anything else was beyond him.

After law school, he had finally ventured out on his own as a full-time freelance outdoor photographer. His luck changed dramatically.

He had the good fortune of being in the right place at the

right time when a veteran outdoor photographer retired, a man who had been paired with one of the top outdoor writers in the business. Hom-Astubby teamed up with that writer, whom he'd worked with several times in the past whenever his aging, increasingly ill photographer hadn't been available.

A lot of that writer's work involved celebrity outings, fishing with famous people on spectacular trout streams, or sometimes for saltwater species, all over the world. It was the kind of break that could jump-start a career and Hom-Astubby made the most of it. In the last couple of years he had skyrocketed to the top of his field while meeting a lot of rich and powerful people.

Then he found he had a curious problem. He couldn't stop having good luck. He had never imagined that he would have so much good luck and that his life would become so complicated that he would have little choice but to become dependent upon other lawyers—on lawyers who specialized in high finance and income taxation for the very wealthy.

He hated the complexity of those fields of law. He hated even thinking about the uncertainty of any field of law—lawyers in any specialty could do little more than make educated guesses about what a court might do with a given set of facts. He especially wished he hadn't learned that he couldn't trust tax lawyers or investment bankers to know for sure what they were talking about.

If he hadn't learned those things, he might have been able to relax and have some peace of mind. He had thought that by not becoming an active, practicing attorney, he could forget what he had learned about the alarming uncertainty of nearly everything having to do with law, as well as its arbitrary deadlines, tedious complexity, and all the other things he hated about the white man's legal system.

He had told his Indian friends that practicing white man's law just wasn't a way of life compatible with doing things on Indian time. He had told himself that he wasn't practicing law because it couldn't compete with the graceful pace of nature, that the life of a lawyer was a hectic, sure path to a white man's self-induced heart attack.

Those things might be true enough, but they weren't the real reason he'd avoided becoming an active attorney. Not long after entering law school, he'd become convinced that if he ever did begin representing any clients, sooner or later, by some oversight, he'd end up in prison. And it would have something to do with money. What he had learned about the law's relentless focus on money had scared the daylights out of him.

Hom-Astubby had always been so indifferent to money, especially to having any more of it than he might need at the moment, that he had rarely ever been able to balance his own checkbook. He had sometimes forgotten to deposit checks even when he had needed the money. He hadn't dared to imagine all that might go wrong if *he* had to juggle client money from court judgments perhaps running into the millions.

That's what had gotten him into trouble with the IRS auditors in the first place—his horrible record-keeping of anything having to do with money. He had not imagined that he could find himself in far worse trouble with the IRS, for things *other* than just failing to keep good records.

But during the last several months he'd become convinced that he was going to end up in prison for tax fraud—all because he hadn't known that he should stop trying to have good luck.

The unbridled extent of that good luck had manifested itself most dramatically when he hit a fantastically huge jackpot in a New Mexico Indian casino while on his way home to Oklahoma for Thanksgiving last year. He would have been happy with just a few thousand extra dollars to spend for Christmas. But with one spin of a slot machine he had become one of the richest Indians in the country, possibly the richest. He had no idea how many Indians counted their money in the millions, but he was pretty sure there weren't very many.

He had begun joyously spending that windfall when it quickly turned out to be merely a stepping stone to having the stupendous good luck of being in the right place at the right time to buy a huge horse ranch in western Oklahoma that was worth tremendously more than he paid for it. That fabulous ranch had everything that anybody could ever possibly want, and much more, except that it didn't have any horses.

That was where he was pretty sure his run of good luck had run out. Buying that ranch had cost him virtually his entire remaining fortune, leaving him nearly dead broke—what his investment bankers called a serious cash flow problem, so serious he barely had gas money for the trip he was now on.

It had also created tax complications so mind-boggling that he'd had no choice but to get an extension for filing his income tax return. The complexities of his tax situation were such that his own blood-sucking tax lawyers had nearly driven him crazy. *That* sort of thing was why he hadn't practiced law in the first place.

The anxiety of the past several months had been hard on him. By early August he had needed a break in the worst way. His delayed tax return was due near the middle of the month, but he was paralyzed with indecision about whether he should follow the advice of his tax lawyers.

The convoluted, borderline-legal-sounding schemes that his tax attorneys were recommending, which they assured him would reduce his tax liability to practically nothing, had scared him so bad he could barely function.

His investment bankers kept telling him to take out a big mortgage on his ranch and invest the money and he'd get all the operating capital he needed. But the complex maze of shady-sounding tax shelters and tax-deferred investments that their mortgage plan depended on made it hard to tell when he was listening to them or listening to his tax attorneys.

Hom-Astubby was far from being an expert in those fields of law or in anything else having to do with finance. But he couldn't help wondering if his own tax lawyers and investment bankers had ever actually met any IRS auditors. The longer he listened to the things they recommended, the one thing he couldn't figure out was why the whole bunch of them weren't already in prison.

He was worried that his luck had changed. He was worried that hitting that casino jackpot had been his death knell and he just hadn't realized it. He couldn't undo the things he had done. He had spent the money. He owed taxes. Maybe a lot of taxes. The only question was how much he owed.

It was so tempting to do what his tax lawyers were recommending. He'd had no choice but to compute his taxes according to their recommendations in April, because in order to get the extension for filing his tax return he'd had to pay the paltry amount of their estimated tax at the time he requested the extension. He had no money to pay what he might really owe.

In moments like this he wished he were not a lawyer himself, wished he weren't burdened by the knowledge that, no matter how much advice he got from how many tax attorneys, he, and he alone, was responsible for the tax return he had to file.

He didn't want to go through life never having a moment of peace, not knowing for sure whether he had settled in for a leisurely stroll along Easy Street or might be headed for a long stretch in a federal penitentiary.

He had a photo assignment on the Crystal Fork coming up in a few days. He had arrived in southwestern Colorado a little early, just wanting to have some time alone to try to relax and commune with nature.

He hadn't counted on finding a body in the woods—about as clear a sign as he could imagine of how bad his luck had changed. He wasn't feeling very relaxed. He wished the cop he was waiting for would hurry up.

He had just about decided he should call the sheriff's office a second time when he saw a white Bronco, caked with dried mud, come speeding around the bend of the highway to his left. It came from the south, from the direction of Alpine, the county-seat town of only a few hundred permanent residents, which was located about three miles down the highway. The Bronco slowed and pulled into the parking lot of the Purple Pentagon. It had DEVON COUNTY SHERIFF'S OFFICE emblazoned on the door.

The Bronco crunched across the gravel and rolled to a stop beside Hom-Astubby, coming to rest at an angle just right for him to see something that made him frown. He didn't need to encounter any of his bad omens at this moment. But he could see all the way through the vehicle to a corner of the back window. There, barely discernible, being dust-covered and seen in reverse, was a faded Notre Dame Fighting Irish football logo.

A much older man wearing a tan uniform and a well-seasoned but smart-looking western hat rolled down his window. Mirrored sunglasses concealed his eyes. The small amount of space between his ears and his hat revealed a haircut that might have been done by a Marine Corps barber. His long, frowning face had been thoroughly roughened and creased by the sun and the wind. He didn't look like someone who would be a lot of fun to spend much time with.

He said, "I'm Sheriff Klewlusz. You the one who found the body?"

Hom-Astubby nodded. "My name is Bill Mallory," Hom-Astubby said, as he pointed toward the west, across the restaurant parking lot, across the highway bridge spanning the Crystal Fork of the Dolores River, and down the dirt road on the other side of the bridge that led to the river bottom downstream. "I was down there hiking along the Crystal Fork taking photos when I found her, just before the river enters the gorge. I went back to my truck and drove right back up here to the pay phone and called your office."

"You didn't see anyone else down there?"

"Two guys in a boat, fly-fishing. But they'd gone downstream when I saw her."

"Did it look like the body had been there a long time?"

"No, sir, it didn't."

"Anything unusual about it?"

"Yes, sir. She doesn't have on any clothes from the waist down."

The sheriff's frown deepened. "Let's go take a look. We'll use my Bronco."

"Let me stow my stuff," Hom-Astubby said, indicating his backpack and cameras. "I'd intended to be gone most of the day."

The sheriff took off his sunglasses. As he was putting them in his shirt pocket, he gave an appraising look at the two cameras secured to Hom-Astubby's chest and stomach with wide elastic bands that kept them held tightly in place, a third camera hanging from his neck on a strap, and his photographer's vest bulging with lenses and accessories. He said, "You a pro?"

"Yeah," Hom-Astubby said. "Outdoor photographer. I'm here on assignment for *Field and Stream*. Gonna do a shoot this weekend with Harry Birdwell, the outdoor writer who grew up around here. I got here a little early to take some vacation time."

"You know Harry Birdwell, huh?" the sheriff said.

"Yeah, I've worked with Harry a lot the last few years. He's topnotch. You know him?"

The sheriff chuckled. "We went to high school together. Hell, if anybody knew half of what Harry knows about me, I'd never have gotten elected to this job."

"That bad, huh?" Hom-Astubby said, a little surprised at the sheriff's easygoing candor. He looked closely at the man, seeing a softness about the eyes that the sunglasses had concealed. There was also something genuine about the smile that transformed his face into one that might make people feel more at ease about putting their trust in him.

"We had ourselves a time. Harry's not back here already, is he?"

"I don't think so," Hom-Astubby said. "I think he's planning on getting here late Saturday afternoon. First time we're supposed to get together is for dinner Saturday night. He was going to drive down here from Wyoming. He just bought a place in Jackson Hole."

"Yeah, so I've heard," the sheriff said. "I haven't seen him for awhile, since he was here Christmas, I guess."

Hom-Astubby relaxed a little. If the sheriff and Birdwell were old buddies that would make things a lot easier. He said, "Let me stow my stuff and I'll be right with you."

Hom-Astubby walked to his truck—a brand-new, cream-colored, huge, super heavy-duty suspension, all-wheel drive, four-ton truck with a powerful diesel engine. Mounted on the long, wide, flat bed of the truck was an enormous crimson-colored, luxurious cabover camper that was more than forty feet long, not counting the big portion that extended forward over the roof of the truck. He started putting his gear in the back seat of the roomy, four-door king cab.

The camper was so wide and so tall that both sides and the back of it extended out over the truck bed and down to the wheels all around, completely hiding the truck except for the front end and the cab. The camper had aerodynamically engineered rounded corners, giving it an appearance more like a big fat motor home than a truck and camper combination.

Hom-Astubby had waited impatiently more than six months for the custom-designed rig to be built and delivered. This trip was his first chance to take it out on the road, and so far nothing about it had disappointed him. It had some special features that might do wonders for his love life, and he was dying to try them out, hoping for an opportunity to test some of those things while he was in Colorado.

"Better make sure your truck's locked up good," the sheriff said. "We've had two cameras stolen out of this parking lot recently."

Hom-Astubby stopped unstrapping his cameras and frowned at the sheriff. "Two different thefts?" he said.

"Well, two different vehicles, both broken into at the same time. Looks like we've got a camera thief around here. One of them was a very expensive telephoto."

"Jesus," Hom-Astubby said. "I can't lose any of this equipment."

"Better bring it with you then."

"Are you kidding? The camper's full of it. You and me both couldn't carry it all."

Hom-Astubby took all of his gear out of the truck cab and put it in the camper, keeping only his backpack to take with him. Then he backed up the truck to a light pole until the pole kept the back door of the camper from being opened. "That ought to do it," he said. He double-checked to make sure the truck and camper were locked, then climbed inside the sheriff's Bronco, resting his backpack on his lap.

Before driving off, the sheriff looked at Hom-Astubby closely. He said, "What tribe are you, Mallory? If you don't mind me asking. We don't see many Indians up here other than a Ute or a Navajo now and then. But you don't look like a Ute or a Navajo and your truck's got Oklahoma tags. Are you an Oklahoma Indian, if you don't mind me asking?"

The question gave Hom-Astubby pause. Maybe it was innocent enough, just genuine curiosity. Or maybe the sheriff was wanting to know what an Indian was doing driving a vehicle that had cost quite a bit more than a million dollars to have custom-designed and custom-built.

"I'm Choctaw," Hom-Astubby said. "As for where I come from, the tags on that truck shouldn't be your only clue. Didn't you notice that the paint job on that cream-colored truck and that crimson camper happen to be the exact precise shades of the official school colors of the butt-kickingest football team in the history of college football? And I'll whup anybody who says different."

That brought a long moment of silence in the Bronco. "Huh. You don't say?" the sheriff said, studying Hom-Astubby's expressionless face intently. After a few moments he added, "I'll be damned. You don't miss much, do you?"

"Some things are hard to miss," Hom-Astubby said, watching the sheriff glance in his rear-view mirror, in the middle of his windshield, toward the decal on his back window.

"You sound like you might have gone to school down there."

"I did. Photojournalism and law school. Hardly ever missed a game. They don't let you graduate down there unless you can say who ended our forty-seven-game winning streak. There'll be a payback for that one of these days. If a big game ever comes along that might be worthy of being that payback."

"You're a lawyer, huh?"

"Yeah. But I don't practice law. You'll not find me getting trapped in some office job. You know what I mean?"

The sheriff nodded. "I know exactly what you mean," he said, as he pulled the Bronco out of the parking lot and turned right onto the highway, headed north toward the bridge over the Crystal Fork.

Prominently displayed near the entrance to the bridge was a big, brand-new, brightly colored sign that Hom-Astubby had not paid any attention to earlier: RE-ELECT SHERIFF KLEWLUSZ. Smaller letters across the middle of the sign read: 45 YEARS WITH THE SHERIFF'S OFFICE. And beneath that, centered near the bottom in very large letters, even larger than his name: DEMOCRAT.

They were on the middle of the bridge when the sheriff suddenly said, "Wait a minute. You're not that crazy Indian who accompanied Harry on that trip to Alaska are you? Hell, you'd have to be. How many Indians could there be who know Harry, who are outdoor photographers?"

"Not many, I guess," Hom-Astubby said, shrugging.

"I've heard Harry talk about you. But I didn't recognize your name. Harry always calls you 'that crazy Indian.' He gave me a magazine article he wrote about the two of you, about that trip up there. I guess those were your photos."

"Yeah," Hom-Astubby said. "He's published eleven articles about that so far."

"Eleven?"

"Different kinds of magazines, different angles on the story. Birdwell's a good freelancer, best in the business, knows how to milk a story for all it's worth. Every time he sells an article about that, more of my photos get used. He's writing a book right now about that trip, and it'll probably sell about as well as all of his other books."

Hom-Astubby didn't mention that he had published his first book recently, but he didn't know how many copies it had sold. Probably not many. It was an instructional manual on photography and on processing black-and-white film and printing the photos in your own darkroom.

"That'll be a hell of a book," the sheriff said, while waiting for oncoming traffic to clear so he could turn left off the highway onto the dirt road and begin angling back down through the heavy brush toward the river. "You guys almost died up there."

"It wasn't that bad," Hom-Astubby said. It hadn't been bad at all, really. The bush pilot who'd dropped them off on the Kenai Peninsula had flown back to his base and had a stroke. Instead of picking them up in a few days, he was laid up in the hospital. By the time Birdwell's relatives began inquiring into what had happened to him and the pilot remembered he'd left them out there, Birdwell had cooked up so many different angles about their "harrowing survival experience in the wilderness" that Hom-Astubby had trouble remembering he'd spent most of that time lounging around camp and fishing. He'd gained about ten pounds, there had been so little to do but fish and cook and eat.

"You're just being modest," the sheriff said. "I remember that article pretty well. Harry said you could walk off into the woods with nothing but a pocketknife and never miss a meal."

Ah, thought Hom-Astubby, the thank-god-I-had-an-Indian-with-me angle. He knew now which article the sheriff had read. That one was Hom-Astubby's personal favorite. In spite of himself he found it pleasing that the sheriff knew something about him. And—he reflected again for about the thousandth time—never underestimate the power of the printed word to create its own reality.

The sheriff, however, soon brought him back to a much darker topic. "Tell me more about the body," Sheriff Klewlusz said.

CHAPTER TWO

"**W**ell, it was kind of strange," Hom-Astubby said. "I found her clothes before I found her. There's an old picnic table in a little clearing in the brush."

"I know where that is," the sheriff said. "On down this road."

"That's right. That's where I parked. When I walked up to that table, there were her clothes scattered around on the ground, and some hanging on the bushes. Blue jeans, a pair of low-cut tennis shoes, a pair of panties, a bra, one sock. I was pretty surprised."

"Did you touch anything?"

"Well, yeah, I did. I picked up everything, folded up the jeans and set it all on top of the table. I looked around for the rest of it, some kind of shirt, the other sock, but that's all that was there."

"Did it look like there had been some kind of struggle?"

"Not that I could tell. I really wasn't thinking about anything like that. I didn't know what to think. Then I more or less forgot about it."

"You found the body later?" the sheriff said, as he steered the Bronco away from some deep ruts in the dirt road, causing the vehicle to bounce up and down and scrape against the bushes on the driver's side.

"Yeah, quite a bit later," Hom-Astubby said. "I took some time working my way toward the river, taking telephoto shots of those two guys fishing. They worked that stretch of water for quite a while. They were already there when I got there."

"Can you describe her?"

"She's lying on her stomach. Her arms are cradled underneath her head, but her legs are outstretched wide. Very revealing, really, of her genital area, like she'd been posed like that, the way some killers will pose their victims. She's hidden among some black driftwood and white rocks not far from the edge of the river. Not really hidden. What I mean is—she blends into that background so completely she absolutely *disappears*, because she's got long black hair, shoulder length, and all she's wearing is a white, long-sleeved sweatshirt, the same color as those rocks."

Hom-Astubby discreetly didn't mention that her thick black pubic hair, clearly visible even though she was lying on her stomach, also helped break up her silhouette, blending in with the pieces of black driftwood beside her. But that powerful vision of that secret part of her body was hard to shake from his mind. It angered him that she'd probably been violated before being killed. But he also didn't understand how that could have happened with the woman's dog there. There was more the sheriff needed to know.

"It doesn't sound good," the sheriff said.

"It was quite a while before I noticed her. The first thing I saw—"

Hom-Astubby was trying to tell the sheriff about the big black dog sitting beside the woman, but the sheriff interrupted him. The dog had been enormous, a Newfoundland of massive proportions that had to weigh close to two hundred pounds.

The dog had blended in so curiously with the black driftwood and offered such stark contrast to the white rocks that Hom-Astubby had switched to his camera that was loaded with black and white film. He had been concentrating so much on getting good shots of that black dog that he hadn't even noticed the woman for quite a while.

The dog had watched him intently as he got closer and closer. The curiosity on the dog's face had been something to see—expressed by cocking its head to one side and then to the other, as Hom-Astubby kept changing lenses and filters, trying different settings, different shutter speeds, moving ever closer, getting shot after shot that he could hardly wait to get developed and printed.

Finally, the dog had whimpered and come trotting to him, wagging its tail, when he'd been crouched down, having gotten to within about ten feet. The dog licked his face with a big wet tongue, bowling him over backward, wanting to play. Even though the dog was huge, it must have been just a big overgrown teenager, still a puppy at heart.

Hom-Astubby had petted the dog, ruffing the hair on its head, speaking softly and gently to it, thoroughly enjoying meeting such an extraordinary animal. He was wondering who it belonged to and what it was doing at the river all by itself when he saw the woman. He was so startled he couldn't move, couldn't do anything but stare at her.

The dog had finally given his face one last big wet licking and then gone trotting back to the woman. It lay down beside her, put its massive head on its huge paws, let out a big sigh, and stared intently at Hom-Astubby again. But before Hom-Astubby could mention the dog, the sheriff interrupted him with another question.

"You see any blood?"

"No, sir. But I couldn't see her face hardly at all, with her lying on her stomach like that, and her hair had kind of fallen over her face."

"Age?"

"Oh, twenty-five, thirty, maybe. Definitely a young woman and very shapely. Very athletic-looking, too. I thought maybe she might be a dancer, maybe a ballerina or something."

The Bronco came to a little clearing in the brush and Hom-Astubby recognized the area. He knew that the picnic table wasn't far ahead. "There," he pointed through the brush toward the river. "She's right down there."

Before they could get out of the Bronco, Sheriff Klewlusz got a call on his radio. Hom-Astubby listened as the sheriff told one of his deputies, a Miss Wellesley, who was just getting back from vacation, that everyone was now on overtime, on twelve-hour shifts.

A woman had been attacked night before last, coming out of a self-service laundry in Alpine. She'd temporarily blinded her attacker with pepper spray and had gotten away, but he had swung what looked like a heavy pipe at her and had stolen her purse.

The woman had described her assailant as a young white male, mid- to late twenties, with short blond hair and a thick southern accent.

The sheriff wanted all of his people on the lookout for him, everyone on overtime until they caught him. He also mentioned the cameras getting stolen out of the Purple Pentagon parking lot.

When Sheriff Klewlusz got off the radio, he turned to Hom-Astubby. "I don't like it," he said. "That woman getting attacked the other night in town. Now we might have one who got killed down here." His face showed the worry. "Now where is that woman, exactly?"

Hom-Astubby led the way through the brush toward the river. As they emerged from the thicket, he directed the sheriff to some black driftwood scattered around among big white rocks that were almost at the riverbank.

But when they got to the edge of the rocks, Hom-Astubby stopped suddenly. He said, "She's not here."

"Are you sure this is the right place?"

"Yes, I'm sure. I was standing beside that crooked tree over there, the one with the twisted fork at the base—"

"Well, I don't see any blood," the sheriff said, "or anything else. This ground is pretty hard-packed."

"Jesus, she was right here," Hom-Astubby said, " pointing at their feet.

The sheriff knelt down, looking closely at the ground, which was densely packed gravel. "I don't see any drag marks." He looked up at Hom-Astubby. "Could that woman have just been passed out or something?"

"Half-naked like that?" Hom-Astubby said. "I mean, she was buck naked except for that sweatshirt."

The sheriff stood up. He shrugged as though he had seen stranger things. "Maybe she was just good and drunk."

"Drunk I could believe," Hom-Astubby said. "But buck naked?"

The sheriff rubbed his chin and glanced around at the brush and the river. "Well, if she was drunk maybe she fell in the water and was waiting around for her clothes to get dry. Didn't you say some of those clothes were hanging on the bushes?"

"Yeah. It looked like maybe the wind had blown some of them off."

"Well, maybe she was still a little too drunk and she wandered too far away from that brush over there. Might have gotten surprised out here in the open when those fly-fishermen came floating around that bend. Maybe ducked down here among these rocks and then either passed out or just fell asleep waiting for them to leave."

Hom-Astubby looked upstream where the river came around the bend, and down at the rocks, and at the brush, and at the river again. He said, "That makes sense, I guess, sort of. I guess she could have been asleep. It never occurred to me that she might have just been passed out." Hom-Astubby was beginning to feel foolish.

"You didn't see any vehicles on this road after you found her, did you?"

"No. I watched the road from the pay phone up there. There was no traffic on this road. You can't see the river right here or much of it upstream toward the bridge, but you can see most of it on downstream from here all the way to the gorge, and you can see the road and that brush over there. That picnic table is just on the other side of that clump of brush."

"Yeah, I know," the sheriff said. "Well, it doesn't seem likely that anybody just picked her up and carried her off. This road dead-ends down at the gorge. She must have just woke up and walked away."

They stood looking all around and up and down the Crystal Fork. The wind stirring the leaves in the trees and the gurgling and splashing of the water were the only sounds disturbing the quiet.

Across the river, about a hundred yards back from the river-bank, a steep cliff rose sharply for several hundred feet to the top of a hill. Up there the wind was whipping the tops of the trees around.

Hom-Astubby, gazing at the river, said, "This water is even shallow enough to wade. Those fly-fishermen were wading all around in it."

"Yeah. This time of year, this stretch of water, it's no more than knee-deep. She could go anywhere from here, upstream, downstream, across the river. Hell, the only place she couldn't go very easily would be up Grimpin Hill over there." He gestured toward the cliff across the river. "Let's go see if those clothes are still on that table."

CHAPTER THREE

The clothes were gone. Hom-Astubby was embarrassed by it all, but the sheriff was obviously relieved. Some half-naked woman out cavorting around is one thing. A dead woman is an altogether different kind of thing.

Hom-Astubby took off his backpack and pulled out a thermos of coffee and two lightweight cups. The sheriff offered him a cigar, a Bradley Cheroot, which Hom-Astubby accepted, it being tobacco offered by an elder. It was a brand that Hom-Astubby had never seen before, and he noticed from its wrapper that it was imported from a tobacco shop in London. They sat down at the picnic table, relaxing for a moment.

"God, I feel so foolish," Hom-Astubby said.

"Don't you worry about that," the sheriff said, lighting his cigar. "I'll take this, compared to what we might have had, any time."

"Maybe I can still be of some help," Hom-Astubby said, trying to get his cigar lit. "If you can tell me what kind of cameras those were that got stolen, I might spot them for you. Being a photographer, I notice cameras."

The cigar was the strongest tobacco Hom-Astubby had ever tasted. And there was something strange about it. With one drag of that smoke, he felt as though something were happening to him, something frightening and threatening. He shook off the feeling, chalking it up to not using tobacco very often, and to the strength of the tobacco.

"Well, one of them was a pretty good Nikon," the sheriff said. "Fairly new, 35 mm in a small camera bag with a few lenses. I don't know what kind of camera the other one was, but it had a 2000 mm telephoto lens."

"A *2000 mm lens?*" Hom-Astubby said, his voice registering disbelief. "Are you sure about that? That lens is more than six feet long. It takes special tripods just to hold it up and get it anchored solidly. With that magnification it has to be rock solid. But if somebody knows what they're doing, they can get close-ups of people with a 2000 mm that they can barely see with the naked eye."

The sheriff glanced at Hom-Astubby. But he sipped his coffee and puffed on his cigar, saying nothing.

"A 2000 mm lens costs a fortune," Hom-Astubby said.

"Tell me about it. The guy was pretty irate about losing it."

"That's a surveillance lens," Hom-Astubby said. "They don't gather enough light to get publishable-quality prints, at least not high-quality prints. They're used mostly for undercover work. No tourist would have a 2000 mm lens."

The sheriff looked at Hom-Astubby, a long, appraising look. Hom-Astubby's eyes met the sheriff's.

"I used to be a police photographer," Hom-Astubby said, "a civilian auxiliary photographer when I was doing newspaper work. I've shot a lot of crime scenes, seen a lot of homicide investigations, been around a lot of police departments, mostly in small cities all over the West."

"I'll be damned," the sheriff said. "You ever work with any private investigators?"

"No." Hom-Astubby shrugged. "Just with a lot of cops and reporters."

"Well, the guy that owned that lens was a private investigator. Seriously private. Wouldn't even tell me his name or his firm."

"That's getting pretty private," Hom-Astubby said.

"If I hadn't been pulling into the parking lot at the Purple Pentagon when he discovered the theft, I wouldn't know about it. He wouldn't have reported it. He refused to make out a report about it. Said he didn't want any official record that he'd even been in this county. Said his work was very sensitive. He was upset that I'd been around when he saw that his van had been broken into and that he'd said as much as he had. Told me just to forget about it, like that's likely to happen."

"So, the thief just gets away with that lens? Even if you catch him with it?"

"Not much I can do." The sheriff shrugged. "The guy refused to report it stolen, wouldn't tell me any registration numbers or anything else. I don't even know who he was to contact him if we did find it. But I'll tell you what—thieves are stupid. We'll catch the guy who stole that lens, and when we do he'll have other stolen property that we can prosecute him for, like that other camera bag."

"Was the other guy a private investigator, too?"

"No. He'd apparently just been having dinner with him at the Purple Pentagon. He's somebody I wish I didn't know. He also lost a briefcase with some business papers. He was a lot madder about that than anything else. Gave me a lot of grief about it. He's a high-powered business executive named Wally Street. He said he had his name and address in both the camera bag and the briefcase. But if you run across any of his stuff you tell me first. You don't want to have anything to do with that guy, trust me."

"Not a nice guy?" Hom-Astubby said.

"He's Nelson Towers' right-hand man in this part of the country. More like hatchet man."

"Nelson Towers? *The* Nelson Towers?"

"Yeah. *The* Nelson Towers. Anything you've heard about Towers, you just magnify it for Street. Helps you understand how Towers got so much money. No, Wally Street is not a nice guy. I would have found out who that private investigator was if it hadn't been for Street. He got between us, got on his cell phone, got company lawyers on the way out here. Had them coming in from their new office over at Telluride by helicopter. Can you imagine that? So I backed off. Besides, I figured I'd find out who that other guy was by running the tag on his van. Turned out to be a rental car, rented to the government of Malaysia."

The sheriff shook his head. "You go up against Nelson Towers' people, you better have more than just a few billion dollars in the bank. I'd sure as hell like to know what they were up to, though. I'd bet money it's dirty."

"Nelson Towers," Hom-Astubby said, his face contorting into a grimace. "You don't have to tell me anything about Nelson Towers. You don't want to know how many good newspaper jobs I lost because of him."

Hom-Astubby told the sheriff how he'd gotten crosswise with one of Nelson Towers' mining companies, back before he went to law school, back when he'd first gotten out of college, when he thought he was going to be an investigative journalist, at the first newspaper he'd worked for, in Montana.

"After that, every newspaper I tried to work for," he said, "would get bought by Towers' media empire and I'd get fired. Blacklisting, it's called. But I didn't know that Towers had any interests around here."

"He didn't used to," the sheriff said. "But lately he's been trying to buy up half the county. A lot of people around here won't sell to him. He hasn't bought our little weekly paper yet, the *Devon County Chronicle*, but I heard he tried to. He's apparently here to stay. He built a big new house last year, not far up the highway. Comes here quite a bit now."

"Nelson Towers comes here?"

"In the flesh. He's not so bad to talk to. Neither is his butler, Barrymore, who's the one who actually lives in his new house and manages the place for him. But that Wally Street, who runs Towers' new office over at Telluride, causes me so much trouble I've thought about giving up this job. They had the president of the United States out here last fall."

"Jesus. The president?"

"Yeah, and he doesn't travel alone. You wouldn't believe the headache that causes. This job isn't what it used to be, just a few years ago, when nobody ever came up here but fly-fishermen and deer hunters. I never had to deal with people like Wally Street back then, or the whole damn traveling White House."

"God, I can barely imagine what that must have been like."

"I'm afraid it's only going to get worse. Alpine's beginning to get discovered. The talk is that Towers wants to put in a big ski area on this side of Mt. Wilson. The ranchers around here have fought that idea for years, but there's never been somebody like Nelson Towers pushing it."

Hom-Astubby sat thinking about all the grief Nelson Towers' people had caused him and how relieved he'd been when he'd finally gotten out of newspaper work and had gotten those people off his back.

As they sipped their coffee, the afternoon silence was suddenly broken by a faint, distant howling, so eerie and so prolonged it raised the hairs on the back of Hom-Astubby's neck.

"What the hell was that?" Hom-Astubby asked. He looked up-river, toward the highway bridge, where the sound seemed to have emanated, from somewhere beyond the bridge, from farther upstream.

"What?" the sheriff said.

"I thought I heard something."

"My hearing's not so good anymore. What was it?"

"Some kind of animal, I think. You didn't hear it?"

"I didn't hear anything."

Hom-Astubby stared upstream, listening intently, but he heard nothing more.

The sheriff changed the subject, asking him about the police departments he'd worked for.

Hom-Astubby told him how he'd gotten involved in crime scene photography. At that first newspaper job in Montana, a part-time photographer for the paper, Warden Hibdon, had been semi-retired after a long career as a crime scene photographer and forensics specialist for the Detroit police department. Hom-Astubby had become Warden Hibdon's protégé, as Hibdon had remained active in retirement, conducting workshops for Montana law enforcement agencies and doing part-time forensics and photography work on their cases. Then Hom-Astubby had spent a few years moonlighting for law enforcement agencies on his own as he'd moved from city to city. During summers in law school he had organized seminars in crime scene photography, featuring Warden Hibdon, for law enforcement personnel all over the West.

The sheriff remembered hearing about those Warden Hibdon seminars and seemed impressed by Hom-Astubby's role. As they talked, they discovered they had several mutual acquaintances in law enforcement, among them Delbert Lawson.

Delbert had been a Colorado Springs cop when Hom-Astubby moonlighted for that police department. He knew that Delbert had moved to the Colorado Bureau of Investigation—the CBI— because he'd run into him in Pueblo in southeastern Colorado a few years back, and had dinner at his house when Delbert was working at the CBI Pueblo field office. Delbert's wife, a southern country gal, could really cook.

From the sheriff Hom-Astubby learned that Delbert had later moved to the CBI Montrose field office in western Colorado, and from there had been promoted to head the CBI Durango substation for the southwestern Colorado area. The sheriff had gotten well acquainted with Delbert.

"I wouldn't mind running into Delbert again," Hom-Astubby said. "Try to get back some of my poker losses."

"You, too, huh?" Sheriff Klewlusz said. "Is there anybody Delbert hasn't taken to the cleaners?"

"The cops in Pueblo were going to bust him a few years back, but none of them wanted to admit in court that they'd been playing poker, too."

"Yeah. He's got the perfect bunch of suckers to bleed dry. Damn good man, though. We have to rely on the CBI quite a bit. It was a lot harder on us before they came along."

"The CBI has been around for quite a while now, hasn't it?"

"Well, yeah, by now I guess they have. Doesn't seem like it to me. Seems like yesterday. The state legislature created them back in the mid-sixties sometime, a few years after I became a deputy. I remember what it was like before we could call on them for help."

He glanced at Hom-Astubby. "I'm old enough to *remember* that 1957 Notre Dame—Oklahoma football game that you were talking about awhile ago. My Fighting Irish *skunked* your Sooners seven to nothing, *at* Owen Field in Norman, Oklahoma, as I recall."

Hom-Astubby frowned and he looked away from the sheriff, shaking his head.

"But the CBI has never had any direct jurisdiction for any kind of case," the sheriff said, watching Hom-Astubby intently. "They have to be invited in by the local authorities. We have to do that a lot. Pretty much anything that's not routine."

"Well, what would you expect," Hom-Astubby said. "You *are* the sheriff of a real *tiny* county, right? Not much tax base up here, huh? To fund the county government?"

"Hardly anything at all to speak of," the sheriff said, grinning at Hom-Astubby. "If it weren't for the City of Denver also being the County of Denver, we would be the smallest-sized county in Colorado. We *are* the smallest in population, just barely. We've only got about 750 permanent residents in the whole county, and that's counting the babies that are due pretty soon. We've got about 50 people less than Hinsdale County and about 80 people less than Mineral County. But we don't have anywhere near the resources of either one of those counties."

"What do you have up here?"

"Well, about all we've ever had are a few ranchers and the Crystal Fork. We get fly-fishermen in the summer. Deer and elk hunters in the fall. Quite a bit of tourist traffic through here the whole summer. Some winter traffic, too, folks going from Dolores and Cortez to ski up at Telluride. Makes the Purple Pentagon a popular watering hole. But you take it all together, it's a nice, quiet place and folks want to keep it that way."

"Be hard to do if Alpine is getting discovered," Hom-Astubby said.

"Yeah. That damn Towers. Do you have any idea the changes that follow like aftershocks from an earthquake when somebody like Nelson Towers starts taking over a place like this?"

"You mean bringing the president out here?"

"Well, that alone overwhelmed our resources and nearly caused me to quit. And if he ever does it again I damn well might just hang it up. Hell, maybe I'll finally get turned out to pasture in this election and won't ever have to worry about it again. Towers is running a candidate against me, a retired army colonel named Upwood, putting a lot of money in his campaign. He's a Republican who lives here, who owns a couple used car lots down in Cortez and Durango, Nonpareil Motors." The sheriff grunted his disdain. "They're nonpareil, all right. He's lucky somebody down there hasn't shot him by now. But I mean other things about Towers."

The sheriff waved his cigar toward the north. "That new house of his is only about four miles up the highway, toward Telluride. He calls it Dartmoor Manor, like he thinks we're in medieval England or some damn place and everybody around here is just one of his serfs. You can't see the house from the highway. It's set back a ways. But you'd have to be asleep to miss Towers' gate. Towers' gate has been the talk around here ever since he put the damn thing up. It's so tall if it ever collapsed it damn well might set off an earthquake."

"Towers' gate is that big?"

"Just wait until you see the damn thing. It dominates the skyline. Folks around here kind of view it as a symbol of how he's trying to take over the whole damn country and put the profit motive ahead of every other consideration, no matter how long the local people have been living on the land or how dead set they might be against outsiders coming in screwing everything up."

"You don't have to tell me anything about that," Hom-Astubby said. "That's what caused us to lose all of our Indian land. Outsiders, guided by the profit motive, coming in screwing everything up."

"Yeah, well," the sheriff said, "we've begun to feel like we're now the Indians out here."

"Nelson Towers is really trying to take over up here?"

"Hell, he's got Wally Street working on it around the clock. We're on Towers' land right now. He bought this piece not too long ago from old man Jezail. His work crews will close access to it soon. Soon as they can get to it to build a gate across the entry road. Before long people won't be able to do the things they've always done, things they've always taken for granted."

"You know what?" Hom-Astubby said. "About two hundred years ago my Choctaw relatives were beginning to say the exact same thing."

"Well, I guess so. But for us it means it'll be a lot harder to get on the Crystal Fork. Outfitting and guiding fishermen is a big chunk of our economy."

"Will it affect the deer hunters, too?"

"Yeah. It'll have a big impact, kind of indirectly. A lot of the deer hunting around here is on public land, but the best access to most of that is through private land. What Towers is doing will make it a lot harder to get in there and guide all those damn Texans from those big cities down there. They spend a fortune up here so they can shoot up the whole countryside trying to hit a deer or damn near anything else that moves. Used to be that was about our only excitement around here and just about our only worry. Hell, a few years ago one of them brought a dead mule he'd shot to the deer check station."

"A dead mule?"

"Yeah. And that's not all. He shot him *inside* the rancher's corral. It was a real old, sickly mule, so the rancher's son, young Stamford, and some of the ranch hands just helped him load it into his pickup and then they followed him to the check station so they could watch him try to check it in. Hell, Mrs. Holborn, who used to be one of our schoolteachers here, until she opened a café down at Orontes, wouldn't wear anything but fluorescent orange from head to toe *inside* our schoolhouse during deer season. Now she just closes up the café and goes away on vacation when those Texans start pouring in."

"A dead mule." Hom-Astubby shook his head.

"Yeah, but I guess we can't complain too much. Those Texans pump a lot of money into our economy."

"Nelson Towers is a Texan."

"That's right. But they don't look at land the way we do out here."

"How's that?"

"Well, down in Texas, where Towers was raised, they don't have hardly any public land to speak of. For deer hunting they lock up all their private land in expensive, exclusive hunting leases. That's why so many of those city Texans come up here. They can do that cheaper than try to find a hunting lease down there. But I guess Towers looks down at all those fellow Texans as peons and freeloaders who'd have their own hunting leases down in Texas if they amounted to anything. He's locking up all the land up here that he can get his hands on, but especially anything that provides access to the public lands."

The sheriff looked at Hom-Astubby. "Then—and you mark my words—he'll use his influence with the government to get a lot of the public access roads closed. He'll turn this whole county into his private estate. He'll take over the local government and make life so miserable for the few remaining old landowners that he'll run them right out of here."

The sheriff shrugged. "Just like we did to the Indians, I guess. But there's nothing we can do to stop him from buying land up here."

"He's doing it systematically?"

"Yeah. It's a calculated thing if you look at what he has concentrated the hardest on buying and what he does with it once he gets it. He's transplanting that Texas hunting culture regarding access to land to our land up here. He thinks he's got the right to do that, thinks that's just the way the world works. He doesn't understand how to be a good neighbor around here and he probably doesn't care. It's just going to make it harder on folks to make a living. If he's even aware of that, he probably thinks he'll be doing us a favor if he ever gets approval for that big new ski area up there at the north end of the county. Create lots of jobs, mostly for a flood of new people, who'll live in his new apartment buildings and housing projects, and shop at his new businesses. He doesn't understand or care why we don't want that, why we like things the way they are, and why we value that wild area up there."

"There's nothing up there now?"

"Nothing much but marmots and mountain goats. Some summer sheep range. Traces of a few old ghost town mining camps. It's pretty much the end of the road except there's really no road going up there. Bunch of jeep trails. Wild and rugged and beautiful country. Like a lot of places used to be."

He looked at Hom-Astubby. "Maybe you're too young to know exactly what's happened to places like Aspen, Steamboat Springs, that whole valley up at Vail, Durango, Telluride. Hell, there's a whole new city now at Crested Butte. Used to be nothing up in that high little mountain valley but a quaint, mostly abandoned, little old mining town. When I was a kid, I knocked around the mountains quite a bit. I know what it's done to those places. Now you might as well be in downtown Denver. The Californication of Colorado they call it."

Hom-Astubby grunted his agreement, an expressive Choctaw sound that needed no translation. They finished off the last of the coffee and drove back to the Purple Pentagon in silence, the quiet communion of two kindred spirits.

Sheriff Klewlusz dropped Hom-Astubby off at the restaurant parking lot and thanked him for calling in, even though it had turned out to be a false alarm.

He said, "Mallory, I've really enjoyed meeting you. I wouldn't mind getting together with you and Harry this weekend. Maybe drink a few beers Saturday night. You might learn some good background material on old Harry."

Hom-Astubby grinned. He said, "I'd like that. Join us for dinner Saturday night, too, if you can. Is this a good place to eat?" He gestured across the parking lot to the Purple Pentagon.

"Best steaks in the county," the sheriff said. "Got a big ole bacon-wrapped filet mignon that'll melt in your mouth. But it's pretty expensive and it gets a little loud on Saturday night. That's when the younguns pretty much take over the place. Mama Garcia's, in town, has got great Mexican food. Nobody can cook like Beryl Garcia. That's Harry's favorite place. She knows how to cook that New Mexican—Pueblo Indian variety of Mexican food, knows how to make green chili and green chili sauce."

"I love that food," Hom-Astubby said. "Let's go there."

He watched the sheriff drive away, staring at the Notre Dame football decal on his back window. Hom-Astubby had never noticed before, but the little Irishman in the decal was smiling, a distinctly smug and mischievous little smile. It was rather cute, and Hom-Astubby thought—you know, maybe some of those Fighting Irish aren't so bad. He'd hardly ever actually met any of them, and he realized he was looking forward to drinking with the sheriff.

Then he shook the thought out of his head. If a man got to thinking like that, next thing you know he'd be looking forward to drinking with those damn, obnoxious Texas Longhorns. And he'd met *plenty* of them.

He turned to go, then stopped. He stood for a moment, gazing back down the river, staring at the clump of brush that hid the picnic table.

He let out a long sigh, realizing how relieved he was that the woman hadn't been dead and wondering what in the world she had been doing down there half-naked like that. He remembered, too, how she had looked. If the top half of her was anything like the bottom half—man, oh, man.

He got the back door of his camper opened just enough to squeeze his backpack through the opening, then locked the door again.

He walked toward the restaurant men's room to get rid of some of that coffee.

CHAPTER FOUR

Hom-Astubby climbed the log steps to the big front porch of the Purple Pentagon. As he approached the front door, he glanced in one of the windows—tall plate-glass windows that ran nearly the whole length of the porch. The window was as far as he got.

There she was! The woman in the white sweatshirt was sitting at a table with two young cowboys.

He stood there, staring. After a few moments he pressed his face right up against the window, cupping his hands around his eyes to get a better view.

There couldn't possibly be two women in that county wearing that same sweatshirt. She had the same luxurious, long black hair. But down at the river he'd not been able to see her face. Seeing her now took his breath away. She was a knockout. He watched as a waitress brought another round of drinks to the table and the two cowboys nearly fought with one another to see which one could get the waitress to take his money first.

She saw him at the same time he saw her. She had been glancing around the room when she saw him approaching the window. He had watched her take a long second look at him, smiling, before returning her attention to the two young men, who were so focused on her they didn't seem aware of anything else.

Hom-Astubby couldn't take his eyes off her. He could see that she was wearing blue jeans and a pair of low-cut tennis shoes, the exact same pair of shoes with little pink flower imprints all over them that he'd placed on that picnic table beside her jeans and her panties and her bra and her one sock that he'd been able to find. Looking closely, he could see that she wasn't wearing any socks. He knew why. She couldn't find that other sock, either, and nobody wears just one sock.

Hom-Astubby was lost in a reverie—remembering her thin and skimpy and feminine panties and bra as he held them in his hands, and how he hadn't been able to resist smelling of those panties, and how *very* good they had smelled, her distinctive natural scent, which had stirred something deep inside him—when he became aware that other customers were staring at him.

He realized he must be making a spectacle of himself, pressed against the window, staring into the place like that. But before he could pull away, she glanced toward him again, and when she saw that he was still at the window and was now pressed against the glass, she stopped smiling and stared at him. Their eyes met. Moments passed before Hom-Astubby could break away from that eye contact.

He stepped away from the window, stepped between the window and the door, behind the log wall where she couldn't see him. He stood there, his heart pounding in his ears, wondering what to do. He felt foolish for staring at her like that. It had apparently made her uneasy. But he couldn't forget how he had seen her down at the river, and now seeing how incredibly beautiful she was—he just hadn't been prepared for that.

He stood on the porch, looking all around, wondering what to do. He noticed a plaque on the wall in front of him: HISTORIC SITE. It had a photo in a glass case showing an old building that had been painted purple. The inscription read: "On this site, historic location of the Devon County chapter of the Veterans of Foreign Wars, affectionately known as the Purple Pentagon, destroyed by fire in 1989. Photo courtesy of Sgt. John Murray, Fifth Northumberland Fusiliers, Royal British Army, a guest of the VFW in 1971."

A poster farther down the wall on the other side of the door caught his attention: "Live! On Stage This Saturday Night! In the Criterion Bar of the Purple Pentagon, LEA* Voted Best Band in Devon County!" It had some smaller print at the bottom but he couldn't make that out from where he stood. He walked to the poster until he could see what it said: "*LEA—Loudly Exploding Assholes."

That's charming, thought Hom-Astubby, and no doubt what

the sheriff had meant about the place getting a little loud on Saturday nights.

He thought about the woman again. She must have walked upstream to the Purple Pentagon while he was down at the river with the sheriff or maybe even while he was standing in the parking lot waiting for the sheriff. If she had taken the path beside the river, under the bridge, then she could have gotten here without him seeing her. But what in the world was she doing down there half-naked like that? And what had she done with her dog? Could it have been her dog he had heard howling?

He had a few moments of awkward uncertainty. Should he go on in, try to strike up a conversation with her? How would he do that with those two cowboys already there? Should he ask her what she was doing down at the river? How could he ask her about something like that? Should he pretend as though he hadn't seen her down there?

Maybe he should try thinking this thing through. Did he really want to have anything to do with this woman? At the very least she was probably some kind of head case. Wandering around half-naked like that. She was probably on drugs or something. A woman *that* good-looking who looked *that* good naked, well, she was bound to be trouble. Use some common sense here, he told himself.

He was now worth a lot of money. A good way to lose that money would be to get involved with the wrong kind of woman. Did he really want to take a gamble on a woman like that?

It wasn't as though Hom-Astubby was any kind of stranger to gambling. He wouldn't be in his present situation if he had been capable of driving past a casino without stopping. In recent years his growing addiction to slot machines had kept him strapped for cash nearly all of the time, and had caused him to lose all of his credit cards. Slot machines were the main reason he had still been driving a thirty-one-year-old Honda Civic when he bought his new camper. That battered and rusty old Honda had topped 400,000 miles sometime before the odometer and speedometer had broken, joining the gas gauge, air conditioner, heater, radio, passenger-side door, and the driver's-side window among the things that no longer worked.

But everything had changed last fall. It had all happened because of a blizzard. He'd been hurrying home to Oklahoma for Thanksgiving in that old Honda Civic when an early winter storm completely shut down the Texas panhandle. He got stranded in Albuquerque waiting for Interstate 40 to be reopened so he could limp on into Oklahoma. He spent that day in the Pueblo Indian casinos on the outskirts of Albuquerque. Late that evening the payline on his five-dollar slot machine hit a progressive jackpot for 8.8 million dollars.

He had celebrated with the intensity of someone who had remained nearly dead broke down through the years by playing back everything he'd ever won in any casino. He had never hit a payline bigger than what he could play back.

His euphoria had lasted until he began inquiring into the income tax consequences of having hit the jackpot.

That's when his old fear of the IRS had resurfaced, nearly paralyzing him with anxiety at the thought of making even one tiny false step in dealing with this kind of money. But he was determined not to become even the least bit vulnerable.

When his tax attorneys quickly drove him nearly nuts, he set aside five million dollars for taxes, just so he could have the option of telling all of them to go to hell and easily be able to pay the maximum amount he might owe and never have to worry about it again.

It took him less than three weeks to spend the other 3.8 million. Ordering the custom-made truck and camper, buying a new laptop and a lot of photography equipment he'd been wanting for years, a specially tailored wardrobe, fleets of new pickup trucks distributed to relatives and friends, and the mounting bills of his tax lawyers and investment bankers made a big dent in it. By the time he'd paid off some mortgages and a lot of other debts for a number of relatives, had set up his nephews and nieces and younger cousins for college, and had paid off all of his own debts, the 3.8 million was nearly all gone. He had not even gotten himself a cell phone, one of the things that had been high on his list.

He couldn't believe it had gone so quickly. It had been so much fun spending it that he started thinking about how he might get some of it back. He still had the five million he'd set aside for taxes, and that was more than he would need. What he should do was visit another casino.

And then that December, the week before Christmas, just before he was scheduled to leave on a long trip to Las Vegas, one he had planned out in minute detail, a man made him an offer to sell him a ranch that he could not turn down, even though the purchase left him nearly dead broke.

It was a horse ranch located a few miles off Interstate 40, about an hour beyond the western outskirts of Oklahoma City, one that was worth a lot more than the five million dollars Hom-Astubby paid for it.

Putting together that ranch had been only one of several expensive, eccentric, harebrained hobby projects of Arlington Billington, a crazy old oil-patch veteran who had more billions of dollars than he knew what to do with. That old fart had barely gotten all of the ranch components put together before selling it to Hom-Astubby.

Hom-Astubby had gotten acquainted with the contrary old geezer when he had been the focus of a barracuda-fishing article in the Florida Keys that Harry Birdwell had done. To his delight, Hom-Astubby discovered that Arlington Billington was a fanatical follower of the Oklahoma Sooners football team. Old Arlington had enjoyed his company so much and had liked the photos he'd taken so well that he had hired him to travel with him occasionally, when Hom-Astubby was between newspaper jobs, and take photos of him all over the world for a biography that he was having written about himself.

They had become good drinking buddies.

Arlington Billington was also a dedicated, lifelong enemy of Nelson Towers, and whenever Hom-Astubby had gotten together with him, cussing Nelson Towers had been their favorite sport.

The old man had been enormously tickled about Hom-Astubby hitting the casino jackpot. They had gotten good and drunk together when Hom-Astubby told him about it. Before the night was over, Arlington told him what he needed to do now was settle down on a place of his own before he gambled away everything he had won. He had backed up what he'd said by asking Hom-Astubby how much of the jackpot he had left.

Arlington Billington had died on New Year's Eve, a few days after the transaction had been completed, leaving Hom-Astubby a truly sad man at his passing and more than a little bit in awe of all that had happened. After thinking about it, Hom-Astubby figured out that the obscenely rich old codger must have known that he was dying, and that selling that ranch to him had just been Arlington's way of saying good-bye.

It was one hell of a good-bye. The ranch was sixteen full sections of land, 10,240 acres, some of it heavily timbered creek bottoms and spectacularly beautiful, rugged canyons, but more than 9,000 acres of it in prime horse pasture and hay meadows. There were dozens of new barns, stables, and corrals, some of them huge, and a towering entryway gate to the ranch, at the mouth of a canyon, that had to be seen to be believed.

The ranch had a large maintenance garage stocked with all the equipment that anyone could possibly ever need to work on any kind of vehicle, including all the tractors and other motorized farm vehicles on the place. Hom-Astubby could not even guess at the exact use for which much of that farm machinery had been designed.

The back side of the maintenance garage was connected to a huge airplane hangar, which sat at the end of a concrete runway that was so long it looked as though it had been built specially for Air Force One. Arlington had said, indeed, that the runway had been designed to accommodate that very airplane.

There was a brand new small jet sitting in the hangar, with seating for eight passengers and a crew of three. The jet was parked beside a twin-engine prop plane. Beside it was a single-engine bi-wing contraption that looked like some kind of stunt plane. Off to the side were two helicopters, one of them quite large. There was room in the hangar for quite a number of other big airplanes.

There were more than six dozen other outbuildings and structures, all of them bigger and better places than anywhere Hom-Astubby had ever lived.

The capstone of the whole place was a massive, towering, sprawling, brand-new, state-of-the-art seven-story house. It had six passenger elevators and a full-size service elevator. There were two additional floors, full double basements, below ground. The lower basement was mostly a huge parking garage with an entryway at ground level on the back side of the house.

The exterior of the structure had been minutely and faithfully patterned after some drawings of a grand old mansion on a Civil War–era cotton plantation that the old fart had seen in some comic book. The house had towering, stately white columns that supported the sprawling roof of a front-entry circular driveway.

The double front doors were easily tall enough and wide enough for Hom-Astubby to drive his truck through. That hallway led to a cavernous, high-ceiling ballroom on the ground floor that was as big and as tall as an ordinary three-story building all by itself, with six full stories above it. The second floor housed a huge library. The next four floors contained two hundred bedrooms.

The seventh story was about half devoted to a mammoth penthouse apartment and several spacious guest suites, and about half given over to office space for running the ranch. The roof of the penthouse had a heliport large enough to accommodate a helicopter larger even than the big one in the airplane hangar. Beside the heliport, an airplane control tower loomed several more stories into the sky. On top of that was a big glass-walled, eagle's-nest office with a spectacular view of everything.

There were quite a number of large single-story drawing rooms and sitting rooms flanking three sides of the first-floor ballroom. The ballroom itself had a grand, sweeping double-staircase worthy of the splendor of that room. While Hom-Astubby was being given a whirlwind tour of the ranch, so he could see what he was buying, Arlington had told him that he had specified to the architects who designed the staircase that each side of it be wide enough and long enough to accommodate every member of the Oklahoma Sooners' P-u-r-r-r-i-d-e of Oklahoma marching band.

Hom-Astubby had asked him what in the world he had intended to do with the house and with everything else on the ranch. But Arlington had said that what he'd intended to do didn't matter anymore. It was now Hom-Astubby's to do with as he pleased.

The house alone had to have cost god only knows how many tens of millions of dollars. Like everything else about the ranch, a lavish outlay of money characterized every aspect of it. Anything that could be done had been done, if it required nothing more than money.

Hom-Astubby hoped that some day he might be able to get the house furnished. It had carpets and drapes and blinds, but there was not a stick of furniture anywhere in the house, except for the huge, fully-furnished library that occupied the entire second floor. That was where Arlington had started furnishing the house, in grand style. Among many other things, the library had a globe of the world that was taller than Hom-Astubby and it had thousands upon thousands of books, some of them apparently quite rare.

All of the appliances and utensils in the fully equipped eight kitchens had also been installed, one on every floor except the library, including the two basement floors. The kitchen on the back side of the ballroom on the first floor was so big that it took quite some time just to walk all the way across it.

All of the fixtures had been installed in the 298 bathrooms in the house. There was a private bathroom for every bedroom, including a large portion of the top level of the basement, where many compact apartments had apparently been intended to house several dozen servants.

Every bathroom had a full-size shower and bathtub. It had been sobering for Hom-Astubby to contemplate that if he showered in a different bathroom every morning, it would take him nearly ten months to work his way through the entire house.

If he took a leak in every urinal and toilet in the house and in every building and barn on the ranch, using a different one each day, he estimated it would take him nearly two years to test the plumbing of the entire ranch.

He wasn't sure how many urinals and toilets there might be altogether in the biggest single structure on the ranch—the main barn and stables, not far from the house, which had a full-size rodeo arena with a wraparound grandstand under its roof, among many other things. He had not yet managed to explore all the many different parts of that building. His most recent discovery there had been a hidden staircase to an underground passageway that led to the parking-garage basement level of the house. He had no idea what else there might be on the ranch, both above and below ground, that remained to be discovered.

No one had yet been able to figure out how many miles and miles of indestructible, concrete-anchored, heavy steel-pole horse fencing had been required for all the many different horse pastures and corrals throughout the more than ten thousand acres of the entire ranch. But Hom-Astubby had been assured that the cost of the horse fencing alone had far exceeded the cost of the land.

Arlington Billington had employed architecture and engineering firms from different countries for each component of the ranch. He had contracted with different construction companies from Sweden, Germany, Australia, and Singapore to build the various components. They had imported every one of their workmen, had produced turnkey jobs, and had gone back home. There did not appear to be a single living person anywhere in the world who might know what the ranch in its entirety might consist of.

There was nothing that could be done about that except to survey and explore and inventory and try to catalog everything, a job for which Hom-Astubby had limited time—but which his tax lawyers were eager to do, at a price. The uncertainty regarding the value of the property was one of the biggest complicating factors in Hom-Astubby's mind-boggling tax problem.

Hom-Astubby had taken up residence in a few rooms of the house's bottom, parking-garage basement, which apparently had been intended as accommodations for more than one chauffeur. He had set up a darkroom there to process his film, and he had moved one of the dozens of leather-covered couches down from the library so he could have something to sleep on.

It was the first house Hom-Astubby had ever owned, several dozen houses altogether if one excluded all the barracks-style bunkhouse areas in the barns and just counted all the other outbuildings that were suitable to live in. Many of them actually were small houses intended apparently for the married ranch hands and their families.

Hom-Astubby had rented out a number of them in order to have some way to pay the utility bills on the whole place. He had nearly fainted when he'd been shown what the estimated annual property taxes would be, and he'd rented out all the hay meadows in order to have enough income to cover that.

Hom-Astubby's tax attorneys had been trying to get the ranch appraised. The house alone had tentatively been appraised at forty-seven million dollars. That had not included whatever value the books in the library might have.

It also hadn't included any of the paintings hanging on the library walls. They were everywhere, taking up every space where there was room to hang a painting. For all anybody knew, some of them might be worth something.

Hom-Astubby didn't think so; neither did his tax lawyers. Hom-Astubby knew nothing about art, but many of them were far too weird to be worth much money. It was just one more thing they hadn't had time to find out about.

Hom-Astubby's imagination, however, had been fueled by a news item about a recently discovered work by the Dutch master Vincent van Gogh, which was thought to be only the second painting the artist had sold during his lifetime. Nelson Towers had paid a fortune for it that summer at an auction in England.

The article said that Nelson Towers had the second-largest private collection of old masters in the world, with an estimated value somewhere in the neighborhood of two billion dollars. The article said that he coveted van Goghs most of all, with Picassos being a close second.

Hom-Astubby had heard of van Gogh and Picasso but had no idea what their paintings looked like. He had carefully read the description of the newly discovered van Gogh, trying to imagine what that one might look like.

He had then dug around in his library and found a book about art history, with some photos of van Goghs. A lot of the paintings in his library sure *looked* as if they might be van Goghs.

And the really weird ones *looked* as if they might be Picassos. Surely that guy had painted *something* that had made him famous other than the disjointed head-scratchers hanging all over Hom-Astubby's library walls. But the examples in the art book of Picasso's most famous work all looked somewhat similar to the paintings in Hom-Astubby's library. Several of them even looked *exactly* the same as the photos in the book.

A lot of the paintings in his library *seemed* to be either somewhat similar to, or *exactly* the same, as the examples of the work of many of the old masters in the art history book—especially a lot of the van Goghs.

They had to be copies. That's what his tax attorneys had said. But *somewhere* among them might be *something* of value.

He had decided definitely to get some expert to evaluate the paintings when he got sidetracked by his most recent discovery—the secret wine cavern. He had stumbled upon the entrance to it while trying to figure out why the service elevator descended far below the two basement levels, to a level that appeared at first to be nothing but a small room at the elevator exit.

The contents of the labyrinthine wine cavern were now being appraised. Just before leaving for Colorado, Hom-Astubby had been told by those appraisers that—if they had discovered all of the parts of the wine cavern—he owned at least fifty thousand bottles of wine, that some of the rare bottles might be worth as much as twenty-five thousand dollars each, and that it looked as though the total appraisal for all of the wine was going to be somewhere in the neighborhood of 37.5 million dollars.

The appraisers said that Arlington Billington might have been collecting and hoarding wine for as long as fifty years. It had been the discovery of the wine that had convinced Hom-Astubby that he could finally take a vacation.

He was eager to begin selling off the wine so he could pay his mounting legal expenses and get some operating capital, but he'd been told it would take time for it to be done right, for him to get the best price, and he wouldn't want to flood the market with the rare vintage wines in the collection. It should be done slowly, in increments, and it would take time to set up the first sale. It wasn't money he was going to begin seeing immediately, but it wasn't far off, near enough he had finally felt he could get out of there for a few days.

His lawyers were still trying to arrive at an estimate of the value of the entire property. Their estimates kept changing every time something new was discovered. Their latest conservative guess, with the discovery of the wine cavern, and with everything else they'd had time to get appraised and catalogued, had been 157 million dollars. But they had also told him that the IRS appraisers might say that the amount, just for those things, should be more than two hundred million. His lawyers were aware of a lot of things they hadn't had time to get appraised. Nobody had any idea what the final total might be. After the discovery of the wine cavern, anything seemed possible.

Given the great disparity in the value of the property and its purchase price, Hom-Astubby's attorneys were trying to find out if Arlington Billington might have paid gift taxes on the transfer. If so, then Hom-Astubby might not have any tax liability, not for the ranch. There would still be the matter of that casino jackpot.

But Billington had died so soon after the transaction, it didn't seem likely he'd done anything about gift taxes, or that he'd even thought about it. He certainly hadn't said anything to Hom-Astubby, and surely he would have said something. Those gift taxes would have been enormous, if they'd been for the full value of everything that had been transferred.

If Billington hadn't known he was dying, he'd probably thought there was plenty of time to deal with things like that later, if he had even intended to pay any gift taxes. And if he had known he was dying, his mind undoubtedly had been on other things. The sale of that ranch had happened so suddenly, after a night of drinking, and then he'd died so soon afterward, that anything requiring much forethought or afterthought didn't seem likely. But the slim hope that Billington had paid gift taxes was all Hom-Astubby could cling to.

Hom-Astubby's attorneys hadn't had any luck finding out what Billington might have done, if anything, about gift taxes. The Billington estate was tied up in court, the subject of several lawsuits, and the attorneys for the estate were slow in communicating with everyone. If Arlington Billington had left his own lawyers the kind of mysteries he'd left Hom-Astubby, which seemed likely, given his eccentricities, then there was little wonder why those attorneys weren't moving very swiftly. It was all one big complex mess.

As Hom-Astubby stood on the porch of the Purple Pentagon, debating whether to go inside and try to meet that woman, he felt overwhelmed by all the uncertainties in his life. He needed to get his life in order and try to adjust to his new circumstances before he got involved with any woman, especially some wild woman like that.

He decided that she was none of his business. He remembered, too, that it had taken most of his available cash just to get to Alpine, and that if he didn't get some checks in the mail soon, he would be flat broke. He had plenty of food and supplies in the camper. He could spend some money in the Purple Pentagon if he really wanted to, but he hated spending money for anything when he started running low.

He got in his truck and drove away, headed toward the main business area of Alpine, about three miles down the highway. But as he was pulling out of the parking lot, he glanced in the rear-view mirror and saw that the woman had come out of the Purple Pentagon and was standing on the front porch. She was watching him drive away.

He almost hit the brakes, but he'd already begun making the left turn onto the highway and there was traffic coming from that direction, far enough away for him to make the turn, but not far enough away for him to stop in the middle of the highway without getting broadsided. By the time he got straightened out of the turn and could look in the rear-view mirror again, he could no longer see the front porch of the Purple Pentagon.

What did she want? Did she want to talk to him? Had she awakened in time to see him leaving down at the river? Maybe she wanted to explain what had happened. Maybe she had seen him headed down there with the sheriff and was worried about that. Or maybe she'd seen him leaving down there with all of his cameras and was worried he might have gotten a photo of her.

He decided he should turn around and go back. But there was no convenient place to turn his big, long truck around for more than a mile, until he got to a gas station called the Shady Rest, sitting all by itself out on the highway, about halfway to Alpine. By then he wasn't so sure he should go back.

He pulled into the big gravel parking lot beside the Shady Rest and sat there debating what he should do. Finally, he went inside the gas station and used the men's room, then chatted for a few minutes with the attendant, a tall, friendly, freckle-faced kid named Dylan.

Dylan gave Hom-Astubby directions to the post office. He had decided he needed to go there before doing anything else. If his mail service in Oklahoma had overnighted anything to him, it might be one of the checks he was looking for. If so, then it might not be so bad if he went back to the Purple Pentagon and spent some of his cash.

If he could just get acquainted with that woman enough to satisfy some of his curiosity, that would be a big help. He had probably been jumping to conclusions about her. Maybe she was just a free-spirited, fun-loving gal.

By the time he got to the post office, he'd talked himself into going back and having lunch at the Purple Pentagon, even if none of the checks had come in. That notion lasted until the postal clerk handed him his mail.

CHAPTER FIVE

Except for the sports section from the *Sunday Oklahoman*, where Hom-Astubby followed the Sooners' preseason football practices, there were only two other items in the overnight package, but he groaned when he saw the first one.

It was a letter from his tax lawyers. He opened it to find *another* bill for legal services, this one for a little more than eleven thousand dollars, and a reminder that his income tax return was due in the middle of the month. The attorney was recommending that Hom-Astubby authorize him to appear before the IRS and request an additional extension of time to file his return, which would not be granted automatically, as the first extension had been. To present a compelling case for the additional extension would require quite a lot of work on the part of the law firm and an appearance of the attorney at the hearing, and all that would be expensive. However, in view of the amount of money involved . . .

Hom-Astubby groaned. There was no end to this. By the time all the bloodsuckers got finished with him, he'd be lucky if he had anything left. And every extension he got from the IRS would just prolong his agony that much more.

Hom-Astubby hadn't always been afraid of the IRS. There had been a time when he hadn't even been able to imagine how much trouble he could get himself into, thinking he was safe simply because he knew he didn't have any intention of doing anything wrong.

In his first job out of journalism school he'd been hired by a crusading newspaper editor in Montana who had encouraged him to do much more than just photography. He'd spent nearly two years investigating a mining company, uncovering a convoluted story of corruption and abuse involving the manipulation of National Forest permits to avoid environmental legislative protections, a story that was likely to get some people sent to prison.

His editor had encouraged him to turn his findings into a book.

He took her advice, working on the book at the same time he was preparing his investigative series for publication in the newspaper.

Hom-Astubby and his newspaper editor had both been blissfully unaware that the mining company was ultimately owned by one of the largest multinational corporate conglomerates in the world, with that ownership obscured through a complex tangle of holding companies involving an array of other corporations. One of those other corporations was a media empire.

They found out about that the hard way. When the newspaper began publishing Hom-Astubby's investigative series, the corporate conglomerate took care of that problem by having its media empire buy the newspaper. It fired him and his editor.

Suddenly, they found themselves out of work, with bills to pay. She encouraged him to continue with his half-finished book, to try to get the story out that way. But she couldn't help him with that anymore. They went their separate ways, job hunting.

He had been debating whether to try finishing that book when a letter arrived in the mail. It was from the Internal Revenue Service, notifying him that his income tax return was being audited and telling him where and when to appear with all of his income, business, and banking records.

The timing of the audit seemed a little too much of a coincidence to Hom-Astubby. When he found out that his former editor was also being audited, he was pretty sure that they were being sent a message by people powerful enough to get their names slipped quietly into the pool of taxpayers that were being audited by the IRS, probably without anyone at the IRS even being aware of it.

By then he had learned enough about the frightening power of the many-tentacled, international corporate monster he had pissed off to know that its influence extended to the highest levels of government in many different countries all over the world.

At the top of that corporate empire sat megamultibillionaire Nelson Towers—something of an enigma—a teetotaling, Bible-thumping, money-hoarding Texan, an impulsive, daring, risk-taking, wildly lucky bachelor, so pitiless, so coldly calculating and ruthlessly unprincipled that he was feared by presidents, kings, and prime ministers in every corner of the world. He had accumulated more wealth than anyone who had ever lived—and perhaps as much power. And what he clearly wanted was more of both.

One article Hom-Astubby had read, "If the Richest Man in the World Likes Your Country, He Just Might Buy It," had been particularly sobering. The more he learned about Nelson Towers and the more he contemplated the mess he had gotten himself into, the more it scared the daylights out of him.

But he didn't fear the IRS. He knew that he had been scrupulously honest with his tax returns, declaring every bit of his income, including all of the freelance outdoor photography he'd been doing on the side in Montana, an activity that had earned him quite a bit of extra money. His freelance photography had supported him all the way through college, when he had kept busy as a wedding photographer.

The tax audit, however, soon turned into a nightmare, mostly due to his horrible record-keeping. He discovered that his position was so precarious that for him to stand any chance of surviving the audit he had to hire a Registered Agent, an expert at advocating the position of taxpayers to the IRS. But his audit was greatly complicated by the puzzling lack of cooperation from his bank in refusing to make his checking account records available to him.

In setting up his checking account, he had chosen the less expensive option of not having his monthly statements include the return of his canceled checks. Now the IRS auditors wanted to see all of those canceled checks, and he had to buy copies of them from his bank. But the bank wouldn't make them available to him, wouldn't even return his phone calls. After long, frustrating months of getting nowhere with them, he finally had to hire a law firm to sue the bank and get a court order just to get his own checking account records.

To his horror, he learned that his bank was owned by another arm of the same corporate conglomerate that owned the mining company that he'd been investigating. The long delay in producing his banking records for the IRS caused its auditors to suspect that he was intentionally dragging his feet, trying to delay the audit process, because he had something to hide.

Then he got fired again. He had moved to Arizona, where he had found a job as a newspaper photographer and where he had also begun moonlighting on his own as a civilian auxiliary crime scene photographer, so he would have as much additional income as possible to pay the mounting costs of his tax audit. One day when he arrived at work, he discovered that Nelson Towers' media empire had bought that newspaper and that he had been the only employee who got fired.

That was just the beginning of it. Before long he would have difficulty keeping track of how many newspapers had fired him.

When the IRS auditor finally saw the mess that Hom-Astubby's business records were in, his eyes lit up as he expanded the audit to include the two previous years. Hom-Astubby ended up having to sue his bank again to get those records.

The auditor had finally ruled that all of the photography he'd been doing on the side had been a hobby rather than a business, mostly because he hadn't set up a separate business checking account for it and hadn't maintained adequate records of his business expenses, which created a presumption, the auditor ruled, that he had not been engaging in the activity with a profit motive. The auditor disallowed all of the business expenses that Hom-Astubby had claimed on his Schedule C, "Profit or Loss from Business," for all three years of the audit, and he levied heavy penalties for each year.

Hom-Astubby might have been willing to concede that taking photos on spectacular trout streams might be something he would do whether or not it turned a profit, but he could not believe that anybody with any common sense could actually think that he had been doing all of that wedding photography during college as a hobby. His Registered Agent tried explaining to him that government bureaucrats didn't think like ordinary people, that Hom-Astubby might have been thinking of himself as a photographer, because that's what he had been, but that had been his critical mistake. To the IRS bureaucrats he should have been thinking of himself as the record-keeper for a small business, because to them that's what he had been.

By the time the IRS finished computing all of the back taxes, with interest, and all of the fines and penalties, the amount was whopping for someone with Hom-Astubby's income level. He soon found all of his bank accounts frozen and he would have had all of his assets seized if he'd had any assets remaining by then to be seized.

Hom-Astubby appealed the rulings of the auditor to Tax Court, where, to his overwhelming relief when the case finally came before the court, he was vindicated. There, the basic honesty of his tax returns was rewarded by a sympathetic judge, who sternly warned him to learn something about standard small business accounting practices.

By that time Hom-Astubby had been so thoroughly wrung out that he could hardly believe the ordeal was finally over. It had dragged on for so long and had scared him so badly and had drained him so completely of both energy and money that he never had gotten completely over it.

As he stood in the post office in Alpine, reading the last page of the letter, he learned that his law firm wanted to put a team of lawyers on this phase of his tax problem right away, working around the clock if necessary to make sure that he would have the best chance possible of being granted that additional extension by the IRS. All they needed was his authorization to delve into it and they would get started without delay . . .

Hom-Astubby walked to the window of the post office and stood staring at the mountains, trying to estimate, at three hundred dollars per hour, per lawyer, what that bill might look like.

He shook his head. These bloodsuckers were incredible. He knew he could get that extension himself with little effort. It was such a routine matter that he'd never heard of one being turned down.

He tossed the letter back into the overnight mailer. He didn't want to think about this right now. He was *trying* to take a vacation. He opened the other letter he had received.

It was from his publisher. To his astonishment, he learned that his book, *Basic 35 MM Photography*, had sold out of its initial press run almost overnight and had then gotten so many back orders so fast that it was now nearly sold out of a second printing, which had been four times larger than the first one. The letter said that schools all over the country had been ordering it as a textbook for summer session and fall semester photography courses, based on glowing reviews of the book in the photography journals and the prepublication galleys the publisher had sent to photography instructors that winter. With advance spring semester textbook orders due soon, the publisher anticipated that a still larger third printing wouldn't last long.

The success of the book had caused them to reconsider his proposal to do a second book, on photojournalism, which they had originally rejected. They wanted to know if he was still interested in doing the second book, with an advance payment against royalties nearly ten times what he'd gotten for the first book.

He went outside immediately to the pay phone and called the publisher. He told his editor he was still interested in doing the second book, and his editor said he was going to take it to the editorial director with a recommendation that they buy it, based on the proposal Hom-Astubby had written and the success of the first book. He'd have an answer for Hom-Astubby within a few weeks.

Hom-Astubby hung up the phone with mixed feelings, happy about the prospects of getting a second book contract, but worried about his immediate cash-flow problem. He wasn't scheduled to get a royalty check for the first book for several more months. It looked as though he might be getting the advance payment to do the second book, but a check was several months away, even if everything went smoothly. In publishing, things rarely went smoothly.

He realized that he probably should have stayed in Oklahoma this week and arranged some kind of bank loan that would have put some money in his pockets right now. But he had been desperate to drive out of there and that's what he'd done. He really didn't regret having done that. He *had* to get away from there.

His immediate situation was nothing new. He'd been nearly dead broke all his life. He could get by again without having much money in his pockets.

He ducked back into the post office long enough to ask the postal clerk where he might be able to camp.

The clerk said that his son, James, ran a private commercial campground called the Cloud Nine, about seven miles down the road, one that had electrical and water hookups, showers, laundry facilities.

Hom-Astubby told him that he was pretty much self-contained and didn't need all of that. He just wanted someplace nice to park his truck. The clerk suggested a dirt road running beside the Purple Pentagon that went upriver a little bit, not far, to some good places to camp in the trees, down close to the river.

As the clerk was talking, Hom-Astubby thought about the place downriver from the bridge, the picnic table where he'd found the woman's clothes. He asked him about that.

"Sure," he said. "Folks camp there all the time."

Hom-Astubby headed out the door for his truck, knowing now where he'd be camping tonight. The thought of getting a free night of camping on Nelson Towers' land appealed to him, and there was also a chance that woman might come back down there. After all, she'd been there once, and Hom-Astubby knew where she might be found right now if she was still there. He could at least afford a cup of coffee, maybe get a chance to talk to her a little bit.

He had just started down the log steps off the porch of the post office when he saw the sheriff's Bronco passing by. Sheriff Klewlusz saw Hom-Astubby at about the same time. The sheriff stopped immediately, backed up, and pulled into the parking lot. He parked beside Hom-Astubby's truck and said, "Mallory, I was just coming to look for you."

CHAPTER SIX

om-Astubby waited for the sheriff to get out of his Bronco, wondering what was up.

"I just got this in," the sheriff said, holding up a sheet of paper. "I was wondering if this woman might be the one you saw down at the river this afternoon."

As he handed the paper to Hom-Astubby, the sheriff got a call on his radio. "I'll be right back," he said.

Hom-Astubby stood staring at a photo of the woman he had seen at the Purple Pentagon. It was a statewide police bulletin headlined "CONFIDENTIAL," from the Colorado attorney general's office.

He read the bulletin carefully. Avalon Blanche O'Neill, female Caucasian, age 28, 5'6", 125 lbs., black hair, green eyes, from Denver, Colorado, was wanted as "a material witness in a sensitive government investigation." If seen, the officer was not to make any contact with the suspect whatsoever, but was immediately to notify Deputy Attorney General George W. Langley, Section Chief, Criminal Law Section, at any hour of the day or night. Langley's office phone, home phone, and cell phone numbers were listed, as was a pager number. The woman's car was described as a blue late-model Honda Accord, with a Colorado license plate. A notation in bold print warned that the nature of the investigation was so sensitive that officers were expressly forbidden to reveal that the suspect was being sought "TO ANY MEMBER OF THE MEDIA WHATSOEVER." An additional note cautioned that the woman might be traveling with "a large, vicious, black, female dog."

If the sheriff had been standing there beside him, rather than talking on the radio in his Bronco, things probably would have gone differently. Probably Hom-Astubby would have identified the woman right away as soon as he'd seen the photo. But he had time to read the whole thing, and characterizing that dog as "vicious" stuck in his throat. He stood there, remembering his encounter with that big overgrown puppy.

As he thought about it, he started getting angry. They had the dog wrong in a way that could be dangerous to the dog. He shuddered at the thought of that dog getting shot because of some mistake like this.

He thought about protesting to the sheriff about how the dog was being represented. Then he remembered that he hadn't even mentioned the dog to him. The sheriff didn't know that Hom-Astubby had seen the dog. He didn't know that he'd seen the woman at the Purple Pentagon, either. Hom-Astubby realized he didn't have to get involved in this at all. He didn't have to say anything.

He heard the sheriff ending his radio conversation. Hom-Astubby looked at the woman's photo again, a little wistfully, but also with sudden relief as he realized how lucky he was to find out about this now rather than later.

As the sheriff walked up beside him, Hom-Astubby handed him the paper and shook his head. He said, "I'm sorry, but that woman down at the river was lying on her stomach and I couldn't see her face."

Narrowly, that was the truth, but Hom-Astubby knew he was telling the sheriff a lie and that made him nervous.

Sheriff Klewlusz took the paper and shrugged, saying, "Well, I thought I'd give it a try. A famous woman like that. If that had been her, I'd sure want to know."

"Famous?" Hom-Astubby said.

"Yeah. Doesn't her name mean anything to you?"

"O'Neill?" Hom-Astubby shrugged. "An Irish name?"

"Don't you recognize her picture?"

Something registered for Hom-Astubby for the first time. "Avalanche O'Neill? The Olympic Gold Medalist? The skier?"

"Yeah," the sheriff said. "What was it they used to say about her? 'The most famous face in Colorado.' First American woman to ever win the Olympic Gold in the women's downhill. Still the only American woman to ever do it. That's been awhile, but I can remember when you couldn't turn on the TV or open a newspaper or a magazine without seeing her. Then she just sort of faded away. There was something about that. Can't remember exactly. Something about her turning down some kind of super model contract and leaving the state. Wanted to get out of the public eye, be a career woman or something like that."

Hom-Astubby looked at the photo again, realizing now that his chances with a woman like that would have been less than zero—someone who'd been wined and dined by the most eligible bachelors in the country, maybe all over the world. He would have made a fool of himself even trying to talk to her, probably like those two cowboys were doing right now at the Purple Pentagon. He was lost in a reverie of disappointment thinking about that when the sheriff gave his nerves a jolt.

"If she's traveling with this big black dog, like it says here, that should make her a lot easier to spot. I need to find her if she's anywhere around here. This George W. Langley who put out this bulletin—'Dubya' they call him—will make my life miserable if it turns out she's around here and I didn't find her. Don't tell anybody I showed this to you."

It was the mention of the dog that made Hom-Astubby uneasy. He'd already lied to the sheriff about the woman. He didn't want to lie to him about the dog, too.

"Wouldn't she likely be around some ski area somewhere?" Hom-Astubby said, trying to steer the conversation away from the dog. "Even in the summer, someplace where she knows people?"

"That Telluride ski area is just the other side of Lizard Head Pass up there," the sheriff said, motioning toward Mt. Wilson in the distance to the north. "There's only two ways to get to Telluride and one of them's right through here. It's not all that far away."

"I've been wondering about that. Couldn't you also get to Telluride from here by going west?" Hom-Astubby said, trying to distract the sheriff even more, get him talking about anything besides that woman and her dog. "You know, up over that ridge out there, then circle up north around the mountains out that way, hook up eventually with some road that goes up into Norwood and then east through Placerville and on into Telluride that way?"

"Well, not from right here, not from this part of the county or anywhere north of here," the sheriff said. "Not without four-wheel drive. You can go south down the highway a little ways and before getting to Orontes go west on a county road over that ridge you're talking about, over into Dolores County. From there you can go anywhere, up north into San Miguel County like you're talking about, or south down into Montezuma County toward Cortez, or on out west in Dolores County all the way to the Utah border."

"I've got all-wheel drive," Hom-Astubby said, pointing at his truck, "and a boosted, raised, heavy-duty suspension and a powerful diesel engine, a truck built to go nearly anywhere. I'd been thinking, when I leave here, about trying to get some shots of this valley, from up on that ridge over there if there's a way I can get up there."

"Well, yeah," the sheriff said, looking at Hom-Astubby's truck. "In the summertime you ought to be able to get up there. But it's not even maintained by the county, just a jeep track over Maiwand Ridge that some of the ranchers use. That's it right there, Maiwand Road." The sheriff pointed at the side street beside the post office. "Not far out of town it starts getting pretty rough. It's certainly not anything a car can get up, not through those ruts. But if your truck's not too long to get around those sharp turns on the switchbacks you'd probably get up there okay."

The sheriff looked at the police bulletin again and seemed about to say something, maybe ask Hom-Astubby another question.

Hom-Astubby said, "Hey, look here," handing him the letter he'd gotten from his publisher, as though the thought of doing that had just occurred to him, which it had. "It looks like I'm going to get to write another book about photography."

"You wrote a book on photography?" said the sheriff as he began looking at the letter. He seemed genuinely interested in that.

"Yeah, and look," Hom-Astubby said, pointing at the first paragraph in the letter. "It's already sold out of its first printing. I've got some extra copies. Let me sign one to you."

While the sheriff was looking at the letter, Hom-Astubby dug around in the camper and found a copy of the book. He called out to the sheriff, "How do you spell your name?"

"K-l-e-w-l-u-s-z," the sheriff said.

"How about your first name?"

"It's Kerry. K-e-r-r-y."

Hom-Astubby wrote on the title page, "To Sheriff Kerry Klewlusz, with best wishes, William H. Mallory."

The sheriff seemed delighted with the gift, especially when he saw the chapter on crime scene photography. Hom-Astubby jumped on that and started talking about how he'd used a lot of his experience with different police departments for examples and exercises in the book.

Sheriff Klewlusz said that he did most of the crime scene photography for the Sheriff's Office when he didn't have a deputy who liked to do it. But it wasn't needed very often. They didn't have much violent crime in Devon County and only rarely had a criminal trial of any kind. Most of the cases were plea bargained.

It had been several years since he had needed to take photos to trial as evidence, so he spent some time going down Hom-Astubby's list of recommended procedures for proper cataloging of each shot, saying, "Boy, I know we should, but we don't do half of this stuff."

Hom-Astubby asked the sheriff if he'd ever had a photo challenged in court by a defense attorney. He hadn't.

Hom-Astubby talked about some of the reasons for recording date, address, the view being shot, time of day, brand of film, film speed, shutter speed, any filters used, and other things for every shot taken. He told him how some photos had been successfully challenged by defense attorneys because the photographer could not say exactly how the photo had been created. Hom-Astubby noted that the sheriff's concerned expression was growing more pronounced the longer he listened.

Hom-Astubby told him it was easy to alter photos, and for that reason it was easy for a good defense attorney who knew what he was doing to raise serious doubts about the integrity of a photo. Prosecutors needed to be able to convince a jury that there was little doubt about how a photo, and especially its negative, had been created, or the prosecution might leave itself vulnerable to having that jury disregard some critical piece of evidence.

He told him that was why law enforcement should never use digital photography, which created no negative at all. The very nature of the digitization process made it virtually impossible to prove that a digital photo had not been altered, unless perhaps every member of the jury was a computer geek who might understand the gobbledygook a prosecutor would have to rely on in trying to convince them that it hadn't been altered. A good defense attorney could complicate the proceedings with counter-gobbledygook, which was why people like O. J. Simpson were walking around free.

Finally the sheriff said, "Whew, boy. I need to read this chapter very carefully tonight, brush up on this stuff. I almost bought us a digital camera last month." He thanked Hom-Astubby again for the book.

To Hom-Astubby's great relief, the sheriff got another call on his radio, an emergency plumbing problem at the jail, a burst pipe with water running everywhere. It was flooding the prisoners in their basement cells and nobody knew how to turn the water off. The dispatcher had tried to call the company that installed those pipes, the Cajun Plumbing Company in Cortez, but the water had already shorted out the phone lines. The county clerk was getting the drunks out of the drunk tank, but he wanted to know if any of the other prisoners were considered dangerous before he tried to get to them. The water was getting deeper by the minute. What should they do?

The sheriff issued a mandatory evacuation order for all the prisoners in the basement, and then he peeled out of the parking lot, headed toward his office at the courthouse.

As the sheriff drove away, Hom-Astubby could see the decal on the back window of his Bronco. He could see the little Irishman in the Notre Dame football logo. The little Irishman was laughing at him. As the Bronco bounced across the ruts in the gravel parking lot, it looked for all the world as though the little Irishman was dancing up and down, laughing and laughing.

Hom-Astubby felt goose bumps running up his spine and shook himself to get rid of them. He frowned, staring at the decal until the sheriff's Bronco was out of sight.

He closed his eyes and shook his head. That would be all he needed, one of the Little People stepping into his life right now. Especially *that* kind of little one. But that didn't make any sense. What possible interest could that little Irishman have in any of this? Surely Irish Little People weren't anything at all like Choctaw Little People. Hom-Astubby tried to calm his nerves by reassuring himself that he had merely seen some kind of optical illusion. But he didn't feel very calm.

He felt the stress of his effort to keep the sheriff distracted from talking about that woman. He didn't want to think about how he might have impeded some investigation, how he might have obstructed justice by not telling the sheriff the truth about not recognizing her photo.

But he forced himself to consider for a moment the potential seriousness of what he had done. He had lied to a law enforcement officer. An overt act. He winced. It was always overt acts that did it, even if this one had been mostly an act of omission. The officer had asked him a direct question while conducting a criminal investigation.

Hom-Astubby closed his eyes and shook his head. It was moments like this that he wished he were not a lawyer, wished he didn't fully realize what he had done. What he had done was no small matter. He could get prosecuted for obstruction of justice, a felony, if it was ever found out.

He was pretty sure the odds were against its being found out, let alone his being prosecuted for it. But if that ever did happen, even if he could plea-bargain the thing, he could get kicked out of the bar association.

He had made himself vulnerable. A potentially serious aspect of his future was now out of his hands. It depended only upon whether anybody found out about it. He had no control over that. He had thrown it to fate—for all he knew, maybe to that damned little Irishman in that Notre Dame logo.

He shook his head. That woman was bad luck. No doubt about that. He'd never even spoken a word to her and now he had made himself vulnerable because of her.

But probably no harm had been done. He'd steer clear of her, forget about her, and try to steer clear of the sheriff for awhile, and that would be that.

He winced again when he remembered he'd be having dinner with the sheriff Saturday night. He shook his head again, wishing he'd waited to come to Alpine with Harry Birdwell.

CHAPTER SEVEN

Instead of leaving the post office parking lot, Hom-Astubby climbed in the back door of his camper and heated a can of soup. He dug out his files and found the book proposal he'd written on photojournalism, reading it while he ate the soup. It had been fun working up the proposal, but now he might actually have to write the book. If they did offer him a contract, he needed to figure out how long he'd need to write the book so he could negotiate the delivery date for the manuscript.

He turned on his laptop computer and was soon deeply absorbed. Traffic came in and out of the parking lot, but he paid little attention to it. Before he knew it, the sun was dipping toward the west. He put his paperwork away.

He saw a van pull into the parking lot and stop beside his truck. A tall, slender teenager got out of the van and filled a newspaper vending machine on the porch of the post office. From the camper Hom-Astubby could barely make out the name of the paper on the machine: the *Devon County Chronicle*.

When the van left, Hom-Astubby bought a copy of the paper. He stood on the porch, stretching his legs, leafing through the weekly, published every Monday. It was mostly advertisements, classified ads, local news, obituaries, engagements, weddings. Not much happening in August, with school out, no local school sports or activities to cover. A filler item at the bottom of a page caught his eye: "*Denver Daily Sun* sold."

He read the short item, which appeared to be a greatly abbreviated wire story. "Texas Planetary Network Productions announced the acquisition of the *Denver Daily Sun*, largest newspaper in the Rocky Mountain region. Texas Planetary Network executive Alexander Kelley was named the new publisher. Clarence Myers was named the new executive editor."

Hom-Astubby looked up from the paper, staring into the

distance, lost in thought. Texas Planetary Network. TPN. Nelson Towers' media empire.

He looked at the bank of newspaper machines. The *Daily Sun* machine was empty. Beside it was a *Colorado Leader-Enterprise*, for decades the *Daily Sun*'s biggest rival, with a circulation almost as large. He dug more coins out of his pocket and got the last copy out of the machine. The story was first-page news in the *Leader-Enterprise*: "Nelson Towers buys *Denver Daily Sun*." He took the paper to the camper dinette table and read the story quickly.

This time a Towers newspaper acquisition had raised a big stink, and the editors at the *Leader-Enterprise* had made no attempt to be gentle in lambasting their new rival. The top editor at the *Daily Sun* who'd been fired was none other than Earl Paggett, a legend in the industry, someone Hom-Astubby knew only by reputation. He was surprised to learn that Paggett had been running the *Daily Sun*. He thought he was still with one of the big dailies in California. But Hom-Astubby had been out of the business for awhile, and he hadn't kept up with things in the newspaper world.

Hom-Astubby was possibly the least surprised person in the country to read that Earl Paggett had been directing an investigation of Towers' business dealings. The stories had been set to start running soon in the *Daily Sun*.

There was more. The *Daily Sun* lead investigator for the series, Pulitzer Prize–winning reporter Linda Ruben, had sold a book about Towers, titled *Shadow on the Land*, to Granier Press in New York—an unauthorized biography of Nelson Towers. Towers' media empire, TPN, had also bought Granier Press and had canceled Ruben's book contract.

It was a bit more complicated, more devious, than that, as Linda Ruben had angrily told the *Leader-Enterprise* reporters. Towers' people hadn't exactly canceled her book contract, which might leave her free to publish the book somewhere else. They were canceling the press run, saying the book needed extensive editorial revisions "to correct serious factual errors." They cited clauses in

Ruben's book contract giving the publisher final editorial control of the book's contents.

Linda Ruben was livid, saying that getting back the rights to the book might take years of court battles and money for lawyers that she didn't have. Granier Press had been in serious financial difficulties, and she had signed a contract that didn't pay any advance against royalties. She was now unemployed. Towers' lawyers were also claiming that the *Daily Sun* investigative series was the work product of *Daily Sun* employees, and as such remained the property of the *Daily Sun*, effectively blocking Earl Paggett or Linda Ruben or any of the other *Daily Sun* reporters from taking any of the series anywhere else until that issue might be litigated in the courts.

There was much more. Hom-Astubby skimmed several more articles, columns, and editorials, most of them focusing on pre-publication censorship aspects of the story and speculation about what the courts might do.

Hom-Astubby put down the paper, knowing what would happen. It was a big stink right now and Nelson Towers was taking a big hit. But he would hunker down and ride it out. Before long, the next big media event would push the story out of the public eye. It would dry up quickly once it got into the courts, amid the delays of the legal process and the complexity and confusion of legal arguments—things not tailor-made for thirty-second sound bites on TV, and too tedious even for an interested reader.

The big hit on Nelson Towers was today. By tomorrow, it would be yesterday's news. The press had told the story of Linda Ruben and Earl Paggett. Repeating it wouldn't be news. By this time next year, only serious news junkies and dedicated Nelson Towers haters would have any awareness of how it was playing out. Few others would remember much about it. Nothing would change. Towers would have one more black mark on his reputation for his unauthorized biographers to play with, but they'd be writing history, and history isn't news.

In the end, if Linda Ruben got anything at all she might get some kind of out-of-court settlement, its terms secret, the whole thing by then largely forgotten.

Hom-Astubby felt a kind of kinship with Linda Ruben. He had learned the hard way the price of trying to investigate a Nelson Towers company, and he too had once thought he would publish a book like hers.

But he was also a little envious of her, and, he had to admit, maybe even a little resentful. Her firing was news, and she'd likely end up with some kind of settlement, offered by Towers' people just to make the problem go away, and accepted when she was too weary and depleted to fight any longer. Hom-Astubby had been fired repeatedly by Towers' people, and nobody had ever even noticed, let alone cared. Of course, he had to admit, he hadn't been a Pulitzer Prize winner, either, and the papers he'd worked for were small potatoes compared to the *Daily Sun*.

He got in his truck, feeling small and inconsequential, but soon turned his thoughts to more immediate matters. He had to find someplace to camp for the night. He saw the postal clerk locking up the post office and waved to him, noting that it was already five o'clock.

He pulled out of the post office parking lot. No way was he going to camp down at that picnic table now. And he wasn't going to spend any of what little cash he had left on some commercial campground. He headed up the highway toward the Crystal Fork.

At the Purple Pentagon he made a right turn and took the dirt road beside the restaurant into the woods, heading upstream on the Crystal Fork, for the other campsite the postal clerk had told him about. As he passed the Purple Pentagon, he could see that a blue Honda Accord was parked behind the building, out of sight from the highway. He shook his head, wondering what kind of mess he might have gotten himself into if he had not run into the sheriff at the post office, if he had pursued that woman. What if she had turned out to be come-and-get-it friendly? Maybe he would have gotten arrested along with her when the police caught up with her.

He hadn't traveled far on the dirt road in the woods when he came to a fork. He stopped. The postal clerk hadn't said anything about a fork in the road, or which one might lead to the campground.

The river was to the left, and the clerk had said the campground was near the river. Hom-Astubby took the left fork. He hadn't gone far when he came upon half a dozen pickup trucks blocking the road. Some of them were parked in the woods on each side of the road, and some were parked right in the middle of the road. There was no way to get around them. Up ahead of the pickups, he could see a big cement truck.

He stopped behind the last pickup and stood on the running board of his truck, where he could see better. A work crew was busy pouring cement to anchor two big steel corner posts for a large steel gate that stretched across the road. Others were busy erecting a high cyclone fence that would connect to the corner posts on each side of the gate.

Hom-Astubby noticed that all of the pickups had Texas license plates, but the cement truck was from a local company. It seemed a long way to bring a work crew, all the way from Texas.

He got back in his truck and was about to back up and try to find someplace to turn around, when another pickup, this one looking brand-new, pulled in behind him.

The pickup parked behind him, and three men got out and started walking toward the gate, two young construction workers and an older man, who was expensively dressed in elegant casual slacks and shirt.

When they walked past Hom-Astubby, he rolled down the window and said, "Hey, you've got me blocked in."

One of the younger men said, "Mr. Street, you've got that guy blocked in."

Street, who had been driving the pickup, kept walking toward the gate.

The younger man gave Hom-Astubby an apologetic shrug and then followed Street and the other construction worker.

Hom-Astubby got out of his truck and stood staring at the three men, hands on his hips, as they walked away. Wally Street, he said to himself. Nelson Towers' hatchet man who had gotten his camera bag and briefcase stolen, the sheriff had said. A big shot too busy to move his truck for some peon like Hom-Astubby. Years of anger at Towers' people welled up inside him, and he had to take several deep breaths to calm himself down.

Hom-Astubby walked to the back of his truck to see if he had any room to maneuver. There might be just enough room for him to back up to where he could then get the truck turned into the woods, to the right. He would have to maneuver the truck, backward and forward several times, to get it angled to where he could then drive out between the trees, but there appeared to be room for that, just barely.

He had gotten his truck turned completely around and was trying to get a better angle to drive out between two trees when he backed up a little too far and the back end of his camper nudged the back bumper of the pickup that had been parked in front of him.

"Hey!" yelled one the workmen, a very short, scrawny-looking fellow. "You hit my truck!" Everyone at the work site stopped what they were doing and stared at Hom-Astubby.

Hom-Astubby pulled his truck forward several feet then stopped and got out. He walked back to look at the other vehicle, but he knew the contact with it hadn't caused any damage.

"There's no damage," Hom-Astubby said, looking at the man's bumper. "If there was going to be anything damaged, it would be the back end of my camper, but you can't even tell where it touched your bumper."

"Like hell," the short guy said. "It probably screwed up my u-joint."

"They barely touched," Hom-Astubby said. "Your bumper's not even scratched."

"We won't know what's been damaged until I get it in the shop and get it checked out. I want your insurance information."

"What?" Hom-Astubby said. "There's obviously no damage. Have you got a u-joint going out, and you think you're going to use this to get me to pay for a new one?"

"Are you going to abide by the law or not?" the man said, squaring his shoulders and bristling and stepping toward Hom-Astubby like a strutting banty rooster. With his hands on his hips and his protruding chest brushing against Hom-Astubby's belt buckle, he said, "You hit my truck, and I demand to see your insurance."

Hom-Astubby just stood there, looking down into his eyes.

"You need any help, Bobby?" asked one of the other workmen, a big rough-looking man.

"No, I don't need no help. Did you see this redskin hit my truck?"

"Yeah, I saw it. He hit it pretty good."

Hom-Astubby couldn't believe it, but he had no choice. He had to exchange information with the man. As he went to the glove box in his truck to get his papers, he remembered that in order to save money on his insurance he had elected to take a large deductible policy. The first thousand dollars for any claim would come out of his own pocket. When he got his insurance papers, he also got one of his camera bags.

Hom-Astubby exchanged driver's license and insurance papers with one Bobby Joe Connolly, of Borger, Texas. Then he opened his camera bag and took out a twin lens reflex camera, with a 135 mm lens, and began taking photos of the back end of his camper and the back end of Connolly's pickup.

"What are you doing?" Connolly said.

"Recording the lack of any damage."

"I ain't sure you can do that without my permission. That's my truck you're taking pictures of."

"Why don't you call the sheriff?" Hom-Astubby said. "I'd like to hear you tell him that."

Connolly glared at him, and then he turned and stomped off toward the gate.

Hom-Astubby had put the camera back in his truck, along with his insurance papers, when it occurred to him that he should also get some documentation to establish where and when the photos had been taken. He didn't think Connolly would go through with the claim now, but he didn't like it that all the other people were Connolly's coworkers, who might support a claim.

Not all of them, though. The guy driving the cement truck wasn't one of them. Hom-Astubby got another camera bag out of his truck, one that had a variable 70–280 mm telephoto lens. He carried the bag up the road, behind Street's pickup, trying to find the best place to get shots of the cement truck at an angle that would also show Connolly's pickup and his own camper. Before he could figure out the best place for that, another brand-new pickup came down the road and parked behind Wally Street's pickup.

Nelson Towers got out of the vehicle, not ten feet from Hom-Astubby. He was a lot shorter than Hom-Astubby had imagined. He was, in fact, about normal height, several inches shorter than Hom-Astubby.

Towers glanced at him and said, in a pleasant voice, "Howdy. How are you doing today?" Then he walked away, toward Wally Street, who was talking to the cement-truck driver.

Hom-Astubby said nothing, his mouth hanging half-open. He stared at Nelson Towers' back. For all the photos he had seen of Nelson Towers, and for all that he had read about him, he still could not believe that the man was real—that he was a living, breathing human being.

Nelson Towers drives around alone? In a pickup truck? God, he really is a Texan.

Hom-Astubby continued staring at Towers until Towers got to the cement truck. Then he opened his camera bag, adjusted the telephoto lens, and took several shots of the cement-truck driver, who was now standing beside his truck with both Wally Street and

Nelson Towers. He backed up a little more and got good shots of the cement truck, also getting the back end of his camper and the rear end of Connolly's pickup. He got a shot of the cement truck's license plate.

He was in the cab of his truck, putting away his camera bag, when Wally Street and Nelson Towers came back to their pickups and drove away. Street left with the same two young construction workers who had arrived with him.

Nelson Towers also left the same way he had arrived, all alone, leaving Hom-Astubby shaking his head that somebody that rich and famous didn't seem to have any concern for his security. As Street turned his pickup around in the trees, Hom-Astubby heard one of the young men in the vehicle say, apparently to Street, "Yeah! Mama Garcia's. That sounds great, especially if you're buying!"

With Street's pickup now gone, Hom-Astubby had no trouble getting on the road. He drove back to the fork and went down the other branch, hoping it would lead to the campsite.

He was tired, and the argument with Connolly had left him feeling irritable. Seeing Nelson Towers in the flesh had unnerved him. He hadn't been prepared for that, and the last thing he wanted to think about right now was all the grief that Towers had caused him. He just wanted to get parked for the night and fix something to eat, maybe take a long walk down by the river.

The other fork soon made a big curve around to the left and took him in the direction of the river. The campsite wasn't hard to find. It would have been ideal, a lovely, peaceful place in a clearing, surrounded by tall trees, within sight of the Crystal Fork, but someone had already erected a tent there.

Hom-Astubby frowned as he got out of his truck. There was room for more than one person to camp, but did he want to disturb another's privacy? And did he really want to be camped so close to someone else?

He was standing beside his truck, looking all around, debating what to do, when he thought he heard a dog bark.

The sound came from somewhere in the trees, in the woods behind where the tent had been erected. He was looking in that direction when he heard it again. No doubt about it. That was a dog bark.

He went to have a look. To his astonishment, about thirty feet into the woods behind the tent, tied to a tree, was that woman's giant black Newfoundland dog.

The dog must have been there all afternoon, the way she started jumping for joy the minute she saw him. Maybe she had remembered the sound of his truck from down by the river and that's why she had barked. Maybe she was just happy to have somebody come along, anybody.

He walked over to the dog. When she stood on her hind legs, she was as tall as he was, and she washed his face with her big wet tongue before he could stop her. She was the most massively proportioned Newfoundland he had ever seen, bigger than any dog he had ever seen. He could barely believe that a dog that big could be a female.

She had turned over her water dish, so he took it back to his camper and filled it from his outside water tank. She drank nearly the whole bowl of water. He filled it again.

She was straining at the leash, wanting to play. He didn't see any harm in untying her for a few minutes. She barked with joy and ran to the clearing. Hom-Astubby followed her. She ran all around the clearing, burning up stored energy.

Apparently, she hadn't wanted to foul the area near the tree where she had been tied, but now she squatted to relieve her full bladder. Then she went sniffing around the clearing, investigating all the things that only dogs find fascinating.

As he watched her, Hom-Astubby thought about the Newfoundland breed. They were foreign, cold-climate dogs, Canadians, and a fairly rare, specialized breed at that, one of the best swimming dogs on earth. They had been bred especially for guarding children, and for rescuing them on land or in water. They were supposed to be one of the most highly trainable, docile, affectionate dogs in the world—a big teddy bear kind not worth a darn for guarding property, or for living in apartments or houses, or anywhere the climate wasn't cold.

Their body proportions were so massive and their hair was so thick that they looked awkward and ungainly, like greatly over-weight Keystone Kops frolicking around. And the poor things had definitely not been bred for beauty. Some of the more pure-blooded ones looked as if they had been dropped on their faces at birth, giving them a dumb-looking dog face. This one had the dumbest-looking dog face Hom-Astubby had ever seen.

But when it came to children, stories of Newfie courage and heroism were legend. More than once had a big Newfie put itself between a bear and some child, sacrificing itself in doing what it had been born to do. They were truly in their element when racing ahead, finding lost children, and keeping them safe until human help could arrive.

When the dog returned to Hom-Astubby, she wanted to wash his face again. It made him laugh. She stood up on her hind legs and locked arms with him, and they danced around the clearing, the dog licking his face and hugging him so that he couldn't get away from her and couldn't stop laughing.

Finally, he took her back into the woods and tied her to the tree again. He sat there petting her, talking to her soothingly, as he had done earlier that afternoon down by the river.

What a dog. But that woman was camped here. He had seen the car tracks beside her tent. She would be coming back here soon. He couldn't stay here. He couldn't camp anywhere near this place.

So this was how she was trying to avoid the cops. Camping out, avoiding motels, probably avoiding her friends and relatives, her known acquaintances, all the places the cops might be looking for her. Pretty smart woman, Hom-Astubby thought, grudgingly admiring her tactics.

But she must be some kind of alcoholic, and a wild one at that, in trouble with the law, and up there right now working on those two young cowboys, drinking up all their wages, in the middle of the day, after having passed out from being good and drunk a few hours ago down at the river. If she had half a brain she'd be getting the hell out of this state.

Maybe she was waiting for dark, when her car wouldn't be so easily identified, her license tag not so easily read. Maybe she'd driven all night to get this far. Maybe that's why she'd fallen asleep down at the river. Maybe she hadn't been drunk after all.

But if she planned on trying to drive out-of-state after dark, why would she be sitting up there at the Purple Pentagon all afternoon getting snockered with those two cowboys? She probably really had been drunk down at the river. She was probably still drunk, and getting drunker.

By dark, she'd probably be so drunk she wouldn't even know where she was, or care. This might turn out to be the luckiest night those two young cowboys ever had. By the time she finally sobered up, sometime tomorrow, she might have a big, lop-sided grin permanently plastered on her face.

"Women," Hom-Astubby said, shaking his head.

He said goodbye to the dog and got in his truck, more than just a little bit miffed that this ski bunny seemed to be directing his life—where he couldn't camp, where he couldn't go for a cup of coffee, causing him now to be tense and nervous when anywhere near the sheriff, who was someone he had been looking forward to getting better acquainted with.

He went looking for another place to camp, determined to put that bimbo behind him for good.

CHAPTER EIGHT

Tuesday, Noon

Hom-Astubby didn't know that a Colorado state patrolman was behind him until he saw the flashing red light. Hom-Astubby knew he wasn't speeding, but that didn't keep his pulse from accelerating as he pulled over to the side of the road.

A traffic ticket was bad enough, but then your insurance rates go up. He couldn't imagine what he'd done wrong. He rolled down his window and watched in his rear-view mirror as the patrolman got out of his car and walked toward him.

"Mr. Mallory?" he said.

"Yes, sir," Hom-Astubby said, surprised that the patrolman knew his name.

"Good afternoon, sir. I'm Jim Mortimer. Sheriff Klewlusz is looking for you. He asked if you could meet him down by the river, where the two of you were yesterday."

"Is something wrong?"

"Yes, sir," Mortimer said. "They've found a body. But that's about all I know, except that it's got something to do with a big dog track. Will you follow me?"

Hom-Astubby told him that he would. He wondered how the trooper had been able to find him. Hom-Astubby hadn't noticed the sheriff writing down his tag number, but that's what he must have done. The thought made him a little uncomfortable. Maybe the sheriff had gotten the tag number by running his name through the Oklahoma vehicle registration records. Or maybe the patrolman had just been told to look for a big crimson and cream truck that looked like a motor home, with Oklahoma plates.

The trooper had stopped him while he was heading upstream, driving back to a small primitive campsite near a highway bridge, where he'd camped for the night, quite a few miles upstream from the Purple Pentagon. He'd spent all morning hiking up and down the river, photographing fly-fishermen, a short drive downstream from where he'd camped, and now he'd been ready to park his truck again in the good shade at that little campsite, relax for awhile, and fix a big lunch. But they turned around and headed down the highway toward the turnoff to the picnic table.

Hom-Astubby had located Towers' gate yesterday evening, on his way up the river. He looked again as he passed it now and recalled what the sheriff had said about it.

Towers' gate was built on a grand scale, with its two side sections consisting of tall twin towers constructed of rocks and mortar, capped, high above the ground, with a long section of a big fat, peeled and polished log, nearly as long as a whole tree. An inscription was blazed into the log in big letters: DARTMOOR MANOR.

Imposing as it was, however, Towers' gate was not the biggest one Hom-Astubby had ever seen, not by a long shot. It was with more than just a little bit of smug satisfaction that Hom-Astubby had noted that the gate to his ranch in Oklahoma was a lot bigger, a lot taller, a lot more massive, and one hell of a lot more impressive than Towers' gate.

Towers' gate was just downright puny compared to Hom-Astubby's gate, and someday he'd like to have the satisfaction of showing that bastard just how puny his gate really was. Hom-Astubby wondered if all of Nelson Towers' houses might also be more puny than his biggest house. Towers might not even own as *many* houses as Hom-Astubby now owned, and if by any chance the son of a bitch *might* own more houses, he'd damn sure bet they didn't have as many toilets as Hom-Astubby could claim. Maybe Towers had one of those medieval castles over in Europe somewhere, but even that might not necessarily be bigger, or more impressive, than Hom-Astubby's biggest house. And if the bastard had a ranch somewhere, he might have more acres, but he would have to have one hell of a big barn to have one as big as Hom-

Astubby's biggest barn. If nothing else, Hom-Astubby would bet money that he now had a wine cavern bigger than any wine cavern that bastard might have. That might be a sure bet, given Nelson Towers's well-known reputation as a teetotaling Bible thumper.

When they got to the turnoff, just before the bridge, across the river from the Purple Pentagon, Hom-Astubby could see several vehicles in the distance, parked downstream at about the location of the picnic table. As they got closer, he could see that most of them were official vehicles of one kind or another—the sheriff's Bronco, two other Sheriff's office vehicles, a Colorado Division of Wildlife pickup, another Colorado State Patrol car, a Fire Department vehicle, along with several other unmarked cars and trucks. The trooper and Hom-Astubby parked behind the line of vehicles, quite some distance from the picnic table.

"I think those two guys found the body," the trooper said. Hom-Astubby looked where Mortimer was pointing, seeing two fly-fishermen still wearing their chest waders, being interviewed by two Wildlife Division officers and a sheriff's deputy at the back end of the Division of Wildlife pickup.

They walked past them, toward a man and a woman who were stringing bright yellow crime scene tape in a wide circle around the picnic table area. Hom-Astubby saw Sheriff Klewlusz standing behind his Bronco with two men, one of them puffing away on a large pipe.

The sheriff had run his Bronco through a car wash somewhere. As Hom-Astubby was approaching the vehicle, doing his best to ignore that damned Notre Dame logo on the back window but unable to resist a glance, he could have sworn that the little Irishman's eyes twinkled at him. But then he saw that it had just been the glint of the sun reflecting off that decal.

The sheriff saw Hom-Astubby. He turned to the other men and said, "Howard, Oliver, here's the man I want you to meet."

As Hom-Astubby walked up to them, the sheriff said, "Mallory, thanks for coming. I want you to meet Dr. Howard Watson, our new coroner, who moved out here from New Hampshire last year, and Oliver Holmes, who's been our district attorney for a long time."

Hom-Astubby shook their hands, then looked at the sheriff, quizzically.

"It's not pretty," the sheriff said. "She's been horribly mutilated. Beside the picnic table."

"My god," Hom-Astubby said. "The woman I saw yesterday?"

"It might be," the sheriff said. "I want you to take a look. But we also need your help on this one. We've got to get crime scene photos before the wind comes up. It's supposed to blow again today. I don't trust myself to do a good enough job with a camera for what we need here, and the CBI is tied up on another case and might not get here in time."

The sheriff pointed down the road. "We've got some fresh car tracks in the dust that we can't risk losing. There's something else, too. It might be a long shot, but I found a large dog track back there in the brush in some loose dirt, and if this turns out to be that O'Neill woman, it would be big news in this state. Our work on this case would be put under a microscope. We want a professional to do this crime scene. Howard usually does his own autopsy photos, but we want professional work on that, too, when he does the autopsy in the morning. We called Delbert Lawson at the CBI to ask his advise. He said there's nobody better than you. We want to hire you to take all the photos."

"Sheriff," Hom-Astubby said, "I'll be more than happy to help, but it'll draw me away from other work I need to do. I'd have to charge regular rates, and I'd need an assistant to take the notes."

"I can assign a deputy to help you. As for payment, we'll need to make it two separate charges, from two different budgets, and it might take a couple months for you to get the checks, but would two hundred dollars for each one be sufficient?"

"Well, my regular rates would be more like four hundred dollars for each one. But I'll tell you what, if I could get the money when I finish the job, rather than having to wait for it, I would do it for two hundred each."

That caused the sheriff and the new coroner to huddle together for a few minutes while they figured out how they could do that. They finally decided they could probably get a check for Hom-Astubby by the next morning, and Hom-Astubby agreed to that.

They talked awhile about the photos they would need, agreeing that Hom-Astubby would give the undeveloped film to the deputy who would be assisting him and taking the notes. "That will preserve the chain of evidence," said Holmes, the district attorney. It would also make it unnecessary for Hom-Astubby to appear in court simply to establish the chain of evidence. The deputy could do that. "The deputy will witness all the photos being taken," Holmes said, "and then will be in possession of the film until it's delivered to the processing lab or to the CBI when they get here."

The Sheriff's Office would pay for all the processing of the film and printing of the photos. Hom-Astubby would have only to provide the film and shoot the photos. If Hom-Astubby had to testify at trial about the photos, the county would pay for his travel and accommodations.

"Is there anything else we need to get straightened out now?" Holmes said. "I don't want any glitches when we get to trial."

"There's one more thing," Sheriff Klewlusz said, "that I don't want to have any misunderstandings about. That weekly newspaper here will probably want a photo—maybe other papers, too—and since you do freelance work, we need to be clear about something. I don't want any of the newspaper photos to show that woman's injuries. I don't want her parents opening a paper and seeing her like this. Is that agreed?"

"Yes," Hom-Astubby said. "That's fine with me. That weekly paper just came out yesterday, didn't it?"

"Yes, every Monday," said Watson, the coroner. "The guy who does it, Dan Druther, is pretty much a one-man show, at least for the news, and he takes all the photos himself. I know he had to go out of town last night, so he'll be needing a photo. But I don't think they can pay very much."

"Okay," said the sheriff. "Let's go look at the body, but be careful where you step. Walk behind me. That fresh set of car tracks is over this way. Let's take a look there first, since that's where you'll need to start. We'll be taking some molds of them, and we'll have to get that done, too, before the wind comes up. The wind is forecast for late this afternoon. I'm hoping the CBI will get here in time to do that, but we'll have to do it ourselves if it starts getting too close. I'm hoping that by you having the photos done, that'll free them up to get right on the tire tracks first thing."

Hom-Astubby followed the sheriff, stepping carefully over the tire tracks when they got to them.

"It's a passenger car," the sheriff said, as they knelt down, looking at the fairly narrow set of tracks in the dust. "It turned around right over there, where we might be able to get all four tires. But those fly-fishermen who found her walked right through the best part of them."

They looked closely at where the car had turned around. "There's enough here for me to work with," Hom-Astubby said.

"Good. Where did you park yesterday?"

"Over there, beside that big rock." Hom-Astubby pointed to a spot just off the dirt road.

"Let's have a look."

Hom-Astubby led the sheriff to where he had parked. The tracks were already barely discernible, pretty much filled in with dust. They were in sharp contrast to the fresh tracks. His truck tires were also much wider than the other set of tracks.

"That's what the wind does here," said the sheriff. "Was it blowing when you got here yesterday?"

"Yes, it had just started. It wasn't blowing at all when I stopped up at the pay phone at the Purple Pentagon and made a couple of business calls. But by the time I got down here it was blowing pretty good."

"It's a good break for us that it's not blowing yet today. Chances are we'll be able to make a positive ID on the car, if we can find it. There's a good chance it'll turn out to be her own car, once we find out who she is. Let's go look at the body."

They had turned to go, when the sheriff said, "Wait. Look over there. It's another dog track."

They walked to where the sheriff was pointing, to where Hom-Astubby's tire tracks had been sheltered from the wind by the big rock he'd parked beside.

A very large dog track was distinct, on top of Hom-Astubby's tire track.

"It's a huge beast," the sheriff said, "and it was here sometime after you left."

Hom-Astubby said nothing, staring at the dog track.

"Let's go look at the body," the sheriff said.

Hom-Astubby followed the sheriff to the picnic table, but despite all the crime scenes he had worked, he wasn't prepared for this one. This time the woman was dead. There could be no doubt about that. Whatever had been used to bash in her skull must have been very heavy, and her throat had been horribly torn open.

There was more blood than Hom-Astubby would have thought possible. A river of it had spread out all around her head, where much of it had seeped into the ground. The surface layer had dried, and flies and other insects were buzzing everywhere.

There were blood splatters and bits of skull and brain matter all over the legs of the picnic table, on the side nearest the body, even though she was lying with her feet toward the table and her head was a good eight feet away from it. It was obvious to Hom-Astubby that she'd been struck repeatedly while she was lying on the ground, probably after she'd been knocked down, after having had her throat ripped out.

The ground all around the body, and all around that end of the picnic table, had been raked over vigorously and thoroughly, apparently with a branch from one of the nearby bushes. The raking had streaked the pools of blood and spread them out all around the area.

Hom-Astubby turned his head slowly, his eyes following the distinct trail of scratch marks across the ground, leading away from the picnic table, toward the tire tracks.

"He wiped out all of his shoe prints," the sheriff said. "All the way over there to where the car was parked. That bloody branch is over there in the bushes, where he tossed it."

Hom-Astubby looked at the woman again. She was lying on her stomach in very nearly the same position he had seen her the day before, except her arms were outstretched, one above her head and one below, and she was fully clothed.

She had changed clothes or at least had changed into a pair of high-topped, bright reddish-brown leather boots, and a light green long-sleeved shirt. The blue jeans might have been the same. The long black hair was a mess, matted with blood and stuck to the side of her face. Her head was nearly detached from her body.

Hom-Astubby felt an old queasiness in his stomach and remembered why he'd stopped doing this kind of work. The stillness of the body, and the buzzing of the insects, was almost as revolting as the blood and the crushed skull.

"Do you think it's the same woman?" asked the sheriff.

"I think so," Hom-Astubby said. "I can't be sure, but it looks like her." But he knew it was that woman. He turned away, breathing deeply.

CHAPTER NINE

"I'll get Albert to help you," the sheriff said, staring at the buzzing flies and the gore. "We need to find something useful for Albert to do. He ran for the legislature a few years ago and got defeated by one vote, and he just sort of gave up on life after that."

Hom-Astubby was soon joined by Albert, an older deputy who didn't seem to have much interest in what they were doing. They went to Hom-Astubby's truck for his cameras, then to the tire tracks. But when Hom-Astubby explained to Albert all the information he would have to record for each shot, Albert said he had to go to his vehicle and get a lot more note paper.

While Albert was gone, Hom-Astubby shot a roll of 35 mm color film for himself, a panorama—something he always did, if there was any chance he might be called to testify about his photos—so he could orient himself to the other photos he'd be shooting. It might be years before a case came to trial, and memories fade a lot faster than photos.

He shot eight slightly overlapping shots around the horizon with a 28 mm wide-angle lens. Once they'd been developed and printed and laid end to end, they would show the complete crime scene, would show what a person would see if he stood near the body and turned slowly around in a full circle.

The photos also captured all the activity at the scene, all the people busy at their separate tasks, all the people coming and going, all the vehicles. The photos would help him remember exactly what the crime scene had been like.

After changing lenses, he did the same thing again, with a 50 mm lens, it requiring twelve slightly overlapping shots to get the complete circular panorama. But that was often the most useful one of all, with the 50 mm lens most closely approximating what the human eye saw.

He dropped that roll of film in a vest pocket, noting that in one of the 50 mm shots he'd gotten the sheriff, the district attorney, and the coroner huddled together near the body and the picnic table, with only the victim's legs in the frame. That one would probably work for a newspaper photo.

He took out a notebook and got the attention of the district attorney, getting from him the proper spelling of their full names—Dr. Howard Dean Watson and Mr. Oliver Hardy Holmes—and their formal titles, the way they'd want them listed in the paper, so he could get the photo caption right.

Hom-Astubby then did something he ordinarily didn't do. Influenced by what the sheriff had said about the scrutiny the crime scene work might get, he shot a panorama of the horizon one more time, with a 135 mm lens, using the twin-lens reflex camera he had used the day before to take photos of Connolly's pickup. It had been loaded with a fresh roll of thirty-six exposures of color film when he'd shot the pickup, and there were enough frames left on the roll to finish it out now with the panorama. He dropped that second roll of film in his vest pocket with the other one as Albert returned and they started to work on the tire tracks.

The car might be one of the main pieces of evidence in the case, so they took great care in what they were doing, shooting several rolls of film, getting shots of the tracks all along their length, up to where they'd been obscured by the official vehicles arriving at the scene. They gave a lot of attention to where the car had turned around, trying to get shots of all four tires.

The grimmest part of the business was shooting the body of the victim. They shot close-ups and views from every angle, while taking great care to disturb the area as little as possible. Concentrating on the technical aspects of what he was doing helped reduce the horror of what he was seeing in the viewfinder, but not by much. It was slow work, with all the information Albert had to record about each shot.

When he was finished, he figured he had probably shot about twice as much film as was necessary, taking great care in what he was doing, changing lenses and cameras frequently, bracketing some shots one or two stops above and below the meter reading, making absolutely certain that at least one of the frames would be as sharp as possible and perfectly lighted.

The sheriff wanted a lot of shots, not just of the body and the tire tracks but of the area all around the body and all around the picnic table. He also wanted shots of the two dog tracks he'd found. Hom-Astubby thought that was a waste of time, but he said nothing, taking careful shots of both tracks.

For some shots of the body and the immediate vicinity and the tire tracks, Hom-Astubby used the 2¼ by 2¼ twin-lens reflex, with its fixed focal length, the 135 mm lens, the same camera he had used for the additional, more detailed, panorama.

Hom-Astubby explained to the sheriff that the inability to change lenses had caused the twin lens reflex to be a lot less popular than 35 mm cameras, but that the larger negative gotten with the twin-lens reflex would allow him to have much better quality enlargements made from it than would be possible with the smaller 35 mm negative. That could be important if he needed a blow-up of some portion of one of the prints, to show some small detail in the tire tracks or anything else that might need enlarging. The sheriff seemed very pleased about that.

People arrived and departed the whole time Hom-Astubby was at work. Near the end, an ambulance arrived, but they weren't ready to move the body. They didn't even want to turn the woman over until the technicians from the CBI had arrived.

Dr. Watson gave Hom-Astubby the address of his new funeral parlor in Alpine and told him to meet him there at eight o'clock the next morning, when he thought they'd be ready to start the autopsy.

During the time Hom-Astubby was at the crime scene, he learned that if the woman had a purse or wallet with her, it apparently had been stolen. She had no identification, unless there was something in the front pockets of her jeans or perhaps something underneath her. He heard a state patrolman say it looked to him as though both the woman and her killer had arrived at the scene in the same vehicle, but Hom-Astubby didn't overhear much more, and he didn't want to ask any questions.

The only odd thing he heard came when the district attorney knocked the ashes out of his pipe and said to Dr. Watson, "Howard, I've got some predictions about the dog in this case." The two of them then walked down to the river, where the coroner sat down on a rock, took out a notebook and began scribbling in it as Holmes was speaking.

Hom-Astubby gathered up all of his equipment while Albert double-checked the labeling on all the exposed rolls of film and organized the notes he'd taken. They went to find the sheriff.

He was at his Bronco, talking on the radio. Hom-Astubby heard him instructing someone to call George W. Langley at the Colorado attorney general's office and tell him that a murder had occurred, that the victim might be Avalon Blanche O'Neill, that the woman matched the description, but that her car had not been found.

Listening to the sheriff, Hom-Astubby wondered if he should tell him that he knew where the woman had been camped and that he had seen her at the Purple Pentagon the previous afternoon with those two cowboys. Those cowboys might be the ones who killed her. He wished he'd paid closer attention to their appearance.

But he had lied to the sheriff about not recognizing her photo. How could he now know so much about her, when yesterday afternoon he'd acted as though he didn't know anything at all? That one little lie was starting to get complicated. Maybe he should just come clean with the sheriff and tell him that, at the time, he hadn't wanted to get involved, that none of it seemed important then. After all, outside of seeing her lying beside the river, he'd had no involvement with the woman.

With or without Hom-Astubby's help, the sheriff would soon confirm her identity, and it wouldn't take him long to learn that she had been at the Purple Pentagon and that she'd been drinking with those cowboys. The sheriff would find out whether she had left with them, or whether she'd taken up with somebody else later. It seemed likely she'd met her killer at the Purple Pentagon, but maybe not. She had to change clothes sometime. But she might have had her clothes in her car. She could have changed in the women's room of the Purple Pentagon.

Her killer might even have seen her naked down by the river and followed her to the Purple Pentagon and waited for her to come out. He might have kidnapped her in her own car, taken her back down to the picnic area, and then driven away in her car.

Or she might have left the Purple Pentagon and gone somewhere else and met her killer. She might not have been killed until this morning, but he doubted that. He'd seen enough homicides to get a rough feel for time of death, and the condition of the body suggested that the woman had probably been dead since sometime yesterday afternoon or evening or last night, but he'd also been way off on his guesses before. It was a tricky business, and appearances could sometimes be deceiving.

Right now, there was no way of knowing hardly anything, except that he knew she'd been in the Purple Pentagon yesterday afternoon drinking with those cowboys.

No matter what, the people at the Purple Pentagon knew that Hom-Astubby had never even been inside the place. All he'd ever done was stand on the porch and look in the window.

That's when he remembered how uneasy she'd looked when she caught him staring at her. Would the people at the Purple Pentagon have noticed that? Several customers had seen him. Were they tourists, already long gone from the area, or were they locals who might remember that and tell the sheriff about the Indian who had stared at her through the window? Would they give the sheriff Hom-Astubby's description? Maybe they had even seen his truck and would give the sheriff a description of that.

The woman had come out on the porch and watched him drive away. Maybe she'd gone back in and talked to those two cowboys about that, asking them if they knew who that Indian was. Maybe by the time Sheriff Klewlusz got through talking to the people at the Purple Pentagon the sheriff would have figured out that Hom-Astubby had deliberately lied to him about not recognizing the woman's photo. That might make Hom-Astubby the number one suspect. More than anything else, cops loved exposing a lie because it often led to solving a case.

If he had to try to prove where he had been last night, or yesterday evening, or this morning, could he do so? He hadn't talked to any of the fly-fishermen he photographed this morning. They'd all gone by in boats. No one else had been where he had camped last night.

Yesterday afternoon was the only time he had an alibi. He was at the post office all afternoon, part of the time with the sheriff. The postal clerk had seen him leaving at five o'clock and likely would remember that. They'd waved to each other. Jesus, he'd asked the postal clerk about camping—right here—at the picnic table. That thought made him nervous.

Did he have any kind of alibi for where he had gone after waving to the postal clerk? Yes! He was with those construction workers after leaving the post office. He'd exchanged insurance information with Bobby Joe Connolly. Down here, near the river. Less than a mile upstream from where the woman had been murdered. That thought made him even more nervous.

But she had still been at the Purple Pentagon then, hadn't she? He'd seen her car parked behind the building, or what he had assumed was her car, from the description on the police bulletin, when he'd driven by after he'd left the post office. He hadn't noticed whether the car was still there when he'd driven by again, after finding her dog at her campsite. But that could have been someone else's car. Lots of blue Honda Accords in the world. And even if it was her car, that didn't necessarily mean that she was still inside when he'd driven by the first time. She might have left anytime, either with someone, in another car, or alone, in her own car, or on foot, maybe to go walking down along the river again.

For all he really knew, she might have left the Purple Pentagon right after he had seen her through the window. How did he even know for sure that she'd gone back inside after leaving to find out who that Indian was? That might have been the last time anybody at the Purple Pentagon, or anywhere else, saw her alive.

Maybe it would be better to come clean with the sheriff right now instead of trying to explain everything later, after he'd become a suspect. If he did become a suspect. But he would have to admit to the sheriff that he had lied to him about not recognizing the woman's photo, and he did not want to do that.

What happened next completely unnerved Hom-Astubby. The sheriff thanked him for his help and said he'd see him at the autopsy in the morning. Then he said, "Oh, one more thing, Mallory. The CBI will be dusting everything for prints, and looking for hair, cloth fiber, a dozen different things. Since you were down here yesterday, right there at the picnic table, we need to be able to eliminate any of your prints they might find. I want you to go with Miss Wellesley"—he motioned to one of his deputies, a fairly plump, middle-aged blonde—"and she'll take your fingerprints."

"If you'll follow me, sir," Miss Wellesley said.

Hom-Astubby said, "Sure," and followed Miss Wellesley to her vehicle, where she got out her fingerprint kit. It didn't take long and they didn't engage in any chit-chat. There was a grim air of determination on the part of everyone involved with the investigation.

Hom-Astubby left then. The sheriff was busy attending to a dozen different things, and Hom-Astubby's work was done. He wanted out of there.

On his way up the dirt road toward the highway, Hom-Astubby met the CBI crime lab van on its way in. His old buddy, Delbert Lawson, was driving. They stopped abreast of each other, rolled down their windows, and talked from their vehicles.

"Hey, Bill," Delbert said. "Long time, no see." He introduced two other men in the van, whom he said were visiting Interpol police offices observing CBI crime scene procedures—Geoffrey

Lastrade, from Scotland Yard, and Alphonse Bertillon IV, from France. He asked, "Did they go ahead and hire you to shoot this one?"

"Yeah. I just finished. Thanks for putting in the good word for me."

"No problem, buddy. You're topnotch."

"The sheriff is worried about the wind getting up and the dust ruining some fresh tire tracks. They're hoping you can get some molds of them."

Delbert nodded. "Thanks for the help. That'll free us up to get right on those tracks. What's it like down there?"

"It's a bad one. You'll see. I guess I better not hold you up."

"Yeah, we better get on down there. Hey, I heard you had some bad trouble up in Alaska. Nearly got eaten by bears? Barely got out alive?"

"I'll tell you all about it sometime if you'll buy the drinks."

"You're on, buddy. I'm in Durango now. Drop by whenever you get a chance. Maggie still makes that cornbread dressing you like so well. And hey, we've got a little game going on the weekends."

"Tell Maggie I'll dang sure get by before long. You still play that Low Chicago?"

"It's the only game there is. Hey, that's a hell of a rig you're driving. Where'd you get that?"

"Won it in a poker game," Hom-Astubby said, and he winked at Delbert as he drove away.

At the highway he met another State Patrol car heading down toward the picnic table. He was debating which way to turn on the highway—whether to go back upstream to where he'd camped, or go somewhere else—when he remembered the woman's dog.

That big ole overgrown puppy. What would become of her? Could she possibly still be tied to that tree? He turned to go find out.

When he drove by the Purple Pentagon he was surprised to see that it was closed. There wasn't a car to be seen anywhere on the property.

When he got to the woman's campsite the tent was gone, and there was no sign of her car. But when he looked in the woods behind her campsite, sure enough, the dog was still there. And boy was she happy to see him.

The dog had turned over her water dish again. Hom-Astubby could see it lying upside down beside her food dish. He leaned against a tree watching the dog jump up and down with uncontainable anticipation as a great wash of sadness came over him.

Never again would the dog see her mistress. She had no idea that life would never be the same, that everything would now be different.

Hom-Astubby walked slowly to the dog, each foot feeling as though it weighed a hundred pounds. He unfastened her and watched her run around. She stopped in the edge of the trees near the clearing to relieve herself. He sat down on the ground, too weary to stand any longer.

When the dog came to him, she first wanted to play, but he didn't respond. She seemed to sense his mood and sat down beside him while he stroked her head.

He felt her collar and took a closer look. She had current dog tags, from the Ross and Mangles Veterinary Clinic in Denver. The collar itself felt as if it might have writing stitched into it. He parted the dog's hair and took a close look.

Heavy stitching in large letters read LADY. But there were smaller stitched letters that continued all around the collar. He couldn't make out what it said.

He took the collar off the dog and held it out to its full length as he read the stitched inscription: GLENNGLAVIN'S SPURLING BASKERVILLE BLOSSOM. What in the hell did that mean?

When he said, "Lady," the dog responded by licking his face. She stood up and wagged her tail. He put the collar back on her.

Her mouth looked dry so he took her water dish to the truck and filled it from his outside tank. She drank nearly all of it, then sat down, looking up at him as if to say, "What's next?"

Hom-Astubby wondered how accustomed she really was to riding in vehicles. Would she get in the camper?

He opened the back door of the camper and said, "You want to go somewhere?"

She jumped up the steps into the camper, bounded down the long hallway, jumped onto the dinette booth seat, and jumped above it into the oversize bed at the front of the camper, on top of the truck cab. She turned around facing him, sprawled out on the bed, stretched out nice and comfortable, let out a big sigh, and lay there looking at him.

Hom-Astubby stood at the door of the camper debating what to do. He couldn't take the dog with him. She wasn't his dog or his responsibility.

He should probably tie her to the tree where he had found her and then go tell the sheriff that, while looking for a place to camp, he came upon the big black dog mentioned in the police bulletin.

After all, that woman had camped here, and the sheriff would probably want the crime lab technicians to comb this site for anything they might be able to find. This was a murder case, and this campsite might figure into it in some way that he couldn't even imagine. For that matter, so might the dog.

He said, "Come on, girl. Let's go."

The dog didn't move, didn't so much as change the expression on her face.

"Lady! Come on, girl. Let's go!"

This time the dog heaved another sigh, stretched out a little more comfortably, and closed her eyes.

He climbed into the camper and sat down in the dinette booth. Reaching up to stroke her head, he said, "You can't stay up there. You can't go with me."

The dog opened her eyes and nuzzled his hand. She lay there looking down at him with big baleful eyes.

He could hardly blame her for not wanting to get tied to that tree again. Maybe it was just as well. He could take her with him tonight, then take her to the sheriff in the morning and tell him where he'd found her. The sheriff would know what to do with her.

"Okay, girl." He stroked her head. "You win, for now."

He collected her water dish, food dish, and her long leash from the tree and set them just inside the back door of the camper. The dog never moved from the bed.

He remembered he needed to go into town and check his mail and climbed behind the wheel. There was a little grocery store in Alpine on the courthouse square. No need to buy a sack of dog food, but he could pick up a few cans. Maybe he'd get a big pack of hamburger meat, too, some buns, fresh onions and tomatoes, some charcoal briquettes. He had some extra money coming in tomorrow morning so he could spend a little tonight.

There had been an old barbecue pit where he camped last night. With a little cleaning up it would charbroil some mighty tasty burgers. It was quiet and peaceful there, with nobody else around and only room for one camping spot. If still vacant, it would be just the place for a nice, relaxing evening. He hadn't had a good hamburger cookout in a long time, and the dog ought to have a special treat.

Only then did he realize he hadn't eaten since breakfast, and neither, probably, had the dog.

CHAPTER TEN

Wednesday Morning

Hom-Astubby woke up enveloped in fur. The dog was sprawled across the top of him. Her massive head, snuggled down on his shoulder, rested warmly against his neck.

He batted his eyes a few times, looking at his face in the mirrored ceiling above his bed, in the early morning light. The dog remained sound asleep.

He lay there for a few minutes, thinking about the dog and the dead woman. They must have slept like this, all cuddled up together. Probably, from the time the dog was a little puppy, she had slept wrapped in the arms of that woman.

Remembering the woman brought a melancholy turn to his thoughts. He was not looking forward to the autopsy. No matter how badly he might need the cash, he wished he had not agreed to do it.

But he had committed himself, and he knew he had to adopt a professional attitude and just get through it. Besides, it would provide an opportunity to turn the dog over to the sheriff and tell him where he had found her. He knew he should have done that yesterday. It certainly could not be put off any longer.

He would have to develop some detachment about that, too. Just do it. Try not to think about this big ole puppy spending time locked up in the pound. Probably the woman's relatives would claim the dog. If not, somebody would adopt her and give her a good home.

He stroked the dog's head. She woke up, stretching and wagging her tail and licking his face all at the same time. Hom-Astubby figured she was probably still thinking about the hamburger cookout they'd had last night. He had discovered that this dog had an unlimited appetite for hamburger.

He got up, showered, dressed quickly, and then took the dog for a long brisk walk along the Crystal Fork. They shared a big breakfast of oatmeal, a few leftover hamburgers, and toast. Then they loaded up and headed for the funeral parlor. The dog seemed to prefer staying in the bed in the camper, so that's where she rode.

Hom-Astubby was a little early when he pulled into the parking lot of the funeral home, but there were already a number of vehicles there, including the sheriff's Bronco and two white sedans with State of Colorado insignias on the doors. He parked beside one of the state cars, and when he got out of his truck he could see that the insignia further identified the vehicle as belonging to the attorney general's office.

He reached down in the floor of the king cab and got the long leash the woman had used to tie the dog to the tree. He climbed into the back of the camper, closing the door behind him. The dog was lying on the bed, her head raised, looking at the leash suspiciously.

He sat down in the dinette booth, reached up and stroked her head. "This is where we have to part company," he said, feeling around in the thick long hair on her neck until he had found the ring on her collar and snapped the leash in place. He sat there stroking the dog's head, delaying the moment, feeling sad.

Through one of the side windows of the camper he saw a man wearing a three-piece suit emerge from the back door of the funeral home and walk briskly in his direction. He seemed visibly upset. When he got to the state car parked beside Hom-Astubby's truck, he yanked open the driver's door, but then stopped and leaned against the car. He placed his elbows on the roof of the car, buried his face in his hands, and stood there, breathing hard.

An older man, slightly balding, wearing glasses and a business suit, came out of the funeral home and yelled, "George!"

George, leaning against the car, turned and watched the older man walk across the parking lot.

When he had gotten almost to the car, the older man said, "Are you all right?"

George wiped a hand across his face and said, "It just hit me all at once." He clenched his teeth and looked around at the mountains in the distance. "What I wouldn't give for a bottle of Jim Beam right now." He took a deep breath. "Thank god it wasn't Avalon."

At the sound of George's voice, the dog's head snapped around in his direction. The rumbling of a low-throated growl startled Hom-Astubby. He had never heard the dog growl before. He quickly put a hand on the dog's muzzle and whispered, "Shhhhh. Hush!" The dog quieted down, but her hackles were raised, and she stared intently at the man out the window.

"So what do we do now?" asked the other man.

"We keep looking until we find her."

The other man sighed and put his hands on his hips. He said, "She's gone. She's got sense enough to get out of this state. She drove out of state the first night."

"The hell she did. She's more stubborn than that." He was about to say something more, but the ringing of a cell phone interrupted him. George dug in the pocket of his coat, pulled out a phone and said, "This is Langley."

A moment later he said, "What?" He snapped his fingers a couple of times in the direction of the other man, and said, "Dick, take notes."

Dick pulled out a notebook and a pen.

George said, "The Purple Pentagon. Where is it from the funeral home? . . . about three miles north of town . . . yeah, how long ago? . . . Monday. She said that, huh? . . . yeah . . . right . . . don't you worry about that. I'll handle it. I'll put Dick on it. You stay right there. Interview everybody. Find out anything you can about where she might be staying, who she talked to, who she danced with, especially if she left with anybody, or made any phone calls, if anybody she talked to paid with a credit card. Find out if anybody was there the staff doesn't know, and who all the locals were who were in the place while she was there. Find out if any staff was there Monday who's not there today and where we can find them right now. I'll be there in a minute. Good work, Paul. Damn good work." He clicked off the phone.

George turned to Dick. He said, "She's here, right here in this town."

"What?"

"She's been hanging out at a place called the Purple Pentagon, a bar and restaurant, about three miles out of town, north up the highway at the first bridge over the river. She was there two days ago, Monday, drinking, dancing, acting like she didn't have a care in the world, from about 2 P.M. until around midnight. And she said she would be back today. The place was closed yesterday. Closed every Tuesday. When we get there, you get the numbers of every phone in the place and then you get Beverly to get the record of every call going in or out of there Monday, and I want that quick. She's got to be right here, somewhere in this town, or somewhere in this county."

"If she's here, we'll find her."

"You're damn right we'll find her. Seal the county."

"What?"

"I said seal it! And I mean right now. State Police roadblocks on every highway. They've already got her photo and all the info about her car and the dog. But I want a new bulletin put out. Have her arrested on sight, as a material witness. You call Beverly right now and have it go out as an emergency dispatch from State Patrol headquarters. Tell Beverly then to contact the sheriffs in each neighboring county. Have those sheriffs coordinate with the patrol districts, get their deputies to throw up the roadblocks at the county borders right now for any place the patrol will be slow to reach."

"George, if we put up roadblocks, there's no way we're going to keep this quiet from the media. The patrol will have to be able to say something."

George looked thoughtful for a moment. "Okay. We've got a

good cover right here, tailor-made. We're searching for this murderer. That'll take care of the media. Now, what was the name of that guy they wanted to question about that murder over in Salida last month, but they couldn't find him?"

"Hussein. Mohammed Khalid Hussein, I think was his full name. But they're not looking for him anymore."

"Well, as of right now, he just became a person of interest again. We are searching for this guy, Hussein. Do we have info on his car?"

"I think so. I think we've got information that he's got a BMW."

"Okay, have Beverly headline Hussein's photo and the info on his BMW, which the patrol can tell the media if necessary. Then tacked on below that—strictly confidential to be kept from the media—Avalon and the dog and the info on her car. I'll call Bob at the State Patrol, fill him in on what's coming, get them snapping on it right away from the top. Now go!"

Dick sprinted to the other state car and was soon busy on the radio, while George used his cell phone, pacing back and forth beside his car.

The dog started growling again. Hom-Astubby had to take hold of the leash and use some muscle to pull her head away from the window, until she was facing him. "Shhhhhh," he whispered.

He held his breath, not knowing what he'd do if the dog started barking. The two men wouldn't be able to see inside the camper very well from where they were, with the screening on the windows. But if they walked up beside the camper, they'd be able to see inside just fine. Hom-Astubby held his grip on the leash, holding the dog's head toward him, but she rolled her eyes toward the window and strained her head in that direction.

Dick finished at the radio and returned to George about the same time that George finished on the cell phone. Dick said, "It's done. Beverly's got it all going out. But, Dubya, are you sure you know what you're doing?"

George looked thoughtful. "We'll emphasize Hussein's BMW.

The Salida people will think we know something from over here, and these folks will think we know something from over there. We'll be okay."

"That's not what I mean."

"Don't mess with me, Dick. We've already had that discussion. You just pay attention, because I want you to handle this, and I want it done right. When they get her, I want her separated from the dog. I want her driven to Denver in a State Patrol car, to my office. I'll deal with her there. But I want that dog dead, do you hear me? You figure out some way to do that so it can sound like an accident—maybe the dog breaks loose and runs out in traffic and gets run over. Something that I can be blameless about. But that goddamned dog has got to go, and this is the perfect opportunity to get rid of it. That damn thing won't let me get near her. I'll buy her a poodle or something. Make up for it."

Dick raised his hands. "I don't want anything to do with that," he said, shaking his head.

"I didn't ask what you wanted to do. I said do it. Look, I wish there were some other way, but I'm worried that someday that dog is going to react to some little kid the way it reacts to me. I've got a responsibility here to do what's got to be done. You'll be doing the dog a favor. It's a vicious animal that ought to be put to sleep. She can't see that. But we'll be doing her a favor in the long run. It's something that has got to be done, and you are going to take care of that damn dog for me."

"George," Dick paused, as though considering his words. "It's not just your career that's at stake here. You'll take a lot of us with you if you go down. We've got a stake in this, too."

"I'm the one with the stake," George said, his face reddening. "Goddamn it! I announced our engagement to my family. Do you have any idea how stupid that makes me look if she doesn't go through with it?"

"You might have asked her about that. Didn't you think she might have something to say about it? Could you possibly be the only one who doesn't know that the reason they call her Avalanche is because she buries her would-be boyfriends? The woman is a world-class ball-buster."

George's jaw tightened, but he didn't say anything.

"You're vulnerable on this. If the press gets wind of it, you're dead meat."

"The press!" George scoffed. "If it ever comes out, we'll say this is how we really started getting acquainted. A misunderstanding that led to romance. They'll eat that right out of my hand. And she'll come around. She's not going to throw away the chance to go where I can take her. She wants that as much as I do. Right now she's just negotiating the terms of the marriage, testing me to see what I'll put up with, what kind of risks I'm willing to take to nail her butt. There is nothing about her that has ever been the least bit normal. Why should her courtship be any different?"

George wiped his hand across his face and stared at the mountains. "But she's also frightened. Frightened that I might wimp out on her. Frightened that there really might not be anybody who can plant the word 'wife' on her ass. It's the big chase, Dick. She just wants me to know that she's making me sweat bullets for her. But this won't go on forever. She wants me to win, and we're going to be one hell of a team, once we get in harness."

George turned back to Dick. "You can either hide and watch, or you can take care of that dog and let me worry about the rest. I know what I'm doing. But if it's too fast for you, Dick, too risky, if you really don't want to go where we're going, if you want to bail out now, then just say so."

"Okay, okay," said Dick, throwing his hands in the air. "I'm in. Jesus, don't get riled at me. Who the hell else has got the guts to try to make you stop and think once in awhile?"

"That," George said, putting his arm around Dick's shoulder, "is why you're going to be my chief of staff."

"So what happens if we don't find her and the roadblocks don't get her?"

"Then we'll sit right here in this county and turn it upside down until we do. We've got the perfect excuse with that woman's murder. We'll keep finding connections with that girl who got killed over in Salida last month and another one somewhere else. Besides, with a woman killer loose around here, Avalon is at risk. She might be hell on wheels, but she's not bulletproof. I'm going to call in more people, get Donald and his staff over here. We'll give this sheriff more help than he ever imagined possible. And when we find Avalon, you'll take care of that dog, without us ever having this conversation again. When I hear that we have got that dog and have separated it from her, I'm going to know right then that the dog is dead. Are we perfectly clear about that?"

"I'll take care of it," Dick said.

"Good. Now you get down to that Purple Pentagon and help Paul. We'll use it as our base of operations. After you get those phone records, you concentrate on finding out where she's been staying. She's got to sleep somewhere. Let's just hope she's still there." He looked at his watch. "It's still early, and she is not a morning person. She's probably still asleep."

"George. This is awkward. But what if we find her sleeping with somebody?"

"Well," George said, "what do you suppose the odds might be that this turns out to be his unlucky day? Now I'm going back in there and start working on that sheriff, in case we don't turn up anything today. I'll be on down there with you guys in a minute."

"Be careful with Klewlusz. He's been around a long time."

"Dick, you worry too much. The guy is a hick. He hired some clown to take the crime scene photos, for Christsake. That's where I'm gonna start reaming his ass. When I get finished with Sheriff Kerry De Nada Clue, we'll be off on the right foot, and from now on, he won't even reach for toilet paper without wondering if that's okay with me." He turned, walked back across the parking lot, and reentered the funeral home.

Dick got in his state car and drove away, in the direction of the Purple Pentagon.

CHAPTER ELEVEN

The dog was still straining at the leash, trying to turn her head toward the window. Hom-Astubby released her, and she immediately scooted closer to the window, staring through it, focusing all her attention on the door that George Langley had disappeared through.

Only then did Hom-Astubby realize he was holding his breath. He had hardly dared breathe the whole time the two men were arguing. He put his head in his hands, saying, "My god, what have I gotten myself into?"

He sat there for a few minutes, thinking about what he'd overheard, until the dog whimpered slightly and nuzzled the side of his neck with her wet nose.

He put his arms around the dog and hugged her to him. He ruffed the hair on her head, saying, "You really don't like that guy, do you?" She licked his face.

"What happened, Lady? Did you see him hit your mistress?" That had to be what happened. He could picture the scene. George Langley, domineering, controlling, thinking love was a game of raw brute power, must have thought he could slap some sense into Avalon O'Neill. He must have been the most surprised man in the world when her cute, monstrously huge pet suddenly sprang between them, teeth bared, growling a threat that was no bluff, maybe backing him all the way across some room, until the O'Neill woman, probably as startled as he was, called off the dog.

The Newfoundland breed was prized for almost never showing hostility toward people. Newfies weren't supposed to act the way this dog had reacted to George Langley. "You're a mess," he said, roughing her head again, "a lot like your mistress."

He wondered how much of what George Langley had said about that woman was even remotely close to the truth. Whatever the truth might be, she had to be some kind of head case. And the guy was obviously a manipulator. He'd played Dick like a fine-tuned violin, and in real time, too, at the speed of face-to-face argument. He was damn good at running over people, getting them to do his bidding. And his position in the attorney general's office made him the most powerful cop in the state.

Hom-Astubby stared deep into some middle distance, trying to form a vision of the risks of getting crosswise with somebody like George Langley. The longer he stared, the more things he thought of that he would have to worry about. He shook his head, shuddering at the resources the man had at his disposal, the most sobering being the sheer force of his personality.

The dog whimpered again, and she gave his face another lick. He looked into her big baleful eyes, saying, "Girl, I don't know if I can get us out of this." The dog seemed unconcerned, just sat grinning at him, licking her lips and beginning to pant, beginning to come down from the stress herself.

"One thing I know," he said, sliding out of the dinette booth. "We've got to get you out of this parking lot."

He told the dog to stay. He got in the cab and drove about three blocks, until he saw an old-fashioned gas station named Eldons, with a garage and a sign that read MECHANIC ON DUTY. It also had a diesel gas pump.

Hom-Astubby's new truck was due for an oil change, and he knew now there was a good chance he might have a long drive ahead of him. He looked up at the steep ridge that overlooked the valley, wondering if he could really get his truck up that jeep trail the sheriff had told him about, over into Dolores County. That might avoid the roadblocks.

He pulled into the gas station. The attendant, apparently the owner, a friendly, middle-aged man with a potbelly and a shirt-pocket nametag, ELDON, turned out to be an Okie. He put his hands on his hips and stood back, admiring the Boomer Sooner color scheme of Hom-Astubby's truck in open-mouthed wonder, saying, "That's the purtiest paint job I ever seen." He said, sure, he'd fill the truck with diesel and change the oil, while Hom-Astubby took care of some business in town.

Hom-Astubby walked back toward the funeral home, loitering in front of the grocery store, where he could see across the sprawling courthouse lawn to the funeral home parking lot and George Langley's car.

He wished he'd already gotten that check from the sheriff, and wished he didn't need the cash. But he did need it.

From where he stood, he could see a portion of the front of Dr. Watson's new funeral home, a side view of the whole building. He could see a sign at the front, one that he hadn't noticed before: ALPINE CLINIC, HOWARD D. WATSON, M.D. He could also see the sign on the back side of the building: ALPINE FUNERAL HOME. He wondered how many people going in the front door would end up coming out the back door.

He had a little time to do some thinking, to absorb the information that the O'Neill woman wasn't the one who'd been killed. That would be an enormous relief to the sheriff. Langley's road-blocks might stir some media interest, maybe. Some local coverage probably, but nothing like the Denver media swarm if the dead woman had been the O'Neill woman. The sheriff would now have to deal with Langley instead of the media. He probably would have preferred the media.

Hom-Astubby had no idea what really might be going on between the O'Neill woman and George Langley, except that, whatever it was, he was now right in the big middle of it. He had her dog. She must be frantic by now, with her dog missing. There was a good chance she was still at that campsite, searching for her dog.

But he couldn't just go there to find her and return her dog to her. The woman was going to get caught. That much was obvious. And when she did, that would be curtains for the dog, if the dog got caught with her. The only way to save the dog was to get it out of the state.

He saw George Langley come out of the funeral home, get in his car and drive away, toward the Purple Pentagon.

Hom-Astubby crossed the courthouse lawn heading toward the funeral home. Before he'd gotten halfway there, Sheriff Klewlusz came out the door, looking distracted, walking toward his Bronco.

"Sheriff," he said, as he got closer to him.

The sheriff stopped. He said, "Mallory. Didn't even see you." He looked all around. "You afoot these days?"

Hom-Astubby gestured down the road. "Getting an oil change."

"Listen," the sheriff said, "I'm afraid there's been a change of plans. I just talked to George Langley, the deputy attorney general who heads up the Criminal Law Section. He wants the CBI to do the autopsy photos, and that's probably a good idea. Says there might be a link with another murder over in Salida."

"That's okay by me," Hom-Astubby said. "Any luck identifying the victim?"

"No. Not yet. It's not who we thought it might be, not that Avalanche O'Neill I showed you that police bulletin on. We don't know who she is. But listen, I've got some other news. I was able to talk to all the right people yesterday and got it all squared away on your payment for the crime scene photos. We really appreciate your work on that. If you want, I can write the check now."

"I'd appreciate that," Hom-Astubby said.

At his Bronco, the sheriff wrote Hom-Astubby a check for two hundred dollars. "It's drawn on that bank right there. They'll cash it for you, when they open at nine o'clock."

Hom-Astubby looked where he gestured, to a bank beside the grocery store. "That's handy," Hom-Astubby said. It was a lot more than just handy. It was a godsend.

"It looks like I'm going to have a change of plans, too," Hom-Astubby said. "It looks like I might have to make a run back home, to Oklahoma, take care of some business. I'm not sure if I can get back up here to go fishing with Harry Birdwell this weekend. Looks like I'll probably have to take a rain check on that dinner Saturday night."

"That's okay," the sheriff said. "The way things have heated up around here, I doubt I'd be able to make it, either."

"I was wondering, also, that road by the post office you were telling me about. I'd sure like to get some shots from up on that ridge on my way out. Are you pretty sure my truck can make it up there?"

The sheriff rubbed his chin. He said, "It's been dry lately. I don't think your truck's too long to get around those switchbacks. Be slow going. But you might get out of the county quicker that way than taking the highway. Langley is putting up roadblocks on all the highways out of here. This time of year, with all this summer tourist traffic, they'll be backed up."

"Roadblocks?" Hom-Astubby tried to sound surprised.

"Yeah. He thinks he's going to catch that woman's killer." The sheriff sounded dubious.

"Isn't it a little late for that? What's it been? About twenty-four hours, at least, maybe thirty-six hours?"

"It's the damnedest thing I've ever seen," the sheriff said, looking distracted again. "But, I hope you have a good trip back home, Mallory. And I hope you get back up here. We'll have that dinner with old Harry sooner or later."

Hom-Astubby thanked the sheriff for the check and walked back to Eldon's gas station. While he was counting out the money to pay the bill, Eldon startled him by saying, "That's a damn good guard dog you got there."

Hom-Astubby lost track of the money he was trying to count. He stared at Eldon, finally saying, "Huh?"

"I been needin' to get me a good watchdog. One that'll bark like that. Keep him locked up inside the garage at night. You wouldn't be wantin' to sell him, would you?"

"The dog was barking?"

"Barking, I reckon. He scared the shit outta me."

Hom-Astubby just stared at Eldon, not knowing what to say.

"What kind of dog is that, anyway? It looks like a damn gorilla."

"You saw the dog?"

"Well, I reckon. The way he pushed aside them winder curtains up there. Hell, I thought he was gonna come through that glass and land right in my lap."

Hom-Astubby looked at the camper bed above the cab, but all

was quiet and still. His brow wrinkled. Newfoundlands weren't supposed to act anything like that. They were, arguably, the worst guard dogs on the planet, except for guarding children. He told Eldon that the dog was just a big mutt, "a duke's mixture," a family pet who wasn't for sale.

Eldon wanted to "visit" for a while with a fellow Okie, and Hom-Astubby tried his best to act casual and relaxed. Eldon had a theory that what the Sooners needed to do was get themselves a left-handed punt returner, "because he'd be left-footed, too. And see, he'd start off different from all your right-footed people, and that little bit of difference might spring him free." Hom-Astubby agreed that special teams play was one area where the Sooners could use some improvement.

"The kicking game is one-third of football, you know," Eldon said, to which Hom-Astubby gravely nodded in agreement.

He finally tried getting away from Eldon by looking at his watch and saying he had to make a phone call. Eldon insisted that he use the telephone in his office.

"But it's long distance."

"Hell, I don't care," Eldon said.

At the phone, while trying to think of who he might call, with Eldon hovering nearby, watching helpfully, Hom-Astubby remembered he needed to tell his mail service in Oklahoma to hold his mail. He found out that they had not routed anything to him yesterday.

When he finally got out of the gas station, he drove straight to the turnoff at the Purple Pentagon, worried sick because Eldon had seen the dog. He noted that there were three white state sedans in the parking lot of the Purple Pentagon as he cruised past it and entered the forest road behind the restaurant.

He had made up his mind what he had to do. Somehow, he had to talk the O'Neill woman into getting in the truck with him. He had to get both her and the dog out of state. When she heard what he had overheard, he was pretty sure she would come with him. It would be the only way to save the dog. He tried not to think about what would happen after he got them out or if he got caught with them. He was already in a lot deeper than he wanted to be.

When Hom-Astubby had passed the fork in the road and was on the branch that led to where the woman was camped, he found that branch of the road blocked by the same pickup trucks he'd encountered on the other fork Monday afternoon. They were erecting a gate across the road, just like the other one. They weren't as far along on this one, apparently just getting started.

He parked his truck, this time out of the way so he couldn't get blocked in, and walked to where the new gate was being laid out. He saw Connolly with a group of men who were carrying rolls of fence wire into the trees. Connolly saw him and stared for a moment before going back to work.

Hom-Astubby saw a man who might be in charge of the crew, someone dressed a little better, a man he'd seen talking to Wally Street Monday afternoon. He got his attention. "Can I walk down this road to that campsite down there? I want to see if someone might still be down there."

"Nobody's still down there," the man said. "This is private property, and it's now closed to the public. You people will have to find someplace else to camp."

"Are you sure there's no one else still down there? It would only take a minute for me to go look."

"There's nobody there. We went down there this morning to run everybody out, but there was nobody there." He turned his back to Hom-Astubby and walked away.

For a moment, Hom-Astubby stared down the road beyond the gate, but there didn't seem to be anything further he could do. The woman apparently was just gone.

He climbed into his truck and turned it around. As he drove past the Purple Pentagon again, a glint of reflected light drew his attention to the back end of one of the vehicles in the parking lot, and he clenched his teeth upon seeing that the sheriff's Bronco was now parked beside the state cars.

He wondered if this very minute somebody in the restaurant

might be telling the sheriff about the Indian who had stared at the O'Neill woman through the window before driving away in a big crimson and cream cabover camper.

Maybe somebody was telling George Langley about that. Maybe they were looking out the window right now and saying, "That's him, right there."

He spotted another Sheriff's Office vehicle in the parking lot and saw Miss Wellesley, the deputy who had taken his fingerprints, get out of it and start walking toward the restaurant. She saw him driving by and waved. He waved back, wincing because she had seen him driving out of the woods where the woman had been camped.

He drove through town, feeling conspicuous, feeling that everybody was looking at him. He went to the bank, but he had to sit in his truck for a while until it opened. He almost didn't wait for it to open, but he needed that cash. When it finally did, he was the first customer in the door. He had no trouble cashing the check.

He drove to the road beside the post office and headed out of town, wondering if there was any way he really could cancel his assignment with Harry Birdwell and not have to come back here. Maybe he could use some of the photos he'd taken this week of fly-fishermen on the Crystal Fork. He'd have to get that film processed soon and find out.

Leaving on the dirt road, he thought about the dog inside his camper, wondering what in the world he was going to do with her. And he thought about the woman, wondering what was going to happen to her.

At least he could try to save her dog. Beyond that, he had no idea what he was going to do. He let out a sigh, glancing in the rear-view mirror, watching the empty road stretch out behind him, taking comfort in that emptiness.

He said, "Good luck, Avalon Blanche O'Neill. You're on your own."

PART 2

The Bull-Riding Barber

(Wednesday)

A camera can be an awful liar. I remember as a boy flipping through a magazine to a photo spread of Turner Falls. I had been to Turner Falls. It was nice, but it wasn't that nice. Elegant waterfalls, emerald green water, shimmering cliffs. That's what the photos said. They were beautiful. But where was the clutter? The run-down concession stand, the rusty iron guard rails, the parking lot, all the things you could see when you were actually there that weren't so beautiful. That photo spread of Turner Falls made a lasting impression on me. When I do a shoot, I always get some clutter, just for me, so I can remember what the place actually looks like. If every photo had a little clutter in it, the world would be a more honest place.

—WILLIAM H. MALLORY
Basic 35 MM Photography

CHAPTER TWELVE

Wednesday Morning

Sheriff Klewlusz had been right about the road—or the lack of one. The road ended not far out of town, at the foot of the heavily timbered ridge, becoming a steep jeep trail, with switchbacks that snaked their way up the ridge.

Hom-Astubby had to shift into all-wheel drive and into his lowest gear. But the powerful big truck crawled right up the mountainside, even through the places where the ruts got deep and the jeep trail was the steepest.

Twice he had to do some maneuvering to get his long truck around the two sharpest switchbacks. But there was room enough, barely, to back up just far enough into the trees to get his truck angled so he could make the turn.

He had hardly gotten started when it was clear why no ordinary car would ever make it up that hill, especially through the ruts. He knew there would be no way his truck could go up that hill after a rain. But the road was dry, and in no time at all he had climbed to the top of the ridge and started down the other side, passing out of Devon County and into Dolores County.

The trip down the other side of the ridge went much more quickly because the jeep trail wasn't nearly so steep and there were hardly any ruts on that side. At the foot of the ridge he came to a junction with a Dolores County gravel road.

He turned left, going south through scrub-timber country, heading out of Colorado, toward New Mexico. He should be out of Dolores County very quickly, into Montezuma County and down through Cortez to the Colorado state line, on the highway to Shiprock, New Mexico.

He should be deep into the desert country of far west-central New Mexico, at Gallup, by sometime around the noon hour, where he could hook up with Interstate 40 and have a straight shot to the east across New Mexico and the Texas Panhandle into Oklahoma. He might be home around midnight, even with losing an hour at the New Mexico–Texas state line, where Mountain Time changed to Central Time.

He would have time to stop in Gallup for lunch. He could unwind a little bit before tackling that long drive on into Oklahoma via Interstate 40.

But he wondered if the Dolores County road he was on was safe. Somewhere to the south was a county road the sheriff had mentioned, connecting Dolores County with Devon County. That road would probably intersect the Dolores County road he was on. That intersection might be a good place for a roadblock.

Maybe there would be a way to turn to the west before he got to that intersection. If he could just get to the west a little bit, he was pretty sure he'd be entirely in the clear.

There wasn't any way to turn west before getting to the intersection, but he didn't discover that until he topped a small hill and saw the intersection in the distance. It was in the middle of a long, narrow valley, one that had a little stream winding its way through meadows filled with cattle.

Not long after Hom-Astubby topped the hill, when it was far too late to stop and turn around, he saw a Colorado State Patrol car racing toward him from the opposite direction, with emergency lights flashing.

The State Patrol car got to the intersection before Hom-Astubby, and it turned toward Devon County. When Hom-Astubby went through the intersection he could see the roadblock, a few hundred yards up that county road, to his left, right about at the county line. It looked like a lone Dolores County deputy sheriff standing in the middle of the road beside his vehicle, watching the State Patrol car pull up beside him.

Hom-Astubby breathed a big sigh of relief and said, "Lady,

this is your lucky day," glancing toward the roof of the truck cab, where the dog was riding in the camper bed.

Fifteen minutes later he was coming into the outskirts of Cortez. A few minutes after that he was headed south out of town, leaving the scrub-timbered landscape behind, entering the starkness of the high desert country, with the New Mexico border only about fifteen miles away.

He glanced wistfully and longingly at the Ute Mountain Indian Casino on the south edge of Cortez as he drove by, one of his favorite little casinos. There were a few slot machines in there that he'd had a long-standing argument with. He'd only properly disciplined two of those machines so far. But it hardly mattered this trip. He didn't have any gambling money at the moment.

Soon he passed the junction with the highway that came in from Arizona from the west, from Toc Nos Pas in the Navajo Nation, and crossed the unimpressive, nearly dry wash of the Mancos River. He couldn't keep from glancing upstream, where, not so far away, in the headwater canyons of the creek, the spectacular ruins of the cliff dwellings at Mesa Verde National Park had inspired him with awe every time he had seen them. He soon crossed the Colorado state line, entering the Navajo Nation, in the far northwestern corner of New Mexico.

He relaxed a little, but he also felt the immediate frustration of the speed limit dropping from 65 to 55 mph. He slowed to the speed limit, watching his rear-view mirror, hoping for a vehicle to come up behind him, wondering why the speed limit was so low across the rolling hills of that empty desert landscape.

He saw a car behind him in the distance. The car soon caught up with him and passed him. Hom-Astubby let it get out in front of him about a half-mile and then he hit the gas pedal. He held his truck about a half-mile behind the car, settling in at about 75 mph, letting the car run interference in case any radar traps might be ahead. There weren't any, and the sixteen miles from the New Mexico border to Shiprock went quickly.

The car turned off in Shiprock, headed east toward Farmington, when Hom-Astubby turned south toward Gallup. On that stretch of highway, south through the Navajo Nation, the speed limit was 65 mph. He settled in at about 68, content with that pace for awhile.

Soon, he was almost all alone, rolling across the high desert plateau with an occasional secluded Navajo sheep ranch in the distance—old country, and a land of old ways, with almost every ranch having a distinctive Navajo hogan somewhere among the cluster of buildings, with the door of the hogan, and the door of every other building, always facing east.

Far to the east, the spectacular, fast-moving violence of a heavy thunderstorm—the "male rain" of the Diné summer landscape— was centered somewhere near Chaco Canyon. Water would be flowing again through that canyon, where many centuries ago ancestral Puebloan peoples had built the largest stone-masonry apartment building in the world, and then had suddenly and mysteriously abandoned it.

All along the western horizon the seemingly endless line of the heavily timbered Chuska Mountains dominated the skyline for as far as the eye could see. Up there Navajo families in isolated summer sheep camps would be watching their children absorb the very essence of being Navajo.

Far south of Shiprock, he watched his rear-view mirror as he topped one of the series of hills that had given the shiprock its Anglo name. If he were going the other way and coming down the hill he was approaching, he could watch the tall base of the shiprock slowly disappear behind the hill he was now descending, leaving, gradually, only the upper portions of the rock formation in view, until, momentarily, only the top portion remained, and there, suddenly, would be a tall-masted clipper ship in full, billowing sail, outlined starkly against the sky. It was an illusion that happened only at a distance, when only the top portion of the rock was in view.

Someday he'd get a shot of that view when the color of the sky and the surrounding cloud formations were just right. Someday, but not today.

CHAPTER THIRTEEN

Wednesday Afternoon

I t was a little after twelve noon when Hom-Astubby rolled into Gallup, New Mexico. As he'd gotten farther away from the Four Corners region of the Colorado Plateau, and as the morning advanced, the heat rose. By the time he got to Gallup, he had the air conditioner going throughout the truck and the camper.

He'd stopped briefly near Sheep Springs to let the dog out to pee, noticing then how hot it was getting. He dreaded what that August heat and humidity would be like in Oklahoma.

He had done some thinking. If he stopped for lunch in Gallup, he'd have time to get his color film processed. He had to find out if he could use some of those shots of fishermen on the Crystal Fork and avoid going back to Alpine this weekend.

Black-and-white film he processed himself in his own darkroom. But there was little reason to do that with color film. The color equipment was expensive, and the results were the same at the automated places. Few photographers processed their own color film anymore, not since it had become so automated and so fast at the one-hour centers. It was black-and-white film that was now hard to get processed commercially, even if one was willing to pay the exorbitant cost.

He'd also have time to make a quick phone call or two. He had noticed while reading the *Colorado Leader-Enterprise* that a young woman he'd once worked with in California was now on the staff of that paper in Denver. She was a sports reporter named Carol Jenkins. Carol might be able to tell him something about Avalon O'Neill.

He pulled into the Wal-Mart parking lot, reached behind him

in the king cab for his camera bags, and dug out the rolls of color film he'd shot in Alpine. But when he opened the door of the truck the heat in Gallup nearly knocked him over.

He went inside the camper and opened every window. He visited with the dog for a few minutes, telling her to hold on for a little while longer and they'd go somewhere and take a walk.

He dropped off his color film for one-hour processing, then found a pay phone and dug out his long-distance calling card. As the *Leader-Enterprise* operator was connecting him with Carol Jenkins, he was hoping this call wouldn't take long, and remembering how Carol had been such a good young reporter.

"Carol Jenkins speaking."

"Carol, it's Bill Mallory."

"Well, speak of the devil. You owe me a pair of pantyhose."

"Pantyhose? Huh? Aw, geez. We haven't talked since then?"

"You cad! You *said* you'd call me."

"I am calling you."

"That was seven *years* ago."

"Hey, what can I say? We'd gotten fired. I had to leave the state, try to find another job. So did you."

"Don't try confusing me with facts."

"I had no idea where you'd gone!"

"It took you *this long* to find me, huh?"

"Well . . ."

"Look, just tell me you're in town, you're picking me up for dinner, and that somehow, amid the tears and the anguish, by the time the sun rises over Denver, I'll have forgiven you."

"I'm in New Mexico."

"Shit! Another lonely night. Hey, I heard you went freelance. Heard you nearly got killed down in the Amazon, or some damn place. A plane crash. Had to hike out of the jungle on broken legs. Saved some guy's life."

"It wasn't anything like that. But, yeah, I'm freelance now. And listen, I need a favor. I'll owe you big time."

"You already owe me big time."

"I'll owe you bigger time."

"How much bigger time?"

"Bigger than you ever dared dream. Bigger than any woman ever dared dream. Bigger than—"

"Aw, hell! What do you want?"

"I'm hoping you can fill me in on some background on somebody."

"Who?"

"Avalon O'Neill."

"Avalanche O'Neill?"

"Yeah."

"How far back?"

"How about right now?"

"Well, she's back here these days, in Denver. Was gone for years. Works for the *Daily Sun*. Or at least she did, until that big housecleaning over there this weekend. Don't know if she's one of the ones who got fired."

"No kidding? The *Daily Sun*. She does ski reports? Or what?"

"She won't have a thing to do with sports reporting. Or with sports reporters. Or with TV or radio. She will have you know that she is no longer news. She most particularly is no longer sports news. She will thank you not even to inform her when the Olympics take place, let alone ask her anything about it. She is now a professional. She is a journalist. She is a print journalist. And if you have slept with her, I'm gonna cut your balls off."

"I haven't even met her."

"Then why the interest?"

"Can you keep a secret?"

"I'm a woman. What do you think?"

"Then I better not tell you."

"Does this fair maiden have any idea she's about to be deflowered?"

"No way that could ever happen."

"He said, speaking to the innocent, fair farm girl from Kansas who—"

"Aw, cut it out. I need to know more about O'Neill. Think you could dig up her background, where she was, what she was doing those years out of state? I'd do it myself, but I'm on the road, in Gallup. Got to drive straight through to Oklahoma, and I need to know really bad."

"Can you give me a few hours? I've got some other stuff cooking."

"Yeah. I've got to scoot to get through Albuquerque ahead of rush hour. I could call you from the other side of Albuquerque. That truck stop at Moriarty would be the best place. Let's see, about four o'clock or thereabouts?"

"I'll see what I can dig up. Let me give you some contact numbers in case you get delayed." She gave him her direct number at the sports department, her home phone, cell phone, and pager. He gave her his home number in Oklahoma.

"Thanks, Carol. I really appreciate it."

"You'll be doing more than appreciating it, mister. You'll be coming to Denver soon. Don't you dare forget."

"We'll have that dinner, and we'll get all caught up. I'll look forward to it. Hey, you like horses? I've got a horse ranch now in Oklahoma."

"A horse ranch?"

"Well, no horses yet. But I've got the ranch."

They chatted for a few more minutes, mostly about the trials of her job search after Nelson Towers' Texas Planetary Network bought the *Long Beach Daily Trumpet*, where they'd worked together briefly. She told him about a short, stormy engagement she'd recently broken off. But she was busy, in the middle of a story, and Hom-Astubby was pressed for time. They didn't talk very long.

Hom-Astubby hung up the phone and stood thinking for a moment, watching the customers, many of them Navajos, going in and out of Wal-Mart.

Avalanche O'Neill worked for the *Daily Sun*? Doing what? It made no sense at all. She sounded like somebody who, for some reason, simply could not capitalize on her celebrity, couldn't be in the spotlight, couldn't be on TV.

Maybe she made a fool of herself every time she opened her mouth. It damn well couldn't be because she was too shy. He'd only seen the brazen hussy twice in his life, and she'd been half-naked the first time. If she insisted on going around half-naked, half the time, that might explain a lot of things.

For all he knew, she might be a committed nudist or something—something wacky that limited her employment potential. They probably called her "Avalanche" because of how reckless and unpredictable she was. It was probably that recklessness that got her a Gold Medal—the one place where that might pay off, straight downhill at breakneck speed.

But if she did work for the *Daily Sun*, what was she doing in Alpine? All the way across the mountains from Denver. Surely not anything related to her job.

The *Daily Sun* was notorious for its Eastern Slope bias, the attitude that Colorado's worries, and its sophistication, ended at the Front Range of the Rockies. Nearly the whole population of Colorado was packed into one long narrow corridor, practically within the shadow of the Front Range.

That corridor extended from Fort Collins in the north, down to Denver and Colorado Springs, and on down to Pueblo. There was hardly anything but arid high plains east of it, all the way to Kansas. West of it, the Rocky Mountains extended all the way across the state.

Outside that narrow urban and suburban corridor, in the mindset of most of its inhabitants, was nothing of concern. Nothing but ski slopes and trout streams and small town rubes. Denverites, and the *Denver Daily Sun*, had never shown any interest in Western Slope issues. The mountains existed to serve Denver, which was what Sheriff Klewlusz had complained about.

But maybe Earl Paggett, as the new editor at the *Sun*, had brought fundamental changes aside from just investigating Nelson Towers. Hom-Astubby had assumed that an investigation of

Towers by the *Sun* would be a Denver-based investigation. Towers' international headquarters was located there.

They called Denver "Little D.C.," partly because of its high concentration of regional federal governmental centers, and partly because of all the big government defense contractors that constituted its primary industry. It was a white-collar industry that gave Colorado one of the highest ratios of college graduates of any state in the nation. And the biggest defense contractor of them all was Nelson Towers.

But maybe Earl Paggett had his reporters looking into what Towers was doing beyond Denver. Hom-Astubby wished he had a contact who had been on the inside at the *Sun*, but he didn't know anybody there.

Maybe that didn't matter. How could the O'Neill woman have been involved in an investigation of Towers? Of what use would some ski bunny be for that?

The whole world had come crashing down on the *Daily Sun* last weekend, and the bimbo had promptly taken up residence in some bar, dancing the night away, between nude bathing in the Crystal Fork. She probably couldn't even type, let alone actually read.

She might not even know that the *Daily Sun* had been sold. She'd apparently just dropped everything and fled Denver, in a big snit over her relationship with George Langley, apparently just about the time the news broke about the *Daily Sun*, probably a little before the news broke.

She's a *white* woman. They live for the moment they can find themselves in a "relationship." And a white woman in a relationship is a thing to behold.

Hom-Astubby reflected for a moment on what he had learned about white people, especially the curious and primitive way they used sex to perpetuate their economic system.

The white people's way of doing that seemed about as backward and illogical as anything a Choctaw could imagine, but the white people called their wasteful and silly notions "civilization," and they had tried to force all the Indian people to become like them. The white people couldn't imagine why everyone wouldn't want to be like them.

The life-goal of white people was to pair up into a man-woman unit called a "couple," with each unit being a separate legal and economic entity. The sociologists called that entity, along with its offspring, a "nuclear family." Everything in the culture and law of the white people was based on that narrow, exclusive entity.

They had put up legal roadblocks to keep Choctaws from being Choctaws, especially in the way Choctaws protected their women from their husbands and their children from their parents. Choctaws had figured out how to do that—by having a husband become a member of the wife's extended family, where the wife would be surrounded by her male relatives, making spousal abuse practically impossible, and by having legal authority for a child rest with the oldest maternal uncle, not because parents didn't love their children, but because they loved them too much, were too emotionally close to them to be able to see what was best for each child.

The white people put their women and children at potentially grave risk, at the mercy of a father-patriarch, without built-in family and community safeguards, and they insisted that everybody be like them. They did everything wrong. They didn't even trace descent through the female line. They didn't even share with one another.

Instead of living a leisurely life in the modest but adequate midst of a cooperative and sharing community, which the white people called a state of "poverty," not placing any value on the time it allowed for nurturing extended family and community ties—the very things that made life worth living—each white couple lived in carefully guarded and very expensive seclusion, in the most wastefully large and pretentious house they could "finance," which they used as a base from which to work and worry themselves into nervous exhaustion, in their quest to acquire and hoard as much wealth as they could from all the other couples, with whom they competed for everything.

Hom-Astubby shook his head. He had allowed himself to fall into that same trap. Trying to live with the financial complications of owning that monstrous house was going to drive him nuts. He could kick himself. He had *known* how to avoid becoming a white person. He had just let down his guard for one little moment, had succumbed to temptation, and here he was, getting dragged into the nightmare existence of the white people. What would be next? Start pretending as though he didn't have sex?

The thing that truly distinguished white people, the thing that made their bad situation much worse—and downright threatening to the earth—was their pretense that they didn't have sex. Their children were raised so they were ignorant about sex and were led to believe that their parents didn't have sex, or, if they did, that they certainly didn't enjoy it and probably wouldn't do it again.

When the white children became teenagers and got interested in sex, their parents panicked and drove them out of their homes, which created the enormous economic waste—and the ever-escalating strain on natural resources—of the sexually active white children then having to get their own separate homes, just to have someplace where they could have sex. They would eventually form pairs and become isolated, wealth-hoarding couples, so they could then pretend as though they didn't have sex and could raise another generation of white children who wouldn't believe that their parents had ever had sex, or, if they had, that they certainly didn't enjoy it and probably wouldn't do it again.

It was a system that benefited nobody but bankers, a system calculated to create enormous economic waste, which the white people called economic "growth"—and which the earth would not be able to afford indefinitely—and it all depended upon keeping the white people ignorant and embarrassed about sex.

But it was the young white women who played the critical role in perpetuating the system. *Everything* depended upon subverting the universal attitude of young males—that when they engaged in sex, they simply had sex—by encountering the overwhelming certainty of the young white women that when they engaged in sex, *they* had entered into a "relationship."

George Langley had gotten into Avalon O'Neill's panties. That's what had happened. And now he was paying the price. Langley was smart enough to know that, too. He knew he had no choice but to play the game, unless he wanted to turn loose of her.

Langley obviously had political ambitions, and a wife like Avalon O'Neill would be worth a lot of votes in Colorado, no matter how much of an airhead she might be. Probably the bigger the airhead, the better.

She might not even be smart enough to realize that Langley would be riding into political office on her skirt tails. She might be aware of very little right now except whatever was going on in the emotional world between her ears.

How long ago would it have been that Langley finally nailed her? Probably about six months, give or take a few weeks. Maybe after having had to work pretty hard to get there.

Hom-Astubby almost felt sorry for him. Once Langley had finally made that big breakthrough it would have been so good and it would have seemed so free for so long, until, suddenly, the bill came due.

She would now bring his whole world to a standstill until she had made him demonstrate to her satisfaction that their relationship was every bit as all-consumedly important to him as it was to her, which had no chance of actually ever being the case, because he was a man, not a woman. But she would allow herself to buy into that delusion if he played his cards just right.

Langley would do that by tiptoeing around her "feelings," like walking on eggshells, until she was convinced that, no matter what kind of mood swings she might go through, her feelings were the critical, central pivot of his universe, which, for awhile, would be the god's truth.

Then she would bear his children and allow him to play golf once in awhile. Or, she would shitcan him and wait for the next fool to come along.

Maybe George Langley had her pegged just about right. Maybe he did know what he was doing. Maybe he would—what did he call it?—"plant the word wife on her ass."

Maybe that's exactly what she wanted him to do. Maybe they deserved each other. Maybe they'd been attracted to each other so they could dance this very dance.

Hom-Astubby unconsciously pushed his hand away from his body in front of his chest as though pushing away a situation that was none of his concern. Heaven help him if he should ever become ensnared by a white woman. He shook his head. He knew how to avoid that kind of trouble. But the one who might do him some harm was George Langley. He had to get a line on Langley, find out something about him.

CHAPTER FOURTEEN

I f anybody could tell him about Langley, it might be Gordon Zimbel, the legendary political-gossip guru, now at the *Littleton Outlook* in the south Denver suburbs.

When Hom-Astubby got Zimbel on the line, they exchanged a few pleasantries, caught up on a few things. But Zimbel already knew about Hom-Astubby's big hit at the casino, and he also knew that he'd bought sixteen sections of land in Oklahoma.

Hom-Astubby didn't know how he knew that, and he didn't ask. He hadn't exactly tried to keep either one a secret. But he was impressed that Zimbel didn't need to be brought up to date on him and confident he'd called the right person to find out what he wanted to know.

"Gordy, I'm trying to get a line on a guy named George W. Langley, a Colorado deputy attorney general."

"That would be Mister Dubya. The Republican Favored Son. His daddy used to be governor, you know."

"No kidding. I didn't know that."

"You meet him?"

"Didn't exactly meet him, just got a view from the cheap seats. He cost me some work."

"What happened?"

"I was at Alpine yesterday. Got hired by the sheriff to shoot the crime scene at a murder they discovered yesterday morning. I was gonna shoot the autopsy early this morning, but Langley came blowing into town and nixed that. He came in like a hurricane."

"That's his style. Don't be looking the wrong way when the eye passes and the wind changes direction."

"He's that kind, huh?"

"Category Five. If the storm surge doesn't get you, the wind shift will. He's Hurricane Dubya. Whether he's headed somewhere or drifting aimlessly, he's just as dangerous."

"Well, the guy pissed me off, the way it happened. He was pretty high-handed."

"You want my advice, forget about it. You think he was high-handed with you? Imagine how those local authorities in Alpine are feeling right now. That's a nest of Democrats over there. But Langley's taken that murder investigation completely away from them by declaring it multijurisdictional. I'm not sure exactly how that works, but it gives the attorney general's office statutory authority in the matter. All the media just got a release from Langley's office, a multistate bulletin they're wanting publicized—be on the lookout for a big black dog. And a man with a BMW. Got a mug shot of a guy named Hussein and a generic photo of what a black Newfoundland dog looks like. And get a load of this—the two of them not necessarily traveling together. Figure that one out. They've got to be onto something."

"A man and a dog, huh? A multistate media bulletin, with photos of both of them?"

"Yeah. Had they developed that Hussein lead when you were there? You're not still in Alpine, right?"

"No. I'm on my way home, in New Mexico. They didn't have anything when I left, not that they told me about, anyway, not even an ID on the murder victim."

"They still don't have that."

A man and a dog. No mention of the O'Neill woman. It was obvious to Hom-Astubby that they'd caught her. But she didn't have the dog with her. She would have told Langley about her dog getting taken. And Langley, the son of a bitch, was proving to her just how hard he was trying to find her dog.

"Bill, you're doing the right thing, heading home. Just stay out of Langley's way and let this one go. You apparently saw his bad side, at least from your point of view. He's got more than your interests to consider, and running the attorney general's office is not for the meek. But if he had needed to charm you, you'd have had a hell of a time not being charmed, as difficult as that might be for you to believe. But trust me. He's ambimanipulatory. He can eat your lunch behind your back, or he can get you to hand it to him. Sounds like he only took a snack from you. Don't let that whet his appetite. You don't want him for an enemy. He's practically the attorney general right now."

"What do you mean?"

"The attorney general is at home, bedridden. Terminal cancer. He's only got a few months left. Langley's been running the office for quite a while. The governor's all set to appoint Langley attorney general, as soon as Haroldson dies, if Haroldson can hang on past this midterm election in November. Then Langley can be appointed to fill out the rest of that term, for a couple of years. There's more, but you won't like it."

"What?"

"Langley won't be the attorney general for long. He's Governor Wade's handpicked boy to succeed him as governor in the next general election."

"Oh, Jesus. If he's Charlie Wade's boy, that means he's Nelson Towers' boy, too."

"You got it. Four more years of Nelson Towers owning the governor's office."

"Does Langley really have a chance at that?"

"Are you kidding? With Towers' money, the governor's backing, his daddy's name, and all of that old political network? He'll be the favorite for the Republican nomination, probably only draw nominal opposition in the party primary. For the general election, who can say? Politics is a crazy business. He's made a lot of enemies, but he's also made a hell of a reputation as a hardline crime fighter. All street stuff. Gang activity, some murders, drug rings. Nothing white-collar. Nothing meaningful, anyway. He's got statewide statutory responsibility for complex white-collar crime. Man, oh, man, does Nelson Towers have the right boy in the right place. Oh, he's busted some big white-collar crime cases, all right, some of Towers' people stealing from Towers. But Langley's got a real knack for finding multijurisdictional reasons for horning in on some of the headline street crime. All that stuff that TV news devotes half its time to making sure the public stays afraid of, so it won't occur to them to ask about anything else. All he needs now is to get himself a wife, but I hear he's working on that. You wouldn't believe who he's after."

"Who?"

"Avalanche O'Neill."

"The skier?" Hom-Astubby tried to sound surprised.

"Olympic Gold Medal. In this ski-crazy state, worth god knows how many votes if Langley pulls her in. Real curious angle about that, illustrates some of what I've been saying about Langley. Did you know she was one of the *Daily Sun* reporters working on that big Towers investigation?"

"You've got to be kidding."

"That's about how Nelson Towers responded to the situation. He was not amused. Word around the campfire is that Towers took Langley on a little trip to the woodshed for letting his pecker do his thinking for him. But Langley convinced Towers that if he married O'Neill, it would be a good thing for Towers. How could anybody accuse Langley of being a Towers puppet if his new wife was a known Towers hounder? Politics is a crazy business, Bill. Did somebody say strange bedfellows? Can you appreciate the moxie it took for Langley to pick a woman like that and then sell the idea to Nelson Towers? Nobody I know is real eager to see Langley in the governor's chair, but nobody I know is real eager to get in his way. Now aren't you glad you asked me about Langley and that you're on your way home?"

"I damn sure am, Gordy. I owe you one. You take care."

"You too, Bill. Don't be such a stranger. We'll kill a bottle of Wild Turkey. Next time."

"Next time," Hom-Astubby said.

Hom-Astubby hung up the phone. The O'Neill woman had actually been working on the Towers investigation? Doing what?

Gordy was a good source of information for a lot of things, but much of what he'd said had to be just gossip, speculation, rumor. There was no way to know how reliable the gossip might be.

He shook his head. He had more immediate things to think about.

Jesus, a multistate media bulletin on the dog, complete with a photo of what a black Newfie looks like. There was no way to keep the general public from seeing the dog. He'd have to let the dog out to pee once in a while. A big conspicuous dog.

Every cop for hundreds of miles would be on the alert for the dog, in connection with a murder case. They'd be taking a hard look at every big black dog they saw. What would he do if he got stopped, just for something like a taillight being out, and the dog started barking, and the cop wanted to see the dog? If the dog got caught, however that might happen, the dog would die.

Maybe he could try changing the dog's appearance. That might work.

He dug out his notebook and found Johnny Begay's work phone number, not knowing if the number was still good. Johnny, a half-Navajo, half-Comanche, had been determined to join the all-Indian rodeo circuit the last time Hom-Astubby had been in town, and he might be god knows where by now.

Johnny had a way of ending up doing the things he talked about doing, at least giving them a try. He took a little bit of pride in that, of not being all talk, and he was as good as his word. He knew horses, too, and was somebody Hom-Astubby had in mind for help with running his ranch and for help with buying breeding stock.

If there was anybody in Gallup who could help him it might be Johnny. Long ago, Johnny had gone to barber school. He'd flunked out, but he'd gotten at least some training, maybe enough to give the dog a good haircut, cut off enough hair to make it easier to dye the rest of it a different color, change the dog's appearance just enough to get by. They studied hair coloring in barber college. It might work, if Johnny was still in town.

He dialed the number. A female voice answered the phone, "Garage."

"Is Johnny Begay there?"

"Sure. Hang on a minute." Hom-Astubby listened to faint but distinct hammering and banging in the background, the roar of an engine being revved up, and the whine of a torque wrench.

Pretty soon Johnny said, "This is Johnny."

"What are you doing, still in this town?"

"Man, I do not know who this is, and I am hanging up now."

"I thought you were going to hit the rodeo circuit."

"I am telling you, this is a wrong number. The person you want is not here."

"The person I want was going to become a bull rider. That person didn't do that?"

"Okay, I did that. Even got my buddy to video it, so I could prove it. But that didn't work too good."

"How come?"

"Man, he stayed focused on the bull. You gotta look quick to see me. What are you doing in town? You are in town, aren't you?"

"Yeah, and I need a big favor."

"Man, I do not have any idea who I am talking to, and I am going to hang up the phone, right now."

"Do you still have your barber clippers?"

"What?"

"You're not going to believe this, but I have stolen a dog in Colorado because some woman's boyfriend, who is a cop, wants the dog killed, and I've got to change the dog's appearance before the boyfriend figures out that I might have the dog and gets the cops after me, so if they do catch me, they might not think it's the same dog."

"Man, the only part I believe is that some woman's boyfriend is hot on your tail."

"Then why do I need the clippers?"

"You got me there."

"You got the clippers?"

"You're not serious?"

"I am dead serious. They've got a bulletin out on the dog. They're saying the dog might be part of a murder case, just to get the cops to be on the lookout for it. I just pulled in at Wal-Mart, just dropped off some film here for one-hour processing, and I'm in a hell of a hurry. I got to go back inside and try to figure out what kind of hair dye I can use on the dog. And I've got to be back on the road by the time that film is done. Can you meet me here?"

"Oh, man. How do I get talked into these things? Tell me that you don't have any midgets with you."

"No midgets."

"You promise? No midgets with car trouble, right?"

"Hey, what could I do? They were broken down out there. Somebody had to help them."

"I didn't hear you promise."

"Okay. I promise. No midgets of any kind."

"No cute little *nymphomaniac* midgets, *damn you!*"

"No midgets whatsoever."

"It took me *three days* to get rid of them! Do you have *any idea* what those three days were like?"

"I have not seen any midgets of any kind anywhere."

"Okay. But if I see either one of those horny little midgets, I'm outta there. Are we clear on that?"

"We are clear on that."

"Okay. I ain't had any lunch yet, so I guess I can clock out for that. I got no wheels right now, but I guess I can get somebody to drop me off. But, listen, Hom-Astubby, don't get any Wal-Mart hair dye. You don't know what you're doing. I got a cousin who's a vet. I can call and ask her about that, see if there's anything we might need to know about for use on a dog. You just wait there in front of the store, and I'll be there in a flash. It's not far."

In hardly any time at all, the tow truck from the garage dropped Johnny off in front of Wal-Mart. He said, "Man, I can't wait to see this dog. Where is it?"

"This way," Hom-Astubby said, leading Johnny through the parking lot. The sun was blistering. He wished there had been somewhere in the shade to park the truck. Even with all the windows open in the camper, the dog just wasn't accustomed to this kind of heat, and it wouldn't get any better where he was headed. Giving the dog a haircut would be a good idea, even if nobody was looking for the dog.

"This is it," Hom-Astubby said, when he got to his truck. He started to lead Johnny to the back door of the camper, but Johnny was still standing in front of the truck, staring at it.

"Holy shit!" Johnny said, glancing quickly all around the parking lot. "Man, you only told me about taking the guy's dog. The dog we can deal with, but we'll do hard time if they catch us with this. It's kind of conspicuous, you know?"

"No, no," Hom-Astubby said. "No problem. It's mine."

"Hom-Astubby, who do you think you're talking to? It's me, Johnny! You think I got struck blind or something?"

"No. Really. It's my truck."

Johnny looked from the truck to Hom-Astubby and back to the truck again. He said, "Holy shit! What did you hit?"

"Double Diamond. Double Diamond. Double Diamond."

"Y-e-e-e-e h-a-a!" Johnny slapped his knee. "At Sky City?"

"At Sandia."

"No shit? A dollar machine? Three coin max? Big progressive?"

"Johnny, you haven't seen the horse ranch, yet."

"Horse ranch? You bought *this*," he pointed at the truck, "*and* a horse ranch?" He stared at the truck for a moment. "Holy shit! You hit a five-dollar machine!"

"Yeah, a big Mini-Bertha. Two coin max. Cost me ten dollars."

"You hit the progressive? How much? A million?"

"8.8 million."

"Holy shit! And you still shop at Wal-Mart? Man, you Choctaws got Wal-Mart on the brain. They ought to rename them Choctaw Cultural Centers. Let's see the inside of this thing. It looks like a palace."

Hom-Astubby unlocked the back door of the camper and held it open. Johnny scrambled up the steps and hurried through the long hallway to the front of the camper. He plopped down in the dinette booth, his eyes wide, staring all around—at the kitchen, at all the cabinet space. He said, "Hi, poochy," and he reached up and gave Lady's head a ruffle, then did a double-take at the dog.

He looked at Hom-Astubby. "What in the hell kind of dog is this? Are you sure it's not half gorilla?"

"She's a Newfoundland, like the one that accompanied the Lewis and Clark expedition all the way to the Pacific Ocean."

"Man, I always wondered why all those Indians didn't kick their butts. Now I know. They were too busy trying to figure out what in the hell was walking beside them."

The dog was feeling the heat at Gallup. She was lying on the bed, panting, grinning at Hom-Astubby.

"You want to drive the truck?" Hom-Astubby said.

"You bet your ass I do!" Johnny scampered out of the camper and Hom-Astubby handed him the keys. He quickly closed all the windows in the camper and pulled the curtains over them.

Once the engine was running, Hom-Astubby got the air conditioning going again throughout the pickup cab and the camper.

"Good idea," Johnny said. "Man, that dog's got such a heavy coat of hair, she's gonna die in that Oklahoma heat. In August, with all that humidity out there? I tell you what. You want to change her appearance? I got just the ticket. Lucky for you, you came through Dinetah to get where you're going. Man, did you come to the right place."

"What?" Hom-Astubby said.

"Sheep shears. You hold the dog's head and keep her calm. Five minutes later, not even you will recognize her. I might not have got too far in barber college, but wait'll you see me with those sheep shears. Prepare to be amazed."

"No kidding? But she'll still have some black hair," Hom-Astubby said. "On her face and ears and tail and whatnot. I don't know how much she'll stand for us messing with her. And I'm in a hell of a hurry."

"No problem. My cousin told me what kind of dye to get, at Hosamma's Beauty Salon. It's on the way home. Hang on." He began pulling out of the parking lot. "What color do you want?"

"I don't know. Brown?"

"Yeah. There's lots of brown dogs. A pooch brown color."

Half an hour later they were lifting the wet, sheared dog out of the bathtub at Johnny's house and carrying her outside to dry off, while Johnny's sister tried to rinse the dye out of the tub. Even wearing rubber gloves, they had gotten nearly as much brown dye on themselves as on the dog.

They stood the dog on some newspapers they'd spread out on the ground in the hot sunshine, having anchored them with rocks to hold them in place against a steady breeze. They stood back to admire their handiwork.

The dog looked something like a tall, wet, skinny, bearded drowned rat. She stood on the papers, a look of stunned disbelief on her face, looking all around at her naked body, as the dye quickly dried into the most god-awful mud-brown color that Hom-Astubby had ever seen. The sheep shears had left nothing whatsoever right down to the skin. But there was abundant evidence—in Johnny's hurried touch-up work with a pair of dull scissors, in the leftover hair on the dog's face, head, ears, lower legs, and tail—demonstrating why Johnny had not been destined to be a barber.

"What do you think?" Johnny said.

Hom-Astubby couldn't believe it. The dog had been mostly hair, and with the hair gone, there wasn't much dog left. "Doesn't look like the same dog." He shook his head. "Doesn't even look like a dog. Not a Newfie anyway. Maybe some weird kind of Afghan."

"You'd be smart getting new vet tags for her, too."

"Yeah, wish I had time to do that."

"No problem. I'll call my cousin again, tell her we're coming, what we need. She can have 'em ready. But we'll need a new name for the dog."

They thought of Joe Babe, Rosalita, Lolita, Hot Mamma.

"How about Hosamma?" Johnny said. "In honor of the beauty salon."

"Hosamma it is," Hom-Astubby said. "Hosamma, the licensed,

tall, skinny, bearded, brown dog from Gallup, New Mexico, who doesn't even look like a dog, let alone a black Newfie. Johnny, you're a genius."

"That's the danged truth, ain't it?"

"You might have just gotten me out of a real bad pickle. I'll tell you what. You've got no wheels? I've still got that old Honda Civic. You want it?"

"Want it! Man, I could win every Indian car contest in the country with that thing. Where is it?"

"It's sitting in my maintenance garage, on my ranch in Oklahoma. I've got everything there you'd need to work on it, if you wanted to tune it up, change the oil, or whatnot."

"Let's go! I got some time coming at the shop."

"It could get dicey. What if they're waiting for me when I get there?"

"Then I could have the camper. You wouldn't be needing it anymore."

Hom-Astubby laughed. He let out a sigh. "I sure hope that old Honda will get you back here."

"Man, you tried every way possible to put that thing out of its misery. It's indestructible."

Johnny called his boss and his cousin, and he threw some socks and undershorts and T-shirts in a bag, while his sister made them a big sack of sandwiches. By the time they'd cleaned up and changed out of their dye-stained clothes, the dog was dry.

On their way out of town they ran by Wal-Mart, picked up Hom-Astubby's processed color film and prints, topped off the gas tank, and got the dog tags at the vet clinic, all in one big rush.

They were pulling out of Gallup onto Interstate 40 before 2 P.M., headed east toward Moriarty, New Mexico, with a tall, skinny, butt-ugly brown thing riding in the back seat of the king cab, its nose sticking out of a partially lowered window, sniffing the strange and wondrous odors on the breeze.

CHAPTER FIFTEEN

A s soon as Interstate 40 emerged from Gallup, the speed limit jumped to 75 mph. The traffic in the fast lane was going between 80 and 85 across the dry, rugged, brushy desert landscape, with a seemingly endless line of spectacular red cliffs running parallel to the highway, only about a mile or so to the north.

Hom-Astubby blended into the traffic in the fast lane. Albuquerque was only 140 miles away. If all went well, they'd be there in less than two hours, just barely ahead of rush hour.

He turned on the radio, while Johnny pulled sandwiches out of the sack. They munched in silence while Hom-Astubby set the radio on scan, stopping it for awhile at every station that was doing anything that sounded like news.

By the time he'd scanned through all the AM and FM stations several times, they had finished eating and were crossing the low crest of the Continental Divide, about twenty-five miles east of Gallup. There was nothing on any radio station about anything unusual anywhere on the highways, nothing about any roadblocks, police bulletins, nothing the police were asking the public for help with. He turned off the radio.

"Man," Johnny said, "you are one nervous hombre. Relax. Colorado is a world away from here."

"Yeah. I guess so," Hom-Astubby said, watching Johnny feed the dog bite-size pieces of a peanut butter sandwich.

They had barely started eating when Hom-Astubby felt a cold, wet nose touch the side of his neck. The longer he ate, the more pressure he felt from that nose. He'd glanced in the rear-view mirror, in the center of the windshield, seeing the dog with her nose resting on his shoulder, her eyes shifting back and forth between him and Johnny every time one of them took a bite. Finally, Johnny had offered her a piece of his sandwich, and she was now over on that side of the back seat, with her nose resting on Johnny's shoulder.

When they were less than an hour from Albuquerque, they passed Acoma Pueblo's Sky City Indian Casino.

"Look," Hom-Astubby said. "That guy coming out the front door. You can tell that he lost money."

Johnny squinted and stared at the man as they were driving by. "Oh yeah? How can you tell?"

"He's coming *out* of a casino."

Johnny laughed and slapped his knee. "That's the dang truth, ain't it?"

Half an hour later, they stared at the sea of eighteen-wheelers in the big sprawling truck parking lot at Laguna Pueblo's Route 66 Indian Casino.

"Man," Johnny said, "I wish we could stop in there for awhile. Can't you just hear the sound of those slot machines?"

"Yeah," Hom-Astubby said. "There's nothing like walking through those casino doors and hearing the sound of the machines."

It was a little before four o'clock when they topped the last big hill and abruptly hit the western edge of Albuquerque. Johnny read the sign, "Albuquerque. Next 17 Exits," and added, "Man, it's getting to be a big town. An hour from now, we'd play hell getting through it."

"Yeah, we're hitting it just about right, barely."

Albuquerque had a curious growth pattern. Hemmed in on the east by the Sandia Mountains, it was also hemmed in on the west by a large, ancient petroglyph preservation area that kept it from sprawling into the desert very far to the west of the Rio Grande River. Coming into Albuquerque from the west, one minute it's hello nothing, and the next minute, from the top of a big hill, it's hello big city.

Interstate 40 was already getting congested, but not enough to stall the traffic. They were able to get all the way across the city doing the speed limit and soon found themselves in heavy traffic, climbing up through the long steep canyon beside Sandia Peak at the eastern edge of the city. After finally popping out at the top of the canyon, the vehicles gradually thinned out as they got farther east, until, fairly quickly, the Albuquerque traffic was well behind them and they were once again rolling across the rugged, mostly empty, arid high plains.

It was getting on toward five o'clock when they pulled off the Interstate, at Moriarty, and halted for gas at the truck stop.

"Can you fill it up with diesel, Johnny? Then I'll pay for it and move the truck. We can feed the dog her regular dinner and take her for a walk in that park over there. I've got to get hold of somebody before she leaves the office."

"You bet. Let's get some coffee and snacks, too."

"You pick out all that stuff, okay? I'll be right back."

Hom-Astubby hurried to the pay phone, hoping that Carol Jenkins had been able to find out something about Avalon O'Neill, if Carol hadn't already left. Getting the dog taken care of in Gallup had caused him to be a little later than he'd thought when he'd called her at noon.

He'd been set on getting to Moriarty, knowing there was a good place there to let the dog romp around a little bit. Maybe he should have stopped somewhere as soon as he'd cleared Albuquerque. But Carol answered the phone on the third ring.

"Bill, you barely caught me. I was on my way out. Something's come up. Listen, I was able to work the phones a little bit, and I got lucky, several times. But I'll have to give it to you quick."

"Okay. What did you get?"

"Do you know about her undergrad studies?"

"No."

"She went to CU-Boulder. B.A., double major, physics and French language and literature. NCAA champion in the women's downhill."

"Physics?"

"Yeah. She might have had a future in quantum mechanics, if she'd continued on down that path. And she hasn't gained a pound in ten years. I hate her."

"Quantum mechanics? Christ! And French?"

"Yeah. CU is one of the top schools for Romance languages. Has been for a long time."

"I didn't know that. She's fluent in French?"

"Well, duh. What do you think? She was probably fluent even before she got to CU. In high school, she spent her junior year abroad, did that year of high school in Paris. She's had a knack for getting ahead of the game for a long time. But Bill, there's more about language, so to speak. At CU, she minored in accounting, the language of business."

"Jesus. No 'Theory of Recreation,' huh?"

"No. This was one focused woman. No jock courses. No boyfriend. No sorority—lived at home with her parents in Boulder all the way through CU. That's not all. Few varsity athletes manage to graduate in four years, or even five. The demands on their time, the travel, the training—it's just too much. She graduated in three."

"How'd she do that?"

"Started at CU the summer after high school. Advanced placement. Tested out of a lot of stuff. Took overloads. Went to summer sessions the last two summers at universities in France."

"What was the fire under her ass?"

"That's just the way she is. They call her 'Avalanche.' She was determined to get her degree before the Olympics."

"How about after the Olympics? I heard she turned down a super model contract or something."

"She turned down a lot of things. Endorsements, you name it. Bill, I looked at an old video, an interview she did during the Olympics. She has got so much charm, so natural. You can't help liking her. Unless you're a woman."

"So. What? She just disappeared, or something?"

"For all practical purposes. She went to France. Was gone a couple years, but I couldn't find out anything about what she did there. Whatever it was, it had nothing to do with skiing."

"Maybe studying French, wouldn't you think?"

"Well, maybe. If I didn't know the rest."

"What's the rest?"

"She came back to the states, to New York. Went to Columbia University School of Journalism. Got an M.A. there. Then to Yale Law School."

"*Law school*. At Yale?"

"Yeah. Law and business. Got a joint degree. An MBA and a JD. One more thing. Then I've got to go. She's been back here in the Denver area for about a year. One of the first new hires that Earl Paggett made at the *Daily Sun* when he came in. When she had been doing her grad studies in journalism, Earl Paggett was a visiting professor at Columbia. She had several seminars with him. I hope all that helps."

"Geez, Carol. You're terrific."

"One other thing. About her parents. I mentioned that they live in Boulder now, but they're both from Ireland. A guy told me that they grew up on remote sheep ranches in the Irish backcountry. He said they still spend a lot of time in Ireland, and in Europe. He said they've been big-time people in the international show dog business for a long time now."

"Show dogs!" Hom-Astubby groaned.

"Oh, I almost forgot. Funny you mentioned horses earlier. Her passion is horses."

"How do you mean? Show horses? Racing? What?"

"Just riding them, I think. Trail riding, the guy said. I've got to go, Love. You-know-who called."

"Your ex-fiancé?"

"Yeah. Here we go again. Round three."

"Good luck, kiddo."

"Thanks. You take care, too."

CHAPTER SIXTEEN

Hom-Astubby hung up the phone in a daze. In a sleep-walk he sipped his coffee while paying for the gas and the snacks that Johnny had gathered up. He moved the truck, replaying in his mind all the things that Carol had said. He remembered, too, the way Avalon O'Neill had looked the moment he first saw her.

"Man, you get some bad news or what?" Johnny said, after he'd asked him twice where he'd stowed away the dog food.

"I don't know."

"You don't know where the dog food is, or you don't know if you got bad news?"

"Huh? Oh. The dog food's in here." Hom-Astubby opened the camper, then held the door open, staring at the horizon.

"You gonna give me a hint where in there it might be?"

"Huh? Oh. That cabinet there."

Johnny dug out the cans of dog food that Hom-Astubby had bought in Alpine, saying, "If this is all there is, we better get some more before we leave here. This will only feed her one time." He found a can opener and the dog's food dish, shaking his head at Hom-Astubby, who was still holding the door open, staring at the horizon.

"Man, you got woman problems," Johnny said. "I recognize all the signs."

When the dog had finished eating, they walked to the park, Hom-Astubby still lost in thought. He couldn't figure out how he had been so wrong about so many things. He didn't understand this woman at all.

What was she doing with a guy like George Langley? Could it be true that smart women make dumb choices when it comes to men? Maybe she'd realized her mistake and was trying to extricate herself. Or maybe Langley was right, and it was just the big chase, exactly what she wanted. Maybe she was the one calling the shots.

Hom-Astubby realized, for all he'd learned about the woman, that he knew nothing whatsoever, really, about her. There was probably some risk in that, in what he didn't know, risk he'd never even considered.

Maybe she had ice water in her veins, and a heart as cold and calculating as Langley's. She didn't seem to let anything stop her from getting where she wanted to go. Where did she want to go? With her track record, anything might be possible.

Maybe she had political ambitions herself. Maybe *she* was the one playing Langley for all *he* was worth. Maybe she was the one manipulating him into marriage without his even being aware of it, using him to get herself into the governor's mansion, get back into the spotlight on her own terms, become the First Lady of Colorado.

Then what? Maybe she becomes the most active and the most visible First Lady that Colorado has ever had. Maybe from there she gets herself elected to the U.S. Senate. Maybe from there she goes all the way to the White House. Maybe that dumbass Langley would wake up one day and discover he'd gone down in history as the first *First Husband* of the United States!

There was just too much that Hom-Astubby didn't know. He didn't know anything, really, except that, no matter what else, she's a lawyer. Christ! What if she sued him for taking her dog? What if she was really pissed about what he'd done to her dog? Could her dog possibly be a show dog?

Hom-Astubby looked at her dog. He groaned. Was the dye permanent? How long would it take for the hair to grow out? What might a jury do if they got a good look at her dog? Jesus! She might end up owning his ranch.

What if she got so pissed off that she wanted criminal charges brought against him? It wasn't as if she didn't know anybody who might do that. Her boyfriend was the deputy attorney general in charge of the Criminal Law Section, a guy with all the compassion and conscience of a great big shark.

But what were the odds that anybody might really get pissed

off enough to pursue criminal charges? Over taking a dog? When he'd taken good care of the dog? He'd be able to convince a jury of that. Hom-Astubby looked at her dog again. He said, "Oh shit! I better get some legal advice. Some damn good advice."

Johnny, who had sat down on the ground and was roughing the dog's head, heard what Hom-Astubby said. He looked up. "What? You gonna hire a lawyer?"

"I'm gonna talk to one, find out just how vulnerable I might be. The potential civil liabilities I can figure out for myself. That's only money, anyway. But getting thrown in jail is a little bit different. I've been worrying about everything except what I *should* have been worrying about—what happens if that woman gets so pissed she makes it her personal business to do more about it than just sue my dumb ass? I've been worried about the cops trying to find this dog. But sooner or later I've got to return this dog to that woman. *That's* what I should have been worrying about. Hang on a few minutes, okay? I've got to make another call."

He headed back to the pay phone, trying to think of someone to call who might be able to take on George Langley, if it came to that. The only person he could think of was Sam Burnbalm. But Sam was big-time, as big as it gets, and Hom-Astubby barely knew him. If he could even get hold of Sam, would the guy sit still long enough to hear any of the complexities of the thing, once he found out it was a dog-napping problem?

Hom-Astubby stopped. Did he really want to risk making a fool of himself with Sam? Sam Burnbalm wasn't just the biggest gun in criminal law that he knew, however slightly he might know him. He wasn't just the best-known criminal trial lawyer in Denver, and one of the best-known in the country. He was the founding partner of one of the biggest law firms in Colorado, with more than a hundred lawyers—how many, Hom-Astubby didn't know. The guy had to be a multimillionaire, and he'd handled so many headline cases, he was a genuine celebrity, often on TV doing commentary about other big cases.

The lawyers in his firm specialized mostly in personal injury,

consumer product liability, environmental litigation, medical mal-
practice, worker's compensation. They were a bulldog bunch of
advocates for the injured and oppressed, a plaintiff's firm of trial
lawyers, for the most part. But it was Sam's celebrity as a criminal
defense trial lawyer that had built the firm.

Hom-Astubby's only connection with Sam was through Harry
Birdwell. Sam had gone on a fishing trip with them in Montana
when Harry had gotten an assignment to do a trout-fishing article
up there. Harry Birdwell's uncle was one of Sam's first partners in
the firm, and Sam was a dedicated fly-fisherman.

But they'd taken that fishing trip years ago, when Hom-
Astubby was temporarily between newspaper jobs. They'd had
a hell of a good time, and Hom-Astubby had liked Sam a lot, but
he wasn't real sure Sam would even remember him, let alone listen
to his dog problem.

So why worry about making a fool of yourself with some guy
who might not even remember you anyway? The more foolish
thing would be not seeking help. Especially in a criminal matter. It
would be stupid to rely on his own counsel for that. In law school,
he'd learned that a lawyer who represents himself has got a fool
for a client.

If he wanted a shot at getting somebody who might not flinch
at going eyeball-to-eyeball with George Langley, he had to make
the call and hope that Sam would listen long enough to see that it
wasn't just a run-of-the-mill dog-napping problem. He made the
call.

"Burnbalm, Balch, Birdwell, Guterrez, and Brinkley," a female
voice said, rapidly, with clear articulation of each syllable.

"Sam Burnbalm, please."

"May I say who's calling?"

"Bill Mallory. I'm a friend of Harry Birdwell, Jim Birdwell's
nephew."

"Hold please. I'll see if he's in."

Hom-Astubby watched the traffic pulling in and out of the

truck stop, wondering who he should try if Sam Burnbalm wouldn't take his call, until a gruff voice came over the line.

"I hope this is an invitation to get back on the Beaverhead with my fly rod. See myself in *Sports Afield* again."

"That's a standing invitation, Sam. Is yours still open? If I might ever need a criminal lawyer?"

"You bet. What's the problem?"

"I think I might have stolen somebody's dog."

"You're not sure?"

"Well, I thought she'd been abandoned when I took her."

"I sure as hell hope this is not a big black Newfoundland dog we're talking about."

That took Hom-Astubby by surprise. He started to say, "How do you know about the dog?" But then he remembered the media alert that Langley had put out at noon. Sam must have seen something about that on TV. But something in Sam's voice gave Hom-Astubby further pause. Something wasn't right. He didn't want to lie to Sam, but he suddenly felt ill at ease. He said, "A big black dog? It's a skinny brown dog."

"I'm damn glad to hear that. Now what's the problem with it?"

"Sam, uh. . . ." Hom-Astubby's uncertainty, a feeling of a need for caution, grew stronger. He should have thought this through before placing the call. Sam, as a member of the bar, was an officer of the court. Sam could get into big trouble, depending on what he knew and when he knew it. The attorney-client privilege had some exceptions. It wasn't absolute. Hom-Astubby didn't want to bet the life of the dog that they weren't getting into one of those exceptions. Knowledge of an ongoing crime, one in progress, might be something that Sam ought to be shielded from. Hom-Astubby tried to choose his words carefully. "I'm wondering. Since you mentioned it, can you tell me what difference it would have made if it had been a big black dog? You know, just out of curiosity?"

"Oh, no." Sam let out a long, loud groan. "You're not watching TV are you? You and that skinny brown dog?"

"No. I'm nowhere near a TV."

"I've got one right here in my office. Got twenty-four of them as a matter of fact. They cover the whole damn wall. One of them interrupted programming awhile ago for a special news bulletin. A live feed from the network affiliate in Grand Junction, a camera crew out on I-70 at the Utah border showing trucks and cars backed up for miles, due to the Colorado State Patrol putting up roadblocks on the borders with Utah, Arizona, and New Mexico. They've bottled up the entire southwest quadrant of Colorado, or at least they're rushing to do so, started apparently about an hour ago. Roadblocks at every border crossing all the way from the Utah border near Grand Junction on Interstate 70 in the middle of the state in the west, down to the southwest corner of Colorado near Cortez, then east along the New Mexico border to U.S. 285, then up the San Luis Valley to the junction with U.S. 50 near Salida in the middle of the state, and from there to the west all the way back to Grand Junction. They're trying to get roadblocks everywhere that any vehicle might be able to get out of that box. It's already the biggest traffic jam in Colorado history, at the height of the tourist season, getting worse by the minute, and it's going to get a whole lot worse real quick. The governor is mobilizing the Colorado National Guard to supplement the law enforcement personnel."

"Jesus!" Hom-Astubby said. "The National Guard!"

"Would any of that have made much difference?" Sam asked. "If it had been a big black dog? Instead of this skinny brown dog?"

"Uh, no. No difference. I'm not in that box. I'm not in Colorado, not now. But, Sam, how can they do that? That is a huge area. That'll bring a quarter of the state to a standstill."

"The governor is mad as hell, that's how. And he knows the whole world will be watching what he does. Somebody murdered a Pulitzer Prize–winning reporter named Linda Ruben over near Telluride, at Alpine. She's been in the news lately. You remember why?"

Jesus. The dead woman at Alpine was Linda Ruben. It took

Hom-Astubby a moment to digest that. He said, "That *Daily Sun* reporter who got her book squashed by Nelson Towers?"

"Yeah. Nelson Towers, who everybody knows is the governor's biggest supporter and contributor. Nelson Towers, who everybody's going to be wondering about, asking questions about, speculating about, and wondering if his old buddy the governor will be engaging in some kind of cover-up. The body was discovered on Towers' land, within a few miles of his new house over there. And, if we read between the lines, Nelson Towers, who's apparently lit a fire under the governor's ass to get this thing cleared up pronto, no matter what it takes, before the press gets to sniffing around Towers' britches legs. That could turn into a feeding frenzy. He's been asking for it for a long time. But apparently the cops have got a hot lead. They're looking for some guy named Hussein and his BMW, and that big black dog, though what the dog's got to do with it is anybody's guess."

Hom-Astubby groaned.

"TV, radio, newspapers, from Denver, Albuquerque, Phoenix, and Salt Lake City, are rushing to Alpine. Every Denver TV station is now promising a live update from there on the late news tonight. Wait a minute. Yeah, that's a BBC satellite station that just picked up the story. There's a Canadian news station, too. Hell, pretty soon even the New York media will find out about this, and they'll be joining the rush to Alpine. Hold on a minute."

Hom-Astubby waited several minutes, until Sam came back on the line.

"Bill," Sam said. "Somehow Interpol has already gotten involved in this. It's not just a nationwide manhunt, it's international. The BBC is promising a live update from Alpine just as soon as they can get there. So is Al-Jazeera and a lot of other foreign news services. This is going to draw reporters from all over the world. There's not a bigger fish out there, anywhere, than Nelson Towers."

"They can get into Alpine?"

"The bottleneck is getting out of that box, not getting into it, though they'll undoubtedly be setting up a lot of roadblocks inside the box, as soon as the National Guard gets there. It's a big box, but I'll tell you what, it wouldn't surprise me to see them expand that roadblock dragnet into southeastern Utah, and northeastern Arizona, and northwestern New Mexico—the whole Four Corners region. They must have a good reason to think the killer has not yet left the area. I'll bet they're getting spot roadblocks right now in those other states, if they think they need them. The only person in the United States with more power than Nelson Towers is the president, and you know damn good and well they've been on the phone by now. There's no telling who all Towers has been talking to. It looks like every cop in the world is already on the lookout for Hussein and his BMW. And that dog. A rental car, too, from a Telluride agency, the one Linda Ruben was driving. Apparently she was so angry with Towers, and in such a hurry to confront him, that she flew to Telluride and rented a car there."

Hom-Astubby thought hard, trying to read between the lines. By the time they'd identified Linda Ruben's body, apparently sometime this afternoon, and all hell had broken loose, George Langley had already gone public with that noonday media request about Hussein. He couldn't back off from that, when, suddenly, everything had snowballed way out of his control—except that the son of a bitch was still taking every opportunity to make sure he'd get his hands on the dog.

"Bill, are you still there?"

"Yeah, just thinking," Hom-Astubby said. "Sam, the dog's got nothing to do with it. Neither does that Hussein character, who-ever he is. I heard them cook up this whole thing about Hussein and the dog. I was at Alpine when the murder was discovered. The sheriff hired me to shoot the crime scene. Then the state people showed up, and I overheard a conversation I wasn't supposed to. They talked about why they should kill some big ole overgrown puppy, if they could find it, because the dog wouldn't let one of them, an abusive boyfriend, get near his girlfriend. They dreamed up a hunt for this Hussein character just as an excuse to get a whole bunch of cops to find that dog for them. That put me in kind of a sympathetic frame of mind toward dogs. And when I happened to find what I thought was an abandoned dog, well, that's how I ended up where I am now, with this skinny, brown dog."

"Did anyone else overhear that conversation that you weren't supposed to hear?"

"No. Just the two people doing the talking, and they'd both deny it. They don't know I overhead it. Sam, one of them is a Colorado deputy attorney general. They're the ones running the manhunt. George W. Langley and some guy named Dick. They had no idea who the murder victim was when they cooked up this thing about Hussein and the dog. They've got to be the two most surprised fools in the world, the way this Hussein thing has ballooned on them, has gotten way out of their control, but they couldn't very well back off from it once they'd gotten it started. Hell, now that both the governor and Nelson Towers are breathing down their necks, they're probably damn glad they had already cooked it up. They've at least got something to show, a big attention-getter that will dominate the news and make it look like they're right on top of it, no matter how many man-hours and how many millions of dollars are being wasted. But if they get their hands on that dog, the dog is dead. Nobody up there knows I picked up a stray dog, except maybe a gas station attendant."

"Hmmmm. George W. Langley, huh? That Dick would probably be Richard Halliburton, in the Criminal Law Section, Langley's shadow. Well, what do you want to do, Old Hoss?"

"It's my call?"

"It's your call. It's your consequences."

"Sam, their focus is on Colorado. And now, all of their manpower, and all of their attention, is tied up with this massive wild goose chase, organizing it, coordinating it, dealing with the media, with people whose cars run out of gas waiting at those roadblocks, or who have strokes or heart attacks, or women trying to have babies, emergency vehicles that have to get somewhere, and god knows what else. If they were going to make any connection between me being up there and any stray dogs that might have gone missing, they probably would have done that by now. They had a little window of time today when they might have stumbled on something circumstantial, or somehow might have gotten interested in me, but it doesn't look like that happened. Now that Langley has tied up all of his resources, big-time, on this Hussein character, he'll likely not get anything else done. I've gotten kind of attached to this skinny brown dog—you know, just knowing how fragile life might be, if she happened to be a big black dog. I think I'll concentrate on giving her a good home for awhile. See what happens."

"Well, Bill, if it goes sour, you call me, day or night, and then you don't say a word to anybody about anything until I get there. I'll handle this one personally." They exchanged phone numbers, with Sam giving Hom-Astubby some numbers where he could be reached, directly, at any time.

"Thanks, Sam. I hope you don't hear from me."

"Me, too, Pard, until it's time for you and me and old Harry to drop a few more dry flies where dry flies were meant to be dropped. Good luck."

Hom-Astubby hung up the phone. Only then did he realize he'd forgotten to mention the O'Neill woman and his worries about her. But that hardly seemed to matter now. He had Sam Burnbalm in his corner.

PART 3

The King Kong Ranch

(Wednesday night, Thursday)

. . . Mallory is a malcontent, displeased with convenience and speed and effortless ease. In another life, he would have been a crusty, recalcitrant mariner, stubbornly navigating entirely by sextant and chronometer and star sightings and his own mathematical calculations, spurning radio beacon signals and computers and satellites and all else that required little of him to get the ship to its destination. He would insist that every midshipman in his charge learn to navigate the old way, so they could do it in a pinch, should all the fancy equipment fail. . . . If you learn photography from this man, you'll learn it the old way, in black-and-white, with a fully manual 35 mm camera that won't even have automatic rewind, let alone automatic anything else. . . . You'll learn how to put together a basic darkroom on a shoestring budget, with simple, inexpensive modifications to any bathroom . . . and when you've finished with this book, you'll know how to navigate on your own, the old way. . . . At last, an introductory, college-level textbook we can recommend without reservation. We predict that this book will set a new standard for textbooks in this field for years to come.

—review of William H. Mallory's
Basic 35 MM Photography in
*Twin-Lens Reflex: The Journal
of University Photojournalism*

CHAPTER SEVENTEEN

They pulled out of Moriarty, New Mexico, before 6 P.M., headed east on Interstate 40, with Johnny behind the wheel. Hom-Astubby tried to relax while Johnny was driving, but scanning the radio dial produced a steady stream of live updates on the massive traffic jam in Colorado.

The Colorado National Guard had not yet had time to arrive on the scene, but the units were assembling at armories all over the state. Some Guard units from western Colorado were expected to be in place that night. State patrolmen from districts all across Colorado were being reassigned to the southwestern part of the state.

Truckers were being advised to avoid the entire state of Colorado anywhere west of Denver, after reports came in of spot roadblocks by county sheriffs all across central and northern Colorado, one of them as far north in western Colorado as the Wyoming border. In southwestern Colorado, travel from town to town was already becoming difficult and time-consuming.

The advisory for truckers was soon expanded to include Interstate 40 in New Mexico when a live update from Gallup revealed that New Mexico state police roadblocks were stopping all westbound traffic at the western edge of Gallup and all eastbound traffic at the eastern edge of town.

Before long, reports were coming in of Utah state police roadblocks near Bluff, Monticello, Moab, Green River, Price, Duchesne, and Vernal. Arizona state police roadblocks were reported near St. Johns, Holbrook, Flagstaff, Tuba City, Marble Canyon, and Page.

Leaving Moriarty, Johnny had immediately steered the truck into the fast lane, hitting the 75 mph speed limit in no time at all. With each reported expansion of the roadblocks, he had pressed the accelerator a little harder. By the time the governor of New Mexico came on the air, announcing the mobilization of the New

Mexico National Guard, Johnny had the truck nearly flying toward the Texas border.

They listened to reports of roadblocks in New Mexico going up on state highways approaching Santa Fe from the west and north, on all of the western approaches to Interstate 25 throughout northern New Mexico, and on so many other roads in north-central and northwestern New Mexico that they soon had trouble keeping up with what they were hearing.

As they were nearing the Texas border, with the sun having set and the darkness gathering, the radio reception on all of the channels faded away to almost nothing. They entered what was nearly a radio reception dead zone in that part of the country, leaving them barely able to hear a faint report of a roadblock going up on Interstate 40 on the western edge of Albuquerque.

Hom-Astubby breathed a big sigh of relief as they entered Texas and the radio scanning produced little but static and the faint wailing of some country-and-western singer. No one had said anything about any roadblocks in Texas. Interstate 40 westbound truckers headed for California had been advised to detour south at Amarillo on Interstate 27 to the junction with Interstate 10 in far southwestern Texas, and stay on Interstate 10 through El Paso, Tucson, and Phoenix to get to Los Angeles.

They lost an hour at the Texas border, with the change from Mountain Time to Central Time, and the speed limit dropped from 75 mph to the weirdness of Texas: 55 mph at night for trucks. Johnny pulled over to the side of the interstate. They put the dog on the leash and took her out to pee. They stretched their legs a bit, unwinding from the tension of getting out of New Mexico, as a big full moon was rising.

When Johnny pulled back onto the highway, the camper limped along in the slow lane, doing the speed limit, waiting for the truckers' disdain of Texas to show up in the rear-view mirror. Before long, a convoy of more than a dozen eighteen-wheelers, which had formed up in far eastern New Mexico, came flying up behind them going about 80 mph. Johnny pulled in behind them, and they continued sailing across the lightly populated high plains toward Amarillo.

Hom-Astubby had been doing some thinking. He said, "I might have it figured out. What to do about the dog."

"Oh yeah," Johnny said. "What's that?"

"There's really no reason for that woman to ever know that I'm the one who took her dog. The dog tags identify her vet clinic in Denver. All I've got to do is wait for this thing to blow over. Give it a week or two after that. Then put the real dog tags back on her collar, take the dog to Denver, and drop her off at that vet clinic."

"Just drop her off?"

"Yeah. You know, tell them I had seen the dog out on the street, near the clinic, as I was driving by. But I'm in a hell of a hurry, late for a meeting or something. So I just drop her off and leave. Don't tell them my name or anything. Park a block or two away, so they don't see my truck. What do you think?"

"That might work."

"Yeah. It would work even better if somebody besides me did it. So they wouldn't even have my description."

"Oh no, no, no, no, no," Johnny said. "Man, you're not talking me into delivering that dog. With my luck, I'd take that dog into that clinic, and that woman would be standing there."

"That's wildly improbable."

"What's wildly improbable is *you* talking *me* into delivering that dog. Half the cops in the country are looking for that dog."

They were still talking about who should deliver the dog when they stopped at a gas station in Amarillo. Hom-Astubby called his cousin Hop, who was looking after the ranch for him, and told him he was on his way. Hop assured him that no cops had been around, that everything was quiet. They topped off the gas tank, took the dog for a short walk, and were back on the road in little time at all, with Hom-Astubby driving.

Johnny dozed the rest of the way. He lowered the backrest of his front seat until it rested on the back seat of the king cab. The dog stretched out on the back seat and cradled her head on Johnny's shoulder, snuggling up against his neck. Hom-Astubby heard her let out a long, contented sigh.

Johnny woke up when Hom-Astubby pulled off the Interstate in western Oklahoma. "We're almost there," Hom-Astubby said, "just a few more miles."

It was after midnight, with the big full moon high overhead. Johnny put his backrest up and was sipping cold coffee when Hom-Astubby turned off a county road and drove across a cattle guard into a pasture. The road across the pasture topped a hill and descended into a valley. As the valley narrowed and they approached the mouth of a canyon, Hom-Astubby's gate loomed in the distance.

"There it is," Hom-Astubby said, as he pulled up in front of the gate and stopped.

"Holy shit," Johnny said, as he stared at the gate in the moonlight. He opened his door and got out of the truck, as the dog bounded over the seat and out the door behind him. Hom-Astubby got out of the truck, too, stretching his legs.

Hom-Astubby's gate loomed above them, so tall it had multi-story guard houses built into its two massive stone-wall side sections. They amounted to twin, six-story apartment houses, with a single room on each floor, adjacent to spiral stairwells leading all the way up to large, twin, fully enclosed, seventh-story castle turrets that capped the top of each side of the gate. A wide walled, open-air crosswalk across the top of the gate connected the two castle turrets.

The gate itself was two huge, six-story, automated doors, constructed of enough big thick planks of lumber to build a fair-sized ship. The doors had been inspired by the gate that protected the Pacific island villagers from the monsters in the King Kong movie.

The massive stone walls, six stories high, extended all the way across the canyon-mouth entrance to the ranch, giving the whole structure the appearance of a substantial portion of the Great Wall of China transported to the Oklahoma countryside.

It created the impression that the entire ranch might be a walled fortification constructed for the express purpose of keeping King Kong at bay, or for keeping King Kong locked up inside the ranch.

Johnny's head was cranked all the way back as he stared up at the castle turrets on each side of the gate. His eyes followed the stone walls all the way across the canyon. "What in the hell kind of horses are you raising here?" Johnny asked. "Are you into some new kind of genetic engineering?"

"Aw, Johnny, if you think the gate is something, wait until you see the barn."

"Barn, hell. I want to see the saddles!"

Hom-Astubby pushed the remote control in his truck, and they watched the gate slowly swing open. They loaded up again and drove up the long, narrow canyon to the ranch headquarters, which was above the head of the canyon, in a big bowl of a valley with a ridge of hills all around it.

As the colonnaded front of Hom-Astubby's house loomed in the moonlight, he said, "That's where I live."

"You live in a goddamn resort hotel? Way out here in the middle of nowhere?"

"Well," Hom-Astubby said, "it does have two or three hundred bedrooms. I'm planning on having lots of kids."

Hom-Astubby pulled around in back of the house and parked in front of the lower-level parking garage. They got out of the truck as Hom-Astubby's cousin, Hop, and his wife, Bunnie, came up to greet them.

"Halito, Johnny!" Hop said. "Long time no see."

"Yah ta hey!" Johnny said. "Hop, Bunnie. I didn't know you guys would be here."

"How's your chukma?" Hop said, as they shook hands.

"Chukma good," Johnny said.

"We've got a late supper all fixed up," Bunnie said, "over at our house." She gestured toward a cluster of buildings. "Let's go eat and get all caught up."

Wampus, Bunnie's big old fat neutered tomcat, crawled out from behind her legs and cautiously sniffed noses with the dog.

After supper, Hom-Astubby was beginning to wind down, feeling sleepy. It was late, after 1 A.M., and the big meal had made him drowsy. But Hop and Johnny were wide awake. Hop took Johnny on a tour of the ranch headquarters, beginning with the big barn and stables.

Hom-Astubby took a glass of iced tea and sat in the moonlight on the steps of the back porch of his house, unwinding a little more before going to bed. The dog, who had gone with Johnny and Hop, came to him. She sat beside him while he stroked her head.

He thought about his first encounter with the dog. He remembered the black-and-white photos he'd taken at the river, when he'd been mesmerized by the contrast of the black dog against the white rocks, with the black driftwood scattered all around.

Before he had noticed there was a woman beside the dog.

Hom-Astubby was jolted upright. The woman would *have* to be in some of those photos. Could it be possible he might have nude photos of Avalon O'Neill?

He got his camera bag out of the truck and hurried toward his darkroom, with no more thought of sleep.

CHAPTER EIGHTEEN

Hom-Astubby had converted one of the chauffeur's apartments into darkrooms. The bathroom was now a compact processing lab for developing black-and-white negatives. The bedroom held his supplies and provided a place to store all of his cameras and accessories. The combination kitchen–living room contained the equipment for printing photographs. Rows of tables held enlargers, trays for fixing and washing the prints, racks for hanging the prints up to dry, and a lot of space for laying out photo spreads.

Hom-Astubby sat among the rows of tables. He had been in the room for a long time, working to achieve the print he held in his hand. Under the glow of a safelight, he sat on a stool staring at an 8-by-10 black-and-white enlargement of a half-naked Avalon O'Neill.

Black-and-white photographs of Avalon O'Neill lay everywhere around the darkroom. Some portion of her body had been present in nearly all of the frames that he had shot of the dog, but in three of them she had been spectacularly visible.

After processing the negatives, he had printed a contact sheet showing all twenty-four exposures on the roll of film. He then made 4-by-6 prints of the three frames that showed Avalon O'Neill lying beside the dog. Then he made 8-by-10 enlargements of the best frame, cropping it, experimenting with varying the amount of exposure time in the printing, until finally he achieved the print he held in his hand.

He was captivated by the technical aspects of the photo. Never in his life had he taken a photo like this. He could barely believe it had been done in 35 mm. Maybe an Ansel Adams, using a format camera that produced an 8-by-10 negative, where the print would not have to be enlarged—maybe something like that could have achieved this result, but not 35 mm. It just didn't seem possible.

He was contemplatively aware that the photo had been something of an accident, but he wasn't bothered by that too much.
Focusing entirely on the dog's face, he hadn't known the woman
was there, the way she was so naturally camouflaged against that
background. Now the dog had been cropped entirely out of the
print. He had slightly miscalculated the shot. The lighting, the focus, everything had been calculated for the dog's face, which had
been pretty good, but nothing like this. It might be the best mis-
calculation he had ever made.

The black-and-white contrast could not be any better. With a
powerful magnifying glass, he studied the details—every piece of
black driftwood, every piece of white rock, each strand of her long,
flowing black hair, the fabric in her white sweatshirt, the elegant
shape of her hips and legs, the breath-taking detail of her genital
area.

Again and again he put down the magnifying glass, held the
photo at arm's length, and stared at the woman, awestruck by her
beauty, as something stirred inside him. Lying on her stomach,
with her legs spread wide, she could not have been more spectacularly naked.

It bothered him a little that he was violating the woman's privacy, seeing her in a way that only a lover would ever see her. But
he was helpless to do anything but stare at the print.

If he had not seen her through the window of the Purple Pentagon, had not seen her face, maybe he could resist the forces stirring inside him. But there had been something about her appearance in that restaurant that had struck a chord with him. He had
felt it then, before she had become uneasy at his staring. It had
taken his breath, he remembered that. At the time, he had thought
it was only because he had just seen the woman half naked, but
now he was pretty sure it had been something beyond that.

Could it be that they were meant for each other? He didn't
know if he believed in that sort of thing.

He kept running back over the conversation he had heard between George Langley and Dick Halliburton, feeling a coldness

for Langley that made him uneasy, knowing that it was jealousy. He had reason enough to dislike Langley simply because of what he wanted to do to the dog. But the coldness Hom-Astubby felt went beyond that. Langley had been with this woman, had seen her as Hom-Astubby was seeing her now, had known her in a way that Hom-Astubby tried not to imagine.

He put down the photo and stood up. He began pacing in the cramped quarters of the darkroom, oblivious to his surroundings. Could it be possible that George Langley would work his way back into that woman's good graces? Might the two of them be together right now? Maybe they were lying in bed, wrapped in each other's arms. He shook his head to clear that image from his mind. What did he really know about this woman? It was stupid being infatuated like this with someone he had never met.

He knew he should get some sleep. It was the middle of the night, and he was tired from the long drive. Maybe everything would seem different after he had slept.

Looking around at all the prints he had made, it occurred to him that the cops could still show up here. They might even come with a search warrant. He would have to be careful with these prints.

He had begun picking them up when he remembered the color photos he had taken that same morning, shots of those two men fly-fishing. The dog and the woman might be visible on one of those frames. He hadn't even looked at any of the photos printed by Wal-Mart in Gallup.

He left the darkroom and headed for his camper to get the bag that held those prints, passing through his living quarters on the way. The dog was sound asleep on the couch where Hom-Astubby slept, but she jumped up and trotted after him as he headed outside.

On the back porch of the house, Wampus, the old tomcat, was sprawled across the top step of the porch, his big body and his long, flowing tail taking up nearly the entire length of the step. Hom-Astubby had to tiptoe down the edge of the step to get by, but the dog stopped, not quite sure how to proceed. Wampus flapped his tail up and down on the step, daring the dog to step on him.

The dog was still sitting on the porch, looking down at Wampus, when Hom-Astubby returned with his camera bag. He left her on the porch and went back to his darkroom.

An hour later, he held in his hand another 8-by-10 black-and-white enlargement that he was proud of. This one was of a fly-fisherman, standing knee-deep in the Crystal Fork, working a dry fly, with the line stretched out high above him and behind him as he was preparing to hurl the weighted line far out in front of him. Hom-Astubby had turned his camera from horizontal to vertical, getting the entire length of the line, its highest arc above the fisherman, with the starkly beautiful cliffs across the river in the background.

The slant of the sun's rays had been just right to highlight the fly line, a thing of pure luck. He knew he could sell a color print of that frame for a good price. It might even make the cover of some magazine.

To make the black and white print from the color negative, he had switched to an orange safelight and special photographic paper designed for that purpose. It was the only frame from all of the film processed and printed in Gallup that had caught his attention. Only a few of the other photos might be publishable. That hardly surprised him. He had learned long ago to shoot lots of film. His old photojournalism professor had been fond of saying, "Film is cheap, good photos are rare—shoot lots of film." Hom-Astubby rarely found more than one or two publishable photos, if any at all, on any roll of film.

He was too tired to study the flyfishing photos closely, too tired to decide whether their quality might make a trip back to Alpine unnecessary.

He had hurriedly looked through all the color prints, noting that Avalon O'Neill and the dog had not appeared in any of them. In his panorama shots of the crime scene, the one he thought might do for a newspaper photo was well composed. Tension and drama were apparent in the faces of the sheriff, district attorney, and coroner, as they were huddled together near the picnic table, with the victim's legs in the foreground. The *Devon County Chronicle* would have been pleased. Hom-Astubby had shrugged as he put that print aside, knowing he had missed out on the sale, and indifferent to the fifteen or twenty dollars they might have paid for that photo.

The pictures of Connolly's pickup made Hom-Astubby feel pretty sure that Connolly wouldn't be getting his u-joint replaced at his expense. One of the prints of the cement-truck driver was well composed, showing the man standing beside Nelson Towers and Wally Street, with the new gate in the background and a portion of the cement truck showing the company name on the front door of the truck.

Hom-Astubby had stared at Nelson Towers for a few moments, marveling at the power of the man to bring a huge portion of the Southwest to a standstill.

Hom-Astubby yawned. It was way past time for him to be heading to bed. He picked up his magnifying glass and took one last look at the 8-by-10 print of the fly-fisherman. He ran the glass all the way along the length of the fly line.

At the top edge of the photo, something in the background caught his eye. Off to the side of the fly line, in the bushes at the top of the cliff on Grimpen Hill, the sunlight appeared to be glinting off something metallic.

He frowned. He didn't want any flaws in this photo. If he was going to sell it as a black and white print, he could burn out that spot a little while exposing the print, to where it wasn't noticeable, but to have someone else do that while making the color print would be problematical.

He looked closely at the spot, adjusting the magnifying glass as best he could, trying to bring out the detail. The longer he looked, the more convinced he became that he was seeing tripod legs sticking out of the bushes.

CHAPTER NINETEEN

M uch later, Hom-Astubby was still sitting in his darkroom. New photos lay scattered everywhere on the tables. He had started by making an 8-by-10 enlargement of only the upper portion of the frame that showed the metallic object at the top of the cliff. He then made many different enlargements, varying the exposure time and trying to shade the rest of the print while burning down that one spot to reduce the reflective glare of the sun as much as he could without burning out the detail, until he could get the detail as clear and sharp as it was going to get.

The greatly enlarged photo was grainy, but when he finally got it printed just right, there was no doubt what it showed. The tripod legs were distinct enough to be unmistakable. But much more than tripod legs showed up in the enlargement. Sticking out of the bushes just above them was the end of a telephoto lens that was so large it had to be 2000 mm.

Somewhere, someone other than Hom-Astubby had nude photos of Avalon O'Neill. Whoever it was might have a wide variety of them, all close-ups, maybe dozens of them, maybe showing her in every stage of undress, everything she had done at the river that day.

Who had taken those photos? That private investigator who had been in Alpine with a 2000 mm lens? The sheriff had said that the man had been having dinner with Wally Street at the Purple Pentagon when he'd discovered that the lens had been stolen out of his van. Had the man replaced his equipment and returned to Alpine?

Or was that 2000 mm lens the same one that had been stolen? Had it been placed on the top of that cliff by the person who had stolen it?

Could there be a third alternative? Hom-Astubby didn't think so. It was either that private investigator or the person who had stolen the lens.

If it was the thief and the sheriff caught him, what else might be in those photos? Would they show Hom-Astubby at the river? Playing with the woman's dog? Returning with the sheriff, searching among the driftwood for the woman? Would the sheriff look through those photos and know that Hom-Astubby had lied to him when he'd pretended he didn't know anything about the woman's dog?

That could be the beginning of Hom-Astubby getting dragged into the middle of the Linda Ruben murder investigation, something entirely out of Hom-Astubby's hands, something he had thrown to fate.

Was there anything Hom-Astubby could do about that? Maybe try to find that camera thief before the sheriff found him. If it was the camera thief up there on that cliff.

Why would anyone put a 2000 mm lens on top of that cliff? Surely there would be no way of anticipating that Avalon O'Neill would go nude bathing in that portion of the Crystal Fork, down there beneath those cliffs. That had to have happened by chance. Probably, the person behind that lens couldn't resist reorienting it to focus on her when she began peeling off her clothes.

The lens would be just about perfectly placed to monitor all of the people coming in and out of the Purple Pentagon and all of the vehicles coming in and out of its parking lot. That must have been the purpose for its placement up on that cliff. If it was the private investigator, working for Nelson Towers, maybe he had figured that the Purple Pentagon would be the most likely place for *Denver Daily Sun* reporters investigating Towers to show up in Devon County. Towers' new house was only a few miles up the road. There weren't any other public places nearby. Monitoring traffic at the Purple Pentagon would make sense, one way to know when those reporters were in the area.

If Nelson Towers had those photos of Avalon O'Neill, what would he do with them? Hold on to them to destroy her credibility as a journalist, if she ever did come up with something damaging on Nelson Towers? Or use them to blackmail O'Neill into having nothing further to do with investigating Nelson Towers? Nothing good for Avalon O'Neill could come from Nelson Towers having nude photos of her. If it was that private investigator up on the cliff, Avalon O'Neill's career was in big trouble.

If it was the camera thief up there, Hom-Astubby didn't know what to think about that. It could be anybody. It could even be Linda Ruben's murderer.

That's when a chill ran through Hom-Astubby that nearly paralyzed him. If Linda Ruben's murderer was the camera thief, and he had gotten an eyeful of Avalon O'Neill in the nude, he might be stalking her right now in Alpine.

How in the world could Hom-Astubby warn her about something like that? He didn't even know the woman, didn't know how to contact her, wasn't even sure if she was still in Alpine.

But he didn't like the way things were shaping up. Linda Ruben had been murdered right there at that picnic table where Avalon O'Neill had stripped off nearly buck naked. *Somebody* had murdered Ruben, and *somebody* had seen O'Neill nude at that very spot, perhaps only hours earlier that Monday.

If Ruben had been killed late Monday afternoon, or early Monday evening before dark, it was possible the person behind the telephoto lens had still been there and might have seen the whole thing, might even have photos of the murderer, possibly even of the murder itself taking place. They wouldn't come forward to the authorities. The camera thief wanted to avoid the cops. The private investigator didn't want anyone to know he was in Alpine.

Hom-Astubby was pacing back and forth between the rows of tables in his darkroom, trying to think his way through the possibilities, trying to figure out what might have been happening in Alpine, trying to sort out the chronology of the things that had happened, trying to figure out what he might be able to do, if anything, about any of it, when he remembered that he had been back at that picnic table himself, on Tuesday, when he shot the crime scene, and that one of his panorama photos might show the top of that cliff. Could it be possible that the person behind that telephoto lens had been back on top of that cliff on Tuesday? Doing what? Watching the cops trying to solve the murder that he had committed?

It took Hom-Astubby a long time in his darkroom to get the answer he was seeking, and it required all of his skill. It would not have been possible if he hadn't taken the additional, more detailed panorama with the 135 mm lens and the 2¼-by-2¼ twin-lens reflex camera. The larger negative made all the difference, just barely.

It still would not have worked if he hadn't known exactly what he was looking for and exactly where to look for it.

He ended up having to use his document camera to take a close-up photo of an enlargement of a portion of one of the panorama prints, develop the negative for that close-up shot, and then make enlargements from that new negative. The result was so grainy, so indistinct, that only the faintly evident perfect circle of the end of that telephoto lens sticking out of the bushes made it possible to be certain that it had been back on the top of that cliff on Tuesday, when he had shot the crime scene.

By then Hom-Astubby was so exhausted, and his eyes were so bleary and watery, that he could barely function. But he knew what he had to do. He had to get back to Alpine without delay. The man behind that telephoto lens had been on top of that cliff on both Monday and Tuesday. He might still be coming back there.

If Hom-Astubby could get to that cliff top before dawn tomorrow morning and get set up, he could find out if anyone was still coming there. And he could do that without being seen himself. All he needed was a few minutes to set up the camouflage netting of his turkey-hunting blind and he could disappear to where somebody would have to step on him to know he was there. Hiding from wild turkeys was a hard thing to do; hiding from people was easy.

He left the darkroom then, too weary even to think about gathering up all the photos he had printed. He went outside to get some fresh air.

He nearly stumbled over the dog on the back porch. She whined and gave him a reproachful look for going off and leaving her there. Wampus was still sprawled on the top step of the porch, still flapping his tail.

Hom-Astubby picked up the old tomcat, deposited him on the ground, and told him to go home. The dog bounded down the steps and quickly found a place to squat and relieve herself. Dawn was breaking all across the eastern skyline. Hom-Astubby walked around a bit, trying to relieve his cramped muscles after sitting for so long in the darkroom. The dog followed him back inside.

It was nearly 5:30 A.M. He set his alarm clock for 8:45 A.M. and placed it on the coffee table, within reach of the couch. He desperately needed to get just a few hours of sleep. He turned out the lights and stretched out on the couch, wondering where Avalon O'Neill might be at that moment, and if she was sleeping with George Langley.

He forced himself to think about other things. He'd have to put the dog in a kennel somewhere down here. He couldn't just leave her at the ranch. The cops might still show up here with a search warrant. He'd have to get Johnny to drive him back as far as Gallup, towing that old Honda, so he could get some more sleep on the way. He hoped they'd have good weather for the drive back out there.

He reached out in the darkness for the TV remote control on the coffee table, to get a weather report before falling asleep. But the station wasn't doing weather. It was doing news, and what the broadcaster said made Hom-Astubby sit up on the couch and stare at the TV.

"In a copyrighted story this morning in the *Los Angeles Dispatch*, former *Denver Daily Sun* reporter Avalon O'Neill is reporting that billionaire Nelson Towers and one of his executives, Wally Street, were secretly videotaped Sunday night at a restaurant in Telluride, Colorado, threatening the life of Pulitzer Prize–winning reporter Linda Ruben, whose body was found Tuesday morning on Nelson Towers' property in the neighboring county of Devon, near Alpine, where she had been murdered. For an update on this breaking story, we go live to Alpine, Colorado, where Sandy Johnson is standing by."

Hom-Astubby stared at the network correspondent, who was standing on the steps of the Devon County courthouse, a scene brightly lit by klieg lights in the predawn darkness. In the background, in the flood of still more klieg lights, he caught a glimpse of George Langley being interviewed by some other network.

Wherever Avalon O'Neill might be, she wasn't in bed with George Langley. Langley was nowhere near a bed. He was live on TV.

The correspondent told what Avalon O'Neill's story was reporting that morning. Sunday night, Linda Ruben had confronted Nelson Towers and Wally Street while they were having dinner in a Telluride restaurant. Her associate, Loren Michaels, had carried a hidden video camera. Linda Ruben had tried to question Nelson Towers about why he was squashing the *Denver Daily Sun*'s investigative series about Towers and why he was squashing her biography of Towers, but she hadn't gotten very far with that. The network had received a copy of the video. They rolled the tape.

On the tape, an enraged Nelson Towers was pointing his finger in Linda Ruben's face, saying, "You're gonna get yours! And when you do, it won't be pretty!" Off camera, a voice attributed to Wally Street hissed, "You little bitch! You better watch your backside!"

Hom-Astubby flipped quickly through a bunch of satellite news channels. They were all carrying the story. He saw the videotape again and again. One network panned across the lawn of the Devon County courthouse. It was an ocean of reporters and klieg lights. How many live TV updates were being done from Alpine Hom-Astubby couldn't even guess. It appeared that every TV network in the world must be there.

His eyes began watering, making it hard to see the TV screen. He turned off the TV, plunging the room into darkness, too exhausted to watch any longer.

He lay back on the couch, his head spinning. Nelson Towers had threatened Linda Ruben? On videotape? Good god, what a story. It was Avalon O'Neill's story? In the *Los Angeles Dispatch?* How had she done that? This was the kind of story that might get her a Pulitzer Prize. Was she still in Alpine? What in the world was going on? If this didn't build a bonfire underneath Nelson Towers, nothing would.

Hom-Astubby almost fought against sleep, feeling an urgency to get up and get going before he got left out. But he had to sleep, just for a little while.

In the darkness, the dog crawled onto the couch. She stretched out on top of him, put her head on his shoulder and snuggled up against his neck. The last thing Hom-Astubby heard before falling asleep was a perfectly relaxed dog letting out a long, contented sigh.

CHAPTER TWENTY

Thursday Morning

The alarm clock went off at 8:45 A.M., jarring Hom-Astubby out of a deep sleep. The dog was still sprawled across the top of him. She licked his ear as he reached for the alarm clock. He picked up the remote control and turned on the TV, getting a commercial for a laundry detergent.

He stretched out on the couch and closed his eyes again. The dog licked his face. "Okay," he said, protecting his face from further washing, "I'm getting up."

He stumbled off toward the bathroom, stopping on his way through the kitchen to start some coffee and take some aspirin. When he came out of the bathroom, he heard the dog growling. Then she barked, not a friendly bark. He hurried through the kitchen to see what was wrong.

The dog was standing in front of the TV, her hackles raised, an ominous low-pitched growl coming from deep in her throat. On the TV screen, George Langley stood in front of a bank of microphones, addressing a sea of reporters on the lawn of the Devon County courthouse.

Hom-Astubby picked up the remote and turned up the sound. The dog looked at Hom-Astubby and barked. She turned back to the TV and barked again. Hom-Astubby stroked her head. He said, "We don't like that guy, do we?"

"No, sir," Langley was saying, "I ordered roadblocks in Devon County before the victim was identified, before any of these wild speculations in the media even got started. The people of Colorado are not going to tolerate a woman killer."

As Langley launched into a tirade against crime in general, and woman killers in particular, Hom-Astubby muted the TV. He took the dog outside, giving her a chance to pee, while he walked around a bit, drinking coffee and trying to wake up.

He took a quick shower and threw on some clean clothes. He got another cup of coffee and carried the cordless phone to the coffee table, his hair still wet from the shower.

The first thing he had to do was find out about the news broadcast he had heard just before falling asleep. He knew who could tell him about that.

He dialed the *Los Angeles Dispatch* and asked for Sarah Peteski, one of the senior editors. She wasn't in. He looked at his watch. It wasn't quite 7:15 A.M. on the West Coast, two hours earlier than Oklahoma. He dialed Sarah's home number. She answered on the second ring.

"Sarah, it's Bill Mallory."

"Well, speak of the devil," she said. "Some of us gals were just talking about you the other day."

"You're kidding."

"No, I'm not kidding. Can you hang on, Bill, while I finish on the other line? This will take a while. You want me to call you back?"

"No, I'll hold. I'll scramble some eggs while I'm waiting."

Hom-Astubby made toast and scrambled a dozen eggs, sharing them with the dog. He had time to finish eating breakfast and have another cup of coffee before Sarah came back on the line.

"Hello, Bill? Hey, I was over at my sister's house and found out my niece is taking a photography class this summer at the community college. They're using your textbook. You rascal, you didn't tell me you'd done that. I want an autographed copy."

"You got it."

Her phone beeped in their ears. She said, "Hang on a second. Let me see who that is, then I'll turn off call waiting. I want to talk to you." She was back in a few moments. She said, "I'll bet you still haven't gotten any horses."

He laughed. "You're right, but I'm working on it."

"I told you, I'm not coming till you get some horses. What could there possibly be to do on a horse ranch without horses?"

"Sarah, you will be amazed. But listen, I'm calling about this Nelson Towers thing."

"I figured I'd be hearing from you. I couldn't help thinking about you this weekend, when that story broke about Towers buying the *Denver Daily Sun*."

Sarah Peteski had been his editor in Montana, all those years ago, when he had tried investigating a Nelson Towers mining company. She had stood behind him and had gone down with him.

She said, "You know, Bill, you were just like Linda Ruben, only you didn't get killed."

"Yeah. And what happened to us didn't make news."

"It's making news now," she said. "Not about us, but a lot of people like us. All those newspaper acquisitions are now getting a lot of scrutiny. People are coming forward, being interviewed. This story has got so many angles. Towers is taking heat for things he did years ago. As long as this murder keeps the story on page one, it's going to get worse and worse for him."

"Sarah, how did the *Dispatch* break that story by Avalon O'Neill this morning? Do you know her? Did you hire her after she got fired at the *Daily Sun*?"

"No. She's not a *Dispatch* reporter. We made a deal with Earl Paggett. Do you know him?"

"No. I've heard about him, but never met him."

"I've known him for years. He's now working as a freelance editor, investigating Linda Ruben's murder. He's got O'Neill working for him. He's feeding us her stuff. Bill, we're putting together a twelve-newspaper task force that Paggett will direct. Papers from all over the country. The *Dispatch* will be the lead paper. I've almost got it put together."

"Jesus."

"It's going to be just like Arizona, when that reporter got killed out there."

"Arizona?"

"Oh. I forget. You're such a baby. That was before your time."

"You've nearly got the task force set up?"

"Yes. With Paggett working with us, the *Dispatch* is way out ahead of everyone else. That's made it a natural for us to be the one to put it together. God, are we lucky Earl came to us. The whole world is now in Alpine."

"Yeah, I was just watching TV. I hardly recognized the place."

"You were in Alpine?"

"Yeah, I was there to shoot a fishing story. Then the sheriff hired me to shoot the crime scene. I was also supposed to—"

"You shot the crime scene!"

"Yeah, that was before—"

"Bill! *Tell* me you've got a photo for me!"

"Huh? Oh sure. I've got a pretty good one, but I shot it with another paper in mind. They asked me—"

"I can pay ten thousand dollars."

"Ten thousand?" Hom-Astubby was stunned. He realized then that he'd been so absorbed with Avalon O'Neill that he hadn't even thought about his crime scene photo or what he might do with it.

"God, I know it isn't much," Sarah said, "but that's as high as I can go on my signature. *Please* let me have it! The cops won't let anybody at the crime scene. Nobody has got a photo. You've got a good one?"

"It's a real good one. Ruben was killed near a picnic table. It's got the sheriff, the prosecuting attorney, and the coroner huddled together near that table, with the victim's legs in the foreground."

"The *victim* is in the photo! Bill, you're driving me crazy. *Tell* me you'll let me have it!"

Hom-Astubby started to say, "Of course you can have it, Sarah. I wouldn't let anybody else have it." But Sarah was someone he'd learned he could tease. She was unable to tell when he was being serious or not. He couldn't resist teasing her now, at least just a little bit.

He said, "Geez, Sarah, I don't know. Nelson Towers doesn't get accused of murder every day. This is almost like paparazzi. The tabloids will be salivating over this. You remember how somebody in England got 1.4 million for photos of Michael Douglas' wedding? And this—"

"How about if I get the other eleven papers to kick in ten thousand each? That would be one hundred and twenty thousand dollars. It can be our first piece of work as a task force."

"One hundred and twenty thousand dollars?"

"Oh, Bill. Please say yes! It will keep us right out in front on this story. It's just what I need to seal this deal with those other papers, to get that up and running right now, this morning. God, we can make the afternoon edition."

"How soon could I get the money?"

"How soon would you need it?"

"Right now. Today."

"I think we can do that. I'll have to go to my boss, and maybe to the board. My paper would probably have to pay the whole amount for right now because it would be slow getting the money from the other papers. But, yes, I'm sure we can do that. Once those other papers agree to it, they'll be good for the money. My board will do it."

"Sarah, I've still got my L.A. bank account, from when I worked in Long Beach. You'd have to get a courier to deposit a certified check in my account this morning, before noon, your time, so I can draw on that money the minute it's deposited."

"Boy, that would be tight. But we've got enough time to get that done, I think, barely. You can get that photo scanned and get it e-mailed to me right now, with the caption, right?"

"I could do that," Hom-Astubby said. "But I'm still thinking about this."

"Oh, Bill. Don't think about it. Just say yes! This is cash in hand we're talking about. It would take time for you to shop it around. Even if you might get more money for it, you know how quick hot can turn cold. You could end up with nothing. If they catch Hussein and he's driving Linda Ruben's rental car, that photo will be worth nothing. Do you really want to gamble that he'll not be driving her rental car when they catch him? That's the kind of risk

I'm taking. If you will do this for me, you'll get the cash right now, and I will owe you forever and ever and ever. Bill, you don't *need* any more money. God, you are already as rich as sin."

"Sarah, there is one additional thing you can do that might make this worth it for me."

"What?"

"Hire me."

"What? You know I'd hire you in a heartbeat. If I could get you. What's up?"

"Not hire me, exactly. Just send me to Alpine, from the *Dispatch*, to be Avalon O'Neill's partner on this story, her photographer."

"You sly fox."

"You can do that. Can't you?"

"I should have known you'd be working some angle that involved a skirt. That's some skirt."

"So I hear."

"You've got your eye on her, haven't you?"

"I wouldn't mind meeting her."

"God, I could kick myself. I could have saved us one hundred and twenty thousand dollars if only I had remembered that you've got every bit of your brains in your britches."

"This is something you can do, Sarah, and it would make sense. Paggett has struck this deal with the *Dispatch*. His reporter, O'Neill, has got an inside track with the state people, with George Langley, but they've got nothing going with the locals. I've got an inside track with the sheriff. He's the one who hired me. Now the story has gotten really hot. The *Dispatch* could insist on sending in a photographer to team with O'Neill. Paggett could not oppose that. And I wouldn't be horning in on O'Neill's story. My photo will be running with the latest thing she files today. But I was on this story even before she was or at least as early. I was there, in Alpine, right on the ground floor. I shot the crime scene. I was on this story even before the victim was identified. Neither Paggett nor O'Neill can give you any argument about that. They might not exactly welcome me with open arms, might prefer not to have it this way, but that'll be my problem. You can vouch for me and get me in, and I can take it from there. And, who knows? They might welcome the help. But they can't stop you from sending me in, if you'll insist on it. The only other stipulation I want, between you and me, is that I work freelance, even though you're sending me in from the *Dispatch*. You get first right of refusal for my stuff. But if your task force can't pay what it's worth, I'm free to sell it elsewhere. Is that a problem?"

"That's no problem. That will cost us nothing unless you come up with something. You know about Avalon O'Neill and George Langley, huh? How much do you know?"

"I know what I'm getting into. I know they nearly got engaged, but they've hit the rocks lately. Their relationship hasn't been exactly what you'd call a secret. It seems to be a hot gossip item. Have they patched things up?"

"Not exactly," Sarah said. "More like a truce. Paggett said they've both been too busy to talk about it. But she's still got an inside track with Langley, big time. He's trying to woo her back. That gives her a big edge."

"You're not suspicious of Langley's ties to Nelson Towers?"

"We're all suspicious about that. But Paggett trusts O'Neill, and we trust Paggett."

"Do you think that's why she might have gotten hooked up with Langley in the first place? He's in charge of complex white-collar criminal investigations in Colorado. That would have interested Paggett's people at the *Daily Sun*—what Langley was doing, or wasn't doing, regarding Nelson Towers."

"I wouldn't doubt it, Bill, but I really don't know how they met. I'd wish you good luck with her, but please don't break them up until this is over. We *need* her to find out everything that's going on with the state people. They're the ones now running the show. That gives us a big advantage over everybody else. It's the main leverage we've got right now in getting the other papers to throw in with us in forming the task force, to spread the risk. Towers can't buy all of us. How well do you know the sheriff?"

"Sarah, the guy was high school buddies with Harry Birdwell."

"Jesus, Bill. You really do have an inside track, just like O'Neill. But do you know what you're getting into with George Langley? I hear he doesn't play nice. Are you really serious about trying to take his girlfriend away from him?"

"I haven't even met the woman."

"Bill, it's me you're talking to."

"Okay. Maybe I am a little bit interested."

"How interested?"

"I've hired Sam Burnbalm to watch my backside."

"Boy. You really are serious about this, aren't you?"

"I don't know. I hear she's a ball-buster."

"You'd rather she had slept with everyone on the planet?"

"I guess not. What do you know about her, Sarah?"

"What do you want to know?"

"What she was doing in France, not high school or college. The couple years before she took all those seminars with Paggett at Columbia."

"Boy, you are a reporter, aren't you?"

"No. I'm a photographer. But I know some reporters. They found out for me. Except for those two years in France."

"She was an aide to the international investment specialist of the Du Roullet banking family, Nelson Towers' primary international bankers. She traveled all over the world with that staff. She might know as much about Nelson Towers as anybody. And what she knows might be about as sophisticated as what anybody knows, anywhere in the world, outside of Towers' inner circle."

"Jesus."

"Bill, she is potentially Nelson Towers' biggest nightmare, now that Linda Ruben is dead. Knowledge is power. O'Neill was a big help to Ruben and Paggett. Those two had been investigating Towers for years, long before Paggett took over at the *Denver Daily Sun* and started pulling it all together. That's why he took the job at the *Sun*, to get set up right in Towers' backyard. But they didn't understand how everything fit together until they got O'Neill."

"How did Paggett get the rug pulled out from under him? He wouldn't have gone to the *Sun* if there had been that risk."

"The owner died."

"How?"

"Nobody knows for sure. Nobody will ever know, for sure. It happened in Kenya, on safari. A plane crash, a small plane in transit from one hunting camp to another. Paggett really wasn't ready to go public with what he had at the *Sun*, but he made a wild scramble to do that. He didn't make it."

"Did he really have anything on Towers?"

"Well, no smoking gun. Nothing on Towers himself. Paggett said Ruben's biography makes a pretty strong circumstantial case against Towers, and that what the *Daily Sun* had on some of Towers' companies was probably enough to force a congressional investigation. Maybe get some laws changed. Make it harder for Towers to do some of the things he's been doing. Cost him a lot of money. Maybe weaken his power. Cause him a lot of bad press. Maybe get some of his people indicted, and, after that, who knows? If some of them were to make deals with the prosecutors, maybe they could get to Towers. But Paggett didn't think so. He said Towers is pretty insulated and that the really dirty stuff is overseas, and so are the people who might know about that. They're beyond the reach of our courts."

"That's depressing, Sarah."

"Yeah. Paggett's pretty depressed about it, too. He says nobody can get very far investigating Towers without Towers finding out about it, and when he does, he figures out a way to stop it. Paggett was hoping for a lot more time at the *Sun*. He thought Ruben's book might shake some things loose, maybe even get someone to contact them who knows something about the overseas operations, give O'Neill a chance to crack something open. Did you find out about her language background?"

"Yeah. She's fluent in French."

"Bill, she was a very rare child prodigy of some sort. She's got an uncanny ability for learning new languages."

"Jesus. Nelson Towers probably knows all about her, huh?"

"I'd bet he knows which hand she uses to wipe her butt."

"God, Sarah. You're so charming. Do you mean that Towers might have had private investigators keeping tabs on O'Neill and the other *Daily Sun* reporters? Maybe trying to dig up any dirt he could get on them?"

"I'd almost bet on it. Paggett thinks they were being bugged, that Towers knew everything they were doing. But that's something we stand no chance of ever finding out anything about. Towers will know all about you, too, Bill. The minute your name shows up on the credit line for that photo. He'll find out that you and him go back a long way, that you're on his company's blacklist."

"I hadn't even thought about that."

"Even if we credited the photo only to the *Dispatch* or to the task force, he'd probably find out. We're pretty sure he's got people on the inside here. He's got them everywhere. That's how he scouts for newspaper acquisitions. That could have been how he knew what they were doing at the *Daily Sun*. And that's just the newspaper world. They say his overseas intelligence operation is better than the CIA. I doubt there's anything in the world he couldn't find out, if he wanted to know bad enough. Our only chance of surviving him is to form the task force with all those other papers."

"You're smart doing that, Sarah. That might be the only way."

"That might protect our papers. But you and me, we go back a long way with Towers. He made our lives miserable back then. We got blindsided that time. But we're going into this one with our eyes wide open. We've both got a lot more to lose now."

"Yeah."

"Bill, Earl Paggett, Linda Ruben, Loren Michaels, and Avalon O'Neill all got their tax returns audited last year. Remember when that happened to us?"

"God. All four of them?"

"All four of them. That's virtually a statistical impossibility. But it happened. I've made damn sure that when I get audited again

I'll be okay. I hope you don't have anything on your tax return that's the least bit questionable, or you'll need Sam Burnbalm. I imagine your return might have some complexity, after that little trip to the casino last year. You might think about getting with a good tax lawyer and make sure you're okay. You could file an amended return, if necessary, try to head off the trouble. It'll be coming."

"Jesus." Hom-Astubby sat staring at his coffee table.

"We're going to be in a shaky position," she said, "if this murder story falls apart. Towers would come roaring out of that. Personally, I don't think he had Linda Ruben killed. It would have been done a lot more cleanly. This is messy. He doesn't leave messes like this, that he can't control. God, this happened near his house, on his land, the very next day after that ugly scene with Ruben and her video cameraman, Michaels, in that restaurant in Telluride."

"That bothers me, too."

"If he does know that he is innocent, he'll get this thing cleared up in a hurry and then come after us. It looks to me like he's doing everything humanly possible to get it cleared up."

"Yeah. But meanwhile, he's reeling. It's looking worse and worse for him. I thought he'd be able to hunker down and ride out that firestorm over buying the *Daily Sun* and quashing Ruben's book. I figured the next big media event would sweep that out of the news. But the next big one turned out to be Ruben's murder. Then this video surfaces with him threatening Ruben. Sarah, until now, we have never had Nelson Towers staggering backwards. I'm tired of living my life in fear of him. There's no end to it. We might never have another chance to deliver a knockout punch. The guy is human. We build him up like he's some kind of infallible machine. But he's got to be capable of losing his temper, having something go wrong in some way we can't even imagine, and ending up with a mess like this. He's been getting his way forever, using his money to avoid messes. That would make anybody arrogant. God, Sarah, he might even have killed her himself.

He's got a temper. We saw that on the video. He might have run into Ruben somewhere, lost his temper, and killed her before he realized what he was doing."

"Bill, I don't see how. He wouldn't go stalking her. And they lived in different worlds. It was a miracle that Ruben and Michaels even got close enough to him in Telluride to get that video. His security has got to be too good for her to just bump into him somewhere."

"That's not true, Sarah. I've seen him. Maybe when he's traveling he might be hard to get close to. But at home, he drives around alone. In a pickup truck, for Christsakes. He darn well might have just bumped into her somewhere. She might even have spotted him and started following him. He's accustomed to having his dirty work done for him. He probably doesn't have any idea how to do it himself. And if he lost his temper, it could have all been just as messy and stupid as what we've got."

"God, Bill. I hope you're right, and we can prove it."

"Have we got a deal, Sarah? All the way around?"

"Yes. If I can get it all done. Get that photo and caption to me right now. Call me at the *Dispatch* in . . . three hours. I'll know everything by then. What's your cell?"

"I don't have one yet."

"Bill, for Christsakes, get a cell phone and a pager. Do that right now. I have got to be able to reach you, at any time, day or night. When you get the cell, never turn it off. Sleep with it by your ear. Do you hear me?"

"Okay. I'll get that done before I leave Oklahoma, then I'll call you and give you the numbers. But, Sarah, listen, before we ring off, there are some things I need to know. Do you know why O'Neill was in Alpine? What she was doing this week? Why it took so long to get Linda Ruben's body identified?"

"O'Neill went to Alpine because she'd promised Ruben she would meet her there Monday afternoon at a restaurant."

"The Purple Pentagon."

"Yes. They tell me it's not far from Nelson Towers' new house.

But Ruben got delayed in Telluride Monday. Nobody knows why. She made a hurried call to O'Neill at the Purple Pentagon that afternoon and told her she'd be there for supper. But she didn't show. That's about when Linda Ruben got murdered, about suppertime, between late afternoon and early evening, on Monday."

"That's what the autopsy said?"

"Yes. When Ruben hadn't shown up by nine o'clock, and O'Neill couldn't get her on her cell or her pager, she called Michaels in Telluride. He told her that Ruben had been gone for hours, since sometime that afternoon, he wasn't sure exactly when. When Ruben hadn't shown up by ten o'clock, O'Neill called Michaels again. They got worried. Michaels drove to Alpine, looking for places where Ruben might have driven off the highway, trying to dodge a deer or something. When he got to Alpine, O'Neill followed him back toward Telluride in her car. They spent hours looking for any place that Ruben might have run off the road."

"They spent the rest of Monday night doing that?"

"Yes. By daylight Tuesday morning they were exhausted. They called Paggett, and he told them to try finding out if Ruben had really made it out of Telluride. When Paggett found out Tuesday afternoon that a woman's body had been found at Alpine, he feared the worst. He thought O'Neill and Michaels might be in danger, too, so he made them go into hiding in Telluride. By then O'Neill and Michaels were so exhausted they were dead on their feet. They slept until Paggett got there Wednesday morning, after he had driven all night from Denver."

"Jesus, that's a long drive. Why didn't he fly?"

"All the flights were booked, and he couldn't afford to charter a plane. We're talking about newspaper people who had suddenly become unemployed. They're working people. You remember what that was like for us when we got fired."

"Yeah."

"Wednesday morning, they all rode to Alpine with Paggett to see if they could identify the body as Linda Ruben. By then

O'Neill was also worried about her dog that she'd left in Alpine. Bill, somebody stole O'Neill's dog while she was gone. She found out about that, and then found George Langley in Alpine, and he tried to help her by putting out a media alert about her dog. He tacked it on to a media bulletin about a suspect he'd identified in the murder case, this Mohammed Khalid Hussein."

Hom-Astubby wondered how much the press knew about what Langley had been doing before Avalon O'Neill discovered that her dog was missing. If Sarah didn't know about the bulletins Langley had sent to the police, then O'Neill probably didn't know about them either. He said, "That media alert was the first time Langley went public with anything. Right? That would have been right around noon, or maybe a little before noon, on Wednesday— yesterday. Right?"

"That's right."

"But hadn't Langley also put out some bulletins to the police before that?"

"I don't know for sure about that, Bill. We've heard about police bulletins, but we haven't seen them. All I know is that by Wednesday morning Langley had roadblocks stopping all traffic coming out of Devon County, trying to catch Hussein, so I guess there had to be some kind of police bulletin about that."

So, Avalon O'Neill probably didn't know that George Langley had put out a police bulletin on her and her dog, on Monday, with a warning that her dog was "vicious." She probably also didn't know that she and her dog had been part of that early Wednesday morning police bulletin about Hussein. He said, "But those road-blocks Wednesday morning—O'Neill and Paggett and Michaels were *entering* Devon County, so they didn't get stopped at the roadblocks. Right?"

"That's right. They said they saw how badly the traffic was al-ready backed up, but it didn't affect them. When they got to the funeral home, they identified Ruben's body. You shot the crime scene, Bill. You know what condition she was in. It tore them up pretty bad. Paggett, O'Neill, Michaels, they'd all worked with her. Paggett had known her for a long time."

"Sarah, it was worse than anything I've ever seen. It was a rage killing. It wasn't just a murder. Whoever killed her couldn't stop pounding her with something heavy. There had to be intense emotion. Whoever killed her probably knew her, and not just slightly, either. You don't get that kind of rage against somebody you barely know. Strangers don't do that to one another, except maybe some kind of really sick puppy. Did Ruben have a boyfriend or an ex-husband?"

"She was married, with two kids. Paggett knows the family really well. She didn't have an enemy in the world, except Nelson Towers."

"Paggett took it pretty hard, huh?"

"It infuriated him. He got in touch with us yesterday afternoon and we made our arrangement with him. I've never heard him so angry. While we were working things out and starting to put the task force together, O'Neill wrote the story about that Telluride video that we broke in the paper this morning. In the meantime, the governor expanded the roadblocks to that whole part of the state, and called out the National Guard, and TV has been wall-to-wall with nothing but this story since late yesterday afternoon. God, what a traffic mess. TV has been mesmerized by it. Our release of that video this morning has been like throwing gasoline on a fire. Did you see, TPN didn't even show that video—the *only* network that didn't show it. Walter Jenkins has resigned over that. We just found out. Can you imagine, *Jenkins* resigning?"

"Jesus."

"That'll be the top story on every other network today. It couldn't *get* any better! Even TPN will have to say something. Their news anchor is going to be on *all* the other networks, talking about why he quit. It'll be like Elliot Richardson and the Saturday Night Massacre during Watergate."

"That's another one before my time."

"Bill, what a day I had yesterday. I was on the phone, nonstop, till way past midnight. I didn't get much sleep. It looks like today will be a repeat. God, I've had six phone messages while we've been talking."

"Yeah. I've hardly had any sleep myself, and I've got a long day ahead of me, too."

"Listen, we'll charter a plane for you into Telluride or Cortez, whichever works out best. We'll pay for that. I don't know what we'll do for a rental car. There won't be one for two hundred miles. We'll have somebody drive one to you from Salt Lake City, or Albuquerque, or wherever. Christ, there'll be no place to sleep. Everything in Telluride and Cortez is already taken. People are having to take rooms in Durango. That'll be the closest we can get you a room, if there are any still available there. Where do you need the plane to pick you up?"

"I'm not going to fly. I'll take my camper back to Alpine. That will solve the problem of where I sleep. I'll get a buddy to drive me back as far as Gallup, so I can get some sleep on the way."

"Bill, we have got to get you there today. We are competing with every news organization on the planet. The ones that aren't there already are on their way. It's not just the hottest story in the country, it's the hottest in the world!"

"Sarah, I've got something that I've got to do when I get back up there, but I can't do that until just before dawn tomorrow, and I've got to have all my equipment with me. I've got to take my camper."

"You're on to something!"

"Yes."

"What?"

"I can't tell you. It might compromise a source. Something I was told in confidence."

"Is it hot?"

"I think so."

"Does anybody else have it?"

"I don't see how. It's something I stumbled upon while I was up there, coupled with some things I was told, before anybody else was up there. I didn't even know I might have something until I got back home and developed some film."

"Bill, you're driving me crazy!"

"Then let's get the things done that we've both got to get done. I'll call you in three hours. Let me give you the info on my checking account out there, so you can get that certified check deposited."

CHAPTER TWENTY-ONE

Hom-Astubby got the crime scene photo scanned and sent it to Sarah Peteski, along with the photo caption. He then took the dog outside and went looking for Johnny.

He found Johnny and Hop in the maintenance garage, working on that old Honda Civic. They had changed the oil and rotated the tires and were about ready to start giving it a tune-up, but Johnny needed to go to town and get spark plugs for it and a few other things. Hom-Astubby told him that he needed to go to town and get a cell phone and pager and could give him a ride.

They drove into Clinton, leaving the dog to romp around the ranch with Hop. On the way into town Hom-Astubby explained to Johnny about needing to get back to Alpine, and Johnny agreed to drive him back as far as Gallup, towing that old Honda. "But, man," Johnny said, "I hate to leave this place. Hop said it would take him at least a week to show me the whole ranch."

Hom-Astubby asked Johnny to think about coming back and giving Hop a hand with trying to take care of everything. Johnny said he'd think about that. Hom-Astubby told him that he'd probably buy some horses before long and he'd like for Johnny to help him pick them out. He told him he was pretty sure he'd sold a photo that morning for 120 thousand dollars, and when that money came through, he might finally be able to think about getting some horses.

"One hundred and twenty thousand?" Johnny said. "For one photo? On the legit? This isn't a photo of some rich guy coming out of a motel room with some babe who isn't his wife, is it?"

Hom-Astubby laughed. He told Johnny about the photo.

"From ten thousand dollars to one hundred and twenty thousand?" Johnny let out a long, low whistle. "Man, you did some good negotiating on that. Your daddy would be proud of you."

"Yeah, I guess so. But I really wasn't trying to negotiate anything. It just sort of fell into my lap."

"I believe that. Man, you have got some strong medicine working for you." Johnny shook his head. "Everything you touch. I wouldn't have believed that ranch if I hadn't seen it with my own eyes. You are in a state of grace. That's what's happening. I've got a feeling you haven't even hardly gotten started yet. I wouldn't be passing up on any poker games right now, if I was you."

Hom-Astubby laughed, thinking about Delbert Lawson. It just might be a good time to drop by Durango pretty soon and give old Delbert a run for his money. He'd cleaned out dang near every cop in Colorado. It had to be a nice, tidy sum he was sitting on.

When they got to Clinton, Hom-Astubby was about to drop Johnny off at an auto parts store when he saw a cell phone sales company down the street. He parked the truck and Johnny got the things he needed while Hom-Astubby arranged to get his cell phone and pager.

He told the salesman he wouldn't be able to pick everything up and pay for it until later in the day, after a check had been deposited in his account, but he wanted to get it all arranged that morning so it would be a quick stop that afternoon. When the salesman started explaining a bewildering array of choices for equipment and plans, Hom-Astubby told him he didn't have time for that, just to give him the top of the line on everything, that what he needed to know right now were the phone numbers he'd be assigned.

From there they stopped at a vet clinic long enough for Hom-Astubby to be assured it would be a good place to kennel the dog. Orange and black Oklahoma State University "Cowboy" football paraphernalia was everywhere, which made Hom-Astubby a little ill at ease. The formerly named "Aggies" at Stillwater were getting to be a pesky menace for the Sooners on the football field, after decades of being a doormat in the bitter Bedlam Rivalry between the two schools. But they had been turning out good veterinarians for a long time.

The kennel had a deluxe package that included a long walk twice a day outside. Hom-Astubby looked at the pens and talked

to the people enough to feel good about the place. He told them
he'd be back later to do the paperwork and drop off the dog on his
way out of town.

They gassed up the truck, so they wouldn't have to do that
later. Bunnie had given Johnny a list of groceries she needed.
As they drove to the store, Hom-Astubby did some thinking.
How did he know for sure that he really was in the clear with
Sheriff Klewlusz and George Langley? If he was going back to
Alpine, he'd better find out about that. When they got back to the
ranch, he'd better call the sheriff, just to chat for a few minutes.
If anything was wrong, he'd find out. Better to find out now than
later.

By the time they got to the grocery store and Hom-Astubby saw
a pay phone, he had become worried enough that he asked Johnny
to do the shopping. He decided he'd better make that call right
now, from Clinton.

When he dialed the Devon County Sheriff's Office and asked
for Sheriff Klewlusz, a woman told him sternly that the sheriff
wasn't taking any calls. Hom-Astubby thought he recognized her
voice.

"Is this Miss Wellesley?"

"Yes, sir," Miss Wellesley said, sounding surprised.

"Well, how are you doing? Do you remember that southern boy
at the crime scene? The one you were so fond of that you just had
to have his fingerprints for a keepsake?"

"Oh, hi Bill. I'm doing okay. Sorry I didn't recognize your voice.
Hang on a second. The sheriff might talk to you. He's in his office."

Hom-Astubby waited, hoping he wasn't making a mistake by
calling the sheriff. A few moments later, Sheriff Klewlusz came on
the line.

"Hello, Mallory? I've got a question for you."

Hom-Astubby's heart leaped into his throat. He should have
known this wasn't going to work, that the sheriff would find out
something. He was barely able to say, "What?"

"Do you need an assistant? You know, somebody to help carry your cameras? Somebody to do the cooking on those fishing trips? I've got a pension coming. I can work cheap."

"It's that bad, huh?"

"It's that bad. They've now trampled every flower out there on the lawn. Those were my wife's flowerbeds. Her prize rose garden. I just got off the phone with her."

"Yeah," Hom-Astubby said, "I've been watching it on TV."

"Hey, Harry Birdwell called a while ago. He said he was going to call you. Have you heard from him yet?"

"Not yet."

"He's canceling out on this weekend, staying in Jackson Hole. Said there's no way he's coming down here into this madness."

"That doesn't surprise me. I'll give Harry a call. But it looks like I'll be coming back to Alpine anyway. The *Los Angeles Dispatch* is sending me in to get some photos."

"Well, if you get here quick you can get a shot of Linda Ruben's rental car. We found it this morning."

"Where?"

"Somebody rolled it down the boat ramp into our city reservoir, less than a mile out of town. Divers found it in twenty feet of water. The CBI will be hauling it up pretty soon. They're getting a tow truck with a winch to do that now."

"Did the divers find anything in it?"

"No. All the windows were rolled down. Nothing in the car. Looks like the water took care of any trace evidence."

"That might mean the killer is still in the area."

"Might be. Langley's not calling off the roadblocks. He still thinks they'll catch that Hussein character trying to get out of here. But now they don't have the rental car to be looking for, just his BMW. Makes it a lot harder. Hell, with the crowds we've got up here, I could have bumped into that Hussein twice already today and wouldn't know it. People around here are getting very unhappy with me about these crowds, and that's not helping with this election coming up. They're only talking about me now in the past tense, like I'm somebody they turned out to pasture a long time ago, and nobody bothered to tell me. Hey, did you say you'll be working for the *Los Angeles Dispatch*?"

"Yes."

"Then I guess you know that Avalon O'Neill showed up here and that she's now a reporter for the *L.A. Dispatch*. Langley called off that police bulletin on her."

"I'm a little confused about that," Hom-Astubby said.

"You're confused. You ought to hear George Langley try to explain it."

"I'm hoping I can avoid him."

"I wish I could."

"Sheriff, there's something I've been wondering about. At the crime scene, I heard the prosecuting attorney tell the coroner that he had some predictions about the case. Do you know what that was about?"

Sheriff Klewlusz sighed. "I wish I didn't know about that. Holmes has got a reputation around here as something of a psychic. I bet that's now the main thing that guides him in analyzing all the evidence we turn over to him. It wasn't so bad until Howard moved out here from New Hampshire and gave him the big head when Howard decided to become his biographer. Now Howard's even talking about running for chairman of our Devon County Democratic Party and guiding party strategy according to Holmes' predictions. Mallory, I wasn't kidding about me maybe needing another job soon. With people around here acting like they've been waiting their whole life for a chance to vote against me, and now—hang on a minute, Mallory."

Hom-Astubby heard the sheriff talking to someone in his office, but couldn't make out what they were saying. A moment later the sheriff came back on the line.

"Mallory, I've got to go. They want me for a meeting. Drop by when you get back up here. My office is about the only place in town to get away from all this madness that damn Langley has brought down on us. I've got a coffeepot in here."

"Thanks, Sheriff. I hope to see you when I get back up there. Good luck to you." Hom-Astubby breathed a big sigh of relief as he hung up the phone.

When they got back to the ranch, Johnny and Hop went back to work on Johnny's car. Hom-Astubby called Harry Birdwell in Wyoming, and they chatted for quite a while. By then, it was time to call Sarah Peteski.

He learned from her that everything had worked out. The certified check was being deposited in his Los Angeles bank account at that moment. He gave Sarah the phone numbers for his cell phone and pager and told her he'd be leaving for Alpine within an hour or two. He told her he'd be sleeping in his camper most of the way, but Johnny would have his cell phone while driving if she needed to get a message to him.

He walked over to his maintenance garage to see how Johnny was coming along. They had the old Honda purring like a kitten. Hom-Astubby pulled his truck up to the garage so Johnny could hook up the Honda for towing. Johnny said he'd hook up the car and then get his bag from Hop's house, and he'd be ready to go.

Bunnie was fixing them a big lunch to take along. They could eat it on the way into Clinton. There, Hom-Astubby could hit an ATM for some cash, pick up his cell phone and pager, get the dog kenneled, and they'd be ready to set sail for Gallup.

Hom-Astubby walked back to his house to gather up the camera bags he'd unloaded and pack some more clean clothes. The dog trotted along behind him. She seemed to sense that something was happening and had stayed close to him ever since he and Johnny had gotten back from Clinton.

He put all of the nude photos of Avalon O'Neill in one camera bag and all of the other photos in another one. He might want to show her the enlargement of that telephoto lens on top of that cliff, from the crime scene panorama on Tuesday, but he certainly didn't want her to see the nude photos.

He had gathered up everything he needed to load, remembering that his turkey blind was already in the camper, and was headed toward the door, the dog still trotting along behind him, when the phone rang. He had to pile everything he was carrying near the door to answer the phone.

"Hello," he said.

"Hello, Mr. Mallory?"

"Yes."

"This is Avalon O'Neill."

Hom-Astubby almost dropped the phone.

PART 4

A Lady Named Avalanche

(Thursday, Friday)

The fully manual 35 mm camera is a disappearing species, going the way of the Passenger Pigeon and the Great Auk. And like those extinct species of birds, we are the ones responsible for its demise. It is dying because we no longer buy it. We choose convenience over the lessons it makes us learn. Now everything is automatic. We point and shoot and cannot say how the picture was made. We do photography without knowing photography. That's a loss. When we achieve a desired result without knowledge, we devalue our capacity to know. We lose our sense of awe at the power of applied knowledge, and we flirt with a kind of complacent dependency that does not bode well for the future of our species.

—WILLIAM H. MALLORY
Basic 35 MM Photography

CHAPTER TWENTY-TWO

Avalon O'Neill sounded tired, worn out. She spoke slowly as she said, "I understand we'll be working together. Earl Paggett called. He said you had been here in Alpine. He said you were the one who shot the crime scene." Avalon O'Neill sounded tired.

"That's right. I just got home late last night. Paggett's not still in Alpine?"

"No. He and Loren Michaels had to go back to Denver. Late last night. Earl said I should talk to Sarah Peteski. At the *L.A. Dispatch*. I just got off the phone with her. She said you'll be back here tomorrow morning. She said you're working on something. Some kind of lead?"

Avalon O'Neill sounded more than just tired. She sounded depressed. She didn't seem fully engaged with what she was saying. It made Hom-Astubby uneasy. If the guy with that 2000 mm lens had killed Linda Ruben and was now looking for Avalon O'Neill, she needed to be alert and watchful, aware of her surroundings, or she would be easy prey.

She needed Paggett and Michaels there with her. But he didn't know how to tell her about his fears. He didn't want her to know that he knew she'd been cavorting around half naked down by the river. He couldn't figure out how to tell her what he was worried about, without her finding out why he was worried about it. And he didn't want to talk about it on the phone.

He said, "Yes, I'm working on something. I stumbled on it while I was up there, but I'm not sure what I've got. I guess we need to figure out some place where we can meet and talk about that. I'd rather talk about it in person."

"Okay. Can you suggest someplace? I'm staying at the Alpine Inn, not far from the courthouse. But I have to park about eight blocks away. If I'm lucky to get that close. It's insane up here. And getting worse."

"There's that much media?"

"It's not just media. There are hordes of other people. I guess they've come just to watch. The Purple Pentagon has become an absolute zoo. You can't even get in the door. The places here in town are even worse."

Hom-Astubby didn't like the sound of that. If some guy was looking for her, he could get lost in those crowds so easily. She'd never know he was stalking her.

He asked, "Do you have a car?"

"Yes. I'd left it in Telluride. But I rode over there last night with Earl and drove it back. I was hoping to get a little sleep over there, but every room was already taken. I wasted a lot of time trying to find a room. I didn't get any sleep."

"Okay," he said. "Let me think of a good place for us to meet . . . There's a gas station called the Shady Rest, about half-way between Alpine and the Purple Pentagon, out on the highway. We could meet there, be away from the crowds. There's nothing there but that gas station. About nine o'clock tomorrow morning?"

"Okay," she said. "That's a good idea. I know where that is. I bought gas there Monday morning. You'll be driving here?"

"Yes. You barely caught me. I was just leaving, heading back up there. I'll be traveling all night, and I haven't had much sleep either. I've got a friend who's going to drive as far as Gallup, so I can get some sleep on the way."

"I haven't had any sleep at all. I'm so worn out I tried to take a nap, but they just got Mohammed Khalid Hussein in California. I'm trying to write the story now."

"He's under arrest?"

"Well, they're questioning him. He turned himself in. But it looks like a dead end."

"How so?"

"Hussein has apparently been in California for a few weeks. Working out there. He just got out of a hospital yesterday. In Bakersfield. He was in a car wreck Saturday night. His BMW stalled on him, and he got rear-ended real bad. He turned himself in today. When he found out on TV that they were looking for him."

"Boy, that's big. The sheriff told me awhile ago about finding the rental car in the reservoir up there. I guess now they'll be taking down all the roadblocks. That leaves them with nothing to be looking for at roadblocks."

"Yeah, except my dog. They'll not keep them up for that." There was a catch in her voice. She said, "Mr. Mallory, I have to apologize. I'm not feeling well. It was so hard seeing Linda like that. And somebody stole my dog. I've been looking everywhere for her."

Hom-Astubby swallowed hard. That's why she was so exhausted and distracted. That's why she'd gone to Telluride in the middle of the night to get her car. She'd keep looking for that dog, hardly aware of where she was or who was around her. She had probably been doing that all morning, after no sleep last night.

She said, "I'm trying to carry on. But I can hardly concentrate on anything. Sarah said that you were someone who would understand."

Her voice was unsteady. Hom-Astubby took several deep breaths. The most dangerous place for her right now was down by the river, all alone, trying to find her dog.

"Mr. Mallory, these have been the worst two days of my life. There's nothing much we can do now for Linda. Except try to catch whoever did that to her. But I'm worried I'll never see my dog again. I've tried everything I can think of—"

"Miss O'Neill, are you alone right now?"

"Huh?"

"Are you alone? Is there anyone with you right now, where you are?"

"No. There's nobody here. I'm in my motel room. Why?"

"I've got something to tell you. But you have got to promise not to tell anybody. Nobody. Especially not George Langley or Sheriff Klewlusz. But I mean nobody. Not Sarah Peteski or Earl Paggett, or anyone else, or I could get in a lot of trouble. It's the reason I had to leave Alpine. Do you promise?"

"Okay. What is it?"

"I've got your dog."

"*What*?

"She's okay. She's with me."

"*You've* got her! She's okay?"

"She's happy as can be."

"Oh my god. What a relief!"

"She's a wonderful dog."

"Are you sure it's her? A big black Newfie. She's got a collar."

"I'm certain it's her. She's right here. You want to talk to her? Here, say something to her."

Hom-Astubby held the phone to the dog's ear. The dog cocked her head and wagged her tail. She barked. She jumped up and licked Hom-Astubby's face, knocking the phone out of his hand and pushing him backward onto the couch. He sat down heavily on the couch, with the dog licking his face. She barked again. He said, "Whoa, Lady, that's enough. That's enough, girl. Easy now."

He picked up the phone. Avalon O'Neill was crying. He said, "Miss O'Neill?"

"I'm so happy," she said, struggling to regain her voice. "God what a relief. But I don't understand. You took her by mistake? You thought she'd been abandoned?"

"No. I knew what I was doing. I mean, at first I thought she'd been abandoned. I thought she belonged to the woman who got killed. At first, I thought that was you. I was taking the dog to the sheriff. But then I overheard a conversation I was not supposed to hear. Miss O'Neill, this is very awkward for me. It was a very private conversation about your relationship with George Langley."

He told her what he had overheard, by whom, and the circumstances that had put him in a position to hear what was said.

She was shocked, then angry. She interrupted him a lot, asking questions, until he had told her virtually everything he could remember that Langley and Dick had said to each other, even a lot of things he had intended to leave out. There was no longer any trace of fatigue in her voice.

As Hom-Astubby had suspected, she didn't know that Langley had made her and her dog part of the police bulletin Wednesday morning when he first set up the roadblocks. She was livid about that—that Langley had tried to use the police to separate her from her dog.

When Hom-Astubby was fairly certain he had told her everything, she made him go through all of it again from beginning to end—exactly what Langley and Dick had said, as best he could remember.

The only part he left out was Dick's crack about her being called "Avalanche" because she buried her would-be boyfriends. But it occurred to Hom-Astubby that a guy named George Langley was about to get buried.

She told him she had encountered the work crew Wednesday morning, blocking the road to her campsite as the crew was building the gate and fence. Hom-Astubby told her he had gotten blocked by them earlier that morning when he was frantically trying to find her. They had tried to stop her, too, and she had been about ready to whip every one of them if they hadn't finally let her through. But when she looked in the woods behind her campsite and discovered that her dog was gone, it was just the beginning of a long bad day for her.

She had found out that the workers were a Nelson Towers crew from Texas. She suspected that one of them might have taken her dog. If she hadn't found the dog soon, she was going to get Langley to haul the whole bunch of them in "and grill them until they wished that their parents had never had sex, let alone that any of them had ever met George Langley."

Hom-Astubby realized that Langley would have gotten a clear description of him and his camper and whatever else the crew could remember about virtually everything they had seen since they arrived in Alpine. Jesus, that Bobby Joe Connolly even had his name and address, from exchanging the vehicle insurance information.

It would have been only a matter of time, probably sooner rather than later, before he felt the long reach of George Langley. Depending upon their thoroughness, it could have gotten dicey. If they had checked nearby kennels, they'd have found the dog. Just calling nearby kennels would reveal that he had kenneled a dog, and the dog's change of appearance would not have withstood close inspection. If he and Johnny had driven away just a few minutes earlier, and he hadn't been there to take Avalon O'Neill's phone call, he shuddered to think what might have awaited him in Colorado, if he had even made it there. And the dog might have ended up in the hands of George Langley.

Avalon O'Neill blamed herself for not taking the dog with her to Telluride on Monday night. Hom-Astubby could tell that she had been very hard on herself about that.

He told her that if she had taken the dog with her to Telluride Monday night then she almost surely would have driven her own car back to Alpine Wednesday morning, bringing her dog with her in her car, rather than riding to Alpine with Earl Paggett. She wouldn't have been leaving Devon County, and not getting stopped by the roadblocks, but the police were specifically looking for her car, and they would have spotted it, even though it was going the other way.

She would have been separated from her dog right there and taken to Denver by the state police. Those had been Langley's explicit orders. She would never have seen her dog again. The only thing that had saved her dog was that she had left the dog at her campsite in Alpine Monday night.

That made her even more angry, but she stopped blaming herself and realized what a narrow escape it had been for the dog. She also understood the risk Hom-Astubby had taken in getting her dog out of Devon County. She thanked him again and again for that.

He didn't have to ask her any questions. She said she could imagine how confused he must be about the conversation he overheard and she wanted to explain what had happened.

He had guessed right. Her dog had seen George Langley slap her, and the dog had sprung to her defense. That happened weeks ago, but the dog had not let Langley get near her since then. Although that greatly complicated their relationship, she said it didn't have anything to do with the underlying problems.

The breakup had finally come over the weekend. She had left Denver to get away from Langley, to try to give him some time to accept that it was over. She had learned that he was trying to find her, that he was calling her family and friends. She had told them she was okay and not to tell Langley anything, except that she just needed to get away for a few days.

She had thought Langley might use the power of his office to hunt for her, so she had avoided motels and friends, stopped using her bank cards, her cell phone, her pager service. She had been camping out for the very reasons Hom-Astubby had suspected. She knew that Langley had awesome resources at his disposal, if he chose to use them. After withdrawning some cash in Denver, she had made some phone calls, packed her car, and driven to Alpine.

She had planned to call Langley in a few days, after things cooled down. She didn't tell Hom-Astubby anything about her relationship with George Langley that was really private, just enough for Hom-Astubby to understand the things he already knew.

Hom-Astubby told her about the police bulletin that Langley had put out on her and her dog on Monday, characterizing her dog as "vicious." She hadn't known about that, either. He told her that when the sheriff showed that bulletin to him, he lied to the sheriff, not telling him that he had just seen her at the Purple Pentagon. He told her he hadn't wanted to get involved. He didn't tell her that he had seen her and her dog earlier that afternoon down by the river.

She remembered his staring at her through the window of the Purple Pentagon. She went outside to see if he was driving away in a state car, thinking he might be working for George Langley.

But when she saw he was driving a camper, with out-of-state tags, she thought he was probably just a tourist.

He told her how he had played with her dog that evening at her campsite when he'd been looking for a place to camp and that's how he knew where to find the dog the next afternoon when he'd finished shooting the crime scene. He explained that he had thought she was the murder victim, that he hadn't been able to see the victim's face at the crime scene, but he thought it was the same woman he had seen at the Purple Pentagon, the same woman in the police bulletin the sheriff had shown him, which was how he had known that the dog at the campsite was hers.

She asked enough questions to get a clear idea of how it had all happened. He told her everything about what had happened in Alpine related to her and her dog, except that he had seen her down by the river Monday afternoon. He didn't say anything about that, or about calling the sheriff, or about looking for her there. He didn't want her to know that he had seen her naked.

He certainly didn't want her to have any reason to wonder if he had taken photographs of her down there. He also didn't know how to tell her that someone else might have taken nude photos of her and might be stalking her, without revealing that he had seen her naked down at the river.

For right now, it didn't seem she would be nearly so much at risk, since she wouldn't be going out searching for her dog anymore. She was so exhausted, she'd have little choice but to go to bed early tonight. She'd probably sleep until time for their meeting in the morning.

Maybe when he got up there he would find that he'd been worried about nothing, and he wouldn't have to say anything to her about it. But he didn't think that was the case. He had to get back up there and try to find out who had been on that cliff with that telephoto lens. He had to do it without her knowing what he was doing or at least not knowing why he was doing it. Damn. It made everything so complicated trying to keep her from finding out that he had seen her naked.

He also didn't tell her anything about the background checks he'd made on her, and he didn't ask her any questions. He still wondered what in the hell she had been doing half naked down by the river. But if that was something she liked to do and she might want company, he figured he would be willing to give it a try. He didn't have anything against communing with nature in new and interesting ways.

By the time he'd finished explaining everything to her, she understood why she couldn't tell anyone that he had her dog. She understood that he could get into a lot of trouble—with the sheriff, with the bar association, with George Langley. She had calmed down. Discussing all of Hom-Astubby's potential problems, stemming from having taken her dog, had made her thoughtful, analytical, reflective.

She was eager for him to get back up there, eager for him to bring the dog to her. He kept trying to figure out some way to tell her about changing the dog's appearance, how that had happened, what he had been worried about, and what the dog now looked like. But every time an opportunity presented itself, he chickened out. He kept telling himself he still had other things to worry about, and one of them was George Langley.

He said, "Miss O'Neill, George Langley's not stupid. For my sake, I hope you understand that you can't let him know that you've found out what he wanted to do about your dog. You can't even let him suspect that you've found out. He'll know that something went wrong. He might figure out what happened, what had to have happened. He might remember that camper in the funeral home parking lot and know that someone had to be in there. If he connects the dots, he'll not have any trouble finding out that I own the camper and that I left Alpine yesterday morning in a hurry. I've got to be able to work in Colorado. I don't need him for an enemy."

"Boy," she said, "that's going to be hard for me to do. I hate dealing with anyone on that basis. I'd rather confront him about this, get it out in the open, talk about it. I don't see how I could just pretend like I don't know."

"Miss O'Neill—"

"Please, call me Avalon. May I call you Bill?"

"Please do. Miss O'Neill. Avalon. I understand the situation this puts you in. We are both compromised here, in different ways. I can't let the sheriff find out that I lied to him. I can't let him or George Langley or anyone else find out that I took your dog. And you can't let Langley even suspect that you know what you now know. I'm not just worried about myself. I'm also worried about Sarah Peteski. I owe her a lot."

"She told me about your background. About you and her and Nelson Towers, from way back. About you going to law school. How you happened to be in Alpine. How she's so glad she's working with you again."

"Yeah. She's putting it all on the line this time. She's depending on us. She's counting on you to continue being able to get inside information from Langley. I know that puts you in a very awkward position."

"Well, the relationship was over, anyway. George just hadn't accepted that yet. We've agreed not to discuss it any more until this is over. Maybe it won't be so hard. He's so swamped I'm barely able to get a minute with him, anyway. Those roadblocks have created a nightmare. But I guess the roadblocks will be coming down now."

"Yeah. Nelson Towers has got to be eager to get them down. That backfired on him, since it didn't get this thing cleared up in a hurry. All it did was catapult this into a huge media event. But Langley will probably be even more swamped now. With Hussein evaporating as a suspect, and the media already in Alpine, that leaves Towers taking all the heat. And that video this morning was devastating for him. Towers will be on Langley hard to do something."

"Bill, I'm not sure how to say this." She paused, as though choosing her words carefully. "But you need to know some things about George that might be hard to understand, especially after what you overheard. What he wanted to do about my dog was awful, and how he wanted to do it was worse. That saddens me.

But George is not entirely to blame. He is not a bad person. Some of this is my fault. It was my fault he slapped me. I slapped him first. I lost my temper. I've been *trying* not to do that. If I hadn't done that, none of this would have happened. I mean, Lady never has liked him, but god, I thought she was going to kill him. Can you understand what I'm saying?"

"I can try, I guess. It's really none of my business."

"But, in a way, it is. Things have happened, beyond our control, that have made it that way. I am very grateful for what you've done. I don't know how I'll ever be able to repay you. But you need to know that George and I have talked about Nelson Towers. A lot. George is a very complex person. He's been under tremendous pressures, with a lot of responsibilities, and he's very ambitious. He has incredible drive and some awesome talents. I doubt there is anything he cannot achieve when he sets his mind to it. He's also got some flaws. I know what people say about him, and I know some things he's done that I don't like. But I've seen another side of him, too. There are things between George and me that no one will ever know about. I know you've gotten thrust into the middle of this, and that's awkward for both of us."

She paused, as though uncertain about how much to say. "I've learned some things, being with George, that are going to cause me to rethink a few things about myself and about what I might want out of life. I know this is all none of your concern. I'm just saying, don't assume that George is controlled by Nelson Towers, or by anyone else. If Towers is the one who did this to Linda, George will nail him for it. Nobody who knows George wants him for an enemy. He's a driven man. Very few people have any idea what drives him. If Nelson Towers takes him for granted, Towers is a fool."

"Okay," Hom-Astubby said, "maybe I've been speaking out of turn. I really don't know anything about Langley, except some political gossip. As for the things I overheard him say, well, to try to be fair, maybe I wouldn't come off looking so good either, if someone was privy to some of my worst moments. We've all done things, or said things, we're not proud of."

Hom-Astubby wondered if he'd intruded into her relationship in a way he shouldn't have. They might have patched things up, if he hadn't stepped in the way he had. Maybe they might still do that.

Maybe he should try to step back out of this, as best he could. She seemed ambivalent about the man and might still be emotionally entangled with him, despite what had happened.

He wondered why so many intelligent women stayed with abusive men. He wondered what had attracted her to George Langley. What had she meant about rethinking things about herself? He wished he could ask her about that, but he barely knew her. At least she'd had sense enough to try to end the relationship—if Langley really was abusive.

It made him uneasy realizing how little he really knew about George Langley or Avalon O'Neill. He wondered if he could have been wrong about Langley. He said, "I know he was genuinely upset after viewing Linda Ruben's body. And not everyone loves dogs. Even dog lovers don't like all dogs. I can think of a few dogs I've met that I haven't liked. They were unfriendly, vicious dogs, some of them bred that way, some of them probably the product of abuse from the time they were puppies. And he did tell Dick he was worried about how the dog might react one day to some child. He might have really meant that." But Hom-Astubby knew he would never understand someone like George Langley, or be able to sympathize very much with whatever problems he might have. He said, "But I don't think George Langley is somebody I could be friends with."

"I learned," she said, "that he's somebody I can't be married to. I think I was a tremendous disappointment to him about that, if only he would have accepted it. But I appreciate your effort to put yourself in his shoes. Not many people would try to do that, under the circumstances. And I like the way you did that. I have to tell you, that surprised me. It makes me feel a lot less self-conscious in talking with you about all of this. I think I'm going to like working with you."

"Yeah, well, okay. I guess I need to get up there. I'll be driving that big camper. It's crimson and cream. I guess you remember."

What she said next caught him a little off-balance.

"I remember. When I saw the Oklahoma tags, I knew why I hadn't liked the color scheme on that camper. I figured it was just some idiot Sooners fan—our blood enemies at CU."

"Uh . . . I am a Sooners fan."

"I figured as much. We'll have to talk about that."

"Talk about what? Colorado's not our blood enemy. Colorado barely has a football team. Down through the decades, somebody has to beat you once in a while to be a blood enemy. And we don't even *have* a ski team. I'm pretty sure about that."

"Most second-rate institutions don't."

"Oh boy. No Golden Buffalo can talk football with the Sooners, except maybe about that little glitch in the 1990s. We'll have that talk. But hey, there's something else we need to talk about."

Hom-Astubby took a deep breath. "Do you really think it's a good idea for me to bring your dog up there right now?"

"Oh, I want to see her so bad!"

"This thing's not over yet. I could still get stopped for something on the way up there, for anything, and end up getting separated from the dog. I'd hate to put the dog at risk, no matter how much that risk might have been reduced."

"I hadn't thought about that."

"I've already found a real nice kennel down here, at a vet clinic. It's a real good clinic. I can take all the extras, including the options for having her walked twice a day, outside, a long walk. And to be doubly safe, I can get a friend to do the paperwork. Just in case they check on me for any reason, they won't find that I kenneled a dog down here. Do you really have any place up there where you can keep her? You're welcome to come back down here with me to get her when this is over. That would be easy. We could tow your car behind my camper."

"Gosh, I don't know. You might be right. Just knowing she's okay was the big thing, I guess. Darn. I'd have my parents go get her right now, but they're in Europe. Is that kennel air-conditioned?"

"Oh yeah. Completely."

"But when she's outside, isn't it too hot for her down there? Her hair is so thick and heavy. I'd worry about her being out in that heat."

"Uh, say. There's something about that I've been meaning to ask you." Hom-Astubby took another deep breath, and prayed. "By any chance, your dog isn't a show dog, is she?"

"How did you know about that?"

"She *is* a show dog?"

"She's a once-in-a-*lifetime* dog! Lady's registered name is Glennglavin's Spurling Baskerville Blossom. She's the North American Grand National Champion. She's the betting favorite to take the world title next month. You should have seen her at Westminster, among all those poodles and Airedales and a cocker spaniel that everyone thought was unbeatable. But why do you ask about that?"

"Huh?"

"I said, why did you ask about that?"

"Uh, ooooh. I guess it probably wouldn't be a good idea to give her a haircut, huh?"

"A haircut!"

"That's what I thought. Not a good idea."

"God no! Her conformity has to be highlighted just right. We spend more time on her hair than anything. It can't even be thinned out any."

"Oh, well. It was just a thought. She won't be out in the heat all that much, anyway. Say, we'd better exchange cell phone and pager numbers, don't you think? Then I'd better get your dog all nice and cozy at that kennel and get on the road."

CHAPTER TWENTY-THREE

Hom-Astubby slept in the camper from Clinton, Oklahoma, all the way past Albuquerque. He slept the sleep of the dead, not waking up until Johnny pulled off the interstate for gas, a little past 10 P.M., Mountain Time.

Hom-Astubby came stumbling out of the camper, yawning and stretching, to discover they were parked at the gas pumps at the Acoma Pueblo Sky City Indian Casino. Johnny was pumping diesel into the truck.

It had been a slow trip for Johnny, with heavy thunderstorms and high winds across the Texas panhandle and eastern New Mexico, almost all the way to Albuquerque. He wanted to get home by midnight, so he stayed behind the wheel as long as he could.

Hom-Astubby took over pumping the gas so Johnny could go inside the casino to the men's room. After paying for the gas and moving the truck, Hom-Astubby took a quick shower and then found Johnny inside at the self-service coffee bar. They helped themselves to coffee and stood there sipping it, listening to the sound of the slot machines, a sound Hom-Astubby found particularly soothing.

Johnny said, "Come look what I found."

Hom-Astubby followed Johnny down a nearby row of slot machines, until he stopped near the end of the row. "What do you think about this one?" Johnny said.

It was a single-coin, five-dollar machine. A stand-alone, not tied into any progressive jackpot. Hom-Astubby shrugged. "Looks okay. Be expensive to play it. That's five bucks a pop."

"Yeah," Johnny said. "But you got no choice but to play just one coin. I can't bring myself to play max coins on a slot machine, so I guess I don't have much chance at hitting a good jackpot. But here, I'd automatically be playing max coins, and I'd automatically be playing minimum coins, too."

Hom-Astubby looked around. He said, "Well, if you got on one of those dollar machines over there, playing max coins would only cost you three dollars a pop. That would be cheaper than this one. You'd get more plays for a twenty-dollar bill."

"Yeah, but I'd have to hit that max play button, and I just can't bring myself to do that."

Hom-Astubby shook his head. He said, "I got to go to the bath-room."

"Wait a minute before you go."

"What?"

"Hom-Astubby, touch my machine for me."

"What?"

"Just touch it for me. Just once. You can do that."

Hom-Astubby shook his head again. He reached out and touched Johnny's slot machine, then headed for the men's room. He had better make this a quick stop or Johnny would be leaving here dead broke. At five dollars a pop, his paycheck wouldn't last long.

Hom-Astubby had come out of the men's room and had poured himself another cup of coffee when he heard Johnny scream, "Yeeee haaaaaaa!"

Hom-Astubby almost spilled his coffee on himself. He hurried toward Johnny, seeing that a crowd had gathered around him.

"What did you hit?" Hom-Astubby asked.

"I don't know," Johnny said. "It went ape shit on me, doing a whole bunch of free spins. I think I won a thousand dollars."

Hom-Astubby looked at the slot machine. "Johnny, it says HAND PAY 1000 CREDITS. One credit is five dollars. You won five thousand dollars."

"No shit? Five thousand?"

"Yeah. It's a five-dollar machine."

"You mean somebody is gonna come over here and hand me five thousand dollars?"

"Yeah. What do you think they're gonna do, come over here and throw you outta the place?"

"Let's do it again!"

"Johnny, it won't happen again."

"But it might."

"Look, do you want to leave here with five thousand dollars and a story to tell about how you hit five grand on a slot machine, or do you want to leave here dead broke? You'll have the story to tell, either way. The only question is whether you want the five grand that goes with it."

"That's my only choice?"

"That's what the odds say. The more you play, the more you lose. You got lucky. Really lucky. These things will gobble up every bit of it, if you put it back in. You might hit two or three hundred for each thousand you put back in. Maybe. But before long, that whole five grand will be back in the machine. Do you want the five grand or not?"

"I want the five grand."

"Then let's get the money and get the hell outta here. We can laugh all the way to Gallup."

It took a while to get out of the casino. They had to prepare IRS paperwork on the jackpot so the casino could report it as part of Johnny's income tax records.

"We should be in Canada," Hom-Astubby said. "Casino jackpots are not subject to taxation there."

The reminder about income taxes caused Hom-Astubby to think about his own quandary and that dampened his mood a bit. But he wasn't going to let that spoil the fun. He was happy for Johnny.

It was something watching Johnny's face as the slot machine attendant counted out five thousand dollars, stacking them in Johnny's hand, all in one-hundred-dollar bills except for the last hundred, which was in twenties, so it would be convenient for Johnny to leave a smaller tip if he might not be inclined to tip a one-hundred-dollar bill.

Johnny tipped him one dollar. Then he composed his face and

gave the attendant his best Richard Boone imitation, from the movie *Hombre*—Boone's good-bye to the stagecoach driver, after having robbed the stage—saying, "We'll do it again sometime."

"Please play off the jackpot," the attendant said, looking at his one-dollar tip.

"Huh?" Johnny said.

"You have to hit the machine again," Hom-Astubby said, "to clear the jackpot off of it. And you've still got two credits on there, just hit the play button one more time."

"You hit it for me," Johnny said. "Okay?"

Hom-Astubby hit the play button. The reels went spinning, and when they stopped, the machine hit $800.

"Yeeee haaaaaa!" Johnny screamed again. He turned to Hom-Astubby. "Are you *sure* we should leave the casino?"

Hom-Astubby almost wasn't sure, but he talked Johnny into cashing out, telling him he had to get to Alpine.

Johnny hit the cash-out button, and they listened to the heavy five-dollar tokens banging into the coin holder as they dropped out of the machine. Johnny said, "Isn't that a sweet sound?" He cashed the tokens at the cashier's window. They got more coffee, to go, and got back on the road, with Hom-Astubby driving.

Johnny was in high spirits. He had won enough money to pay off all of his debts and have quite a bit left over. He said he was going to quit his job, put his affairs in order in Gallup, and head right back to the ranch. He might try to talk his boss into letting him put that old Honda in his shop for a little more repair before heading out.

Johnny told Hom-Astubby about a couple of calls he'd gotten on his cell phone while he'd been sleeping in the camper, one from Sarah Peteski and one from Avalon O'Neill. They'd both just wanted to make sure that Hom-Astubby was on his way. "Man," Johnny said, "that Avalon O'Neill is one sweet lady to talk to."

"Easy for you to say," Hom-Astubby said. "You don't have to figure out how to tell her about her dog."

They stopped at the Denny's on the east side of Gallup for a long, leisurely T-bone breakfast. Johnny insisted on paying. While eating breakfast, they worked out a deal for Johnny to be Hom-Astubby's ranch foreman. By the time Hom-Astubby dropped Johnny off at his house, and they got the Honda unhooked, it was after 2 A.M.

"I'll see you back at the ranch," Hom-Astubby said. "I don't know when I'll be getting back there. Just leave the dog in the kennel until I get back. Be safer for her that way."

"Okay," Johnny said. "I'll be back there in a few days. I'll call you on your cell or give Hop a call if I get delayed."

Hom-Astubby's drive to Shiprock went smoothly, with the big full moon lighting up the high desert plateau. He didn't push the pedal, content to drive the speed limit. He eased along, listening to a Navajo-language radio station, to Navajo crooners belting out old country standards like "Your Cheatin' Heart" in Navajo.

A Colorado state patrolman and a Montezuma County sheriff's deputy were parked at the Colorado border, standing in the moonlight talking to each other, but there was no roadblock.

Passing the Ute Mountain Indian Casino on the south side of Cortez made Hom-Astubby think of Johnny again. Johnny was going to round up some of his Comanche cousins, all veterans of the rodeo circuit, and put together a ranch crew that knew something about horses. All Hom-Astubby needed to do now was get some horses. Johnny also wanted to get some racehorses. Hom-Astubby wasn't sure about that, but Johnny said that's where the big money was, in stud fees, if they could come up with some winners. It might work.

Every motel in Cortez had its no-vacancy sign lit up. When he drove by the Cortez Denny's, the place was packed, with people lined up at the door and the parking lot overflowing with vehicles.

It didn't take long to get to Alpine. He had to slow down to a crawl to get through town. He was surprised to see that the lights were already on in several businesses, including the grocery store. He saw Eldon pumping gas at his station, with a line of vehicles waiting to get to the pumps.

Near the courthouse, pedestrians almost blocked the road to a point that vehicles couldn't get through. Television sound trucks were parked everywhere, including in front yards. The courthouse lawn was densely packed with people and was so brightly lit with klieg lights it looked like the middle of the afternoon.

Hom-Astubby glanced at his watch. It was getting on toward 5 A.M., nearly 7 A.M. on the East Coast. The morning network TV news broadcasts were in full swing.

Halfway to the Purple Pentagon, he noticed that even the Shady Rest gas station was already open, with cars at the gas pumps. Before he got to the restaurant, he could see that a heavy early morning fog had settled along the river. He could barely see a new flashing neon sign: OPEN 24 HOURS. It was mounted on a small trailer that had been placed on the shoulder of the highway in front of the Purple Pentagon. As he got closer, he could see long rows of cars parked on both shoulders of the highway in front of the restaurant and knew that the parking lot was filled to overflowing.

He eased off the highway onto the shoulder and parked behind the last car in line. He wondered how long it would take someone to get served breakfast in the restaurant.

He ducked into his camper, quickly pulling on his camouflage coveralls. He stuck a flashlight in his pocket and gathered up his turkey blind. Already, two cars had pulled off the highway and parked behind him. He watched until there was no traffic on the highway and then sprinted across the road and into the woods.

He turned on the flashlight and headed up the fairly steep slope of Grimpen Hill, casting around a bit in the fog, hoping to find some kind of trail. Before long, he found a narrow footpath that took him straight up the hillside.

He turned off the flashlight as he emerged from tall trees onto a bald spot on top the hill. He couldn't see the Purple Pentagon from there, but he could see across the river bridge, could see in the gloom the eerily flashing lights of a police vehicle, blocking the entrance to the dirt road that led to the picnic table. Down in the depths of the fog in the dark river valley, he could barely see the flashing lights of another police vehicle at about the location of the picnic table.

There was a faint pinkish glow along the eastern horizon. He was still quite a bit upstream from where he needed to be, but the footpath led him right along the crest of the hill to where he figured the cliffs he was looking for must be.

He sat down then and waited for daylight, wanting to be sure he was in the right place. It wasn't long before he could see where he was. He was farther back from the cliff than he had thought. The footpath skirted away from it, back about forty or fifty yards. There was fairly dense brush on both sides of the path and tall trees behind the brush.

As it got lighter, he eased down to the top of the cliff. The fog had dissipated enough that he could see the picnic table, and he could see that it was a Devon County sheriff's office vehicle parked near it. He guessed that Albert was probably sitting in the vehicle, probably sound asleep. Hom-Astubby could see the Purple Pentagon and all of its parking lot, but he needed to move a little farther downstream.

When he got pretty close to where he thought that telephoto lens had been set up, he could see a small rise behind the footpath, back away from the cliff, a vantage that would offer a commanding view of the immediate area. He went there. It was perfect. He might not even need the turkey blind netting, but he spread it out and got beneath it anyway. He settled in to wait.

CHAPTER TWENTY-FOUR

Hom-Astubby didn't know how long he'd been asleep, but he knew he hadn't dozed off for very long. It wasn't the first time he'd fallen asleep in a blind, and he didn't move anything but his eyes when he awakened.

A young man stood down the hill in front of him, at the top of the cliff, staring through the bushes at the crime scene across the river.

He wore a floppy old green hat, pulled down over his ears, and a ragged gray long-sleeved hunting shirt that was too big for him, with the shirttails hanging out over baggy camouflage pants that also looked too big for him. He wasn't carrying a camera or a tripod or anything.

The man watched through the bushes for a few minutes, then turned away and began walking up the hill. He passed within thirty feet of Hom-Astubby, on a trail that led into the trees.

Hom-Astubby watched him until he was nearly out of sight in the trees, then crawled from under the netting and followed him.

After several hundred yards, the man led Hom-Astubby to a barbed-wire fence at the edge of a clearing. Hom-Astubby got to the underbrush near the fence in time to see the man climb the steps of a sagging wooden front porch and disappear into an old house.

Looking around, Hom-Astubby saw that the clearing wasn't very large. A tractor with a big scoop bucket on the front of it was parked behind the house. A snow blade sat on the ground beside the tractor. There weren't any other vehicles in sight.

On the other side of the house, a dirt road coming out of the trees was blocked by a rusty steel gate that had a heavy chain and a big lock on it, at another barbed-wire fence. This side of the gate, the dirt road went in front of the house to the barbed-wire fence where Hom-Astubby was crouched, and then the road turned to Hom-Astubby's right and went beside the house and up a hill, running beside the fence for about a hundred feet to the entrance of an old mine in the face of a rock wall.

The entrance to the mine was large and had big double doors, as big as barn doors. The dirt road continued on up the hill beyond the mine, still running beside the barbed-wire fence, and disappeared over the crest of the hill.

Hom-Astubby got himself concealed in the underbrush at the edge of the clearing and settled in to wait.

Before long, the man he had followed from the cliffs came out of the house onto the porch. He had taken off the hat and the long-sleeved shirt and was now wearing only a brown T-shirt with the baggy camouflage pants. He sat down on the top step of the porch.

Hom-Astubby got a good look at him—short blond hair, probably mid to late twenties, a match for the description of the young man who had attacked the woman outside the laundry in Alpine.

A vehicle came up the road. A large brown heavy-duty, four-wheel-drive pickup truck came out of the trees and stopped at the gate. An older man, probably in his fifties, tall and broad-shouldered, got out of the truck. He left the engine running, unlocked the gate and swung it open.

The man at the gate saw the young man sitting on the front porch and his face contorted in anger. He yelled, "What in the hell are you doing?"

He had a distinct southern accent, maybe from Alabama or Georgia, from somewhere in the Deep South, but the accent sounded tempered, perhaps by years away from home.

The younger man stood up and slouched against a porch post. He stuck his hands in the big front pockets of his pants and said, "Aw hell, Uncle Charlie, there ain't nobody gonna see me way off up here." His accent was thick and fresh and straight from the Deep South.

The older man got back in his truck, drove it through the gate to the front of the house, and killed the engine. He got out, leaving the gate standing open behind the pickup, and walked to the front porch.

He climbed the steps and hit the younger man with his fist so hard it knocked him off his feet. Then he stepped toward him and kicked him hard in the stomach.

"Goddamn shitbrain!" he said, as he kicked him again.

The younger man tried to roll away, but he rolled against the wall of the house, where he lay clutching his stomach, gasping for breath.

"What if I'd had one of them with me?" the older man screamed. "If they find you here, they'll kill my dumb ass!"

The older man stood staring down at him. Then he gave him one more good kick and went inside the house, leaving the young man lying on the porch, all doubled up, still clutching his stomach.

After a few minutes, the man came out of the house with a small wooden crate that looked very heavy from the way he was carrying it. He put it on the floor of the cab inside the pickup, on the passenger side, and went back to the house, emerging a moment later with a small green tarp.

He stopped on the porch long enough to say, "You get your ass back up in that mine and you stay there. Come Sunday night, I'm gettin' you outta here."

He spread the tarp over the small crate in the pickup, then turned the truck around and drove through the gate. He stopped on the other side to get out and lock it. He said, "I won't be gone long. You be in that damn mine when I get back." He drove away.

After a few minutes the young man rose to his feet, grimacing with pain, and went inside the house. He came out with a pistol in his hand, wearing the long-sleeved shirt and floppy hat again. Even from the bushes, Hom-Astubby could see the bruise on the side of his face.

He stood on the porch, staring at where the pickup had disappeared down the road. He said, "To hell with you!"

He stuck the barrel of the pistol down the front of his pants, then pulled the shirt together and buttoned it, covering the gun. He stepped off the porch and walked to the gate, limping slightly. He climbed through the barbed-wire fence beside the gate and went walking down the road, toward Alpine.

When the young man was out of sight, Hom-Astubby lay staring down the road, wondering what was going on at this house. Why didn't that man want anyone to see that kid here? Had that kid killed Linda Ruben, and the older man was hiding him? But he'd said that someone would kill him, would kill the older man. The cops wouldn't do that, not even for harboring a murderer. It didn't make sense.

There didn't seem to be anybody else at that house. All was quiet, as still as could be. He crawled out of the bushes, climbed through the barbed wire, and walked to the front porch. He peeked inside the house.

The living room had an unmade bed in one corner, and the room was strewn with literature from some organization called the Tetons. He had never heard of them. Newsletters and pamphlets were scattered everywhere.

He glanced through some of them, finding articles about bomb making, assault weapons, survivalist wilderness skills, food storage, water purification, auxiliary power systems, guerilla warfare tactics, and shrill diatribes about a separate sovereign nation status for white Americans—with chilling, hate-filled rantings about the "contamination of white racial purity" by other races.

Hom-Astubby fought against an urge to get out of that house right then. But he had to find that telephoto lens, if it was there, and any film that might have been shot with it.

He peered into a small messy kitchen and a dirty bathroom. The only other room, one as large as the living room, was outfitted with four double bunk beds. All eight beds were made up in crisp military fashion. The orderliness and cleanliness of the room was in stark contrast to the rest of the house. It was spotless.

Footlockers and wall lockers provided most of the furnishings. Boxes of canned food, powdered milk, and other dry goods were neatly stacked in one corner. He looked in a closet, but it was empty. He opened each locker, but they were all empty, except for one footlocker, which was filled with handguns and boxes of ammunition.

He stood gazing all around the room. Someone was expecting company, probably pretty soon.

Stepping back into the living room, he looked inside a closet, but it held nothing but some coats and shirts on hangers, and a few pairs of shoes on the floor. He went outside onto the front porch.

Looking down the road, he wondered how much time he had. Maybe not much.

He walked around the house and followed the dirt road up the hill to the mine. The big double doors weren't locked. They would obviously open up wide enough to drive the pickup inside, or the tractor. He pulled open one of the doors a bit and peeked inside.

It was too gloomy to see how far the tunnel extended. He couldn't see any kind of light or a light switch. He pulled the door open wider to admit more light, frowning while doing so because the doors to the mine could be seen from the house and from the gate on the road. With one door standing open, he could see that the tunnel extended about thirty feet.

Apparently, it was being used more or less as a storage shed and a garage, where maybe the tractor was ordinarily housed. He could see traces of the big tractor-tire tracks on the ground, and there was an open space in the middle of the clutter, big enough for the tractor, all the way to the back wall. The tunnel was at least twice as wide as necessary to park the tractor inside it.

A workbench stood along the right wall, with a lot of tools scattered out all over it—wrenches, screwdrivers, pliers. Shelving above the workbench held more tools and other odds and ends.

He walked down the right wall to the back of the tunnel. Beyond the workbench was a big gasoline-powered generator, an air compressor, gas cans, shovels, rakes, a big pair of bolt cutters, an ax, a pile of garden hose, a stack of fence posts, and an old car engine resting on a pallet.

At the back end of the tunnel the floor was boarded over. Heavy timber framing, above the boards, supported a large pulley, which was threaded with a heavy rope. The boards apparently covered the top of a vertical shaft.

He walked along the other wall back to the front door, along a row of old furniture, beginning with a tall double-door cabinet, and then a stack of end tables and coffee tables. Beyond that was a chest of drawers and then an unmade cot, where someone had obviously been sleeping recently. A pile of dirty clothes, mostly socks and underwear and tee shirts, lay beside the cot.

Beyond the cot was a large padlocked trunk. A coffee cup, lantern, and small propane stove sat on top of it. Beyond the trunk were two kitchen tables sitting end to end, cluttered with old radios and stacks of old dishes. Beyond that, near the front door, was a pile of iron pipes and a stack of wooden chairs with seats that had been woven out of rope. One of the chairs had been taken down and was placed in front of the table nearest the cot. A pair of blue jeans was draped over the back of the chair.

He glanced at the door he had opened. That made him nervous, that door standing wide open. He peeked around the edge of it, at the old house and the gate. Everything was quiet and still.

Pulling the door shut, he took out his flashlight. He started at the back, at the cabinet, which was easily tall enough to hold that telephoto lens.

He found it inside the left door, standing almost as tall as the top of his head. He examined it with the flashlight. It was 2000 mm, in perfect condition, either brand-new or close to it. No camera was attached to it. The tripods for holding it up and securing it in place were in the right side of the cabinet. He looked through the cabinet, pulling out all the drawers, but they were empty. There were no cameras, no camera bags, no film.

He closed the cabinet doors and stood frowning at the cabinet, wondering how much more time he had. He moved to the chest of drawers. In the top drawer he found a briefcase.

He carried it to the front doors and opened one door a bit, glancing around it quickly to make sure no one had returned to the house. He crouched in the bright light at the doorway and examined the briefcase.

It was a very expensive leather case, somewhat worn, but it was still good for years of elegant service. He opened it.

The briefcase was filled with papers. He found Wally Street's American Express billing statement and other credit card bills.

The top of a business card sticking out of a small pouch caught his eye. He lifted it out and looked at it. Embossed, expensive lettering read "Ryerson & Neely, Incorporated" and "San Francisco, London, Hong Kong." Below that was the name "Pat Culpepper" with an international phone number, followed by "Hong Kong." He tucked the business card into his shirt pocket, beneath his camouflage coveralls. It wouldn't be missed.

He rifled through the other papers quickly. Most of them seemed to concern something called the Sunstruck Land Company. Others seemed to be complex financial statements of some kind. There were a number of manila envelopes and folders, but he didn't take time to open any of them. There was a cell phone, a calculator, and several computer disks.

Most of the space was taken up by a thick, elaborately sealed packet. "Ryerson & Neely, Inc." was stamped into the wax of the unbroken seal.

Hom-Astubby wanted to take the briefcase, but he was afraid the young man would miss it. Maybe he could take some of the things that were in the briefcase. The Ryerson & Neely packet looked like a good bet. But what else, and how much should he take? There was no way to know what might be important. He stood up, thinking about what he should do.

He felt the clock ticking. He frowned. He had to find the film that kid had shot before he wasted time thinking about anything else. And he didn't like having that barn door open.

He closed the door again and used his flashlight, putting the briefcase back in the drawer where he'd found it. He opened the next drawer. It was filled with socks, undershorts, and T-shirts. He closed it and opened the next drawers, but they were all empty.

He began feeling panicky. He glanced at the front doors, wondering if he'd even be able to hear that pickup returning. Thinking about the pickup made him remember that kid on the front porch, lying there, getting kicked repeatedly and viciously. And that kid was a relative, a nephew. What would that man do to a stranger? A trespasser? A burglar—caught in broad daylight?

Where was that film? He opened the drawer with the clothing again and patted his hand around on top of the clothes. He felt something in a back corner. He pulled out an old billfold, badly worn.

Inside the wallet he found a Georgia driver's license for a Lawrence Selden Lindquist, of Princetown, Georgia, with an old photo of the young man who had led him to the house. The license had been expired for two years.

He took a notebook and ink pen out of his pocket and started copying the information from the license, but it was awkward trying to find a way to hold the flashlight and license and ink pen and notebook all at the same time, and his nerves were so jittery, he wasn't sure he would even be able to read his own writing. He needed more light, and some kind of writing table.

He didn't want to open the barn door again. Maybe he could move to one of those kitchen tables. But he was getting ever more nervous about how long he had been in there, and he had to find that film. He put the driver's license in his shirt pocket, thinking that Lindquist probably wouldn't miss it.

He put the wallet back where he'd found it and patted around through the clothing some more, wondering what that man had meant about not being gone very long. An hour? Half an hour? Fifteen minutes?

On the other side of the drawer, beneath the clothing, he found ten rolls of exposed 35 mm color film. Bingo.

He put the film in a zippered front pocket of his coveralls. He looked around quickly to see if there was anything else he could search.

The only thing he couldn't get to was the locked trunk. Apparently, Lindquist had stashed the stolen cameras in there. And more film too? He could use the bolt cutters to remove the lock, but then

Lindquist would know right away that someone had been there. He might not miss that film for awhile, or that old driver's license, but he would notice that the lock was gone from that trunk.

He took one more quick look around to make sure he was leaving everything the way he had found it. He was getting so panicky about being in there for so long that he could barely think straight. His nerves were screaming at him to get out of there. He had a bad felling there was something else he ought to do, but he couldn't think what it might be.

He hurried out, leaving the doors closed the way he had found them, and sprinted for the barbed-wire fence. He crawled through it and didn't breathe easy until he was in the trees, beyond the underbrush.

Once in the trees, he stopped and looked back at the clearing— at the house, gate, and mine-garage. All quiet and still.

He started second-guessing himself then. Maybe he should have cut the lock off that trunk. He knew he didn't ever want to come back here—why hadn't he thought about that? He'd had a vague idea about returning soon and substituting ten rolls of bad exposed film for that kid's film. But he knew now that he would never come back here. This was his only chance.

Jesus, he had forgotten to take anything else from Wally Street's briefcase. Maybe he should have taken the whole briefcase. At least, he could have taken those computer disks and some of those papers. The kid likely wouldn't miss any of that, not if he left something in the briefcase. But what should he take and what should he leave?

He was nearly beside himself with indecision, debating whether he should go back in there, when he heard a vehicle coming up the road.

That big brown pickup came out of the trees and stopped at the gate again. This time, the man didn't unlock the gate. He climbed through the barbed wire and began walking toward that mine-garage.

Hom-Astubby eased back through the trees, back toward the

cliffs, not wanting to imagine what would be happening right now if he hadn't gotten out of there when he did.

He picked up the camo netting on the way to his camper and thought about that old house, trying to make sense out of what he had discovered, and kicking himself for leaving everything in that briefcase.

Everything except that business card. Maybe he could do something with that.

At the camper, he fixed himself a quick breakfast and showered. While drying off, sipping coffee, he thought about what he might do.

He had an old girlfriend, Laura Frankland, who had been the manager of the big Lyons photo lab in Albuquerque. He hadn't seen her in a while and had heard she'd gotten married to the wealthy owner of that lab a couple years ago. She probably wasn't still managing the lab, but she might be able to let him in there after hours, late this afternoon or this evening. If so, he would have time to drive to Albuquerque, after his meeting this morning with Avalon O'Neill, arriving by about the time that lab closed.

He looked at his watch. Nearly 8:30. He got his cell phone and dialed the old phone number for her office at the lab. To his relief, she came on the line.

"Laura, it's Bill Mallory."

"Bill. Talk about perfect timing. God, you always have such perfect timing. Are you in town? I just got stood up for tonight. Can you believe that? Want to go have dinner?"

"I heard you got married."

"I did. He ran off to Florida with his investment banker, a skinny redhead with Las Vegas tits. I'm in mourning. I got the new house, the new car, a list of things as long as your arm. The ink's still wet on the decree. You up for a hot time on the old town tonight? I'll treat."

"I'm in Colorado, Laura. But I'm hoping to drive down there later today. Boy, I need a big favor. Could you be at the lab after hours, late this afternoon or early this evening?"

"I guess I could be. That wasn't exactly what I had in mind to do with you. What's up?"

"A friend of mine has got some guy stalking her with a camera. She went skinny dipping and I think the guy might have gotten it on film. I've got ten rolls of color 35 mm that I need to get processed. I took a risk stealing the film from that guy, and I sure need to find out what's on it before he misses it. I'm almost afraid to look at what else might be on there. Any chance we could have the use of the lab, after hours?"

"Bill, I own the lab now. That was one of the things on that list. What time can you be here?"

"I'm not sure right now. I've got a meeting pretty soon. It might be noon or later before I can get out of here. I'm in Alpine."

"Jesus, you're up there in that mess? It looks like a zoo on TV. They even had roadblocks down here."

"Yeah, it's a mess, all right."

"You remember how to get to the lab, don't you?"

"Yes. I can find it again."

"I'll wait here for you after we close. I'll order out after you get here. I remember you like Chinese."

"Geez, Laura. You're an angel."

"Angel, my ass. I've got a couch in my office. I'm so horny I'm climbing the goddamn walls. Tell me something—this bashful, skinny-dipping friend of yours. Any chance she looks like Helen of Troy?"

"Uh . . ."

"Never mind. I'll deal with you when you get here. You're gonna pay your dues for letting me marry that creep. You call me from the road somewhere when you've got an ETA. Okay?"

"Will do."

"And you be thinking about nothing but me all the way down here, you hear? I want you to remember every damn thing I like to do. I want you ready to do your duty the minute you step through the door. Ciao, for now."

Hom-Astubby sat lost in thought for a moment, remembering Laura's appetite for, as she had said, "every damn thing" she liked to do. He exhaled a long breath and looked at his watch.

He got dressed quickly, then hurriedly cleaned up the kitchen and made a last-minute inspection to be sure the camper was all tidy and ready for a guest—a very special guest.

He got behind the wheel and headed for the Shady Rest gas station to meet Avalon O'Neill.

CHAPTER TWENTY-FIVE

om-Astubby arrived at the Shady Rest as Avalon O'Neill was driving up. As she got out of her car, he was darn glad he had dressed in expensive casual clothing, a very trendy pair of specially tailored, matching, cream-colored slacks and shirt.

She was nothing short of stunning.

She had chosen a long-sleeved, thin, almost sheer blouse of some color that struck him as a cross between purple and a dark pink, but more on the purple side. The blouse did little to conceal a skimpy, low-cut bra of matching color. She didn't have the top of the blouse buttoned up.

It was an outfit calculated to highlight breasts that might keep astronauts from leaving earth.

Breasts were what he saw, at a distance, as she got out of her car. His first good look at Avalon O'Neill that day was of her leaning over, stepping out of her car, with the top of her blouse falling away from her body.

But it was when she stood up that he stared in amazement. No drill instructor would ever have to teach that pair how to stand at attention. That didn't necessarily mean they had any future at close-order drill. They stood at attention with such lofty perfection they were clearly unsuited for parade rest.

As he got closer to her, he could see that the cloth of her bra was darn near as sheer as the cloth of her blouse.

She was wearing a very short skirt that seemed to have a life of its own, the way it swished around at the slightest movement. Hom-Astubby had no idea how to describe its color, except that it was lighter than the blouse and looked great on her.

The short skirt revealed long shapely legs that exposed enough bare flesh above the knee they just begged a man to imagine having those warm thighs wrapped tightly around him. He could tell

she wasn't wearing hose, confident those legs could take her anywhere she wanted to go just the way they were.

It also meant she would be wearing panties. Not some damned
panty hose that covered up everything from the tips of her toes to
her belly button, but honest-to-god panties, maybe as skimpy and
sheer as her bra—and meaning, in the heat of action, it might not
require a contortionist to get the damn things peeled off her.

She surprised him by giving him a big, warm, long, tight hug.
He marveled at the amount of body heat she was putting out. She
was almost hot to the touch. This woman was ovulating. Of that
he was certain.

Oh, an ovulating woman could be wonderful. But dangerous.
He made a mental note to keep Mr. Mindless locked up in his
britches, no matter what, or he might risk bringing the pitter-patter
of little feet into his life.

He memorized the day of the month, so he might figure out her
monthly cycle and have that for future reference as some small aid
in the imprecise art of interpreting female behavior—most important, for figuring out when her most infertile moments might be.

Hugging her for so long allowed him to bury his face in her hair
and then along her warm, moist neck, while drinking deeply of her
scent. He had expected some faint trace of perfume, but instead
encountered her natural scent, fresh from the shower. It was an
intoxicating aroma, one he had smelled before, when he had held
her panties in his hands.

He drank deeply of it, trying to imagine how it would be inten-
sified and heightened when she was aroused, when she was wet
with the sweat of lovemaking, when the very essence of her would
be flooding the confinement of some small room.

She cast a powerful spell over him from the moment she
stepped out of her car. He was aware of that, too, and was a little
worried at how he was struggling to maintain his equilibrium in
the face of everything she was throwing at him.

He wasn't too concerned, though. From what he had overheard

Dick Halliburton say about her, he was pretty sure this woman was just a tease. Either she was some kind of head case or she just didn't understand about testosterone or possibly there was some other explanation. He couldn't remember ever encountering a woman who seemed so baffling or so intriguing.

He was also struck by something about her that seemed just a little bit "off." He couldn't put his finger on it. Maybe it was partly how provocatively she was dressed, which had certainly taken him by surprise. But it was more than that, something about her that was just a little strangely different. Something about the way she made eye contact—the intensity of it, and the way she sustained it, almost as though eye contact might be an unnatural thing for her to do and she was overcompensating, forcing herself to remember to do it. It was a fleeting first impression, soon forgotten amid her captivating warmth and charm.

She asked about her dog, first thing.

"Your dog," he said, "is the best-kept lady in Oklahoma. She is lounging around like a queen in air-conditioned comfort, being taken for long walks twice a day, being fed and monitored with veterinary sophistication, being washed and groomed to her heart's content twice a week."

He showed her his camper. She was impressed. Who wouldn't be? He had spared no expense in providing himself with a place suitable to his desires, and one he might enjoy coming home to, whenever he was away from home. He had spent almost as much money on its design and planning as it had cost to have built and equipped.

She could barely believe all the storage space, especially the large walk-in closets, with enough shoe racks to make even Imelda Marcos happy, and the palatial spaciousness of all the living areas, an effect primarily achieved by the strategic location of both large and small mirrors, which created a convincing illusion that those living areas, which were not at all cramped to begin with, continued on forever.

He had gotten the interior of the camper professionally designed and decorated by a hastily-assembled, sophisticated, hand-picked team consisting of both theoretical and practical specialists who had devoted a long, intense weekend to its planning. He had told those experts he wanted them to apply and coordinate all of their combined knowledge in creating an environment that would be calculated to induce a subliminal clitoral itchiness in young worldly women of elegant good taste who might not find anything particularly distressing in contemplating the prospect of a leisurely life of luxury and comfort.

That team had included some prominent female-behavioral psychologists, a neurogynecological research specialist, several kinds of architects, engineers and decorators—all quite distinguished in their specialties—an award-winning erogenomicist, a legendary Madison Avenue advertising executive, two local used-car salesmen, and an elderly, long-retired Hollywood special-effects wizard who had pioneered a multiple reflected image technique that had produced some noteworthy cinematic illusions.

Putting together that team would have been impossible without the help of a number of the celebrities Hom-Astubby had met while working with Harry Birdwell. He also had the help of some of the rich and powerful people he had gotten acquainted with while traveling the world with Arlington Billington. The big names on his team had signed on mostly as a favor for one of those people, though they had all become intrigued with the challenges of the task once they had started working on them.

As the out-of-town members of his team were flying in, he was still racking his brain, trying to think of anyone else who might be able to help whom he'd gotten acquainted with through Arlington Billington, when he suddenly realized the one, critical detail he had overlooked. At the last minute he convinced a well-known international bimbo that he needed her on the team, just to make sure he would have someone who could speak with the authority of the right kind of practical experience.

Ever since the camper had been delivered a few weeks ago, he'd been dying to try it out on a real, live specimen, but he'd been so buried in dealing with all of his problems that this was his first opportunity to find out if it might work.

She ooed and aahed, at times cooing, at the large bathrooms. There were sinks and a stool and a shower and a bathtub in both rooms, and a forty-lightbulb make-up mirror in the everything-a-lady-could-possibly-want larger room, including two small clothes dryers and a compact washing machine.

There was an oversized tub in the other room—large enough and deep enough for two people to enjoy its many Jacuzzi features, with three sides of its rim sporting slatted wooden benches to accommodate the room's Swedish sauna. Additional woodwork along the entire length of the front of the tub provided a table that had been specially designed for the art of massage.

She said she loved a sauna, that there was nothing like steaming oneself to heavenly bliss and then getting a relaxing full-body massage. He told her that massage just happened to be one of the things he had learned how to do.

She was amazed at the kitchen, saying she could cook a full Thanksgiving dinner in it. As she looked around that kitchen, mentioning some additional feature that might be nice to have, he showed her whatever she had thought of, with most of those things so ingeniously and compactly hidden away that flipping a switch and watching them magically appear—either from up out of the floor well, or down from the false ceiling, or from inside one of the rotating, unfolding wall-panel sections—was fun to do all by itself.

He didn't show her the wonders that could be done with the lighting or hardly any of the other features, but he couldn't resist showing her how the flipping of a few more switches sent the various components of the dinette booth rotating and sliding around and being reshaped and rearranged until they formed a long, comfy couch for viewing a large theater screen that dropped down in front of the kitchen cabinets, near the magically appearing hot-buttered popcorn machine, creating a cozy environment surrounded by so much sound that the difficult thing to believe was that you were *not* in the movie you were watching.

He let her flip the switches that sent all of the components of the movie theater back into their places, while watching the delight on her face as the couch was coming apart and the dinette booth was so ingeniously reassembling.

Gazing beyond and above the luxurious, spacious, oval dinette booth, with its inlaid-teak tabletop, she discreetly didn't comment on the oversized bed, perhaps because of the full-mirrored ceiling above the bed.

But she gave the bed a long look, chewing the bottom of her lip and then running the tip of her tongue all around the outside of her lips.

Hom-Astubby made them coffee. They sat in the deeply cushioned comfort of the dinette booth, across from one another, sipping the steaming brown liquid from thick crystal mugs.

She said, "Bill, there's something I want to ask you about. Yesterday evening, when I was talking to Johnny, while he was driving you up here and you were sleeping, he called you Hom-Astubby. When I asked him about that, he told me why your father gave you that name."

"He told you that?"

"Yes. He said that long ago a Choctaw chief named Hom-Astubby signed a treaty selling a large tract of land for one dollar. But in the next treaty, the very next year, when the Choctaws sold some more land, they were able to get a lot more for it. Johnny said your father wanted you to be reminded about that, so you wouldn't neglect to get everything out of life that it's worth. I think that's a wonderful story."

Hom-Astubby chuckled. "Did Johnny tell you much about that next treaty? That what they got was three rifles, some blankets and cloth, one saddle, and one black silk handkerchief?"

She laughed. "No. He didn't tell me that. One black silk handkerchief? Who got that?"

"It was a prize in the ball games for a while, passing from one town to another. My grandmother has it now. She's had it for a long time. Her grandmother got it as a wedding present, sometime around 1812."

"You've seen it?"

He nodded. "It's in fairly good condition. When I held it in my hands I couldn't help thinking, they gave up all that land, and my grandmother ended up with a black silk handkerchief."

"Did they even get any bullets for the rifles?"

"Yeah, they did get some lead to make bullets. And some gunpowder. And they also got a bridle to go with the saddle."

"Well, I guess that's better than one dollar."

"Yeah, I guess they did a little better that year than Hom-Astubby had done. The Americans had gotten him good and drunk."

"How do you spell Hom-Astubby?"

Hom-Astubby showed her. He said, "That's how the American treaty commissioners wrote it on the treaty in 1802, that 'one-dollar' treaty, at Fort Confederation."

"The Choctaws didn't sign the treaty themselves?"

"Well, when they went up to the table to put their x mark beside their names on the treaty, the interpreter would tell the secretary who each Choctaw was, and that guy would write down whatever he thought the interpreter had said."

"The guy writing it down didn't know the Indian language, huh?"

"That's right. For some of those chiefs—or mingoes, as we call them—nobody's sure exactly which Choctaw name the guy was trying to write down. For 'Hom Astubby' there are several possibilities. My dad wanted it spelled the same way it was recorded on the treaty. Somebody at the hospital where I was born added a hyphen. It's the middle name on my birth certificate. William Hom-Astubby Mallory."

"William Hom-Astubby Mallory," she said. "I like that. The

hospital wouldn't let your dad spell your name the way he wanted to?"

"Well, Dad always said he figured whoever typed up the birth certificate didn't think my initials ought to be W.H.A.M."

Hom-Astubby sat listening to her laughter, thinking it was the most captivating music he had ever heard.

Her distinctive scent was beginning to fill the camper. He couldn't seem to get enough of that. He drained the last of his coffee and sat smiling at her. He liked her interest in his heritage. She seemed genuinely interested.

"Is much known about Hom-Astubby?"

"Well, it depends on who he really was, exactly. The different people writing down the Choctaw names back then hardly ever spelled them the same." He shrugged. "All we know for sure is that he was a war leader. The suffix, *ubby*—it's sometimes spelled *ubi* or *ubbee*—is a war honor. He was someone who had achieved distinction in battle."

"But not for negotiation."

He laughed. "No. Not for negotiation. Not that time, anyway. That's what my dad wanted me to remember—try to do better than that."

"I think I'd like your dad."

"He'd talk your ear off. He's got a million stories."

"Really? My dad, too. We're Irish. We've visited Ireland often, ever since I was a little girl. I practically grew up there with my cousins on their sheep ranches in the summers, while my parents were doing the show dog circuits. You know, we're an ancient tribal people, too. Not so long ago, the English were still calling us 'the wild Irish.' "

"I've never known any Irishwomen. Does that mean you're a wild Irishwoman?"

She gave him a look that said, silly boy, wouldn't you like to find out.

She said, "There's no such thing as a *tame* Irishwoman."

She drank the last of her coffee. As she excused herself to go to the bathroom, he reached beneath the table and pushed a button. It turned on the flashing lights in the crystals surrounding an inlaid mirror in the hallway.

The flashing lights caught her eye, and she paused in the hallway to admire the crystals as she passed by the mirror.

She stopped with the top half of her torso backlit by the rear window of the camper behind her, which had bright sunlight streaming through it, an arrangement that one of the used-car salesmen on Hom-Astubby's design team had insisted that the engineers and architects get exactly right.

It was an arrangement Hom-Astubby had taken into account in carefully positioning the camper in relation to the sun as he had been parking it at the Shady Rest.

Hom-Astubby held his breath as he saw the thin cloth of her blouse and bra simply evaporate into wispy, ethereal nothingness, leaving a naked breast in full profile vividly displayed. He could feel his blood rushing to Mr. Mindless.

Without bending, she reached around as she lifted her foot behind her to adjust her shoe. She arched her back, thrusting that backlit breast forward, and she jiggled up and down on one foot, trying to get her shoe adjusted. She couldn't quite get it adjusted the way she wanted, and she kept trying and trying, until finally she was able to go on down the hall to the bathroom.

Hom-Astubby caught sight of a mirror giving a reflection of his face. He had a fly-trap mouth. And sitting in that booth had suddenly become uncomfortable.

He got up and washed his face with cold water at the kitchen sink and he tried rearranging his crotch, cat-footing around in his kitchen, pulling and tugging at the fabric of his pants one way and then another, until finally he could sit down again without discomfort.

When she returned, he forced himself not to look, until she slid into the booth across from him.

He said, "Listen, there's something I want to ask you about.

Sarah Peteski told me that you and Earl Paggett and Linda Ruben and Loren Michaels all got your tax returns audited last year. Did she tell you that happened to us? To me and Sarah, back when we first tried investigating one of Towers' companies?"

"Yes, Sarah mentioned that. God, I hope I don't ever have to go through that again. Where do they get those people? They made me feel like I was public enemy number one."

"Mine dragged on for three years. I had to sue my bank, twice, just to get copies of my canceled checks. I finally found out that my bank was owned by another one of Towers' companies."

"We found out a lot of things like that at the *Daily Sun*. Bill, I have to tell you, I'm losing my enthusiasm for investigating Nelson Towers. When I think about what's happened to Earl. What happened to Linda—I mean before she was killed. If Towers killed her, I want to see him burn for it. But I don't think he did it."

"Neither does Sarah. I'm not sure I do either."

"It doesn't make any sense," she said. "Not the way it happened. But it's scary. When we were investigating Towers at the *Sun*, I thought it was all a game. But this guy plays for keeps. I'm not sure he's a murderer. But I'm not sure I want to live my life like Earl, either, obsessed with Nelson Towers."

"I wish I'd never tangled with him in the first place," Hom-Astubby said. "All I've tried to do since then is get away from him and live my life in peace. But after they blacklisted me, I couldn't seem to get away from him. I finally went to law school just to find out if there was anything I could do about it."

"Really? That's why you went?"

"Yes."

"I went because Earl talked me into it, so I could help him investigate Towers."

"Jesus. We've both been living derivative lives."

"Derivative lives," she said, and she looked at him contemplatively. "I hadn't thought about it like that."

"If you could do anything you really wanted to do, what would that be?"

She sat looking at him.

"I mean, during law school, I figured out that what I really wanted to do was outdoor photography. And, by god, that's what I did. And I wanted to write a book about photography. I did that, too."

"I know about your book. I guess you can imagine, Earl did some checking on you. I don't know who he talked to, but they carried weight with Earl."

Hom-Astubby shrugged. "Probably Sarah."

"You don't know Earl. Not that he doesn't trust Sarah. But he doesn't leave much to chance. It was a one-in-a-million shot that Towers brought him down. Earl is very thorough. He'll bounce back. If anybody ever nails Towers, it'll be Earl. He said your book has got some people talking in a way that surprised him, some people in the business who aren't easily impressed. They said it's about a lot more than photography, almost like autobiography. 'The thoughtful engagement of a life with a problem,' one of them said."

"That's good to hear. It looks like I might get to do another one, on photojournalism. But what about you? What do you really want to do?"

She sat looking at him across the dinette table, as though debating something. Hom-Astubby let the seconds tick away, an interested, quizzical look on his face.

She had said that her relationship with George Langley had caused her to rethink some things about herself. What had she meant by that? He wondered why this woman who could have had the world on a plate years ago had walked away from that.

It was almost as though she'd wanted to start all over again, or maybe she'd been running away from something. Why would she now have nothing to do with skiing? Carol Jenkins had said she wouldn't even talk about the Olympics. He wondered if she had ever told anybody why she left Colorado back then.

"Is that how it works?" she said. "If the first book does well, you get to do another one?"

Hom-Astubby shrugged. "I guess. I've only had limited experience with it. Are you writing a book? What's it about?"

"I haven't told anybody."

"You can tell me."

"Can I? I don't know if I can tell anyone."

He wondered if he could get her to tell him about her book. That could be dicey. She didn't seem inclined to talk about it, and they barely knew each other. Pressing her about it might do more harm than good. He wanted to get off on the right foot with her. But he also wondered how many opportunities he would ever have to talk with her alone. Linda Ruben's murder might be solved at any minute. They might go their separate ways, and this moment might turn out to have been his only chance with Avalon O'Neill.

Maybe he should be trying to make an impression on her, one beyond cordial collegiality. Would he want to find himself looking back on this day, wishing he had tried something, anything? What could he do? Maybe this book of hers was the opening he needed. He might take a shot at that.

He wondered if he could somehow coax her to a point where she *wanted* to tell him about her book. Maybe he could try some game that might draw it out of her. That might be worth the risk. Maybe he could get her a little bit off balance, a little flustered, get her to forget her reticence. Then maybe he could get her to tell him at least something about her book.

There was also the delicate matter that sooner or later this woman was going to see what her dog now looked like. He decided to roll the dice.

CHAPTER TWENTY-SIX

He said, "Avalon, don't they teach you Colorado Buffaloes *anything*? When you write a book, the whole world finds out about it. If you're lucky. It's sort of the general idea of the whole thing. They don't let us out of journalism school at Oklahoma if we don't know that."

"Okay, smartass, I know *that*. That's not what I mean. I mean . . ." Her face became serious. "That's what worries me."

"What?"

She leaned across the table toward him and he leaned toward her until their faces were only inches apart. As she leaned, he glimpsed the top of her blouse falling away from her body, but she held his eyes and there was no way he could look at her chest without being obvious.

In his peripheral vision he could see that blouse hanging open, but he could only imagine the view he would have—this close to her—if he could just glance down there for one little instant.

She said, "If I tell you and you make a joke out of it, I'll kill you."

"But not if it makes you laugh. That's a rule I read somewhere."

"Okay," she said, "but you'd better be willing to bet your life on it."

Geez, her breath smelled *so* sweet, so enticing, as fresh as a *garden*, with just the faintest suggestion of apple blossoms. He looked at those red, delicious lips as she spoke, watching her tongue flickering here and there, as though enticing him to press his lips against hers, in open-mouthed delight, and slowly, ever so wonderfully, learn how talented that tongue might be.

He was nearly mesmerized by that dancing, enchanting tongue and the inviting, pulsating rhythm of the way she was opening and closing her mouth, surrounded by those luscious, blood-red lips. Mr. Mindless didn't see the sharp edge of those teeth that her tongue was flickering against, but Hom-Astubby did.

She lowered her voice almost to a whisper.

"Maybe you can understand. Maybe you had to deal with this. Isn't it presumptuous for someone my age to write an autobiography? A partial autobiography. I don't know if I should."

He said, "I don't know." He shrugged. "How old are you?"

She pulled back and sat up straight, putting her hands on her hips. She said, "You don't ask a woman *that*."

He had glanced downward the moment she began pulling back, getting a close-up, fleeting glimpse of those marvelous breasts, so exposed it exceeded anything he had imagined. Mr. Mindless responded instantly, telling him he *liked* this woman.

He saw that she had seen him glancing at her chest. He saw just a faint flicker of triumph in her eyes and he felt Mr. Mindless really begin rising to the challenge. He reminded Mr. Mindless: not today, not with an ovulating woman.

But it was going to be perfect timing with Laura, with her waiting for him in Albuquerque. This Irishwoman was going to have him all revved up and raring to go.

He leaned back casually against the booth and said, "Why not? You brought it up."

"The specific age was incidental to the question." She put her elbows on the table and looked indignant. "A gentleman would know that."

"You're twenty-eight."

Her mouth fell open slightly and she leaned toward him just a little. "How did you know that?"

"A wild guess. But you just confirmed it. Nobody ever accused me of being a gentleman."

She put her hands on her hips again. "I accused you of *not* being a gentleman."

He raised his finger and danced it back and forth, as though conveying great wisdom. "Did you know you have got a keen insight into human nature? It usually takes women longer than that. You should think about writing a book."

She threw her hands in the air. "*That's* what I asked you."

"You're being much too serious. It's so hard to get a book

published. If you've got something to say, you should assume that you're probably wasting your time and just let fly and write the damn thing. Worry about anything else later."

"Really?"

"Really. I made a million excuses for not writing my book. Too young. Experience too limited. Who did I think I was, anyway? No time to write. Who would ever read it? But I had something to say. And most of what I had to say I'd learned years earlier. I finally just said to hell with it and said it. But you're acting so shy about this I think your problem might be that you just don't have anything to say."

She had a sharp intake of breath. "*What?*" And she sat up straight. "But I've *got* something to say! And I'm not the least bit shy."

Yipes. That touched a live wire somewhere. Maybe that's the way to go at it. Anybody who had won an Olympic Gold Medal would have to be as competitive as hell. She might not back away from a direct challenge.

He decided to take a shot at that. He started loading the gun and luring the target within range.

He said, "If you *really* had something to say, you'd be saying it."

"I've *been* saying it. I'm just not very far along."

Her cheeks were a little flushed and she was glancing around the room as though she couldn't believe she was having this conversation.

"Maybe you've said all you had to say."

"I've got lots more to say."

"Then what's holding you back?"

"I *told* you. I don't know if I should."

"Don't know if you should? Or don't know if you want to?"

"I *want* to."

It was time to see if he could get the bullet loaded into the chamber.

He said, "Sounds to me more like you might be afraid to try."

"What?" She looked at him as though she couldn't believe he had said what she had heard.

"That's nothing to be ashamed of. Lots of people are afraid to try. Especially if they don't think they can do it."

"I'm pretty darn sure I can do it!"

Her cheeks were more than just a little flushed and he thought, boy, this might be working.

He said, "Doesn't sound like it to me. Sounds more like you might have a serious hang-up about it."

"What?" She was staring intently at his face.

"I'm just trying to be helpful here." He shrugged. "People who are in denial don't do themselves a favor by trying to do something they really can't do."

Her brow wrinkled and she looked dumbfounded. She gave him a strange look, a look he had never quite seen before. "You don't think I can do it?"

It was time to see if he could rotate the cylinder until the bullet was lined up right in front of the firing pin.

He said, "I might be willing to bet on that."

She stared at him for a full five seconds before saying, with considerably more than just a trace of an Irish accent, "You might be wanting to bet on that, might you?"

"Yeah. I think I might smell a profit here. Lots of people *talk* about writing a book, but they never quite get around to doing it."

She had another sharp intake of breath and sat up rigidly straight, squaring her shoulders. "*I've* not been talking about it! I've never talked about it to *anyone!*"

"And you haven't quite gotten around to doing it, either, have you?"

Her cheeks flushed again. "You are thinking I might not be *up* to doing it, are you?" She spoke it more like a challenge than a question, as the cross-hair sights of her eyes began seeking a target.

"I think it might be a sure thing. I think I might have to call your bluff about not being shy."

"A *sure thing!*" Her eyes widened. "Call *my* bluff!" She tried to jump up out of her seat, but the dinette table stopped her. She banged her lap against the bottom of the table and that bounced her back into the seat.

The jolt sent the empty coffee mugs flying off the table and bouncing across the thickly padded carpet all the way to the edge of the tiled kitchen floor.

He said, "Yeah. Call *your* bluff."

"You want to bet, huh?" Her cheeks definitely had a flush now. She was breathing rapidly, her mouth half-open, her chest rising and falling with each breath.

He said, "Yeah. What do you want to bet?"

"*You* name the bet, *buster*. But take some advice and make it something you can afford."

"I might have to give odds for it to be fair."

Her eyes widened again. "Give *odds!*" She almost jumped up out of the booth again, catching herself just in time, halfway to her feet, and stood there glaring at the tabletop that held her back, as her whole body was quaking.

Timing was everything, and either the target was in range, or it wasn't ever going to come into range.

He cocked the gun.

He said, "Yeah. But I'd need to know a little more about it."

"Like *what?*" she said, as she sat back down.

He could see, from the intense concentration she was giving his face, that if he had succeeded in doing nothing else, he definitely had her full attention. She couldn't seem to sit still, kept shifting around in the booth.

He put his finger on the trigger.

He said, "I'd wonder if you could even tell me the *title* of the book. That's how confident I am that you might be too *shy* to do it."

She chewed her lip and shifted her weight, scooting around on the dinette seat, looking him straight in the eyes, with a concentration so intense it almost unnerved him.

She dropped her hands beneath the table, apparently even beneath her lap, from the way her shoulders were all hunched up and dropped down. The way those shoulders were contracting, she must have been squeezing her arms between her legs. Her upper arms, hanging straight down in front of her body, were completely covering her breasts.

It didn't look very ladylike, but she didn't seem the least bit concerned about that. Perhaps she was restraining herself from jumping up again.

She said, "Oh *yeah?*"

"*Yeah.*"

Her eyes bore into his and her face was flushed nearly crimson.

"You've already started the book. And you've got a title for it, right?"

"That's right," she hissed.

Her bottom was scooting all around on the dinette booth, and her head was bobbing and weaving.

"And you *claim* you're not the least bit shy, right?"

"That's right," she hissed again.

She was scooting around so much she was nearly floating on that seat. And she was licking her lips, her tongue flickering all around them.

In that instant, Hom-Astubby felt the kind of adrenaline rush that might only be known to a mongoose, just inches away from an agitated cobra that's been coaxed to the spring-loaded cusp of striking—and overshooting its target.

Hom-Astubby would have bet the ranch that she had never seen it coming as he had been loading and cocking that gun.

"Okay," he said, giving it the slight initial *h* sound of the Choctaw *hoke* (*hōkāy*), meaning roughly the same thing in both Choctaw and English, with the slight additional Choctaw connotation in this instance of everything being well in hand and the target being well in range.

He pulled the trigger.

He said, "You tell me the *title*, and I'll tell you *what* I'll bet."

What happened next happened almost too fast for him to react.

She sprang from behind the table and onto the dinette seat, giving the tabletop a good slap with her hand, as though it had damn well better behave itself and stay out of her way. She planted both of her feet where her bottom had been and stood up, towering above him.

The instant she got to her feet she leveled the double bore of her intensely concentrating eyes at a target spot right at the top of his nose and drew in a deep breath. Just before launching herself at that imaginary dot right between his eyes she screamed "*Downhill!*"

Her upper body was flying toward him, picking up speed, when her voice broke forth in a thundering *wild* Irish, backcountry *female* roar—"by *Avalanche* O'Neill!"

Hom-Astubby didn't just sit there watching that avalanche coming. He tried desperately to lean forward fast enough to duck beneath her and get his face flat on the table. He didn't make it.

He *might* have made it, just barely. But, as she was bending down, planting both of her hands on the table, braking sharply to bring herself abruptly eye-to-eye with him, his face had only gotten as far down as the top of her wide-open blouse. He made the near-fatal mistake of stopping just long enough to get a breathtaking glimpse of her gloriously nearly naked breasts—an instant before those downhill-racing, suddenly braking, lethally flopping fangs struck him square on the mouth hard enough to nearly knock him out.

He bounced back to a sitting position and found himself face-to-face and eyeball-to-eyeball with an intensely focused Avalon Blanche O'Neill.

He thought maybe his only chance for survival might be to convince her that he was on her side.

He said, "Hell, woman, don't hold anything back. Go for it!"

She said, "Really?"

"That's what you did, wasn't it? Go for it?"

"Yes, I did!"

"And you got it, didn't you?"

"I damn sure did!"

He watched both of her faces floating in front of his eyes, as one of them drifted to the right, and the other one drifted to the left, before drifting back the other way, lining up momentarily as they met each other in the middle, before floating apart again. He was afraid he was going to go permanently cross-eyed trying to focus on both of them.

His vision cleared up just enough to see her beginning to withdraw across the table. He could tell that the top of her blouse was still hanging open, but he couldn't see well enough yet to get a good look at those downright dangerous weapons that had nearly knocked him into next week.

She sat down again in the dinette seat, but as she was preparing to do that, his vision cleared up enough to see her swiveling around on the tabletop, on her hands and knees, right in front of his face. She reached down, putting both of her hands on the dinette seat, to get down off the table, and as her upper body dropped way down, and her bottom was elevated way up, lifting that short skirt with it, Hom-Astubby saw that her little purple panties were every bit as skimpy and sheer as he had imagined.

He leaned out across the table, getting a *good*, *close* look at what this woman was packing beneath those panties. Mr. Mindless went wild.

Curly damp strands of that thick black pubic hair were sticking out from beneath both edges of those panties right at the base of her crotch, in striking contrast to her creamy, white thighs, bringing vividly to mind his very first sight of this woman and the photograph he had spent so much time staring at.

He managed to lean back to his side of the booth before she got seated. She said, "God, I hate that nickname! But that's what they *insist* on calling me."

Jesus. She was still intensely focused on what she had been saying. And she wasn't finished.

She acted as though she didn't even care if he had seen her panties, or if his face had been *inside* her blouse, however briefly. How could she pretend *that* hadn't happened? That one quick taste of her tits had nearly sent him to meet *all* of his ancestors.

She said, "So *I* am going to have the *last* laugh, by using it to help sell the book."

He said, "Help sell the book? Jesus, the book would sell itself."

"I *hope* so."

He sat gazing at her, marveling again at how stunningly beautiful she was, and how uninhibited. He *liked* a lively, high-spirited woman, and she was definitely the liveliest one he had ever met.

She said, "Okay, buster. Now what are you gonna bet?"

He shrugged. "I wouldn't bet against that."

"What? You said you'd bet!"

"I said I'd tell you *what* I'd bet."

"You fraud!" She almost stood up again. "You said you'd call my bluff."

"Hey, you already knew I wasn't a gentleman." He shrugged again. "I just wanted to know what your book's about."

"You *what*?"

"I wanted to know at least something about it."

"You didn't even *intend* to bet?"

"You think I'm a fool? No American woman ever did what you did. I wouldn't bet against you."

"You *knew* you wouldn't bet?"

"Not if I didn't have to. Not if you were right about not being shy. And you know what? You were right about that all along."

Her reaction to that was where Hom-Astubby began falling in love with her.

She put her hands on her hips and stared at him with a look of stunned, indignant discovery, as though for the very first time she had caught a boy being brazen enough to try stealing an unearned kiss while playing post office and didn't quite know what to do about it.

She sputtered for words, finally saying, as though she was going to go home and tell her mother, "You don't play fair!"

"God, you *are* precocious. You have *really* got this keen insight into human nature."

"If you tell me I should write a book, I'm gonna slap the shit outta you!"

"I already told you that."

She slumped back against the dinette booth, folded her arms across her chest, and sat glaring at him. Beneath the table, he could hear her foot tapping on the floor. She sat glaring all around the room, tapping that foot.

There would be hell to pay now. He sighed. Nothing he could do about that but wait to find out how deep a hole he had dug for himself and whether she was going to busy herself shoveling dirt down on top of him or throw him a line so he could try climbing back up.

This was familiar terrain, but if the energy level apparent in the speed of that tapping toe might be some indication, he had a feeling it might be a little deeper hole—with more slippery, somewhat steeper sides—than he was accustomed to. Maybe he'd been just a tad too focused on making sure he brought the target within range. The longer he listened to that tapping toe, the more he wondered if he was about to find out what it was like looking up from the bottom of a well.

He had been giving his fingernails a long, close inspection, marveling at the sustained energy of that female Celtic tapping toe, and wishing he had gotten just a little longer look at those breasts, and wondering what he might do to make the top of that blouse fall away from that fantastic body again, but without a result so life threatening, when he heard the tapping stop.

She unfolded her arms, straightened up, put her hands on her hips and said, "You were pulling my leg, weren't you? The whole time! And I fell for it!"

"Fell for it? I thought you were gonna climb over this table and kick my butt."

"I *should* have!"

"I was about ready to bolt out the door."

"My mother warned me about men like you."

"That's a smart woman, your mother."

"You are exasperating."

"Hey, I *really* wanted to know what your book's about. And now I know. You should write that book."

She glared at him and folded her arms again.

He went back to inspecting his fingernails and listening to the sound of that tapping toe.

When the tapping had *finally* slowed down and almost died away, he said, "I was pretty darn sure you couldn't possibly be as shy about that book as you were acting."

She let out a sigh and unfolded her arms.

"Whatever might be holding you back on that book, it is definitely not shyness."

She looked at him, chewing her lip.

"And it is definitely not lack of confidence, either."

Her forehead wrinkled and she gave him a strange look, the same strange look he had seen when he had been loading that gun.

Uh oh, here it comes. Whatever she has cooked up, the table is spread and here's the first dish. How many courses this meal might have he had no idea, but he knew damn well he'd better be able to eat it all and ask for seconds.

She said, "Was I really about to climb over the table?"

"When you get focused, you do get intense."

"Damn! I've been trying not to *do* that." She seemed disgusted, but more with herself than anything else.

He said, "Hey, I know lots of people who would be way ahead of the game, if only they could get focused and be intense."

She sat up a little straighter, frowning, almost pouting. She said, "But it's not very feminine."

Jesus. He thought he detected a note of genuine hurt in her voice. He couldn't believe that. "Says who?"

"Not the way other women are feminine."

He hadn't been wrong. There *was* pain in her voice. Avalon O'Neill not confident of her femininity? The very thought was ludicrous. But he trusted his ears.

He said, "Are you kidding? You are way ahead of the game in that category. In every category."

She stared at him for a long time before looking down at her lap. She said, in a quiet voice, "I had my arms under the table, didn't I?"

He shrugged. "So what?"

She swallowed hard, and she looked as though she had just been eliminated from the game of life.

Her voice was dead and so were her eyes as she spoke slowly and softly, "I wish you hadn't seen me like that."

He said, "Hey, look at me."

She looked at him.

"Has that stopped me from flirting with you?"

She gave him that strange look again and her eyes narrowed just a little. He couldn't figure out what the strangeness was in that look. It was something he had never seen before in anyone's face. It reminded him, somehow, of his fleeting first impression—that something about her was just a little bit "off."

She cocked her head slightly and asked, "Do you always flirt this way?"

He shrugged. "Pretty much."

She sat looking at him, her brow furrowed.

He said, "It doesn't often work, probably for good reason."

She just sat looking at him.

"But I'm glad you do realize that I am flirting with you."

She looked at him as though he had said something she very much wanted to believe.

He said, "I like flirting with you."

She looked away and seemed, momentarily, almost embarrassed. When she looked back at him, she smiled. A sheepish little smile that pulled together and crystallized all of her possibilities of beauty.

It wasn't the kind of beauty seen when a stunningly attractive woman became, in an instant, dazzling. It was the kind of beauty that projected a person's inner shadow, her *shilup*—in its truest guise and at its most vulnerable moment. A peeking out of that secret shadow, a shadow that doesn't peek at everyone.

The beauty of that little smile took him by surprise. Its impact on him was unfolding, flowering toward its maximum effect, when she reached out and touched the back of his hand, squeezing it in the warmth of her hand.

A live electrical wire couldn't have jolted him any more. He tingled from the nap of his neck to the tips of his toes.

Wow! What was that? He had never felt anything like that before. It was a little frightening.

He smiled at her and composed himself. He had better try steering the conversation away from whatever had led to that.

He said, "And I wasn't kidding about you writing that book. I think you're being damn smart using that nickname as a pen name. Putting that to work for you. You should write that book."

She let out another sigh.

He said, "It would practically write itself."

She gave him a long, steady look.

He said, "It's got to be a hell of a story."

"But . . ." She sat up straight and then leaned toward him a little. "That's what worries me."

"What?"

"The story of that. It's so self-revealing. I'm not talking about being shy. But it might be too self-revealing."

"That's the *nature* of autobiography! God, you Buffaloes are something. That's where you'll find out if that's really what you want to do. If you can't get past that gate, you'll not get down that hill."

She glared at him. "You sound like Mr. Peters, my middle-school slalom coach."

"Did you like him?"

"I do now. I didn't then."

"I can wait a few years for that."

She laughed, in a way he hadn't quite heard before. She looked at him a little differently, too. She chewed her lip again. "I've never told anybody about this. I don't know for sure if I can write that book."

"Your secret's safe with me."

"Is it?" She gave him a long, steady look. "You'd push me to do it, wouldn't you? You'd try to draw it out of me."

He shrugged. "Only if you really wanted to get it out."

He let the seconds tick away, wondering what she was thinking, then added, "But I'd want to know what's in that story. You've got to tell someone. Why not tell the whole world? If that doesn't get it off your chest, nothing will."

She sat looking at him. It was a deeply contemplative, speculative look. For all he knew, she might be thinking about her book. But she might be thinking about him.

She *was* thinking about him. It was plainly evident, after a few moments, in her self-conscious smile.

He smiled, too. He liked that moment of mutual awareness—that realization, and acknowledgment—that they were sitting there thinking about each other.

She said, "You haven't told me what you did this morning." But he could tell that her thoughts weren't entirely on finding out what he had done.

He had no idea if the dice he had rolled had come up seven or eleven or snake eyes with Avalon O'Neill. But he liked this moment. He didn't regret having given those dice a roll.

He might end up second-guessing himself for a long time, wishing he had never loaded that gun. Maybe that hadn't been the right game to play with her. But at least he had taken a shot.

And if that was all there was to the meal she had cooked up, Mr. Mindless might some day soon be sneaking in and out of her kitchen, tasting for free what one more cook had thought she might sell for a good price.

In his mind's eye he consulted her menu, flipping through the offerings, noting the days her most dangerous dish might be avoided, as Mr. Mindless wiggled with delight at the prospect of sneaking into a glorious kitchen and snatching a rare and special desert.

CHAPTER TWENTY-SEVEN

Avalon O'Neill went to the bathroom again while he gathered up the coffee mugs that had been bounced onto the carpet. He rinsed them out at the kitchen sink while thinking about her. There was a lot to think about, some of it very puzzling.

She returned shortly, looking even more stunning. He stood for a moment, gazing at his face in the mirror above the sink, asking himself if there could possibly be another woman, anywhere, who could cast such a spell over him.

They sat down again at the dinette table.

"This morning," Hom-Astubby said, "I followed up on a lead I stumbled onto when I was back home in Oklahoma. I found something back there when I looked at a photo I had taken up here. It was one of the crime scene photos I'd shot at that picnic table Tuesday afternoon, where Linda Ruben was killed. I shot a few panoramas from that picnic table, in every direction, all around it, using different lenses. One of those photos showed the cliffs across the river. Something at the top of those cliffs caught my eye."

"What was it?"

"A telephoto lens, sticking out of the bushes."

"You mean, a camera?"

"Yes. I had to make several enlargements of that photo to be sure. But there's no doubt about it. Somebody had been up there, watching the cops work that crime scene on Tuesday afternoon. That got me to wondering. Maybe that person had been up there on Monday, too. Maybe he might know something about the murder."

Avalon O'Neill was distracted. She was looking beyond Hom-Astubby into some far distance.

She said, "That telephoto lens had a clear view of the picnic table?"

"Yes."

"And it might have been there on Monday, too?"

"I think there's a good chance of that."

"Oh, no."

"What's wrong?"

"Bill, I took a walk down the river late Monday morning, down to that picnic table. I fell in the water. I had to dry my clothes on the bushes at that picnic table."

"You mean . . . you had to undress at that picnic table?"

She looked uncomfortable. "It was an accident. I'd slept in the tent after a long drive from Denver. I just wanted to freshen up a little. I found a really secluded place to do that. There's a little creek off in the brush behind that picnic table, with thick brush all around it. There was no way anybody could see me, not even from up on that cliff. I wanted to wash my underarms, so I took off the sweatshirt I was wearing. I was crouched down beside the water when Lady jumped at a chipmunk. The big galoot. She knocked me into the creek."

"Your clothes got wet."

"Soaking wet. Everything except the sweatshirt I'd taken off. And god was that water cold. That picnic table seemed the best place to spread everything out to dry, on the bushes there. They were in the bright sunshine. I had to strip off all of those wet clothes, everything, and wait a few minutes to dry off before I could put on that sweatshirt. I didn't get my hair wet, and I got into that sweatshirt as quickly as I could. It's pretty long. I could pull it down over my hips. But still, I was a little nervous about somebody coming along. Then . . ."

She thought for a moment, as though searching for words. She shrugged. "I don't know. I just felt kind of free and daring. Bold. I walked down to the edge of the river. It wasn't far, but god, a couple of guys in a boat came down the river and almost saw me. I had to lie down and hide from them behind some big rocks while they were fishing. I thought they were never going to leave."

"Geez," Hom-Astubby said. "If you got undressed at that picnic table, and then got dressed there, that would be in the direct line of sight of that telephoto lens, if that guy was up on that cliff on Monday morning."

She looked worried. "Bill, we've got to find out. If somebody has got photos like that it could ruin my career. Would they be close-ups? From that far away? Could I really be identified or would it just look like some naked woman at a distance?"

"Yeah, with that kind of lens they would be close-ups. Like the photographer was standing right beside you. This complicates things."

She looked undecided about something, but took a deep breath and said. "I think you might need to know something else. It wasn't just at that picnic table. I took off that sweatshirt down there beside the river. I just wanted to stand there naked. Out there in the open. Just me and the river and that beautiful valley. God, it felt so good, until I saw that boat coming around the bend."

"I can understand that." Hom-Astubby shrugged.

"It was a foolish thing to do. I never thought about anything like this."

"Well, I think I might have taken care of this problem."

"What do you mean?"

"That's what I did this morning. Find out who was up on that cliff."

"You did? Who was it? How did you do that? Do you think they saw me?"

"Well, I figured whoever was up on that cliff on Tuesday might come back again. So I went there this morning before daylight and set up a camouflage blind, to hide and see if anyone showed up. Sure enough, somebody did. A young guy. He didn't have a camera or a telephoto lens or anything, but he came to that exact spot where I figured that telephoto lens had been set up. You can see the Purple Pentagon from there. I figure that's why he had picked that spot in the first place. I think he did that just to have someplace to put that lens to use, to experiment with it. I'm pretty sure the guy stole that lens and the camera that went with it. The sheriff had told me about a powerful telephoto lens stolen out of a vehicle recently."

Avalon O'Neill was concentrating intently on everything he was saying. She had put her hands way down under the table again, in that same posture he had seen earlier, as though squeezing her arms between her legs, with her shoulders dropped down and hunched together. And she was scooting her bottom around a bit on the dinette seat.

She didn't seem to be aware of her posture. What she had said about femininity came back to him. It was definitely not a very ladylike posture. Could she be unaware of how she was sitting? He wondered what else she might not be aware of.

She changed her posture, taking her arms from between her legs and placing her hands beneath her outer thighs, sitting on her hands, but with her shoulders still hunched up.

As he talked, she began leaning toward him, as though she didn't want to miss a single word. The more she leaned, the more her blouse fell away from her body.

She seemed unaware of that. Hom-Astubby swallowed hard. Could she not know what she was doing?

She was staring directly into his eyes, licking her lips. But there was something about her eyes. They didn't seem as alive and alert as they should be. And they didn't really seem focused on his eyes, more like right between his eyes.

Would she even notice if he weren't making eye contact with her?

He lowered his gaze, with a bad feeling he might be violating her. But, despite himself, what he saw took his breath.

Her blouse was covering no part of her breasts, and her low-cut bra barely clung to her nipples. With her shoulders hunched, the bra wasn't tight across her chest. It looked as though the least bit of movement might shake it loose, and she wasn't sitting still.

He looked quickly into her eyes, seeing that she had no awareness of where his eyes had been. He continued gazing into those unaware, innocent eyes, but that didn't erase the image of that frail piece of cloth about to drop away from those nipples.

There was nothing he could do to stop the swelling in his britches. His eyes pleaded with her eyes for help, but got no response. Hadn't anyone ever explained to her that, while most men might have a conscience, no man's Mr. Mindless had one?

He stared at her eyes as he finished talking. He couldn't quite put his finger on what was wrong with those eyes. They seemed to have lost some essential human quality and looked more . . . more . . . hmmmm . . . more reptilian than anything else. She was licking her lips rapidly, so rapidly her tongue was nearly flickering here and there.

Despite himself, he could not keep from looking again to see if that cloth had dropped. The sound of his heart pounding in his ears nearly deafened him, as he glanced at her chest.

The bra had slipped just a little bit more. It could not possibly hang there even a moment longer.

He panicked. "I've got to get a glass of water," he said, as he scrambled out of the booth and went to the kitchen sink.

She said, in a perfectly normal voice, "You think it was somebody just taking photos for kicks? Some kid who had stolen that equipment?"

He ran cold water and washed his face, staring at himself in the mirror. Jesus, is there no way to tell when she is impaired like this, except for her posture and her eyes?

She can think and speak and analyze complex facts when she is locked in the grip of this thing? But she becomes unaware of other things? Becomes vulnerable? In a world that preys on the vulnerable?

How in hell could she have achieved so much and *be* like this?

He said, in an unsteady voice, "I'm pretty sure about that now."

He took a deep breath. "And I don't think he'd try to get that film developed just anywhere."

He took another deep breath. "So I don't think any of it has likely been developed yet."

She said, "Can I please have a glass of water, too?"

His hands were trembling as he filled a small glass with water to take to her. But when it was full he had to set it on the counter and take several deep breaths.

He could not bring himself to turn around to take it to her. He had two problems.

One was what he might see, that he should not see, when he carried the water to the table, if she was still in that trance, or whatever it was.

And the other problem was what *she* might see, that she should not see—the enormous bulge in his britches—if she was back to normal.

As the seconds ticked away, and he stood there, paralyzed, he finally figured out what to do.

He said, "Here's your water," picking up the glass and setting it down a little farther along the counter, slopping out a bit of it over the rim. "I've got to go to the bathroom."

He didn't come out of the bathroom until he had run enough cold water on his face and had cat-footed around enough, tugging at the crotch of his britches, to get himself presentable. But his head was spinning.

When he got back to the kitchen she was as cool as could be, with the water glass sitting empty beside her on the dinette table. Her hands were folded in front of her.

He eased into the booth, seeing that her eyes were alert and alive.

She said, "Boy, it's a relief if you really think none of those pictures might have been developed yet."

He said, "I'd bet money that none of them have."

He looked into those beautiful, shimmering green eyes, marveling again at how stunningly attractive she was. And he glanced at her blouse, draped so thinly over those heavenly pointing breasts.

He felt the beginning of pressure in his crotch again. Damn. This wasn't fair. Women should have to spend just one day in a man's body. Just one day.

He put his face in his hands and rubbed his eyes, thinking about Avalon O'Neill. He felt like a jerk. She must not have been aware of nearly knocking him out with her breasts, or that she had given him a good look at her panties. But he hadn't known. OK. So now he knew. So, now what?

He had never before been in a situation like this. What *was* this situation? She was not *mentally* impaired. Christ, she was a lawyer. She was out in the world, on her own. A talented, competitive, intelligent career woman.

OK. So what were the rules here? What should they be? He could allow himself to feel lust for this woman—when she *wasn't* going cuckoo on him?

"Are you all right?" she asked.

"Huh? Oh, yeah. I'm okay. I was just thinking."

He drew a deep breath and did some more thinking. Damn. She was waiting for him to start talking again. What should he say? Better yet, what should he *not* say? He could feel himself beginning to sweat.

She didn't seem to know much about cameras or telephoto lenses, not enough to realize that the kind of lens he'd been talking about was a rare and expensive surveillance lens that only somebody like a private investigator or some intelligence service might own.

He didn't want her worrying about the possibility that Nelson Towers might have nude photos of her. That seemed unlikely now. No need to have her thinking about something like that. Something she might concentrate on intently.

Hom-Astubby drew a deep breath and said, "When that guy showed up this morning he didn't stay very long."

He watched her eyes as he spoke. As long as her eyes were alert and alive, that might be his best clue.

He continued, "There wasn't much going on down at that picnic table, probably wasn't much going on down there yesterday, either. That's probably why he'd stopped bringing that lens with him."

"Did you follow him?" she asked.

"Yes."

It occurred to him that if he was going to sit here all morning, afraid to take his eyes off her eyes, that might be a pretty good payback for the trick he had played on her about that bet *and* about trying to sneak a peek inside her blouse. Had she manipulated him into this? He remembered she had caught him glancing at her chest before she started going cuckoo on him.

Could she possibly be pulling his leg? Could this be just one more course in a long meal she had cooked up for him? Could she possibly have learned how to do her cooking from Choctaw women, exacting *that* kind of price to get into her kitchen?

His eyes narrowed a bit as he said, "He led me through the woods behind that hill, to an old house. It's really secluded. It's at the end of a dirt road up there that looks like it comes from somewhere down on the highway."

"From down here? The highway we're on?"

"Yeah."

If she *was* pulling his leg, damn she was good. What might she be trying to do? And if she *wasn't* pulling his leg, what might happen? How much trouble might he get himself into with this woman, either way? He'd better be thinking about this.

He said, "That road must come from somewhere down here. One of those roads that go off into the woods between the Purple Pentagon and Alpine. I had a chance to search that house. It gave me the creeps."

He remembered what Granny had been telling him, from the time he was a little boy. Granny knew about witches. She said they ride the lightning, that anything struck by lightning is witched. He remembered the tingling he'd felt when Avalon O'Neill had touched his hand. That felt like lightning. Granny said when a witch casts a spell over a man she can get him to do what he does not want to do, and he would be helpless to resist.

"It was spooky?" she said.

He swallowed hard. "Really spooky. One room was almost like a military barracks, with bunk beds and footlockers full of guns. God, I don't ever want to go back there." Was *that* what a witch would make him do, go back there? He swallowed hard again. "It looks like that place belongs to some crazy white supremacist organization. There was literature all over the house. The most awful kind of hate propaganda against blacks, and Jews, and Chicanos—anybody not Anglo-Saxon lily white. Jesus, they probably think Indians are not much different from insects."

Hom-Astubby was having trouble keeping things straight between what he was saying to her and what he was saying to the gods. He was negotiating with the gods.

He had just promised them that he would never again play another trick on any woman as long as he lived, if he might be allowed to escape from the spell this one had cast on him.

He then expanded that promise to include not playing any more tricks on *anyone.*

He would apologize to Johnny for saddling him with those two little nymphomaniac midgets.

He was trying to figure out what else he might throw in, to sweeten the deal, when Avalon O'Neill said "Bill!" as she reached across the table and put her hands on top of his, squeezing them tightly.

Ooooooooh. He felt all the anxiety leaving his body.

Her hands were so warm, and the pressure she was applying felt so good.

This wasn't the touch of a witch. This was the touch of an angel. Better than that, this was the touch of the warm, beautiful, captivating creature who was holding hands with *him.*

And boy, if she liked to touch, and be touched, he might not care what kind of spells she cast.

He told the gods—time out—maybe he could handle things on his own. No need to be rushing into some rash promises here. Maybe he could afford to find out a little more about this before jumping into some bargain he might not need to be making.

After all, she was a *woman,* and women were to be listened to.

He tried making a lightning-quick assessment of the cross-cultural complexities that might be working against him here.

Where he came from, women ruled the roost. In fact, Choctaw

women had created a problem for themselves that they were having a hell of a time trying to figure out what to do about—all the white women snatching up their men as fast as they could because Choctaw men had been trained from birth to do whatever a woman told them to do. It was all complicated by the kind of dating and mating games the Choctaw women played, which scared their men right into the waiting arms of those white women, where, if nothing else, a man could at least relax.

That's what he should do. Relax. Get a grip on things. Would he even want the gods to know that he had chickened out on his chance with Avalon O'Neill?

She said, "That's a Teton safe house!" as she squeezed his hands again.

Hom-Astubby took a deep breath. Oh, her hands felt so good. He looked around the room. Maybe he wasn't going about this the right way. He ought to think about what kind of impression he was making on this woman. Women everywhere weren't *that* much different about some things. Women liked to be protected. They liked to feel safe.

Tetons, huh? He shrugged nonchalantly. He said, "That's what was on their literature. How did you know about them? I'd never heard of them."

"I hadn't either," she said, "except for the violence of their gangs in the prisons. God, they castrated that poor guy they took hostage last year. You didn't hear about that? You don't know what a risk you took." She gave his hands one last squeeze.

She was withdrawing her hands across the table when he reached out and overtook them and pulled them back toward him. He squeezed them for a moment—then he held them for a long time, turning them over, caressing them, running his fingers lightly over them.

She said, "That feels *good*," and she smiled at him.

She ran her fingers lightly up his forearm as she said, "Most people think the Tetons are only in the prisons. They're very secretive about what they do on the outside. They're paranoid about that. And vicious. George told me about them, and about that house up there." She gave his hands a big squeeze before withdrawing them.

The mention of George Langley made Hom-Astubby frown. What could she possibly have seen in that guy? What might she still be seeing in him? Was it over between them? Jesus, would he want to see this woman back in the arms of *that* jerk?

He took a deep breath. He said to himself: if this woman is just trying to teach me a lesson, perhaps some cockamamie *white-woman* notion about how a gentleman should manage his eyes, no matter *what* the temptation, the thing to do would be to let her win this round.

She just doesn't *understand* about testosterone, no matter how much she might have read about it.

If he let her see that he could be a good sport about this sort of thing, that he could take his lumps when they might be deserved—and, after all, he *had* asked for it—he might turn this to his advantage.

And if she *wasn't* trying to teach him a lesson, then there were a *lot* of things he needed to find out about before he proceeded with anything other than extreme caution. Cordial collegiality might not be such a bad idea until he got a better feel for the situation, a better idea of what he might be getting himself into if he pursued this Irishwoman.

Hom-Astubby began concentrating more on what she was saying.

CHAPTER TWENTY-EIGHT

He asked, "What did George Langley say?"

"George said that some federal agency, either the FBI or the ATF, or somebody, has infiltrated them. The Tetons are not the brightest candles ever lit. They think they are the *Teutons*, but they don't even know how to spell it. The federal people know everything the Tetons are doing. They're going to bomb a federal judge's house somewhere in Arizona pretty soon. That's all George would tell me about that. I don't think he knows very much about that part of it. But the federal people have been all over George to keep Linda's murder investigation away from that house."

"Why?"

"Because those federal agents know that the Tetons had nothing to do with Linda's murder. They know that nobody is at that house except some Teton from Georgia. Some guy named Uber. They know that Uber was in western Montana at a meeting at the Teton compound when Linda was killed. That house you searched is going to be their staging ground for bombing that judge in Arizona."

"Jesus."

"Bill, you took a big risk. Uber's job is to keep that house safe, not let anybody near it. Those federal agents don't want anything messing up their undercover operation. They're already nervous that Linda's murder, so close to that house, and the swarms of people down here, might cause the Tetons to change their plans. They want the Tetons to carry this thing out, as far as getting to Arizona, so they can arrest them there with all the evidence."

"George Langley told you all of this?"

"Yes. He would be furious if he knew I told anybody. I'm pretty sure no one else in the media knows about that house. I'm pretty sure hardly anybody anywhere knows about it—certainly not any of the local people. Those federal agents wouldn't have told George, except they had to. I think he told me just to impress me with how much he knows, to keep me close to him. But god, we've got to be careful what we do. We've got two problems here, the Tetons and the federal agents. We can't let either one of them find out that you were in that house."

"The feds are watching that house?"

She shook her head. "They think there's no need for that. Their infiltrator is apparently somebody pretty high in the organization at that compound in Montana. George said that guy was adamant that nobody, but nobody, except Uber is up there at that house. He said the Tetons are absolutely paranoid about that sort of thing. George said they make Uber go to places like Cortez to buy groceries and gas, so nobody will even know that *he* is here."

"But I followed that young guy there."

She shrugged. "I don't know how to explain that. From the way George talked, Uber is an older guy. He said he'd already done something like a fifteen- or twenty-year prison term."

"Yeah. There was an older guy there, too. The kid called him 'Uncle Charlie.' "

"That's what George called him. Charles Uber. He's letting a nephew stay there? I don't think the federal agents or the Tetons know about that."

"Well, Uber wasn't happy about it. I heard him tell that kid to stay hidden in an old mine behind the house that's been converted into kind of a garage and storage shed. Uber cussed him out and knocked him down when he came driving up and found the kid sitting on his front porch. Uber told him to stay hidden until he could take him somewhere Sunday night. But that kid didn't listen to him. As soon as Uber drove off, the kid left, walking toward Alpine."

"Do you think that kid might have had something to do with Linda's murder?"

"I don't know. I think there might be a good chance of that. If he didn't, he might have seen it. I found the stolen telephoto lens in that old mine-garage. I found that kid's driver's license, too, an expired Georgia driver's license in an old billfold. His name is Lawrence Selden Lindquist."

"Lawrence Selden Lindquist," she repeated.

"Avalon, if he killed Linda, and if he saw you naked, he might be looking for you, might be stalking you. Please tell me you'll be careful. You've got to be alert to your surroundings. Not be going anywhere alone where you might be vulnerable."

"What does he look like?"

"He's twenty-four years old, according to his driver's license. He's five feet ten, skinny, with short sandy hair."

"You want me to find out about him?"

"No need to. I've got a friend who now works at the *Atlanta Star-Herald*. I'm going to call him and have him check on that kid. But I also found a bunch of rolls of exposed film he may have taken with that telephoto lens. I took that film."

"That might be film of me?"

"Maybe."

He watched her eyes closely. Hadn't the possibility of nude photos of her set her off a while ago?

He said, "I don't think that Georgia kid will miss it right away. He had it hidden behind some clothes in a drawer. I was thinking when I took the film that I could sneak back up there later and replace it with some bad exposed film, and when that kid tried to get it developed he'd just think that none of the photos turned out, that something was wrong with that telephoto lens. But now I don't want to go back up there at all."

"God, Bill. Please stay away from there."

"I will."

She seemed OK. She'd been paying close attention, but her eyes were lively and normal. Normal, hell. Those dazzling green eyes were beautiful.

He said. "I've also got a friend who runs a photo lab in Albuquerque. I called her a while ago to see if I could come down to her lab and develop that film. I told her it was very sensitive, something private. But she's a really great gal. She said come on."

"She did, did she?" Avalon O'Neill sat up straight, peering intently at Hom-Astubby. She said, with a trace of an Irish accent, "And might this lass, by any chance, be an old girlfriend?"

"Huh? Well, she used to be. That's what I was planning on doing after meeting you here this morning, go on down there to her lab."

"You were, were you?"

He paused, seeing that she was paying *very* close attention to him now, so close it made him a bit jittery. Her eyes made him a little nervous, too. Something about them reminded him of a trip he had taken to the Oklahoma City Zoo, where he'd been face-to-face through the bars with the spectacular green eyes of an intently curious, full-grown female tiger. He thought—she doesn't want me looking at nude photos of her.

He said, "But that was *before* you told me that you might be in those photos. If you don't want me to see them . . ."

"Don't worry about that," she said. "I'm not *that* bashful. Just don't stare at them too much."

That emboldened him a bit. He leaned closer to those unblinking feline eyes and said, "I don't think there's much chance of me being able to keep a promise like that."

"Okay." She smiled a bit self-consciously, even a little invitingly. "I guess I'll not hold you to that. Just don't let anybody else see them."

"I won't. But we've got some potential problems here we need to think about. What if it turns out that Georgia kid *was* up on that cliff on Monday and he not only got photos of you but also got photos of the murderer, or maybe even of the murder taking place? Or what if it turns out that Georgia kid *is* the murderer? I'm going to be tampering with evidence by processing that film. I might have already tampered with evidence, just by taking it out of that mine-garage."

"Jesus," she said. "That hadn't even occurred to me." She was quiet for a moment. She frowned. "We could really mess up the investigation into Linda's murder, mess up the evidence the prosecuting attorney would need for trial."

"We could get ourselves into one hell of a lot of trouble is what we could do."

Avalon O'Neill frowned again. "Do . . . do you think we should wait about developing that film? Maybe taking it down to that woman's lab in Albuquerque wouldn't be the best thing to do right now."

Hom-Astubby shrugged. "That Georgia kid might miss it before long."

She chewed on her lip. "Do . . . do you think we should put that film back and tell the cops about it?"

"Not if there might be photos of you on that film."

Hom-Astubby was beginning to get nervous again. He didn't know why, just something about the way she was acting.

He watched her eyes closely as he said, "You wouldn't want the cops getting that. They're just a funnel to the prosecuting attorney, Holmes. Or maybe George Langley. Langley's multijurisdictional intervention would include prosecution, wouldn't it? Boy, that could be a mess. Langley, with nude photos of you? He might have to introduce them as evidence in open court."

She shuddered. "God, I'd hate to think what might happen if George got those photos. He might be confronted with violating his oath in trying to protect me, if he'd even be able to do that. If, by then he'd even want to protect me . . ."

She stared at the table. "He hasn't accepted our breakup. He's really only interested in me for a campaign wife. Surely he wouldn't use those photos to try forcing me back to him, to make me choose between . . ." She sat staring at the table.

He said, "And what if it turns out there isn't much on that film except photos of you? There's no way to find out except to process that film."

She looked at him, frowning. "This is getting complicated. There are too many variables, and we're risking getting into trouble."

"If we weren't lawyers," he said, "maybe we wouldn't be aware of some of the problems we might be getting into."

"But Bill, we do know. If this blows up on us, we won't be able to make many excuses."

"Yeah. This could get really complicated. But I'm glad we're in it together. We can draw strength from each other, figure out how to work our way through it."

She put her hands on his and squeezed them tightly. "Bill, I want you to know how much I appreciate the risk you took to get that film."

She didn't withdraw her hands. He took them in his hands and held them, marveling at their warmth.

She said, "I'm a little scared about what might happen."

"We had better keep this just between the two of us. Not say anything about that Teton house or that Georgia kid or that telephoto lens to anybody, until we find out more about what we're dealing with. Okay?"

She nodded. "Okay."

They sat holding hands across the table, smiling at each other.

He was relieved that she hadn't gone cuckoo on him again. They had discussed some fairly complex things, which required a good deal of concentration. That hadn't triggered anything. He wondered what did.

She appeared perfectly capable of functioning normally. He could not for the life of him figure out whether or not she might have been pulling his leg. If so, he knew damn well he should never get into a poker game with this woman or she would clean him out.

But there was more to all of this than she realized. He didn't want to tell her about Wally Street's stolen briefcase. Despite what she had said about staying away from that house, he was afraid she might make him go back and try to get it, and he did not want to go back to that house.

He damn sure didn't want to see her going there, which she might do, if she knew about the briefcase and he wouldn't go get it for her. He'd end up going back there with her.

He also didn't want to tell her that the Georgia kid matched the description of the young man who had attacked the woman at the laundry in Alpine, if she didn't already know about that attack. He had a bad feeling that the Georgia kid was going to turn out to be the one who had killed Linda Ruben.

He didn't want Avalon O'Neill to know how nervous he was becoming that he might already have tampered with evidence, might already have committed obstruction of justice—or how afraid he was that what he was about to do in Albuquerque was going to plunge him a lot deeper into that.

But he had felt compelled to give her some hint of that because she was involved, too. He told himself he just wanted to protect her, especially from Langley, if that kid's film contained any nude photos.

If there were more women who got a thrill out of being naked like she had been, down by the river, the world would be one hell of a lot more interesting place. If anybody was going to see those photos, he wanted to be that person. And if there *were* photos of Avalon O'Neill standing beside that river, buck naked, he hoped to hell that little shit from Georgia knew how to operate that telephoto lens.

He tried not to think about how much trouble he might be getting himself into.

He looked down at their hands, clasped together on the table, so his eyes could stray to her chest, for just a moment, without her noticing.

As he watched, she drew in a deep breath and stretched her shoulders a bit, arching her back, pulling his hands toward her a little, and squeezing them as she stretched, as though she might be getting tired of sitting in the dinette booth. When she stretched, the thin cloth of her blouse pressed against her low-cut bra. He nearly bit his tongue.

And oh, the way she was squeezing his hands felt so good. She stretched even more, pulling him toward her. And then even more, pulling his hands all the way to her.

She held them there for a moment, pressed against her stomach, as she gave a big stretch, and he could feel her heartbeat pounding against his hand. It was pounding fairly rapidly, almost as rapidly as his.

Being so close to her, he suddenly became aware of how over-poweringly intoxicating her scent had become. He just wanted to stay where he was, drinking deeply of that wonderful aroma that spoke a language all its own—saying warm, moist, young, healthy, *fully alive* female.

After she stopped stretching she relaxed her grip on his hands but she didn't let go of them. Several seconds passed before he realized he was leaning far across the table, where she had pulled him, and that he had been daydreaming a bit, staring at her chest, only inches from his eyes. He realized that he had been daydreaming for the whole time since she had stopped stretching.

There was no hope that what he was staring at could be anything but obvious.

He let go of her hands and sat back in the booth, avoiding her eyes, feeling the awkwardness of the moment.

He said, "Well, we won't know anything until I get that film processed and get those photos printed. I don't see what we could do, except for me to go on down to her lab in Albuquerque and do that. We'll just have to hope there aren't any nude photos of you, and then we can take it from there. Maybe we're worried about nothing."

She said, "I hope so."

Then she said, "Darn. My ankle is itching."

She reached down to scratch it, with her blouse falling forward just a little, but not dangerously so.

She smiled at Hom-Astubby as she scratched, and then, looking a bit beyond him and frowning, she strained a little, obviously trying to get herself scratched just right to relieve that itching.

She strained a little more, still frowning, and as she leaned a little more forward, her blouse fell farther away from her body and began falling open at the top. Hom-Astubby averted his eyes, still feeling the awkwardness of the previous moment.

He chewed his lip for a few seconds, and then he glanced at her. She was looking down toward her ankle, intent on her scratching. She wasn't bent all *that* much forward. Her breasts weren't all *that* much visible. But they were *coming* into view. He took a deep breath, pondering the unwritten rules of cordial collegiality.

He said to himself: there doesn't *seem* to be very much that is really wrong with this woman, and there is nothing whatsoever wrong with her at *this* moment—she is just scratching her ankle. She is fair game.

He allowed himself one little peek at those magnificent breasts, marveling at their capacity to engage his attention, knowing that the sight of those breathtaking twins would never fail to arouse his interest anew, no matter *how many* times he might have seen them.

She leaned a little farther forward, and he leaned a little closer across the table, as far as he dared, without being obvious, getting a better look.

He was getting a *good* look as she leaned over a bit more, reached down a little farther. His pulse quickened as every bit of that blouse fell away and there was nothing left covering those nearly-naked breasts but that skimpy little bra, with those nipples so vividly jutting out through that thin little purple patch of cloth, as though they were straining to reach out to him, a sight that filled him with an aching desire that they might somehow do that very thing, and filled him with a worshipful sense of reverence and awe for how they could induce in him such a longing to be allowed just to taste them, just to put one of them in his mouth, if only for a moment. Then she pulled the trigger.

She hunched her shoulders. The bra crumpled up and fell away from her chest, not just for a moment, but long enough for an image to emblazon itself permanently on his brain—two beautifully engorged nipples, swollen blood-red, standing hard and erect, and moving, ever so slowly, straight for his wide-open mouth.

Hom-Astubby's last functionally intelligent thought was an awareness of the ballooning in his britches, just before that drained so much blood from his brain it began relaxing the muscles in his face.

By the time enough blood had been drained from his brain that his tongue was hanging out, his IQ had been lowered somewhere into the borderline range between slobbering moron and drooling idiot.

As that swollen nipple on the nearest breast came brushing past his upper lip and buried itself in the most sandpapery part of his tongue, beginning its scratchy, pressing caress, so much of his blood had gone south, he couldn't even close his mouth.

He wasn't aware that she had climbed across the table, where she got her hands on the back of his head and buried that achingly-itchy breast as deep as she could push it.

Exactly *what* happened after that he would never be able to remember, except for dreamy, wispy snatches here and there.

His next functionally intelligent thought—that one being panic—didn't occur until he lay gazing up at the mirrored ceiling above his bed, admiring how great her naked body looked on top of him, all wrapped around him and all glistening wet with sweat, hugging him so very tightly, when he saw the big grin on his face and heard Avalon O'Neill purring in his ear, "Oh, Bill, that was *wonderful*. Let's do it again."

CHAPTER TWENTY-NINE

When Avalon O'Neill finally led Hom-Astubby to the bathroom he could barely walk. If she hadn't been holding his hand, pulling him along, he might not have made it. She bathed him like a baby and then steamed him nearly to unconsciousness in the sauna.

She seemed to know a trick or two about reviving spent men by following up the sauna with a cold shower, bringing Hom-Astubby gradually back to life.

She made coffee while they were picking up their clothing and getting dressed, and then she sat him down in the dinette booth and pampered him with the hot, reviving brew, while sitting beside him and kissing the side of his neck, his forehead, his hair, his cheeks, his throat, his hands.

She finally took his hand in hers and sat holding it, humming with warmth and contentment and looking lovingly into his eyes.

He said to himself: you know, it could be worse.

She said, "Get yourself some more coffee and relax while I fix my hair. I'll only be a jiff."

She patted his leg and squeezed his thigh, saying, "Oh, Bill, you're a champion. I think I might keep you."

She kissed his cheek before leaving, and he watched every skirt-swishing, high-stepping stride she took, all the way to the bathroom door.

It seemed almost as though she was back instantly, her hair looking the same as it had when she arrived that morning, and he realized he had been so lost in daydreaming he had no idea how long she was gone. He hadn't gotten himself any more coffee.

He did that now, getting a mug for her. They sat beside each other in the dinette booth, sipping their coffee, their bodies pressed closely together.

Now would come *the talk*. He was a past master at avoiding this episode, but this time there were a few things he thought advisable to find out about, at least to get *some* clue about. But he knew he should go about that obliquely.

He told her he'd been impressed by her story in the *L.A. Dispatch*, about the clandestine videotape.

"I wish I could take full credit for it," she said. "But it just fell into my lap. Loren should have gotten the credit. I found out everything from him."

"He got the credit for the videotape. And he's a video guy, right?"

"That's true."

"You guys really nailed Nelson Towers. That's got to ratchet up the heat on him. God, that's an awful mixed metaphor, isn't it?"

She laughed. "You should see some of the ones I write. Earl's pretty good about catching them. But he's not gentle about it."

They sipped their coffee. He admired how the sunlight, streaming through the window, was highlighting her hair. He glanced out the window wondering if anyone might have heard them in bed. He had been surprised at how vocal she had become. At the height of her passion she had hit some marvelously impressive high notes. But they were parked at the far end of the big gravel parking lot, well away from the gas station, and all the windows in the camper were closed.

"One thing, though," she said. "Wally Street didn't show up on that video. Just his voice. I wish I knew what he looks like."

"No problem," he said. "I've got a photo of him I took here Monday afternoon."

"Really? You saw him here? And took a photo? But it couldn't have been Monday."

"Yes. It was Monday. I'm sure."

"But it couldn't have been here."

"Yeah, it was here in Alpine. Well, on that dirt road behind the Purple Pentagon. He stopped by to check on how that work crew from Texas was doing, building that new gate across the road."

Avalon O'Neill was sitting very still, staring at Hom-Astubby as though holding her breath.

She said, "Bill, Wally Street told the police that he never left Telluride on Monday."

Hom-Astubby was lifting his coffee mug to his lips, but he froze. He lowered the mug. "Are you sure?"

"Yes, I'm sure. George showed me the police interviews with both Wally Street and Nelson Towers. They both swore that they never left Telluride on Monday."

Hom-Astubby felt an excitement he could barely contain. He said, "Avalon, I've got a photo of *both* Wally Street *and* Nelson Towers, *here*, in Alpine, on Monday afternoon."

They stared at each another, neither one daring to breathe.

She said, "Bill, *please*. Show me that photo."

"It's in my camera bag, in the cab. Let me get it."

He could barely unlock the door to the cab of the truck, his mind was racing so fast. God, could it be possible that Nelson Towers had lied to the police, and they could prove it? He grabbed the bag and hurried back into the camper.

They sat beside each other again at the dinette table, looking through all the photos. He showed her the photos of the cement-truck driver, standing beside Nelson Towers and Wally Street. He showed her all the photos he had taken at the new gate that day. He told her how Wally Street had arrived with two young construction workers and parked behind him, blocking him in, how he had bumped into the fender of Connolly's pickup truck and had gotten into the argument with Connolly. He told her what he had been doing when Nelson Towers drove up.

"Boy," she said, "this explains a lot."

"What do you mean?"

"There was one guy," she said, "on that Texas work crew who offered to help me find my dog. Just one guy, named Chuck. Yesterday evening, after I talked to you, I called the motel where they were staying to thank him for that. But I found out they had all checked out Wednesday evening. He had given a home phone number in Texas when he'd registered. I got that from the motel clerk and called down there. I got his mother. She said he'd never come home, that he'd flown out of Albuquerque Thursday morning for a job in Costa Rica, with that whole crew that had been up here in Colorado."

"Jesus," he said. "Towers got them out of here in a hurry, and then he got them out of the country."

"Yes. He's not taking any chances on the cops questioning those guys. They know that both Towers and Street were at that gate late Monday afternoon, at about the time that Linda got killed. Not far from where that happened."

He said, "Nelson Towers might really have killed Linda Ruben. I can't believe that. Can you believe it?"

"Boy, I don't know. What time was it when Towers and Street drove away from that work crew?"

"It must have been getting close to six o'clock by then. They left in separate pickups. Towers was alone, but Street still had those two young men with him. I heard one of them say they were going to Mama Garcia's for dinner."

Her brow furrowed. She said, "Here's what I don't understand. Why would Nelson Towers wait until Wednesday evening to get that crew out of here? That's not really getting them out in much of a hurry, is it?"

He shrugged. "Not really, I guess."

"If either Towers or Street had killed Linda on Monday evening, why wait until Wednesday evening to get that crew out of here? They would have known Monday night that they had to get those guys out before the cops could talk to them. Doesn't it seem like they might have just panicked when Linda's body was identified and the time of death was established by the autopsy? All of that happened on Wednesday. That's what seems to be the catalyst here, Linda's body getting identified."

"You don't think they did it?"

"I'm just playing devil's advocate," she said. "Law school ruined us about that, you know? We'll never be able to just look at one side of anything."

"Yeah, that's true. But why would they lie to the cops in the first place? That's taking one hell of a risk. We're about to put their butts in a sling for that. They had to know it was a big risk. As for what you're asking. Think about it. Suppose Nelson Towers did kill Linda. That surely would not have been something he anticipated doing or wanted to happen. Imagine his state of mind after that, when he realized what he'd done. He could have been a basket case for a day or two, not knowing what to do."

"Yeah," she said. "Or Wally Street might have gotten rid of the two construction workers and then killed her, and maybe Towers didn't find out about that until Wednesday."

"Or, if Street did kill her, Towers still might not know about that. Or you might be guessing right and Towers just panicked when Linda's body was identified."

"Boy," she shook her head, "anything could be possible. But we don't have to figure it out. Not right now. We've got work to do. We've got to get your photo out there."

"Yeah."

She said, "This might be the biggest story of our careers."

"For Earl and Sarah, too."

She nodded. "We've got to get it right."

"Are we ready to break this story?"

"Let's go through it, see if we are."

He said, "What do we know—for sure—that you can write?"

"That Nelson Towers and Wally Street both lied to the cops about not being in Alpine on Monday."

"Yes. And it's damned obvious they got that work crew out of here so their lie might stand a chance of holding up. But you can't write that part yet, can you? Don't we need to get more on that?"

"I'll leave that out for now. Sarah will be wanting to make the afternoon edition. I can do a follow-up story for the morning paper, after I've done some more checking on that work crew. But we can nail Towers and Street right now about that lie to the cops. Bill, do you realize what your photo means? It doesn't really matter now whether Towers or Street had anything to do with Linda's murder. This alone can get them sent to prison, for obstruction of justice. That's a felony. They lied to the cops—about something really material, about something that casts doubt on their innocence in a murder investigation. The media will go wild."

"We've got to get independent confirmation. We've got to have more than just my photo. We are about to accuse Nelson Towers and Wally Street of a felony."

"That cement-truck driver can confirm. I can find him. And I can check with the people at Mama Garcia's, find out if Wally Street was really there."

"Good. Sarah will be wanting my photo ASAP. I can get that scanned somewhere in Cortez and get it on the Internet to her. Then I'll go to that photo lab in Albuquerque and be back late tonight or at least by about midmorning tomorrow."

"Bill, try to get back tonight, okay?"

"I'll try."

"You call me, even if it's late."

"I will. God, if Sarah has to, this afternoon, she'll hold the presses until we've gotten all of this in. This is the story she's been waiting on for a long time. I guess we'd better not tell her about all the time this morning we've spent fooling around, huh?"

Avalon O'Neill grinned, and she kissed him. A quick kiss on the lips. He kissed her back, not quite so quickly, and they sat smiling at each other for a moment.

She began looking through the photos again, saying, "You'd better pick out the one you want to use."

He said, "Jesus, you don't suppose Towers has paid for that cement-truck driver to go on vacation to the headwaters of the Nile, do you? And Mama Garcia's has suddenly relocated to Cancún?"

Avalon O'Neill was chewing her lip, looking distracted. She had picked up a photo of Nelson Towers and Wally Street and was looking at it.

She said. "Bill, something's been bothering me. I've seen Wally Street somewhere. I know I have."

"Maybe you've seen a photo of him, but didn't know who he was at the time."

"No, it isn't that. I have *seen* this man somewhere. Somewhere recently."

"Where? Here in Alpine?"

"I can't remember."

"Well, he was here Monday. You were here Monday. Maybe—"

"That's it! He was buying gas when I bought gas. God, that was right here! At the Shady Rest!"

"Do you think the attendant would remember him being—"

"He paid with a credit card!"

"You're sure?"

"Yes! We had to wait for him. God, he was rude to the attendant. He'll damn sure remember him."

They piled out of the camper and ran to the gas station. The attendant, Dylan, the same tall, freckle-faced kid Hom-Astubby had talked to on Monday afternoon, had no trouble remembering Wally Street. Dylan looked at the photo and said, "That asshole? Who could forget him?" He remembered Avalon O'Neill being there at the same time.

"Just a minute," Dylan said. "I've got those credit card receipts for the whole week. The lady doesn't come in to do those until the weekend."

Dylan found Wally Street's credit card receipt. Hom-Astubby got a close-up photo of it. It had Wally Street's signature, and his name and the date were plainly printed on it. Hom-Astubby got another photo of Dylan holding up the receipt. Avalon O'Neill did a quick interview with Dylan.

"That's confirmation right there," Hom-Astubby said.

"Yes," she said, nearly bouncing up and down. "And I'll find that cement-truck driver. Get him to confirm that Towers was here, too. God, we're gonna have them nailed. I can barely imagine how big this is going to be. It's a once-in-a-lifetime story. Can you let me have those photos, except the one you're going to send to Sarah? So I can show them to that cement-truck driver and the people at

Mama García's? Can you call Sarah and tell her what we've got, what we'll be sending soon?"

"Okay, then I'll get on the road to Cortez." They went back inside the camper and gathered up all the photos she would take with her. Hom-Astubby picked out the photo he would send to Sarah Peteski and put it in his camera bag, along with the ten rolls of film he had stolen from that Georgia kid.

Outside, standing beside her car, Avalon O'Neill said, "God, what a story!" She threw her arms around Hom-Astubby and kissed him. She planted a good one on him. When they finally broke it off, he planted one just as good, and just as long, on her. They stood holding each other, smiling at one another.

Then he watched her drive away, toward Alpine, until her car was out of sight. He let out a long sigh. Man, that woman could kiss.

He had walked halfway toward the Shady Rest pay phone when he remembered he now had a cell phone. He called Sarah. She could barely believe what they had.

He asked her how much she could pay for his photo of Nelson Towers and Wally Street with that cement-truck driver. She said she didn't know, but she was pretty damn sure it would be a lot. She would do a conference call with the other papers in the task force.

He told her to get him top dollar for it or he would have to take it somewhere else. She asked him to call her back after he'd gotten the photo scanned and sent to her.

He told her he'd have to find someplace in Cortez to do that, and he could get his new photos printed there also, showing Wally Street's credit card receipt. She told him to hurry, that time was wasting, that she wanted to make the afternoon edition.

Hom-Astubby drove to Cortez. There, he dropped off his film at the Wal-Mart for one-hour processing, sooner if possible. He found a computer service store, got the photo scanned and e-mailed to Sarah, and then sent her a caption that included everything except the name of the cement-truck driver, which she'd have to get from Avalon O'Neill.

He called Sarah to make sure the photo had come through. It had. Sarah was ecstatic. Avalon O'Neill had called. She'd found the cement-truck driver, and he had confirmed that Nelson Towers had been there. Avalon O'Neill was now at her motel in Alpine writing the story.

Wally Street had also paid with a credit card at Mama García's, for a long dinner with those two construction workers, staying with them at the restaurant for hours, doing paperwork while the two young men drank in the bar. The waiter heard them say they were going to Telluride for the night.

Hom-Astubby went back to Wal-Mart, got his new photos, and went back to the computer store and got them scanned and sent to Sarah. He called her again to make sure they'd come through. They had.

Sarah said to call her back in about two hours and she'd make an offer for his photos. He told her he had to go to Albuquerque, and that he would get to Gallup in time to call her from there.

She reminded him that he had a cell phone now and that he could call her from anywhere.

He hurried to his truck and was putting his camera bag away, when he couldn't find the other bag that had been in the cab. The two bags had been together in the back seat. He looked for the other bag frantically, but it wasn't there.

He had stored his nude photos of Avalon O'Neill in that bag. It had to be there. But it was gone.

He stood staring at the mountains in the distance, so nervous he could hardly think straight. When was the last time he knew for sure that bag had been there? It had been there when he'd gotten the other bag out of the cab, at the Shady Rest gas station, to show the photos to Avalon O'Neill.

Oh, Jesus. He'd left the cab of the truck unlocked when he'd gotten that bag. He'd been in such a rush.

He realized then what had happened. What *had* to have happened. That Georgia kid had left that old house walking toward Alpine. He would have walked down that dirt road to the highway, and then he would have walked right past the Shady Rest, where Hom-Astubby and Avalon O'Neill had been parked. Right past Hom-Astubby's unlocked truck cab.

Hom-Astubby pounded his head against the door of his truck. That damn kid had come walking by and had stolen *his* camera bag.

He would have to go back to that old house. He couldn't leave that bag in the hands of that kid, not with those nude photos of Avalon O'Neill in it. Just as quick as he could get back from Albuquerque, he'd have to go get his camera bag.

He got in his truck and drove off toward Gallup, cussing his own stupidity, and cussing that Georgia kid.

PART 5

The Bluff of a Lifetime

(Friday, Saturday)

The difference between studio photography and photojournalism is one of temperament. The studio photographer looks at a print by the photojournalist and sees mostly those things that could be done better. The photojournalist looks at a print by the studio photographer and sees little that could be done under field conditions. The studio photographer is a manipulator of the environment, principally a manipulator of light. The photojournalist must react to conditions as they are encountered, rather than attempt to control them. A photographer who wants control will be an unhappy photographer in the field, unhappy with the conditions, dissatisfied with the results. If you want control, stay in the studio. But if you like the challenge of working within constantly changing limitations—where the all-important factor is how well and how fast you can identify the critical limitation in each shifting light condition—then come join us out in the field. That's where the news happens.

—WILLIAM H. MALLORY
Basic 35MM Photography

A s Hom-Astubby drove out of Cortez, he tried to remember everything that had been in that camera bag. There wasn't anything in it that he couldn't afford to lose, except those nude photos of Avalon O'Neill.

But none of them showed her face. She couldn't be identified from them, except maybe from the ones that also showed her dog. Anyone recognizing her dog would be able to guess her identity.

But what were the odds of someone like that ever seeing those photos?—unless that kid got arrested in Alpine and the sheriff, or George Langley, searched through his things.

Hom-Astubby frowned. That damn kid from Georgia was complicating his life to the point it was getting dicey. He had to find out something about that kid.

When Hom-Astubby had cleared Cortez, heading toward the New Mexico border, he dug out his address book and found the number for the *Atlanta Star-Herald*. He soon had his old buddy Elliot Stevenson on the line.

"Elliot, it's Bill Mallory."

"Can you hold for a few minutes, Bill? We've got a Girl Scout convention going on down the street. Give me a chance to call down there and warn them that you're in town."

Hom-Astubby laughed. "No need for that. I'm not within a thousand miles of Atlanta."

"I don't know. That's still pretty close. Where are you?"

"Colorado, on the road to Albuquerque."

"Well, maybe our girls are safe. Now, let me guess. You're calling in that debt I owe you. Right?"

"Something like that. I need a rundown on one of your fair citizens, a twenty-four-year-old punk. I lifted his Georgia driver's license that expired two years ago."

"Sounds like a jailbird to me."

"Huh? No kidding?"

"They don't get them renewed in prison, you know."

"I hadn't thought of that. I just assumed he was carrying a current one on him. But maybe not."

"Give me the poop on this guy."

Hom-Astubby read the details from the driver's license.

"It'll only take a minute. You want to hold?"

"Sure."

It took several minutes, but it was worth the wait.

"Yep. Jailbird, all right," Stevenson said. "Just got sprung about ten days ago. And if you might know where the lad can be found, the Georgia parole board would be mighty interested in hearing from you."

"I'd rather not say."

"Mum's the word."

"He skipped out, huh?"

"Soon as they turned him loose. Didn't hang around to chat, not even once."

"What was he in for?"

"Most recently?"

"Geez, Elliot, he's not that old."

"Your sheltered life. This convict has a real taste for prison food. In and out since age fourteen, mostly in. His juvenile records are sealed. Since adulthood, two trips to the big house, almost back-to-back. Both for assault with a deadly weapon, last time with intent to maim. I'll bet my ex-wife's boyfriend that both charges were plea-bargained down from god knows what."

"Ex-wife? You and Jeannie split?"

"You didn't hear? She ran off to Florida with her tennis coach, a tall redhead with—how did she put it?—great buns."

"You're kidding me."

"I kid you not. I was looking the other way when it happened."

"Elliot, you're not gonna believe this, but I know a gal in Albuquerque you have *got* to meet. Same thing happened to her. Florida. Looking the other way when a redhead made off with the goods. But it was an investment banker that got her hubby."

"Albuquerque, huh? Sounds like I could hold a chat with that woman. Hell, I'm getting so desperate I'd fly to Timbuktu. Been way too busy to chase anything."

"If you could get here by about five or six o'clock, you could save me from her."

"That bad, huh?"

"Oh contraire. Venus in blue jeans. Her name is Laura. Brunette, freckles, hazel eyes. I dare you to watch her walk across a room without biting your tongue. And a pretty darn good match for you, too, come to think of it. A damn good match."

"So how come you're bailing out?"

"I done been rode hard, all morning, in Colorado. She saddled up and took me through the Triple Crown. Don't remember much about how well I ran in the Kentucky Derby, but I was there all the way for the Preakness and the Belmont Stakes."

"How well did you run there?"

"Like a champion, she said."

"Her opinion is what counts, if you ever hope to get taken around the track again."

"Yeah, but this one waiting for me in Albuquerque likes to take you on the European circuit after Belmont, with a stop at Ascot along the way. And by god, you'd better be ready to run again when she's ready to cross the ocean. She done told me I'm gettin' saddled up as soon as I walk through the door, and I have *got* to use her photo lab. She's all spurs, with a heavy hand on the whip. She'll get you across the wire every time, if you're ready to run. But I've got no hope of gettin' through the Triple Crown again, let alone on to Ascot or anywhere else. I don't know what I'm gonna do."

"I'll pray for you. That might help. Hell, I'll call my friends, get them praying, too. This sounds like an emergency."

"That's exactly what it is. What I need is a rescue. I'll pay for the plane ticket."

"Don't tempt me, hoss. Albuquerque by six might be doable. Maybe even by five. I'd gain two hours flying west."

"You book it right now, and then I'll call your travel agent and pay for it."

"Don't tempt me, pard. I've *got* a travel agent. And I keep a bag packed right here at the office."

"Here's how we'll work it. You take a cab from the Albuquerque airport to a Village Inn Pancake House near her photo lab. I'll pick you up there. Meanwhile, I'll call her and tell her something's come up and I'll have to do a hell of a quick turnaround as soon as she can get some sensitive film processed for me—but, to everyone's mutual, great good fortune, my old buddy Elliot, from Atlanta, is in town, who I've been dying to introduce her to anyway, and that I can pick you up and bring you with me, if that's okay with her, and then the two of you can go to dinner just as soon as we get out of the lab, which won't take long."

"She'll go for this?"

"Hell, I'll tell her I learned everything I know listening to you."

"You *could* lie to her if you had to, you know."

"You gonna book that ticket?"

"You talked me into it. Call me back in ten. What's your cell—just in case? Hey. Do I fly first class?"

"First class, you bet." Hom-Astubby gave him his cell phone number.

"One more thing, Elliot. Think you could make some discreet inquires about this Lindquist kid for me? Find out more about those charges? Anything else you might dig up on him, without anybody thinking you were overly interested?"

"Sure. I can say we're researching a piece on parole jumpers. I got a good intern here I can put on that, too. Young Cartwright. He's sitting over there trimming his toenails right now. Call me back in ten and I'll give you the poop for the travel agent."

"Will do."

Hom-Astubby rang off. He breathed a big sigh of relief.

Half an hour later, Elliot's plane ticket had been taken care of, and Elliot was on his way to the Atlanta airport.

Hom-Astubby chatted with the intern, learning that Lawrence Selden Lindquist had worked for a relative who ran a sleazy photography studio in Atlanta's tenderloin district. The relative had a long rap sheet involving drugs and prostitution.

But it was the charges against Lindquist that fueled Hom-Astubby's imagination. Both convictions were for unprovoked attacks on attractive, middle-class women, on total strangers. The last victim had been a jogger in an Atlanta park, in the early evening, after sunset. She had barely survived a bludgeoning of her head with some kind of heavy object that had not been recovered. Evidentiary problems had kept Lindquist from getting put away for a long time. The Atlanta police suspected him of a rash of similar, attempted attacks and had been relieved to get him off the streets before he killed someone.

Hom-Astubby was pretty sure he now knew who had killed Linda Ruben. His first thought was to wonder what might be inside that locked trunk in that mine-garage. That was something he knew he'd have to find out.

As he was approaching Sheep Springs, in the Navajo Nation, he got a call from Avalon O'Neill. She was excited. She had reached that work crew member named Chuck in Costa Rica and had gotten a phone interview with him. She was telling Hom-Astubby about that when his cell phone began cutting out on him.

"Is that your phone, Bill, or mine?" she asked.

"I think it's mine. I must be—." His cell phone went dead.

He couldn't get it to work again all the way to Gallup. Once, he got it to ring her cell phone, but when she said "Hello," and he said, "Avalon, it's Bill," it went dead again.

"Damn gadgets," he said. He tossed it on the seat and didn't try again. Gallup wasn't far ahead. By the time he arrived there, he had gotten pager messages to call both Sarah Peteski and Avalon O'Neill. Sarah had called six times.

He stopped at the Denny's on the east side of Gallup and ordered a light lunch to go. At the payphone he tried calling Avalon

O'Neill, but when she answered, her cell phone cut out on her. He tried several more times without getting a connection that would allow them to talk.

He called Sarah. She had news for him. She'd been trying to call him nearly nonstop for half an hour. They were holding the presses, waiting for his approval.

With Avalon O'Neill's story that afternoon, they were running three of his photos—one of the gas station attendant holding up Wally Street's credit card receipt, along with the close-up photo of that receipt, on page two; and on page one, his photo of Nelson Towers, Wally Street, and the cement-truck driver at the gate construction site on Monday, accompanied by a banner headline "Nelson Towers lied to police," in a type size the paper hadn't used since the Japanese bombed Pearl Harbor.

All twelve newspapers in the task force were ready to go, or nearly so. The ones that didn't have afternoon editions were putting out extras, including home delivery, and were scrambling to locate their newspaper carriers for that.

The bombshell would be hitting the streets before the evening network TV news broadcasts. By bedtime, the whole world would know about it.

She had a package deal for his photos—particularly the one on the front page showing that the richest man in the world was not only a liar but maybe a murdering liar, with the clear implication being "probably" a murdering liar. The task force would pay Hom-Astubby 2.4 million dollars. He'd have a certified check in his Los Angeles bank account that afternoon.

He agreed. Then he asked Sarah if she could get hold of Avalon O'Neill for him and tell her that he had been trying to call her back but his cell phone wasn't working, and apparently hers wasn't working very well either. Sarah said she'd do that.

He then took a deep breath and called Laura at her photo lab. He had to do some fancy dancing, some fine footwork indeed, but she finally came around to where her intrigue at meeting Elliot outweighed her anger with Hom-Astubby.

By the time he finally got off the phone with her, his sack lunch had been sitting on the counter so long it had gotten ice cold, which was real close to how Laura had said good-bye on the phone. He saw he had another page from Avalon O'Neill. He tried calling her again, but couldn't get her on her cell phone or at her motel. He called and left his cell phone number on her pager. At least she would know he had been trying.

He paid for his sack lunch and was about to head out the door with it when he thought of Eugene Wentworth—the one person who might know something about that business card he had found in Wally Street's briefcase, especially if Ryerson & Neely, Inc., might happen to be a private investigation firm, and in San Francisco, no less.

Eugene Wentworth was practically a California institution himself—spy novelist, former CIA intelligence analyst, wine connoisseur extraordinaire, fly-fishing fanatic, and long-time international investigative journalist for the San Francisco Evening Bugle, which, despite having been a morning-only paper for decades, still clung to the prestige and reputation of its much-respected name. If there was anybody he could ask about Ryerson & Neely, it would be Gene.

They had never worked together, but they had fly-fished together for several days, years ago, on a really sweet assignment with Harry Birdwell to Argentina, when Birdwell's photographer couldn't make the trip. Gene had been in Argentina for some reason and had joined them at the last minute, to Birdwell's and Hom-Astubby's everlasting delight.

Wentworth had contacted Hom-Astubby a couple times since then, trying to coordinate another time when they could get together on some stream, something they were still trying to work out, though they hadn't talked in more than a year.

He called the San Francisco Evening Bugle, but was told that Wentworth had been overseas for about a month. They said he was due to fly back into San Francisco sometime soon. They were expecting him at the Evening Bugle on Monday.

Hom-Astubby tried his home number, leaving a message on his machine that he was trying to reach him. He left his cell phone number and said he'd try to call again.

Between Gallup and Albuquerque he gave up on trying to get his cell phone to work. He also started getting a little drowsy and realized he'd been up since about ten o'clock the night before.

He was at the Village Inn Pancake House near Laura's lab, at the pay phones, trying unsuccessfully to reach Avalon O'Neill, when a cab dropped Elliot Stevenson off at the restaurant. They took time to have coffee and visit for a few minutes, unwinding from their trips before heading for the photo lab.

Elliot seemed a little nervous. He kept asking questions about Laura—what she liked, what she didn't like, how long he had known her, where she'd grown up, gone to school. He had thought of a lot of things to ask while on the plane.

Hom-Astubby gave him a quick tour of his camper. But Elliot was still asking questions about Laura and hardly seemed to do more than glance around at the inside of the camper.

When Hom-Astubby saw Laura, he almost regretted having brought Elliot with him. She had obviously gone home sometime during the day, probably since he had talked to her from Gallup. She was dressed for bear. She couldn't so much as breathe without everything jiggling.

Elliot was drooling as Hom-Astubby made the introductions, and Laura was not looking disappointed. She said she knew a little place where they could do some dancing after dinner, if he liked to dance. At that point, Elliot would have agreed to salt-water crocodile wrestling.

She made Elliot comfortable in her office, with some coffee. Then she ran Hom-Astubby's film quickly on automated machines.

Hom-Astubby stood beside her, watching the photos come out of the machine, seeing a lot of shots of fly-fishermen on the river, and of people going in and out of the Purple Pentagon, and then of Avalon O'Neill at the river on Monday. There were shots of Hom-

Astubby at the river, some of them with her dog, and then of him and the sheriff, and then a lot of shots of the crime scene being worked on Tuesday. The kid was pretty good with a camera, and with that 2000 mm lens.

There were no photos of Linda Ruben.

As one sequence was coming out, showing Avalon O'Neill peeling off her wet clothes, right down to the bare skin, Laura glanced at him and lifted her eyebrows. When a spectacularly good one developed, showing her buck naked beside the river, Laura gave him a long, level look and lifted one eyebrow.

As Laura was putting the ten packets of photos and negatives in a small box for him, he realized that none of the photos had shown Avalon O'Neill arriving at the river, and none of them had shown her getting dressed and leaving. There had only been three or four photos, at the end of a roll, showing her standing naked beside the river.

The kid might have shot an entire roll of film while she was naked beside the river. He might have set aside that one as a special roll. He might have done the same thing with shots of her arriving, when he hadn't known it would get so much better. And shots of her getting up from behind those rocks, maybe rinsing off at the river, and then getting dressed, might have been on another special roll.

There was a good chance that there was still some undeveloped film of Avalon O'Neill naked, somewhere in that mine-garage. It wouldn't be enough just for Hom-Astubby to get back his own camera bag, with his nude photos of her, and to cut the lock off that trunk, and find out what was in it.

He would have to find the rest of that kid's film, wherever it was. Two or three rolls of film could be hidden nearly anywhere.

CHAPTER THIRTY-ONE

Hom-Astubby declined a polite but insincere invitation to join Laura and Elliot for drinks before dinner. He wished them well, getting a sly wink from Elliot when Laura wasn't looking, and then an almost bashful smile from Laura as she kissed him good-bye.

He heaved a big sigh and drove back to the Village Inn Pancake House. In a newspaper rack beside the front door of the restaurant, his front-page photo caught his eye, beside a banner headline on the *Albuquerque Independent-Bee*, in Martians-have-landed type size, proclaiming, "Nelson Towers is a liar," with a Hitler-found-alive type size subheading, "Is he a murderer too?"

He bought a copy of the paper and took it inside. He tried calling Avalon O'Neill again, but had no luck.

He called Sarah Peteski. She had a message for him. Avalon O'Neill was driving to Montrose to pick up Earl Paggett at the airport, which was the closest place to Alpine that he could get a flight that wasn't booked up, but with no rental cars available. They would catch a few hours' sleep there and get an early start for Alpine in the morning.

Avalon O'Neill had told Sarah to tell Hom-Astubby that she hoped he didn't have to spend the night in Albuquerque, that he should try to get at least as far back as Gallup, so he could meet her and Paggett for brunch at the Purple Pentagon at 10 A.M. If Sarah talked to him, she was to confirm that he could do that, so Sarah could let her know, and she and Paggett could plan accordingly.

Hom-Astubby told Sarah to tell Avalon O'Neill that he could do that. He told Sarah about the banner headline in the *Albuquerque Independent-Bee*, which she hadn't heard about, and she told him about some of the others that she did know about. Her favorite, so far, was "Towers caught telling one lie too many" in the *St Louis Packet-Express*.

He said he was about to sit down to dinner and do some pleasure reading. She wished him "Bon appetite!" He had never heard Sarah Peteski so happy.

He tried calling Eugene Wentworth again in San Francisco, but nobody answered the phone.

He had a long, leisurely dinner while reading the newspaper. After dinner he felt lethargic, drowsy. He didn't feel like getting up, so he kept drinking coffee and reading.

He marveled at how much copy Sarah had prepared in advance, just waiting for a story like this one to headline. It recounted every sleazy thing Nelson Towers had ever done that was a matter of public record. There was a rehash of the *Denver Daily Sun*–Linda Ruben book story, as though it were fresh news, which, in a way, it was, much bigger now than when the story had broken on Monday.

The Telluride clandestine videotape now sounded even more devastating, even when only transcribed in print. On TV that video was no doubt being replayed tonight over and over again.

He could barely imagine the scene on the courthouse lawn at Alpine. The klieg lights would have it looking like high noon until way past midnight—and probably, with all the international crews there, until daylight. Alpine had become the little town that never slept.

He sat back, reflecting on what was happening and on what he knew about that Georgia kid. He wondered if Sarah and all the others, including himself, were going way out on a flimsy, rotten limb.

On his way out of the Village Inn, he tried calling Avalon O'Neill's cell phone again, and then Eugene Wentworth, with no luck on either call. He left his cell phone number again on Avalon O'Neill's pager.

He drove to the Denny's in Gallup, fighting to stay awake all the way. He had to stop at Grants to wash his face with cold water and walk around a bit. He couldn't think straight anymore. It took all his concentration just to keep the truck on the highway.

At Gallup, he called Johnny, catching him at the garage cleaning up after a long day of working on that old Honda Civic. Johnny joined him for a while at Denny's, before leaving to pick up his sister when she got off work.

Johnny filled him in on the good luck he'd been having at contacting his Comanche cousins. One of them, in Kentucky, had told Johnny about a young stallion thoroughbred racehorse named Quiet Retreat, for sale at a bargain price, the fastest horse his cousin had ever seen. A series of unlucky injuries had kept the horse from racing much, but if Hom-Astubby could plop down twenty-five thousand dollars, Johnny's cousin could deliver the horse to the ranch late next week, by which time Johnny would be there. Johnny thought he'd be heading back to the ranch Monday or Tuesday.

Hom-Astubby got his checkbook out of the camper and wrote a check to Johnny for twenty-five grand, saying, "What the hell. We can give that a shot."

While sitting at the counter, drinking coffee, talking to Johnny, Hom-Astubby tried calling Eugene Wentworth every fifteen minutes.

When it was time for Johnny to pick up his sister, Hom-Astubby went outside with him to look at that old Honda.

With the help of some of his buddies, Johnny had gotten the air conditioner and the heater working. From his boss's salvage yard, he'd replaced the rusty old gas tank, float, and sending unit, which had the gas gauge working again. They'd started on the speedometer and odometer before quitting for the night.

They'd installed new ball joints, wheel bearings, shocks, brakes, and a whole new exhaust system, including a dandy set of glass-packed tail pipes they'd salvaged out of a wrecked dune buggy.

They'd salvaged out and installed a couple of mismatched doors in good condition, and Johnny said they removed a super-fine set of leather bucket seats from a badly rear-ended Ferrari that they were all set to try getting installed in the morning.

All the rust spots had been sanded out, and someone had been hard at work patching the holes all over the car body. The dents were all gone and most of the paint had been sanded off. The badly cracked windshield had been replaced, and the car had new tires all around.

"Man, I'm gonna paint it fire engine red," Johnny said. "What do you think?"

"Doesn't look like the same car," Hom-Astubby said.

"Doesn't sound like it, either. You just listen to these tail pipes."

Hom-Astubby listened, shaking his head and grinning, as Johnny thundered out of the parking lot.

Johnny hadn't been gone long, and Hom-Astubby was about to give up for the night, when, at 11:45 P.M., 10:45 Pacific Time, Eugene Wentworth finally answered his phone in San Francisco.

"Gene, it's Bill Mallory. I hope it's not too late to be calling."

"Holy cow! A voice from the grave. I heard you got killed in a plane crash in Antarctica. I guess they found your body. Is this cryogenics at work, or what?"

Hom-Astubby chuckled. "It's Antarctica now, huh? And I got killed?"

"Deader'n a damn doornail was what I heard. Hell, I was gonna send flowers, but then I forgot."

"Thanks a lot. But, Gene, there was no plane crash. I'll tell you the story some day, at a more convenient time."

"Yeah, well, old buddy, you just caught me walking in the door. Been gone since Reagan was president, it seems like. But I don't see any dead fish in the fish tank, so I guess they've been getting taken care of okay."

"Gene, I'll not keep you long. I was hoping you might know something about a San Francisco firm, one with international connections, might be a PI firm."

"Bill, you dialed the right number for that. And don't you worry about the timing. Hell, I ain't in that big a hurry to get unpacked, or get to bed. It's still early out here, and even earlier with my jet lag. And it's Friday night. I'm gonna drop off this stuff and go out on the town. I miss it when I've been away too long."

"I appreciate it, Gene. That outfit I'm trying to get a line on is Ryerson & Neely."

There was a pause on the other end of the line, and when Wentworth spoke again, his voice was different. "Mind if I ask what this is in relation to?"

Hom-Astubby felt a need for caution. He said, "Gene, it's way out of my area. I think it has to do with something going on in Malaysia. A rental car, apparently rented to the government of Malaysia."

"In Malaysia, huh? That sounds about right." Wentworth let out a long breath, audible over the phone. "You had me going there for a minute. I thought you might have the scoop of this young century, even bigger than that mess up there in Alpine. Is that where you are?"

"No. Not now. I'm in New Mexico. But I was at Alpine, and I'm headed back there. I've been getting some photos in the papers. Got a good one that's out there today."

"I haven't seen any papers yet. I'll look for it."

"Look on page one. But Gene, a big scoop? What did you mean by that?"

"Bill, not many people know about Ryerson & Neely. Damn few have ever even heard of them. You'd play hell trying to find an office for them, anywhere in the world, I'll tell you that, except right here in San Francisco. They have only got one client—your old buddy Nelson Towers."

"Towers doesn't own the company?"

"No. It's a devil's deal he got into way back. Could be his Achilles' heel, if he's got one. You don't have any idea what they do?"

"Not a clue."

"They are the premier international industrial espionage firm in the world, and you don't want to know what all else, trust me. Of course, they don't call it industrial espionage, some gobbledygook about systems management analysis, or some damn thing, but, by whatever name, it's a cactus patch you don't want to sit down in."

"If it walks like a duck, and it quacks like a duck . . ."

"Exactly. They are prohibited from doing anything but paperwork here in the states, by a gentleman's agreement with the CIA—one that the rest of corporate America would not tolerate being breached. You get my drift?"

"I think so."

"Hell, I thought maybe you had something on them over here. If they got caught operating in the states, the roof would collapse on Nelson Towers. He'd never risk that. He's too smart. And he doesn't need them over here, anyway."

Hom-Astubby's pulse was racing so fast he couldn't speak.

"There's nothing about this that connects them to the states, is there?" asked Wentworth.

"I don't see how. I couldn't make any sense out of that Malaysian thing until now. Doesn't sound like I'd get anywhere trying to pursue it."

"All you'd get would be trouble, if you got anywhere at all. And you don't want their kind of trouble. You'd have to go overseas, even just to try, and people who get too interested in them have a way of suffering fatal accidents overseas. Hell, Bill, I won't even write anything about them, and there's not much that scares me anymore."

"I'm getting the impression that Nelson Towers really is not a very nice guy."

"That's a healthy impression to have. You nurture that impression, and I'll rest easier about you. But let's hope you folks up at Alpine might have him by the tail this time. I hope you'll work that angle and forget about Malaysia."

"That's what I'm going to do, Gene. You have a good night on the town. I really appreciate your help on this."

"No problem, old buddy. Let's talk soon about another fishing trip."

"Let's do that, Gene. Real soon. And hey, I'm sending you a very special bottle of wine."

"Dang, you don't have to do that. How special?"

"Prepare to be amazed. I'll holler at you later."

Hom-Astubby could hardly wait to get to Alpine. But he also could barely keep his eyes open. He had to sleep, at least for a little while.

He climbed into his camper and set the alarm for 4:30 A.M., wondering if old Elliot had gotten spurred beyond Ascot by now, and which European track he'd be on when Laura finally galloped him into the ground.

Hom-Astubby was asleep almost by the time he got his eyes closed, fully clothed except for his shoes.

CHAPTER THIRTY-TWO

When the alarm went off at 4:30 A.M., Hom-Astubby groaned himself half awake and pulled on his shoes. He stumbled across the parking lot of the Denny's in Gallup, accompanied by the sound of an idling diesel engine on a refrigeration truck, as its driver snoozed in the predawn darkness. He got coffee to go at Denny's and then struggled to stay awake all the way to Sheep Springs.

He stopped there long enough to make coffee in the camper, douse his face and head with cold water, and walk around a bit in the crisp morning air, admiring the bursting streaks of color in the sky. That got him on to Alpine.

The sun was up when he parked again behind a long line of vehicles on the shoulder of the highway near the Purple Pentagon. He pulled on his camouflage coveralls and stuck his flashlight in a pocket.

He saw his cell phone and tried getting a dial tone on it. To his surprise, it was working again. He stuck it in another pocket.

He set off through the woods, hiking up the hill. The brisk walk in the cool morning air finally woke him up.

As he approached the barbed-wire fence, he could see that one door to the mine was standing open. He could see Lindquist lying on the cot. The big brown pickup was parked near the house.

Hom-Astubby moved up through the trees, nearly to the crest of the hill, where he could still see the pickup and the doors of the mine. He got concealed in the underbrush and settled in to wait.

He had fallen asleep when he heard the pickup starting up. He saw Lindquist come to the door of the tunnel and peek toward the gate, watching the pickup drive away. The kid walked straight to the barbed-wire fence across from the mine, climbed through the fence, and headed off through the trees toward the cliffs.

Hom-Astubby knew he couldn't count on having much time before Lindquist might return. It wasn't far to those cliffs. But at least he wouldn't have to work in the dark. The kid had left the barn door standing wide open. He wondered if the kid still had that pistol.

Hom-Astubby climbed through the barbed-wire fence and sprinted to the mine. He went straight to the chest of drawers and opened the top drawer.

The briefcase was there. He opened it. The Ryerson & Neely packet was there. The contents of the briefcase did not appear to have been disturbed since he had replaced it in the drawer.

He carried the briefcase to the trunk, setting it on the ground beside it. He got the bolt cutters from the other side of the tunnel and cut the lock off the trunk. He put the bolt cutters back and took a look at the lock. Its cut portion fitted back into place nicely, and the lock rested on a lip of the trunk, looking all in one piece. The kid might not notice for a while that it had been cut.

He cleared the things off the top of the trunk, being careful to note how they had been placed, so he could set them back in the same position. He raised the lid of the trunk, seeing his camera bag. He looked quickly in the side pouch that held the photos of Avalon O'Neill. They were there. He rifled through them quickly. They all seemed to be there.

From the weight of the bag, he could tell that his cameras and other things were still in it. He put his arm through the strap, shouldering the bag, and took a close look at the contents of the trunk.

It was filled almost to the brim with candy bars and small bags of potato chips—what might have been the contents of some vending machine. Digging down into the candy bars he found that everything was resting on a pile of blankets that filled about half the trunk. As he stirred the candy bars around, he found two more camera bags and three purses.

He carried one of the purses to the kitchen table and opened it, seeing a cell phone. He picked it up and pressed a button, and a light came on. The battery still had a charge.

He glanced at a telephone number on the side of the phone—then did a double take and peered at it closely, at the black letters on a thin white strip of tape. The phone number missed being his Social Security number by only two digits, by having three digits in the middle cluster of numbers, where his Social Security number had only two, and by the very last digit being only one number lower than his last number.

A shiver ran up his spine. It was almost as though he was being told that he would be next.

He pushed the phone to the side of the purse and stirred through its contents. He saw a fat brown leather wallet. With trembling hands, he set the purse on the table and opened the somewhat worn but elegantly plain ladies' wallet.

He extracted a driver's license from a plastic sleeve and turned it in the daylight to see it better.

He stared at a photo of Linda Ruben, reading her name, her address, date of birth, expiration date—.

"Larry!"

Charles Uber's booming voice, very close, shook Hom-Astubby to the core of his being. He had taken several quick steps backward, nearly tripping over the trunk, before he recovered enough to turn around and run to the back of the tunnel.

He looked frantically for some place to hide, stepping on one of the loose boards that covered the vertical shaft, losing his balance. He was barely able to grab the heavy timber framing above the shaft to keep from toppling over on top of the boards.

"Larry."

Uber *had* to be almost at the front doors.

Hom-Astubby saw a gap between the rock wall at the back of the tunnel and the side of the tall double cabinet. He squeezed into it, sliding along the wall all the way to where he could get behind the cabinet.

Movement at the front of the tunnel caught his eye. Through the legs of the end tables stacked beside the cabinet, he saw Charles

Uber walk around the open door and stop at the front of the tunnel.

Uber put his hands on his hips and stood frowning into the tunnel. He said, "Damn you, boy, where are you?"

Hom-Astubby held his breath.

Uber turned away. He walked back around the open front door, toward the house.

Hom-Astubby breathed a big sigh of relief.

His cell phone rang in his pocket.

It rang so loud it startled him out of at least two birthdays.

Frantically, he grabbed at the pocket that held the phone. He couldn't get it out.

The cell phone rang again.

It was the loudest and longest ringing Hom-Astubby had ever heard.

He got the phone out of his pocket and fumbled with it. How did you turn the damn thing off?

It rang again.

He finally found the off button and pushed it—in the middle of the ring—an instant before Uber's face appeared around the door.

"Who's in here?" Uber said.

Hom-Astubby froze.

He fought against an urge to slip back into the space between the side of the cabinet and the back wall of the tunnel, where Uber wouldn't be able to see him, at least not from the front of the tunnel. But the movement might give him away. In the gloom at the back of the tunnel, he knew his best chance was to remain absolutely still.

Uber stepped around the door, looking quickly all around him, into the tunnel, back toward the house, at the trees across from the tunnel, up the road that ran along the fence up the hill. He eased forward a few steps to the stack of iron pipe near the door and pulled out one about half the length of a baseball bat, and about as thick.

As his eyes darted everywhere, he stepped lightly, his weight on his toes, the pipe swinging slowly back and forth at his side.

Hom-Astubby swallowed hard. He had no doubt that this man had once been an athlete. He appeared to be in superb physical condition. He was several inches taller than Hom-Astubby and outweighed him by at least fifty pounds, much of that being beefy muscle in his upper chest and arms.

Uber stepped to the other door and opened it wide. Sunlight spilled into the tunnel, cutting away much of the remaining gloom, making it possible to see details even at the back of the tunnel.

Hom-Astubby's heart sank. There weren't many places for a man to hide. It wouldn't take long to find him.

Uber came down the other side of the tunnel, where someone might get behind the generator or the air compressor. He passed out of Hom-Astubby's vision, but not before Hom-Astubby saw that the pipe he was carrying wasn't a pipe at all but a round piece of solid metal.

Hom-Astubby had to do something. He heard Uber approaching the cabinet.

Hom-Astubby eased his hand up to his face, so he could see his cell phone, as Uber jerked a front door of the cabinet open.

Hom-Astubby raised his other hand. As he was trying to punch in the numbers, Uber jerked the other cabinet door open.

He thought he had misdialed, his finger slipping off one key, but he wasn't certain. He didn't know if he'd have time to try dialing again.

He was just about to, when, to his horror, he saw the top of the cabinet pulling away from him, as Uber was toppling the cabinet forward, to drop it all the way over onto the floor.

Linda Ruben's cell phone rang.

The cabinet stopped tipping forward—it remained where it was, suspended at an angle.

Her cell phone rang again.

The cabinet rocked back into place.

Uber strode toward the front of the tunnel, to near the kitchen table, and stood listening, looking all around.

Her cell phone rang again.

Uber looked down, picked up Linda Ruben's purse, which had been standing open on the table. He took out the phone. As it was ringing again, Hom-Astubby broke the connection and turned off his phone. He stood staring at Uber through the end table legs, his chest rising and falling so fast he was afraid he might pass out.

Uber put down the metal rod and dumped out the contents of the purse on the kitchen table. He started stirring through them, then stopped, stepped back, and looked down, seeing something on the ground. He bent down and came up holding Linda Ruben's wallet, where Hom-Astubby had dropped it.

Uber stepped back a little more and looked all around on the ground. He bent down again and came up holding Linda Ruben's driver's license.

He turned it in the light, reading it, as his face contorted in anger. He said, "That little bastard."

The sound of a shoe scuffing the ground came from just beyond the door. Uber dropped the license on the table and picked up the heavy metal rod. He concealed himself just inside the doorway, against the front wall, in front of the stack of pipe.

Lawrence Selden Lindquist came walking around the door and into the tunnel. As he walked past Uber, Uber jumped out behind him and screamed, "You *stupid* bastard," swinging the pipe as hard as he could into the back of the kid's neck.

Lindquist crumpled instantly.

Uber stepped to him and shouted, "Bring the Tetons down on me!" as he swung the rod and crushed his neck again with a powerful blow.

Hom-Astubby stood trembling behind the cabinet. Uber's screaming, by itself, in the confinement of the tunnel, had been enough to unnerve him.

Uber stood staring down at Lindquist's body. He wiped the back of his hand across his mouth and looked around. He stepped to the door and looked toward the house.

Then he walked straight toward Hom-Astubby. Hom-Astubby thought he was a dead man, until he heard Uber lifting the boards that covered the vertical shaft.

He peeked around the cabinet just enough to see Uber, only a few feet from him, tossing the boards into the pit. Faintly, Hom-Astubby could hear them crashing against the bottom.

Uber walked to the kid's body, grabbed it by the feet and dragged it to the shaft, tossing it over the edge. He threw the metal rod in after it.

He stuffed the contents of Linda Ruben's purse back into it and threw the purse down the shaft. He dragged the trunk to the pit and pushed it over the edge. Then he opened the cabinet doors and threw the telephoto lens and the tripods into the pit.

He picked up Wally Street's briefcase and the chair the kid had sat on and threw them in, as well as the cot, lantern, propane stove, and coffee cup. He pulled out the drawers in the chest of drawers and dumped their contents into the shaft.

He picked up the kid's pile of dirty clothing and a lot of other small items on that side of the tunnel and threw them in. Then he got a sledgehammer and knocked apart the timbering that supported the pulley above the shaft, erasing all trace of the structure, and dropping all of its parts into the pit.

After looking all around for a moment, he walked out of the tunnel toward the house.

Hom-Astubby slipped out from behind the cabinet and ran to the front door. He peeked around it, seeing Uber disappearing around the corner of the house, toward the front porch.

He clutched his camera bag and sprinted up the hill, up the road, away from the house, not stopping until he had topped the crest of the hill and had gone well beyond it. He crawled through the barbed-wire fence and scampered through the underbrush and into the trees. He sat down then, breathing deeply, catching his breath, his head spinning.

He felt miserable. He shook his head. He was an utter failure. He had seen Wally Street's briefcase going into that pit. Jesus, what he might have done with that briefcase.

He had witnessed the trunk, and everything else, going into that shaft.

Somewhere among those things was the rest of the film of Avalon O'Neill. The cops would find it now. It would be evidence. It would get developed and be introduced as evidence in open court.

How could he look into her eyes and tell her that the whole world was going to see those photos, and that there was nothing that anybody, anywhere, could do about it. Uber's lawyers would force it, if nothing else.

He hoped she didn't have her heart set on a career in journalism, because her credibility was going to be destroyed. He couldn't even imagine the tabloid headlines. They'd never let up.

He sat staring at nothing, until he heard the tractor being fired up at that old house.

He crept down through the trees, well away from the fence, until he could see the clearing. Uber was scooping up a big load of rock and dirt in the bucket on the front end of the tractor. He drove it into the mine and dumped it into the shaft. As he went to get another load, Hom-Astubby slipped away through the trees.

When he had walked past the cliffs, but was still on the ledge overlooking the Crystal Fork, he thought to look at his watch. Damn. It was 10:15.

He dug out his cell phone and turned it on, to try calling Avalon O'Neill. But before he could dial, it rang.

"This is Earl Paggett," said the voice on the line. "I'm sorry we're running late. Are you at the Purple Pentagon?"

"I'm parked close to it."

"We got here early and came on into Alpine. We've been trying to reach you."

"What's up?"

"I'm afraid your photo yesterday has broken some things loose in a way we couldn't have anticipated."

"How so?"

"Nelson Towers wants a meeting with us."

"You're kidding."

"I wish I were."

"You don't sound very happy."

"I'm not. He's got me over a barrel. He's offering to fund the task force, but he wants you and Avalon off the story."

"What?"

"Avalon's not happy about it either—to put it mildly. But I've talked her into listening to what Towers has to say. I hope you'll do the same."

"When?"

"At noon, at Towers' new house—Dartmoor Manor. He's flying in now by helicopter from Telluride. He'll send a car to pick us up at the Purple Pentagon parking lot at twelve o'clock sharp. Will you go with us?"

"Is this offer of his legit?"

"Yes. It's good for everyone, except, perhaps, you and Avalon. I'm trying to get you more money."

"Money?"

Paggett sighed audibly. "That's been Avalon's response. It's a kill fee he's offering—for you and Avalon to withdraw from this investigation. He says that the two of you have personal axes to grind. He offered fifty thousand dollars for each of you. I've tried to get him up to seventy-five, but he won't budge. He says you'll be taking a year's vacation on him, and the value of that should be considered. I think, however, if you insist on seventy-five you might get it. But even fifty thousand is a pretty damn good kill fee, simply to drop out of this story entirely and go do something else for a year."

"For a year, huh?"

"Yes. No contact with anyone involved with the task force for one year, or until the task force completes its work, whichever comes first."

"He doesn't think you have an ax to grind?"

"He is demanding that I remain in charge of the task force. He needs my prestige, my reputation, especially my undisputed reputation for hounding him, as he calls it."

"You could refuse."

"I wish I could. That's where he's got me over the barrel. He's putting up twenty-four million dollars to fully fund the task force, for up to one year—two million dollars for each newspaper. They need the money. They can't turn it down. But they won't get it unless I agree to remain in charge of the task force."

"The money comes with what kind of strings attached?"

"None whatsoever. No restrictions of any kind. It will be spent entirely at my discretion. We will be free even to dig into anything that might only speak to motive, such as everything Linda had been investigating, or anything else—anywhere. The money will be entirely out of Towers' hands. It will be in escrow, disbursed by an independent accounting firm, as we spend it. Sarah's lawyers and Towers' lawyers are putting the finishing touches to the agreement right now. Towers and I will be on the Sunday morning TV news, talk-show circuit back east tomorrow, if we can get this worked out between you and Avalon and him."

"He's really serious about this, isn't he?"

"Mr. Mallory, you have put his back against the wall. He's facing prison time. He's desperate, and he has run out of options. It's really a rather brilliant maneuver on his part, one that might cost him little but money."

Paggett sighed again. "It looks like it might be my fate to prove him innocent, to save him from himself. The irony of that is making me sick. But he insists that he had nothing to do with Linda's murder."

"You believe him?"

"I believe in justice, Mr. Mallory, and in the Constitution of the United States, and in playing by the rules. He deserves a fair hearing, as any American would. I don't want it on my conscience that he got railroaded—that I did the railroading. As much as I despise the man, it's important to me to beat the son of a bitch fair and square—to show him that people of principle can overcome people like him. We will be conscientious and thorough and fair. If he is innocent of Linda's murder, we'll find that out. If he did it, or had it done, we'll find that out. The twelve papers will be publishing our findings day-by-day, and then other media will be picking up many of those stories, allowing the forum of American public opinion to know the facts, as we discover them. There will be two full-time reporters from each paper—cooperating with each other, under my direction, and competing with each other, to solve this case. Each of them will have a staff of their own, as much as the budget will allow, and it's a big budget."

"With no restrictions, huh?"

"Well, in theory."

"What do you mean?"

"Mr. Mallory, we are going to have the full cooperation of George Langley and the Colorado attorney general's office, and of Sheriff Klewlusz and all the Devon County authorities, and of the Colorado Bureau of Investigation, and whoever else we might need. With that support and the crew I'll have working on this, it won't take long to wrap it up. Towers is smart enough to know that he can afford to dangle a big carrot in front of us, without taking much risk, and without it ending up costing him much money, if, in fact, he had nothing to do with Linda's murder and we can wrap this up quickly. He is teasing us with our dreams, while employing us to get him out of this jam. He is a worthy adversary, and he might win this round. You do see what I mean about having me over a barrel, don't you?"

"Yes. Me and Avalon, too. It looks like we would have a lot of people mad at us, if we were the ones who stopped all those papers from getting that money."

"That's what Avalon is angry about," Paggett said. "She can see that she doesn't really have much of a choice, and that I don't either, that this is bigger than any one of us. She is resigned to this, and to facing Nelson Towers with me, and getting through it as best she can. Will you do that?"

"Yes. I'll be there."

CHAPTER THIRTY-THREE

Hom-Astubby showered in his camper and dressed in his finest pair of matching burgundy-colored slacks and shirt. He had time to fix himself a light lunch and have coffee and do some thinking before it was time to go.

He left his camper parked where it was and walked quite some distance down the shoulder of the highway to the Purple Pentagon parking lot.

The line of people waiting to get a seat at the Purple Pentagon stretched all the way around the side of the building. The front porch was now packed with an odd assortment of makeshift tables and chairs.

The customers who had finally gotten seated were virtual prisoners of the Purple Pentagon. The torture on their faces was plainly evident as they made no attempt to hide their disgust at the bumbling army of new, untrained staff, who seemed to have no idea what they were trying to do.

Earl Paggett and Avalon O'Neill arrived in one of the makeshift taxis that had sprung up. That made sense. There was no place to park. The taxi was a battered old pickup truck with a large hand-lettered sign on the door: JOHN CLAYTON'S TAXI SERVICE—Purple Pentagon $25, Cortez $50, Telluride $100, Durango $200.

Avalon O'Neill was dressed in a business suit and looked absolutely smashing. As Paggett was paying for the ride, she gave Hom-Astubby a big tight hug and whispered in his ear, "I missed you so much. So much it scared me, just a little."

He swallowed, gazing into her dazzling green eyes. He gave her a big hug and whispered in her ear, "I missed you, too. I'll tell you what I found out later, okay? I think we'll be all right."

She glanced at Paggett as he joined them and said, "Okay."

"We'd better not say anything in his car," Paggett said. "Towers may be listening."

They nodded.

"If we've got anything to discuss," Paggett looked at his watch, "we'd better do that now."

"Earl's already gotten an earful from me," Avalon O'Neill said. "Do you have any questions, Bill?"

"I think I have a pretty clear idea what's happening," Hom-Astubby said. "Doesn't look like we've got much choice."

She nodded, frowning. "I know."

She shrugged. "I was losing my enthusiasm for it, anyway." She looked at him. "So were you."

"Yeah," he said. "I was—beginning a long time ago."

A sleek black limousine pulled into the parking lot at precisely twelve noon.

Well before they got to the big gate at the driveway to Nelson Towers' new house, both shoulders of the highway were more littered with vehicles than the approaches to the Purple Pentagon. A crowd of several hundred people was swarming in front of the gate.

Everywhere he looked, Hom-Astubby saw television cameras and sound trucks, and reporters doing stand-ups in front of cameramen, with some portion of Towers' gate in the background. He realized then that the courthouse lawn wasn't the focus of the media anymore. Towers' gate had become the new background icon in this made-for-TV-story, at least at Alpine.

The scene at Towers' new corporate office in Telluride, and at corporate headquarters in Denver, was probably much the same. The media event was now a feeding frenzy, and it was feeding time.

Armed guards parted the crowd, making room for the limousine to enter the driveway and pass through the gate. They topped a hill and saw a helicopter sitting on a pad beside a sprawling ranch-style house of massive proportions. A wide circular driveway took them to the front door.

Attendants opened the limousine doors. They were led into the house by an immaculately dressed, dour-faced butler with a full black beard who looked as though he could recite Shakespeare by heart for days on end. Hom-Astubby was so impressed by the butler that he made a mental note to find out where in the world he might get himself a butler like that.

The butler led them at a measured, gentleman's pace through winding hallways to an airy, spacious room with a tall glass-paned wall facing the mountains in the distance.

Nelson Towers stood in the middle of the room, near a cluster of sofas and overstuffed chairs, looking every bit the most eligible bachelor in the world. But his face showed the strain of the last several days and he didn't appear to have slept much recently.

Towers said, "Thank you, Barrymore. I'll call you if we need anything."

The butler closed the door behind him as he left.

Towers turned to his guests and said, "It's so good of you to come. Drink?" He gestured toward a mahogany bar, beneath a van Gogh painting hanging on the wall.

Earl Paggett and Avalon O'Neill shook their heads.

"I'll have one," Hom-Astubby said.

Nelson Towers looked surprised, almost stunned, as though he had never before had anyone take him up on that offer—which well might have been the case, his teetotaling views being well known.

He said, "What shall I get for you, Mr. Mallory?"

"A double shot of brown whiskey, I think."

Towers nodded. He said, "You know, that sounds good. I'm not much of a drinking man, myself, but I've been looking forward to meeting you. I think I'll have one with you."

Towers moved behind the bar. As he looked from one bottle to another, he mumbled, "Brown whiskey . . . hummmm . . . brown whiskey . . ."

He held up what Hom-Astubby recognized as a rare and expensive, barrel-shaped, unopened half-gallon bottle of Old Slobberknocker, a limited occasional specialty item from one of America's oldest and finest distillers, which had been a favorite of the old fart who had sold Hom-Astubby his ranch.

Towers read the label, "Barrel proof. Aged fifty years. One-hundred and fifty-one proof Kentucky straight bourbon whiskey." He said, "Will this one do?"

"Mighty fine," Hom-Astubby said.

As Towers searched for the glasses, Hom-Astubby stared at the van Gogh. There was something about that painting. He couldn't think of what it might be, but it rang a bell somewhere. That nagged at him, but he didn't have time to think about it.

He glanced around the room. On a writing table, he saw a puke-orange-colored University of Texas Longhorns "Hook 'em Horns" paperweight.

Towers returned with two small glasses of fiery brown liquid. He said, "Double shots, I measured them carefully."

Then he gave Hom-Astubby a curious look and said, "Mr. Mallory, I understand you were good friends with my lifelong nemesis—old Arlington." He sighed. "They don't make enemies like that anymore. Shall we drink to him?"

Hom-Astubby raised his glass. "To old Arlington."

"May he rest in peace," Towers said, as he clicked his glass to Hom-Astubby's—then added, "Down the hatch."

"Look out liver, look out lips," Hom-Astubby said.

They downed the shots.

That big, long-flowing throat-full of mule-in-a-bottle kept kicking and kicking and kicking all the way down.

Towers' eyes grew as big as silver dollars. He wheezed and put his hand to his throat, breathing rapidly, his mouth wide open.

After handing his empty glass to Towers, Hom-Astubby let out a big sigh and wiped his sweaty palms on his pants. For the first time, he felt at least a little at ease.

Towers set the glasses on a coffee table and stood breathing deeply for a few moments. Finally he said, "Please, have a seat."

Paggett settled into a sofa. Hom-Astubby and Avalon O'Neill remained standing.

"Very well," Towers said, as he remained standing, too. "Mr. Paggett, I think, has explained to you the arrangement I have proposed for funding the task force investigation into the murder of Linda Ruben." He looked at them, as though expecting them to nod, but they didn't.

Towers sighed. "I did a very foolish thing. I thought I could avoid being involved. I lied to the police. Now I'm paying the price. But I am not a murderer, despite what you might think of me—which is the point of this meeting.

"But before we get to that, let me tell you that Linda Ruben's book is going to be published exactly the way she wrote it, under Mr. Paggett's sole supervision."

Avalon O'Neill looked at Earl Paggett. She said, "Is that part of the agreement?"

"Yes," Paggett said. "It'll be out just as quick as we can get it out. Mr. Towers wanted to tell you that, himself."

"I want you to know," Towers said, "that publishing her book is something I didn't have to do. I'm not thrilled about doing it. I can't stand sloppy work—half-truths masquerading as fact, especially when they're aimed at me. But I'll have a chance to rebut the book. Perhaps that's how I should have approached it to begin with. But that's water under the bridge. What I want you to understand is that this task force is going to be unfettered. There's going to be nothing stopping it or slowing it down. It will get at the truth. I have no doubt of that."

Hom-Astubby saw Avalon O'Neill's cheeks flushing, but Nelson Towers didn't seem to notice. Apparently, he wasn't aware, or had forgotten, that she had been Linda Ruben's right hand in the final stages of doing the "sloppy work" on the book.

"But Mr. Mallory"—Towers turned to Hom-Astubby—"we've had our differences. I'm told we have a history, one that goes back quite a ways. And Miss O'Neill"—he turned to her—"it was your good friend who got killed—an awful thing, but something I had nothing to do with."

He looked back and forth between the two of them. "I'm asking you, in fairness, to recuse yourselves from this investigation, from any investigative thing having to do with me, for the duration of the task force, or for one year, whichever comes first. I am entitled to a diligent inquiry by fair and impartial investigators, the same as any other American would be."

Avalon O'Neill took a step forward, saying, in a thick Irish accent, "You are thinking we'll not be *up* to being fair and impartial, are you?"

Towers seemed taken aback.

She put her hands on her hips and said, "You are thinking you'll be *buying* us off this story, are you?"

Her cheeks flushed even more. She stepped face-to-face with Towers and said, "You are thinking you'll be getting a *bargain* rate, are you?"

Her chest was rising and falling inside her business suit, and her breathing was rapid, through her half-open mouth.

Nelson Towers' face became ever more still the longer he gazed into Avalon O'Neill's eyes. He glanced quickly at Earl Paggett.

"I told Mr. Paggett," Towers said—he stepped back, only to see her step forward, closing the distance—"that I would pay each of you a sufficient kill fee to take a one-year vacation."

Towers stared into Avalon O'Neill's eyes, as though encountering something he had never been face-to-face with before.

He said, "Mr. Paggett, however, insisted that I wasn't offering quite enough. I didn't fully agree with him, but I've had some time to reflect on that. I want there to be *no* question *whatsoever* of my fairness in dealing with you. And I want no ill feelings on your part. Therefore, I shall pay each of you one hundred thousand dollars as a kill fee, and I shall fully fund the task force, for twenty-four million dollars, for up to one year, without restrictions of any kind, but only if you agree to recuse yourselves. Will you accept this generous offer?"

Towers gave a fleeting glance at Hom-Astubby, before looking back at Avalon O'Neill.

"We might be willing to accept a kill fee," Hom-Astubby said. "But I think we need to renegotiate your offer. I don't think you have any idea where this story is about to go."

Hom-Astubby took the business card he had found in Wally Street's briefcase out of his shirt pocket. He extended it toward Nelson Towers, face down.

Towers stepped around Avalon O'Neill and toward Hom-Astubby, watching her out of the corner of his eye as he moved beyond her. He took the card.

Hom-Astubby watched his face closely, as he turned the card over in his hand. Towers blanched, just slightly, but enough for Hom-Astubby to see it.

Towers stood staring into Hom-Astubby's eyes, saying nothing, as though having forgotten completely about Avalon O'Neill, and Earl Paggett, and everything else.

"What's this all about?" Earl Paggett said.

Towers flinched at the sound of Paggett's voice. He turned to him and said, firmly, "This has got nothing to do with your investigation, Mr. Paggett. This . . ." He turned to Hom-Astubby. "This is something else. Isn't that right, Mr. Mallory?"

"That's right," Hom-Astubby said, gazing into Towers' eyes. "This is personal."

"Mr. Paggett," Towers said, "I'm afraid I'm going to have to ask you to wait in the library while we discuss this. If you'll come with me, sir, I'll show you the way. We'll call you in a few minutes."

Earl Paggett remained seated on the sofa, reluctant to move, looking back and forth between Nelson Towers and Hom-Astubby. Finally, he rose, giving Avalon O'Neill a long look before walking with Nelson Towers toward a door at the far end of the room.

Hom-Astubby felt Avalon O'Neill touch his arm. She said, in a hurried whisper, "Bill, what are you doing? What was that card you gave him?"

He turned to her and whispered, "Let me do the negotiating now, hoke? This is my chance. Maybe my *only* chance. This won't be for a black silk handkerchief and a few other odds and ends."

They stared at each other.

As Nelson Towers walked back toward them, Avalon O'Neill whispered, "Hom-Astubby."

Towers stood facing them. He said, to Hom-Astubby, "Now, how much?"

Jesus. The richest man in the world wanted to know—how much? What was in that Ryerson & Neely packet? What was it worth? How much would Nelson Towers pay to keep Earl Paggett from getting it? Hom-Astubby knew he had to make the amount high enough that Towers would think he had the briefcase and knew what was in it.

But how much? He should leave some bargaining room, should say at least twice as much as he might hope for, to have plenty of room to come down. But how much?

The man had billions and billions of dollars. Estimates started at ninety billion. Some thought the total was much more than that. Could Eugene Wentworth possibly have been right about the roof collapsing on Towers? What might it be worth to keep that from happening?

Hom-Astubby had to name a number. He had to do it right now. He grasped for guidance. For anything.

He saw the van Gogh again, hanging on the wall. Now he remembered. A recent news item. Nelson Towers had paid something more than 100 million dollars, at auction in England, for a van Gogh—a light breeze at twilight stirring a darkening hay meadow, with overlaid brush strokes of orange and blue playing the curious trick of those colors upon the eyes, making the field of black and green appear to shimmer in the twilight breeze.

Hom-Astubby had tried to imagine what that might look like, and how it could be worth 100 million dollars.

He gazed at the van Gogh on the wall. Jesus, it was *that* painting—hanging right here in this room. Hanging over a bar the man didn't use? In the sunroom of a house he visited only when it was convenient?

Nelson Towers could raise that kind of cash, if need be—simply by taking something off a wall?

Hom-Astubby took a deep breath. He said, "One hundred million dollars, for each of us."

Towers didn't even blink. He said, "Two hundred million, huh?" He pursed his lips, and his eyes narrowed. "When can we arrange the exchange? You don't have it with you, do you?"

Christ. He hadn't even given the money a second thought. Hom-Astubby could have kicked himself. He could have gotten more.

There had to be absolute *dynamite* in that Ryerson & Neely packet, so potentially devastating for Towers that he wasn't even going to dicker about the money. It *was* his Achilles' heel.

To clean up this mess would cost Nelson Towers 224 million dollars, instead of twenty-four million. Maybe not chickenfeed, maybe he would feel it, feel it a lot, but it was within his means. And the amount had gotten the message across loud and clear.

Towers wasn't worried about money. He had money. He was worried about the briefcase. He was worried about the roof collapsing on him.

Hom-Astubby said, "You haven't heard all of my terms yet. There isn't going to be any exchange. What I've got is security for our future. For one hundred million dollars, for each of us, it gets buried. But for it to stay buried, we get a free pass on our income tax returns, both of us, for the returns we filed this year and for the ones we file next year."

Towers frowned. He said, "I've got no control over something like that."

Hom-Astubby just stood staring at him, saying nothing, letting the seconds tick away.

"What you're suggesting I do," Towers said, "even if I could do it, is a crime. It's a crime even for you to suggest such a thing."

"What?" Hom-Astubby said. "Are you recording this? Maybe even on video? Which way is the camera? You want me to repeat it?"

Towers' lips tightened.

"Let me clarify it. If either one of us ever gets audited, for the returns we filed this year, or for the ones we'll file next year, or if anything happens to us, this gets unburied and it goes to people who'll know what to do with it. There'll be nothing wrong with our tax returns. They'll have been done by damn good tax lawyers. But you're not putting either one of us through that hell again. You know damn well what I'm talking about. That's part of the deal, or we've got no deal."

Towers stood looking back and forth between Hom-Astubby and Avalon O'Neill, with a slightly perplexed expression, trying to get his eyes to focus. It made Hom-Astubby pretty sure that the celebrated delayed effect of Old Slobberknocker had begun kicking in. Towers' thought processes appeared to slow down enough that Hom-Astubby could almost see the wheels turning in his mind. This was going to cost him something. Something more than money. A lot more than money. How much of his influence would he have to spend to get this done? Could it be done? Was it worth it? Was there another way? What could go wrong?

Towers frowned. He looked at Avalon O'Neill, saying, "There's too many people who know about this."

"She doesn't know," Hom-Astubby said.

"She doesn't know?"

"She doesn't even know what you are holding in your hand."

Towers focused all his attention on Hom-Astubby. "So, this is just between me and you."

"That's right," Hom-Astubby said. "Just between me and you. It's personal. But she's part of the deal, or we've got no deal. You write the checks, right now, and this problem goes away."

"For this kind of money," Towers said, "it would have to go away permanently. Not only do you two have nothing to do with Paggett's task force, no contact whatsoever, but I get rid of both of you, permanently. You get out of the business of hounding me. I never hear from either one of you again. You find something else to do, forever. Is that clear?"

"That's what we want. We want to live our lives in peace. We want to forget about you."

Towers looked directly into Hom-Astubby's eyes. "You never say a word about this," he indicated the card in his hand, "to anyone, not even to her."

Towers looked at Avalon O'Neill. "You never ask him any questions about this. If you can't do that, we've got no deal."

He looked back and forth between the two of them. "Neither one of you ever tells Paggett, or anyone else, anything about what we've discussed here, not the amount of the settlement, or its terms, or even that we made an agreement. Nothing whatsoever, to anyone, about anything. We'll tell Paggett nothing, except that you accepted my kill fee arrangement, and you are off the task force, and he is forbidden to speak to you for its duration, beginning right now. If I find out that either one of you has said so much as hello to him or his task force for its duration, or if you tell him or anyone else anything whatsoever about this after the task force has finished its work, our deal is off."

Hom-Astubby nodded. "Neither one of us ever says anything about this to anybody."

"Let me put it this way," Towers said. "If this comes to light," he indicated the card again, "no matter how that happens, no matter if you claim to have had nothing to do with it, our deal is off, and we'll be at war."

"That's a risk I'm willing to take," Hom-Astubby said. "Do we have a deal, all the way around?"

Towers nodded. "If she agrees with it, with everything. I want to hear her say that she agrees with it."

"Give me a few minutes to talk to her, outside." Hom-Astubby nodded toward the patio. "She didn't know this was going to happen."

"Make it quick." Towers looked at his watch. "I want to get this wrapped up." He put the card in his shirt pocket. "Paggett and I have got a plane waiting for us."

Hom-Astubby turned to Avalon O'Neill and motioned toward the sliding door to the patio. She followed him outside.

CHAPTER THIRTY-FOUR

Hom-Astubby led Avalon O'Neill all the way across the patio and then beyond the grass into the edge of the trees, far from the house. When he stopped and turned to look back at the house, he let out a long breath.

Avalon O'Neill also turned to look at the house. She spoke in a whisper. "My god, Bill, what have you got on him?"

"I was running a bluff. I've got nothing on him."

She stared at Hom-Astubby, incredulous.

"That card came from a briefcase that got stolen out of Wally Street's car, about a week ago, in the Purple Pentagon parking lot. I found the briefcase this morning at that old house up on the hill, in the mine-garage behind the house. That kid from Georgia stole it, at the same time he stole Street's camera and that telephoto lens. But the card's all I took. Towers thinks I've got the briefcase, but I don't have it. I didn't even have a chance to find out what's in it. All I know for sure is that the briefcase has got nothing to do with Linda Ruben's murder."

"My god," she said. "You mean we've got to decide whether to take his money, or go get that briefcase and try to nail him with it?"

"That's about it. This deal with Towers is our ticket out, if we want to take it. Or we can play hardball with Towers. Take a gamble. Hope to hell whatever's in that briefcase is worth it. It would be war. We probably can't even imagine how bad it would get. Towers wouldn't fund the task force. I don't know how long Sarah and Paggett can hold it together. But god only knows what Paggett could do with that briefcase."

"Jesus," she said, looking at the house.

"But I negotiated us a deal. We've got a choice." He took her arm and turned her toward him. "Tell me that I negotiated us a deal."

"My god, Bill. Did you *ever* negotiate us a deal."

"I needed to hear you say that. Thank you for letting me take over the negotiating in there. For letting me have my chance."

She smiled at him, gazing into his eyes and shaking her head. "Mister William Hom-Astubby Mallory, I was holding my breath."

"You weren't doing so bad, yourself. God knows what you would have gotten him up to—maybe as much as what I ended up with."

She grinned. Then she glanced at the house. "I'm a little scared. Are you scared, just a little?"

"I was about to pee my pants in there."

She laughed, a release of nervous tension. She glanced at the house again. "Should we go get that briefcase? Before something happens to it?"

"That briefcase is not going anywhere. But I don't know how in the hell we can get it by ourselves. We might have missed our chance for that. The cops might be the only ones who can get it now. When I was finally able to get out of there, Charles Uber was busy with a tractor bucket, burying it at the bottom of a vertical mine shaft at the back of that garage. It's now under god only knows how many tons of dirt."

He took her arm and walked her a little farther away from the house. "Avalon, that kid from Georgia is at the bottom of that mine shaft, too. I saw Uber kill him and dump his body down there, when Uber discovered that his nephew had killed Linda Ruben. I was hiding behind a cabinet in there. I saw it all. Uber found Linda's driver's license among the kid's stuff. Uber was furious that the kid had jeopardized what the Tetons were doing. The kid picked that moment to come walking in. It wasn't pretty."

"Uber's nephew killed Linda?"

"Yes, almost certainly. A buddy of mine in Atlanta checked on him. He just got out of prison down there last week. He had worked in a photography studio. That's why he broke into Street's car, to get his camera. I'm sure the kid was disappointed that the briefcase had nothing but papers in it. But he had been in prison for a brutal attack on a woman. Not a sexual assault. A horrible beating. The cops down there suspected him of other attacks like that but couldn't prove it. He's the big monkey wrench in everything that's happened up here. The sheriff had told me a few days ago that somebody tried to attack a woman in Alpine. A young man with short, sandy hair. That's what the kid looked like. He apparently got Linda as she was arriving at the Purple Pentagon, out in the parking lot. He probably forced her at knife point to drive them down that dirt road along the river. He kept her purse and her cell phone, after he killed her."

"Oh my god." Avalon O'Neill's face contorted into a grimace.

Hom-Astubby looked toward the house. "We were right all along about it not making any sense that Towers would have done that, not this messy, anyway."

She took a deep breath. "Bill, that means that Earl's task force has got nothing to do. There won't be any task force."

"There will be, if we don't tell anybody."

"What? How could we not tell anybody?"

"We let nature take its course. Everything is buried at the bottom of that mine shaft. It's really long odds that Paggett's task force can solve Linda's murder, or the cops, either. The feds are keeping everyone away from Uber and that house. The feds *know* that Uber and the Tetons had nothing to do with her murder. They don't care about her murder. All they care about is their own undercover operation. They don't know that Uber's nephew was there. Uber was trying to keep him out of sight. Uber was scared to death that the Tetons would kill him for letting the kid stay there. If reporters on the task force were to find out about that kid, even if they got him identified, they'd have one hell of a time finding him now. If they did ever develop him as a lead, he'd probably just be one of a thousand leads that never panned out. Uber will probably cover up that mine shaft so you couldn't tell it had ever been there. I'll bet he's finished filling it up with dirt and has already got some of that old furniture moved on top of it."

"You mean . . ."

"I mean, Towers doesn't know it, but he's cutting his own throat by funding the task force and buying us off. Avalon, he was *try-*

ing to get rid of *you* before funding the task force. I think that's the *only* thing this meeting was supposed to be about. There's got to be *something* you know about his financial empire that makes you dangerous to him in some way you're not yet aware of. He was playing poker with us. That's why he made a low initial kill fee offer, so it wouldn't look like it meant much to him. I think he had thrown me into the deal, hoping that would keep us from suspecting it's *you* he *had* to get rid of, and to make it easier for you to leave the task force, so you wouldn't be the only one doing that. Why would Towers have had any fear of me? Does it make sense that he would have *needed* to get rid of me? He hadn't even known about me before today, probably not even my name, or anything about what his people had been doing to me. He said, 'I'm told we have a history.' That was baloney about 'fair and impartial.' He was putting on a show in there, and he's damn good at it."

"This meeting was about me?"

"Does it make sense any other way? Is there any way in hell that Towers would have committed himself to publishing Linda's book the way she wrote it, if he hadn't thought he *had* to do that to get Paggett to go along with getting you off the task force? Towers knows that Paggett can't be bought, not for something like getting you off the task force—not unless the price is something like Linda's book, something you could go along with too. I think Linda's book is our barometer for how desperate Towers is to get rid of you. It was just dumb luck that I got to be at this meeting. I would still be some nameless peon to Towers if he hadn't thought he needed someone besides you to be a part of this. But Avalon—if I hadn't found that briefcase, I think he might have been planning to get you separated from the task force, to get some distance between you and him, and then have you killed, maybe the next time you went overseas, and it would probably look like an accident."

She shuddered. "That briefcase might have saved me?"

"I don't know. Maybe I don't have this thing figured out right. Maybe I worry too much. But I don't like it that it *looks* to me like he's *desperate* to get rid of you. That's never been healthy for anybody."

She stared at him, her mouth half open.

"Don't worry about it. I think we're both safe as long as Towers thinks we've got the briefcase and that he's got us neutralized—as long as we keep our end of the bargain. He thinks we're now just a couple of money grubbers that he's bought. If we take his money, we've got to allow him to continue thinking that."

"You know what that briefcase was about?"

"I have a pretty good idea. I'm not worried that anybody will blow our deal by stumbling upon that information some other way. That briefcase had to be the only way it would ever come to light."

"Towers thinks this task force will save him, doesn't he?"

"Yes. And he's desperate. He's taking a big gamble that they'll solve Linda's murder quickly. He *knows* he didn't do it."

"Jesus, Bill. He's got to be climbing the walls. He knows he's getting nailed for the one thing he hasn't done. He's doing everything he can do, isn't he?"

"Yes. And he'll get a big splash of publicity out of funding the task force and releasing Linda's book the way she wrote it. That will begin in the morning back east when Towers and Paggett make the rounds of all those TV news shows. It'll look like he's got nothing to hide. That'll buy him some time with public opinion."

"But Linda's book is devastating for Towers. I've read it. I worked on it with her."

"I think, for Towers, it might be a matter of timing. It'll take a while before her book can actually come out. She had only gotten the manuscript accepted, and a contract, right? The manuscript probably hasn't even been copyedited. Paggett will have to be involved in that. Then it will have to be set in type, and the page proofs checked for typesetting errors. Then however long it takes at the printers. It'll be months before the book can go into distribution, even with Paggett trying to rush it. Towers might be able to stall a congressional investigation, might even be able to derail it, if they could clear up Linda's murder in a hurry. He could then deal with her book, when it comes out, in an entirely different climate, without the suspicion of murder hanging over his head. He might not want to put off dealing with his own criminal liability, for lying to the cops about being in Telluride all day on Monday. That's a felony. He might want to act quickly and get it plea-bargained down, during this period of good will. I'll bet he'll be doing a mea culpa tomorrow morning on those TV shows, admitting that he made a mistake, that he panicked and lied to the cops. People respond to that. It's something they can understand. And god, it *will* look like he's doing everything he can do to help solve Linda's murder. That will hold up even under the most probing questioning, because that's exactly what he's doing. It will be impressive."

"He's pretty smart."

"He's damn smart. And it might work, if only they could solve Linda's murder. But as Paggett's task force, and the cops, run out of leads, more and more of their focus will be on Towers, and his companies, and what Linda had been investigating, and motives for why Towers might have wanted her killed. For a whole year. For twenty-four million dollars worth of Nelson Towers' money. Two dozen reporters, a dozen newspapers, without restrictions, with Paggett leading it. And Linda's book would come out at about the right time to kick all of that into high gear."

"They might bring Towers down."

"They'd damn sure have their chance. Towers might survive it, but he wouldn't be able to operate the way he has in the past. It would be a disaster for Towers. Whatever Paggett can find. And from what he saw in there a while ago, Paggett knows damn well there's *something* to find. That would turn out to be like waving a red flag at a bull."

"God." She looked at the house again. "Nobody knows but us."

"Well, Charles Uber knows. But the feds are about to bust him and the other Tetons. He's damn sure not going to tell anybody about killing his nephew. And he's got to keep everybody from finding out that his nephew was even there. He knows the Tetons would kill him, even in prison."

She put her hand on Hom-Astubby's arm and looked into his eyes. "Bill, Linda's family wouldn't have any closure. They'd never know who did it."

"That's a tough one."

"Couldn't we tell them? They'd have to know."

Hom-Astubby shook his head. "We could never tell anyone. If we told anybody, the whole thing might fall apart."

They stared at each other.

Hom-Astubby said. "It's not like Linda is missing and they don't know where she is, or what happened to her. They've had some closure. I know it's not enough, but we've got to realize what choice we're making and live with it."

"We'd have to live with this for the rest of our lives," she said, with a look of uncertainty on her face. "And we'd be violating our oath. We'd be committing obstruction of justice. As members of the bar, we're officers of the court."

"I know. But I might not be a member of the bar anymore, if we tell."

She clutched his arm harder. "You might have already tampered with evidence. You took those rolls of film yesterday. And I knew about it. That might make me an accessory. But we weren't certain it would be evidence. Wouldn't it depend on whether we knew it was evidence? Surely we could make the cops understand. We were just reporters trying to do our jobs."

He stared into the distance. "It isn't just that I took that kid's film to Albuquerque—and processed it. I also took his expired driver's license. They'd wonder what else I might have taken. I know cops. They are not incompetent people. They get paid for being suspicious. They wouldn't be doing *their* jobs if they didn't consider every possibility. I know what they would find down in that mine shaft. I left fingerprints all over Wally Street's briefcase. I was so nervous, and in such a hurry. They might have to consider whether I'd been the one who'd stolen that briefcase in the first place, and then maybe that kid stole it from me."

He let out a long breath and shook his head, still staring into the distance. "I haven't had time to think this through, to try to figure out how things might look, depending on what else is being considered at that time, and what lies other people might be telling. If Nelson Towers was at war with us, that could change everything. Christ, my fingerprints are even on Linda Ruben's cell phone, and her purse, and her wallet, and maybe even on her driver's license. I think I was holding it by its edges, so I'm not sure if I left prints on it. But, Jesus, I *know* I left prints on everything else. I was *holding* her wallet and driver's license, looking at the license, when Charles Uber surprised me. I barely had time to drop them and hide, or he would have found me there. I'd be dead right now, like his nephew."

"It was that close?"

"It was that close." He turned back to her. "Avalon, if the cops dig up that mine shaft, and they find my fingerprints on those things in Linda's purse, I don't want to think about what might happen. This whole thing started with me lying to the sheriff about not recognizing your photo on that police bulletin. If the cops were to focus on me, even if they didn't find out I'd lied about that, they'd damn sure find out that I took your dog when I *knew* they were looking for the dog, and that I've been lying about that.

"They would retrace every step I've taken all week long and grill everybody I've had contact with, all the way to Oklahoma. There would be no way to keep them from finding out about the dog. My credibility with the cops would be zilch once they found out I'd been lying about anything. That's how they work. And this is a murder investigation. They find out that you lied once, and then they become unmerciful until they get to the bottom of everything."

"That's what has gotten Towers into trouble."

"Exactly. They'd find out that I evaded all those roadblocks in getting out of here. They'd want to know why. They'd want to be damn sure they knew why. Would they believe I was only trying to get your dog to safety? Do you think George Langley and Dick Halliburton would admit to what I overheard them say to each other? But I'd have no choice other than to tell the cops what I heard, and try to get them to believe it. If I ever deviated from the truth again, I'd be dead meat. They are damn good at catching you in any kind of lie. At that point, your only chance for survival is to tell nothing but the truth. Avalon, at the very least, that would make George Langley my mortal enemy. His whole career might depend on destroying my credibility, and he'd have some things to work with."

"Oh, god. There's no way that George could allow that to go unchallenged."

"It might get ugly. My lawyer might have to leak that conversation I overheard to the press, and find a way to leak those police bulletins that Langley put out on you and your dog, to fight back against him. It might be a godawful mess, and you might get dragged into it."

Hom-Astubby wiped his hand across his face. "I can't even prove where I was when Linda got killed. I was camped upriver, alone. But I had been down there at your campsite, playing with your dog, within a mile of the crime scene, late Monday afternoon. I had that run-in with Towers' work crew on that other fork of the road. Who knows what lies Towers might get one of them to tell. I could find myself in one hell of a lot more trouble than just tampering with evidence or obstruction of justice. I don't think I want to find out what Nelson Towers means by war."

"Jesus, Bill."

"We don't know what might happen. Towers' people might spin some theory about me being consumed by some long-standing hatred for Towers, with them being able to show an employment history that might support that, and claiming that I came up here stalking Towers, but ended up trying to frame him for murder, by killing Linda. They might manufacture a bunch of threats they'd say I'd been making against Towers. Uber might claim that I'd killed his nephew. Towers could probably get Uber to say anything. Uber would be trying to save his own hide. It might look like I killed his nephew because he was screwing up my attempt to frame Towers. If Towers threw all his weight into getting my ass fried, with George Langley madder than hell at me, trying to cover up his own lie, that damn well might happen."

"Jesus, Bill, you're scaring me." Avalon O'Neill appeared nearly overwhelmed, trying to digest everything.

"I hope I'm worrying about a lot of things that might never happen. Maybe I worry too much. Maybe Towers isn't *that* ruthless, or *that* corrupt. Maybe worst-case scenarios are not the way we ought to be looking at it. I don't know. But that's not all we've got to worry about."

"God, there's more?"

"Yes. There are those photos of you that kid took with that telephoto lens. I don't think I got all of his exposed film yesterday. I didn't have time to look for it today. That's why I went back there this morning. But I found Linda's driver's license first. Now Uber has dumped everything into that mine shaft, and I mean everything. All the kid's clothes, the cameras and lenses he'd stolen, Street's briefcase, Linda's purse and cell phone, everything that was in every drawer in all that old furniture. It's all down there with that kid's body. If it gets dug up, it could all get introduced as evidence in open court. Remember when we talked about that?"

She stared at him, her mouth half open.

"I'm worried that there are probably at least two more rolls of exposed film down there, maybe three, of you arriving at the river, and leaving the river, and maybe a whole roll of you standing beside the river. They weren't part of the film that I processed in Albuquerque yesterday. But there were a lot of photos of you at the river. Even if there isn't any more exposed film down there, how could I keep the cops from getting the film that I did process? Tampering with evidence is one thing. But destroying evidence is something else. What choice would I have but to turn over all that film? They'd find out about that. They'd find out that I went to Albuquerque and everything I did there. When these things fall apart, they find out everything."

"I was nude in those photos." Her eyes blinked several times, and she swallowed. "Wasn't I?"

"Some of them."

She stared at the mountains. "I've worked so hard to be taken seriously as a journalist. That would be the end of that, wouldn't it? I have one little moment of revolt against all that discipline, way out in the woods all by myself, and poof, my whole life goes up in smoke."

"Maybe not. Uber might plea-bargain. It might not go to trial. He'd probably plea-bargain. They might not come after me."

"It wouldn't matter. If Towers was at war with us, those photos would get out, somehow. He'd make sure of that. The tabloids. Christ, they'd be on the Internet. I'm not a prude, but this would stay with me forever. My parents . . ."

"And I'd likely get disbarred, if not worse. Wally Street might even get his briefcase back, without Paggett ever seeing it. Why would Earl Paggett, or any other member of the media, be allowed to see it? It wouldn't have anything to do with Linda's murder. Towers might be able to keep anybody from seeing it who might make sense out of whatever's in there. It's probably just a bunch of esoteric business documents that would mean nothing to anyone except someone like you. Towers might end up getting off nearly scot-free. He'd be off the hook for Linda's murder. There wouldn't be any task force. He wouldn't have to release Linda's book, not the way she wrote it, anyway. But he'd damn sure have a kitten when he found out the cops had gotten that briefcase. And when he knows we don't have it, you lose your protection from him."

"He'd be mad as hell at us," she said, frowning. "Bill, from what I know about Towers, we'd better consider worst-case scenarios. I wouldn't put anything past him. If we didn't take his money, and we told the cops instead, he'd probably view that deal you proposed in there as a fishing expedition to get him to confirm that the briefcase was worth digging up. And he'd have no trouble figuring out that even if we had taken that deal, it would have been nothing but a trap for him. He'd come after us with everything he had."

"Yeah." Hom-Astubby was thoughtful for a moment. "I guess if I were the defendant in Linda's murder, or the kid's murder, or maybe *both* of them, maybe I could fight off Towers, maybe force him to throw his weight into trying to get the charges dropped against me, if I threatened to get that briefcase introduced into evidence at the trial. I'd hate to end up having to spend the briefcase like that, and him be able to keep it from coming to light that way. But if that didn't work for me, for whatever reason, and I did get the briefcase introduced into evidence, it wouldn't do me any good against the charges I'd be facing. Would it be worth it to have the briefcase come out that way? And I don't know if I'd want to gamble my life that Towers couldn't get the contents of that briefcase sanitized, somehow, behind the scenes, before it could get introduced into evidence in court."

He put his hand on her arm. "Avalon, George Langley would be in charge of that briefcase. You know him a lot better than I do. You might know him better than anyone. With Towers off the hook for Linda's murder, and with the contents of that briefcase having nothing to do with her murder, and with Langley madder than hell at me, with his career depending on destroying my credibility, would you be willing to bet my life that Langley could withstand whatever Nelson Towers might offer him to let Towers have just a few minutes alone with that briefcase? Would you want to see George Langley subjected to that kind of temptation? Is there any way that could be good for him, either? Unless you are dead-level certain he could withstand that temptation?"

She swallowed hard, and her eyes blinked rapidly. She said, "I say, let's take the money and run! I'd rather say good-bye to Nelson Towers and George Langley and this whole mess. Let's hope it never gets dug up."

"That's what I say. I'd rather live with that problem, and its consequences, than with all the other ones. And I'd damn sure rather watch Nelson Towers squirm, instead of us. We can go do whatever we want to do."

"We can go get my dog! I can start getting her ready for the world title competition next month."

"Oh yeah." Hom-Astubby looked around at the mountains, trying hard not to change the expression on his face. "That big ole puppy. I'll bet she misses you so much. And I can show you my horse ranch. I think you might like it."

"You've got a horse ranch?"

"Well, no horses yet. But I've got the ranch. And the ranch house has got a library you have to see to believe."

"Really?"

"Oh yeah. It might be a good place for you to write that book, if you might want to think about that."

"I might think about that."

She put her hand on his arm and said, "But Bill, there's something I need to tell you."

"What?"

She took a deep breath. "I've got an attention disorder. I've always tried to keep it a secret, as much as I can."

He took her hand and held it. "You can tell me about it."

She swallowed hard. "They think it might be a rare form of autism, so rare they're now calling it O'Neill's Episodic Syndrome. I've had it all my life. I didn't start talking until I was five, even though I could understand several languages by then. You should know that there are things about it that sometimes cause me to embarrass myself, or would, if I were fully aware of what I was doing."

She looked away. "It took a long time to learn how to live with it. The doctors told my parents a long time ago that I would have trouble forming normal relationships, but I think I might be outgrowing that part of it. When I was younger, it would get me into trouble." She looked down. "The other girls made fun of me."

He squeezed her hand.

"I haven't been able to have many male friends. My parents were very protective. Then I was cautious. I've missed out on a lot of things. Lately, that hasn't been working for me very well. I don't want to miss out on everything. I hadn't had an episode for quite a while until I had that one with you yesterday. They're becoming less frequent. But I still have them."

She looked at him. "Dating is something that's been really hard for me. I've been trying to figure out how to do it. I'm still not very good at it."

"Says who?" He grinned. "You charmed the pants off of me, didn't you?"

She smiled, just a hint of that sheepish little smile. "I did, didn't I?"

"You damn sure did."

"And I gave you fair warning about Irishwomen, didn't I?"

"Fair warning."

"But you walked right into it with your eyes wide open, didn't you?"

"I damn sure did."

She gave him a mischievous, triumphant little smile. "You, Mister William Hom-Astubby Mallory, are now a notch on my lipstick case."

"I damn sure am."

She looked into his eyes. "But Bill, I wouldn't have done that, but you saw me have that episode, and you said you didn't care."

"It didn't phase me in the least."

"Really?"

"Really. I don't care."

She threw her arms around him. He gave her a big hug. He held her in his arms, feeling her squeezing him tightly.

When he released her, her eyes were moistened. She said, "There are some other things you should know."

She wiped her eyes and stood looking at the mountains.

"I've been asked to be a spokesperson, do fundraising for medical research. A lot of people have some form of autism, or have children who do. There are so many different kinds of it, though hardly anyone seems to have exactly what I've got."

She looked into his eyes again. "It has some advantages. I've got some special powers of concentration, among other things."

"It's a gift," Hom-Astubby said. "You've been given a special gift. God forbid that every one of us should be exactly the same."

"Really? I never looked at it that way." She was thoughtful for a moment. "I have been able to excel in school. And I've been able to have a career—though Earl did make me go through counseling and therapy for anger management. Having a temper kind of complicates my situation."

Hom-Astubby grinned, but he didn't dare say a word about that.

"George encouraged me to go public about my life, to be that spokesperson. He said he'd give me his full support."

"Maybe he's not as bad a guy as I thought. I'll support you in that, if that's what you want to do."

"I think it might be what I want to do. It's what my book's about. I want a chance to tell my own story first, to see if I can write that book. But I'm a little scared. I don't want to be alone while I do it."

"You can write it in my library."

"Are you sure? You've got a book to write, too. I don't want to crowd your work space. Are you sure your library's big enough?"

Hom-Astubby's grin stretched all the way across his face. "We'll work something out so we don't feel cramped. And we won't have to spend all our time in the library. We can figure out something to do for recreation when we're not writing."

This time that sheepish little smile was full blown. It would never fail to work its magic on him.

A thought occurred to Hom-Astubby. "Do you, by any chance, happen to like wine?"

"Oh, I love wine! I learned all about wine in France."

"I'll remind myself to drop in somewhere that has some vintage wines and pick out something special for you. You might go with me and pick it out yourself."

"Really?"

"Really. But tell me, being Irish, you're not a Notre Dame football fan, are you?"

Her face lit up. "Oh yes! *My* Fighting Irish. Are you kidding? They're my favorite team. Even more than CU."

"We'll have to talk about that."

"What's to talk about?" She shrugged. "We've won more national championships than Oklahoma."

Damn, Hom-Astubby thought, she knows something about football.

"Oh Bill, I don't want to talk about football right now. I want to talk about horses. I love horses. You're going to get some horses, aren't you?"

"Oh, I'm going to get some horses. I'm going to get a lot of horses. You might help me pick the horses, too, if you want. I'll bet you'd like to get one for yourself. If you get a mare and have her bred you can start your own herd."

"I'd love to raise a colt! But are you sure you have enough pasture?"

Hom-Astubby grinned. "My friend who built the ranch made sure it would have plenty of pasture."

"Who's that?"

"Arlington Billington."

"Arlington Billington? The oil tycoon? The famous art collector?"

"I don't know." Hom-Astubby shrugged. "Did he collect art?"

"Did he collect art! Ever since he died last December, the whole art world has been trying to find his collection of paintings. They're supposed to be worth more than three billion dollars, maybe four billion."

Hom-Astubby stared at the mountains. He said, "Well, son of a gun. So that's why Nelson Towers was able to come out on top at that auction to get that new Vincent van Gogh that's hanging on the wall in there."

They walked back across the meticulously manicured lawn to the sunroom of Nelson Towers' new house, and they told Towers what they had decided. They watched him stand beneath a rather remarkable depiction of an eerie shimmering darkness descending upon a hay meadow at twilight, as he used the mahogany bar for a desktop to write two checks for one hundred million dollars, one for each of them. He wrote the checks with a careful, precise penmanship, including a notation on each one that the money was for "consultation services."

But Hom-Astubby wasn't thinking about what he might do with Nelson Towers' money. He wasn't thinking about art collections, either, or football, or buying horses, or writing books, or drinking rare and expensive wine, or where in the world he might find himself a butler as impressive as the one he had seen.

He was thinking that he would have all the way to Oklahoma to hope he could figure out some way to tell Avalon Blanche O'Neill about her dog, before she saw the dog, just on the off chance that her first sight of Glennglavin's Spurling Baskerville Blossom might cause her to focus the full intensity of her special powers of concentration right between his eyes.